Renee
and Jay

Renee and Jay

J. J. MURRAY

KENSINGTON BOOKS

KENSINGTON BOOKS are published by

Kensington Publishing Corp.
850 Third Avenue
New York, NY 10022

ISBN 1-57566-862-9

Printed in the United States of America

For Amy

Chapter One

"Thank you for calling Star City Cable. May I have your name and account number?"

I must say that one hundred times a day as I sit in my ugly-ass Post-it-noted, industrial blue-gray, cloth-covered cubicle. I connect most folks with new service. Other folks? Well, let's say I listen a lot and try not to go off.

"How far is your trailer from the road, Mr. Williams?"

"I dunno."

Another trailer person. Why are white people so fascinated with trailer parks? Maybe it reminds them of circling the wagons during Indian attacks. I make an L with my left hand, notice another chipped nail, and flash the loser sign (left hand to forehead) to Collette Johnson in the next cubicle. She winks and comes over to listen in.

"Okay, Mr. Williams, how far is your trailer from the trailer next to you?"

"Dunno."

I hit the mute button. "Collette, this man is trippin'. Doesn't know how far his trailer is from the road or from his own next-door neighbor."

"Ask him how long it takes him to walk next door," she says.

I press the mute button again. "Mr. Williams, how long does it take for you to walk next door?"

"Well," he says, "I walk kinda slow. And it depends on the weather, too."

I need this job, but I don't need people like Mr. Williams calling at 5:59 P.M. when I'm off at six and I'm hungry and gotta pee and it's been snowing all day and I know VDOT isn't going to have the roads clear and a Jetta isn't exactly a Range Rover.

"Mr. Williams, if you walk out on your front porch—"

"Don't have a porch."

I can't imagine living without *something* out the front door. "Okay, Mr. Williams," I say, as Collette tries not to fall out laughing, "let's say you stick your head out the door."

"Okay."

"If you were to spit," I say, and Collette walks away waving her hands. "If you were to spit out your door, would it hit the trailer next to you?" Silence on the other end. "Mr. Williams?" Fool is probably out trying to lay a loogie on his neighbor's trailer.

"I'm just doin' some figurin'."

"Take your time, Mr. Williams." Collette has now collected a few coworkers from other cubicles, each making nasty *p-tui* sounds. Collette removes one of her dagger earrings and picks up my handset.

"Well," Mr. Williams says finally, "I guess if the wind was right, I could hit it."

I stifle a laugh, push Collette toward the others, and type "50 feet or less from nearest dwelling" on my computer screen. "Uh, thank you, Mr. Williams. I have all the information I need. The cable technician will be by sometime Monday afternoon, weather permitting. If you have any more questions about this order, please call the toll-free number, and when instructed, dial six-seven-six-eight"—Collette's extension.

"No, you didn't," Collette says.

"That's right. Six-seven-six-eight. My name? Collette Johnson. Thank you, Mr. Williams. You have a nice evening."

I quickly log out and push back from my computer. "He says he'd be 'sho 'nuff callin' back Monday,' Collette."

"That was cold, Renee."

"Oh, like you never done that to me." I gather my purse and coat.

"Honey," Collette says, "I only give your extension to the men with sexy voices."

"Right, and every one of them fools is married."

"What about that minister?"

"Puh-lease. Man wanted to lay some hands on me, said he was sorry he couldn't since we were on the phone."

"Just tryin' to get you a new man, girl. What you got planned for tonight?"

Another Friday night with nothing to do and all night to do it, nowhere to go and all night to get there. Another date with Mr. Remote Control. At least he's a slim black man who doesn't mind getting his buttons pushed.

When I don't answer, Collette pouts and shakes her head. "Girl-friend, you gotta stop thinkin' about that dog. He gone, you ain't, you got legs and a fresh paycheck. Put on some decent clothes and come out with us."

"Us" is Collette and her forever-man, Clyde Dunbar. I call him "forever-man" because Collette says he's for-*evuh* doing this, that, and the other. He's okay-looking in a "Charles-Dutton-as-Roc" sort of way, and he's funny sometimes. He has a job, a Lex, and his own condo. All paid for. And he's for-*evuh* reminding everyone of that.

"You driving?" I ask, looking at the snow drifting down.

"You coming?"

I want to go—really. Well, not really. Clyde will go on and on about being one of the few brothers at the executive level of the N&W railroad, play kissy-face with Collette, dance like a fool, order drinks with names like "screaming orgasm" too loudly, and over-tip the waitress or waiter. Collette will be checking out every breathing or barely breathing dog at the club, trying to find me a new pet.

The last time we go, she flirts with this dreadlocked Coolio wannabe—right in front of Clyde—until Dread Man comes over. Collette excuses herself, grabs Clyde's hand, and drags him to the dance floor, leaving me and Ziggy Marley alone at the table.

"You alone?" he asks.

I want to say, "Uh-duh," but I only roll my eyes and say, "My man will be here soon."

Then he checks me out. You know what I'm talking about. He steps back, checks out my legs under the table, leans in and checks my titties, all done like I don't know he's doing it. It's nice to get attention now and then, but sometimes these dogs go too far. Whatever happened to a man looking in my eyes and calling them "limpid pools" or something romantic? I know that's cornball, but at least it's better than being felt up by bloodshot eyes.

"Where he at?" he asks, shaking his dreds in my face. Maybe he's Whoopi's long-lost son.

I don't need this. "Where he *be*," I say, taking a sip of my strawberry daiquiri.

He gulps his drink, sets it on the table, and holds out his hand. I see rings on every finger, every damn ring with a diamond. Except for a class ring, my fingers are naked. His have to be CZs. "Wanna dance?" he asks. Rico Suave he's not.

I curse Collette in my head and catch her eye as she dances with Clyde. She means well. After R. J. left for D.C., Collette decided to find me a hookup. And this is what she finds for me. The black Liberace.

I hate being cold to people I don't know, and I'm sure "Rings" isn't a total dog, but sometimes you have to show who's master.

"Sure. I want to dance," I say with a smile. He smiles and grabs my hand. "But not with you."

His hand lingers for a moment, then slides off. "Touché," he says.

As he walks away I wonder if I've made a mistake. I mean, he's in Roanoke, Virginia, speaking French. Maybe they are diamonds, maybe he is Bob Marley reincarnated. I gulp the rest of my strawberry daiquiri and think, *Naah*. Besides, I'd never go out with a man with hair longer than mine.

"Renee? Hello? Earth to Miss Howard. You trippin' or something?"

"No. Just reminiscing."

It's snowing something fierce now. I can barely see my Jetta in the parking lot from Star City's main entrance.

"When you gonna get rid of that purse?" She taps my Liz Claiborne purse with a long, curly nail. "You heard what that heifer said on Oprah."

I have no intention of getting rid of it, even if it isn't made especially for *my* people. "You know Liz will have to change her mind after she loses money," I say.

"Whatever," Collette says. "So, you coming?"

I put on my coat and pop my umbrella. "I got some groceries to pick up."

"You and everyone else in town."

"Maybe I'll get on channel seven at Harris-Teeter." In Roanoke, a long line at a grocery store becomes the top story. "Then Prince Charming will see me, fall immediately in love with my bomb of a body, and rescue me."

"Child, you need Jesus. Besides, Prince Charming was a white boy. You mean Prince, or The Artist or whatever."

"You know what I meant. You and Clyde have fun."

Collette gives me her "uh-huh" smile. "I'll call you tomorrow. Oh, there he is now."

I envy Collette for Clyde. Yeah, he's chubby and loud and dresses like he's on *227*, but he takes care of Collette—like tonight leaving early from work to drive her home in the snow. I've never known, much less been with, a man who would do that for me. Then again, I've never known exactly what I've wanted in a man, but whoever he might be, I know I haven't found him yet because I'm still alone.

I can't think of a time that Collette didn't have a man. In kindergarten, she had the boys helping her paste shit down or do her finger painting for her. Me, I went home with crusty nails. In middle school, they carried her books while I lugged a book bag. In high school, she hooked up with most of the linemen on the football team—simultaneously—while I had only one real date my entire high-school career. And the ho ain't even all that pretty. Big teeth, big hair (mostly her own), big body, and big feet. She's keeping Weight Watchers in business all by herself. I tell her she's in their "Frequent Fryer Program." As a result, I can't borrow shit from her, not that I'd want to. Collette dresses like she's part of a perpetual circus, wearing every damn color of the rainbow every damn day. When she spins around, she looks like a kaleidoscope. The girl is loud even before she speaks, and when she does, daa-em, *everybody* looks her way.

I'm no diva-in-waiting like Collette. I know I'm at least somewhat cute, I'm better-educated, I'm soft-spoken, I know how to dress, and yet . . . Collette's got another man, a good man, driving her home on a snowy night.

I trudge through the slush, soaking my white Nikes, to my Jetta, kitted out with rims, spoiler, and a bumpin' sound system. No matter how long it takes to get home, I will be jammin' to UNV and Babyface, my "dates" for the evening. I know Babyface is married, but what that ho don't know won't hurt her.

I only live six miles from the Star City Cable operations center, but tonight it takes forty-five minutes to get from Hershberger Road to 581 to the Elm Avenue exit to Franklin Road to my neighborhood in Old Southwest thanks to no plowing and a whole bunch of fools in four-wheel-drives thinking they can drive the speed limit. I enjoy watching them leave the road here and there to get around traffic and get ass-deep stuck in the snow.

Roanoke, Virginia, the Star City of the South. More like the Most Segregated Town in the South. Even the bowling leagues are segregated. Go to Hilltop Lanes any Wednesday night, and you'll see white folks on the left half, black folks on the right. Population's less than 100,000 so 'Noke isn't a city in my mind. "Big Lick" (I love that nickname) is divided off into sections, kind of like D.C. Most of the white people live in three of the four quadrants (NE, SW and SE), and most of *my* people live in Northwest. One out of every four Roanokers is black, and we live in one of four sections. Nah, we ain't segregated—just separated. I grew up in Northwest and now live in Old Southwest with Mama. Around here, that almost makes me a traitor to my people.

Roanoke is an all-American city. Really. We've won this award five times to tie Cleveland for top honors. That should tell you something, huh? And no offense to anyone from Cleveland. I mean, at least Cleveland has a professional football team (who thought up the name "Browns" when the team was all-white back in the day?), a professional baseball team (still called the Indians—what's up with that?), and a professional basketball team. Roanoke used to have a semi-pro football team (the Rush), and now has an indoor football team (the Steam) and a minor-league hockey team (the Express). Steam? Express? It's a railroad-town thing, you wouldn't understand.

Our all-American city council (mostly white) recently built a seven-million-dollar footbridge over the damn train tracks, like they're scenic or something. The bridge connects the Hotel Roanoke, staffed by my people, to downtown, a place my people avoid. Had a brother pepper-sprayed and beaten for one blown taillight down there. Wasn't quite Rodney King, but it sent a message: "Y'all just keep to yuh-selves, now." As for the police, seems like

7

99 44/100 percent of them are ivory white. They always seem to cruise Northwest, yet when the shit really happens, it takes them forever to get there.

Whenever I get out of Roanoke, which isn't often, and I tell people where I'm from, they always say, "That's in Georgia, right?" I correct them and get asked, "What's it near?" I have yet to be able to answer that one to anyone's satisfaction. It's north of Blacksburg (where the Virginia Tech Hokies play) and south of Lynchburg (where Jerry Falwell lives), about four hours west of Richmond, and three hours north of Charlotte, North Carolina. The border of West Virginia looks like a belly, so consider Roanoke the tip of West Virginia's "outie" belly button. In other words, we're in the middle of nowhere, connected to the rest of the world by I-81. Yep, I'm stuck between *Blacks*burg and *Lynch*burg, two towns you can get to from Lee (as in Robert E.) Highway, yet I'm only eighteen miles away from the Booker T. Washington National Monument.

If I were moving into Roanoke from somewhere else, I'd have lots of questions. It was once called Big Lick? Isn't that a bit suggestive? Oh, it was a salt lick for deer. That's still kind of suggestive. It's also an all-American city? In what sport? Oh. The *city* is all-American. And you have a big star on a mountain? There's a zoo there? Sounds nice. Just one tiger? What happened to the other one? Oh, Roanoke's just a one-tiger town. Any other animals, like bears? You shoot bears. Why do you do that? They tie up traffic. This is a joke, right? It's not a joke. On Hershberger Road, you say? But never on Carolina Street. Why not? There's a really big tree in the middle of the road. Why is there a really big tree in the middle of the road? Oh. No one's thought to cut it down. You say that snakes occasionally get loose and end up in Laundromats? And people have kept pet pigs in their backyards? Within the city limits? Oh, I don't doubt they make good pets. Kinda puts a damper on barbecues, though, huh? Well, I thought it was funny. How about shopping? I'll be able to see all the stores as I land at the airport? Especially the sidewalk sales at Valley View? Isn't that dangerous? Oh, only the prices are falling at Valley View Mall. Catchy. What about places to eat? You recommend Texas Tavern. Sounds good. What do they serve? A cheesy Western and a bowl with. A bowl with what? A bowl of chili with lots of onions. Okay, uh, what's a cheesy Western? You have no idea. Okay. Tell me about the people. You had a minister with two wives. Isn't that sacrilegious? Oh, only if you're caught. I see. And you have a bank robber who dropped his wallet in the parking lot of the bank he was robbing, and another bank robber who went to a local hospital complaining that a strange red dye was burning his skin? Caught red-faced, huh? Any colleges in the area? I'd like to live near one, maybe take some classes. Roanoke College. How do I get there? I drive to Salem. Um, I go to Salem to get to Roanoke College? Oh, I understand. Kinda like going to Philadelphia to get to the University of Pittsburgh. What about R&B or rap shows? Unless I like country or fake wrestling, I have to drive to Greensboro, North Carolina? Why is that? What about cultural events for my people? The Henry Street Festival? So I go to Henry Street, right? No, I go to Elmwood Park. Why don't I . . . never mind. Has Roanoke ever been in any movies? *Crazy People*. No shit. But I thought that movie took place in New York City. It did, but Roanoke was cheaper. Any other films? *Dirty Dancing, Sommersby, What About Bob?, In a Shallow Grave*, and *Hearts in Atlantis* were filmed around here? But Roanoke is in *Crazy People*—as New York City.

To say it in a countrified way, we is right conflicted.

Is there anyone famous enough to put Roanoke on the map after nearly 120 years of existence? Let's see . . . singers Jane Powell, Wayne Newton, and Derrell Coleman (the brother who won seven times on *Star Search* before Sam Harris beat him), the Barber brothers (Tiki and Ronde) in the NFL, Tony Atlas (who wrestled the shit out of Hulk Hogan back in the day), George Lynch in the NBA, and actress Debbie Reynolds used to live up on Mill Mountain where we have that one tiger, Ruby, in the zoo. If I were Ruby, I'd be pissed. It can be lonely enough in Roanoke (there are only seventy-one men to every hundred women in this town), but to be a tiger all alone on top of a mountain? That shit would depress me. And during my lifetime, we've been on CNN only three times that I can remember: the flood of '85, that minister with two wives (one old and the other sixteen), and the killing of a gay man at the Backstreet Cafe. We've been on ABC's *Nightline* once when a kid was selling his Ritalin to his friends. Muddy water, unholy man, shooting at a gay bar, Ritalin-snorting—my hometown.

But . . . I like Roanoke and wouldn't think of moving. Really. Yeah, I talk bad about Roanoke, but I have a right to since I am a Roanoker, born and raised. This is my home, for better or worse. My mama is here, my people are here, my best friend is here, my church is here, my roots are here. I know this place, and according to some national magazines, Roanoke is in the top ten for health, least stress, and best place to raise a family. And Roanoke is beautiful (whenever we aren't on water restriction during a drought), especially in the fall, with more colors in the mountains than you can imagine. And when a snowstorm gets stuck between the Appalachians and the Blue Ridge Mountains, we get tons of snow. They're predicting over a foot from this storm, which is ten inches more than we got all of last year.

As I'm watching the Chevette in front of me sliding down Franklin, I remember that Mama and I have no food in the house. Yeah, we're messed up: black folks living in the wrong part of town with no food in the house. And since it's her bowling night, I know she didn't do any shopping. Can't do much with condiments, sauces, and an expired bottle of ranch dressing. Instead of making my debut on local TV at Harris-Teeter, I turn right on Walnut Avenue to see if I can get something at Luchesi's on Fourth Street. My people don't normally eat there (at least *I* have never eaten there), and Connie, my heifer supervisor at work, is always raving over their Italian sandwich with banana peppers, their carrot cake (is that Italian?), and their hot, fresh amaretto-flavored latte (whatever that shit is).

Just as I'm making the left turn off Walnut to Fourth Street, I start sliding and get stuck sideways on a puny little hill right in front of Luchesi's. I mean, I could have at least slid to the side, and then I could play it off like I'm trying to parallel park. But no, I'm stuck and spinning in the middle of the damn road. No shovel, cat litter, flashlight. Nothing. No boots, either, just some white Nikes that I'll have to bleach when I get home.

Then someone's tapping at my window, making me jump even though I know Old Southwest isn't all that bad a neighborhood. Yet. I press the down button on the window, and a sheet of snow falls into the car. Serves me right for dreaming about carrot cake.

"May I help you?" a white boy asks. After brushing the snow off my lap, I look up at a butcher . . . only there's no blood on his apron. He waves. "Hello. Do you need any help?"

Uh-duh. At least he doesn't ask if I'm stuck. "If you can," I say, looking at his too-orange hat, his rusty snow shovel, and his flour-covered face. At least I hope it's flour. Otherwise, he's the whitest white boy I've every seen. An albino white boy?

"I'll try. Better roll up your window."

He goes around the back of my car and starts digging under my rear tires. Fool doesn't know I have front-wheel drive, but oh well. I check him out in my rearview, you know, because looking is free. He isn't that bad looking—for a white boy. Kinda tall, but I'm only five-four so everyone is tall to me. Not all that buff, and that apron ain't happenin'. But mostly, that orange hat has *got* to go. Fool looks like a wooden kitchen match.

He comes back to my window and wipes some snow off it before signaling me to roll it down. "Okay, I want you to turn all the way to the right"—I do—"and go in reverse. I'll push from the front. Hopefully we can get the front of your car pointing downhill."

"You gonna dig out under my front tires?"

He smiles. Has all his teeth. Dark eyes, too. "Uh, there's nothing but ice under them from, uh, the spinning. Let's see if this works."

He starts to walk away when I yell, "Hey!"

He leaps back to me and says, "What's wrong?"

"What do I do once I start going downhill?"

He smiles again. "Just aim, I guess."

How stuuu-pid of me. He goes to the front of the Jetta and gets ready to push the right side. I put the car in reverse and hit the gas pedal—hard. He waves at me and yells something. Now what? He comes around to my window again, and as the window rolls down, I start laughing because he is covered with snow and slush. "Sorry," I say. I look in the back seat for a towel, and all I can find is one un-used Burger King napkin. "Will this do?" He takes the napkin and smiles again. This is one of the smiling-est boys I've ever met. Maybe he doesn't have a brain cell in his head. Either that or he's really a serial killer with a rusty shovel who—

"Go easy on the gas," he says, interrupting my daymare, and returns to the front of the car.

"Go easy on the gas," I say, mimicking him as the window rises to the top. How was I to know? Ain't no snow in Africa! Snow-storms ain't in my culture! He nods his head once, and I tap lightly on the gas pedal while he pushes.

After no movement at first, the car begins moving down the hill. Good thing there's no traffic (or black people to see me). In about thirty seconds, I'm facing downhill toward Allison Avenue.

He comes over to the window, gives me the okay sign, and just stands there, still dripping. Oh, now what? Just like a dog. He saves me and wants his reward. And me without my Scooby Snacks.

"Thanks," I say quickly as the window slides down halfway and is on its way up when he puts this large hand on it. Daymare returns.

"Uh, if you still need to go toward Elm"—he just had to say Elm as in *Nightmare on*—"you might try Fifth Street. It's not as hilly, and I'm sure they plowed it since it has a traffic light."

I know the neighborhood, fool. "Actually," I say coolly, "I'm going to Luchesi's."

"Luchesi's?" I freeze my eyes from rolling and nod. Then he

smiles that doofy Opie grin. Maybe he's Mr. Williams's neighbor out for a spree in the big ol' town of Big Lick.

"Should I leave it here? I'm off the road, aren't I?"

He checks. "Close enough." Then he just stands there. What's he going to do? Make sure I get inside okay?

"Giovanni!" some fat man yells from the doorway of Luchesi's. The guy could have played goalie for the Roanoke Express and never would have had to move to stop the puck. Not that I watch hockey games anyway. I mean, it's a racist sport, right? Ain't no black people out there. Oh, I know it ain't a cultural sport of my people because there are no ice rinks in Africa, but neither is basketball if you think about it. Besides, if my people did what those white men did to each other on the ice, we'd be pepper-sprayed, locked up, and beaten some more. We been on our way or in the penalty box since Jamestown.

"Giovanni?" Fat Man yells again, but Giovanni isn't moving himself or his hand from my window. What kind of name is that? I check out his face, and although it's sweaty and slushy, I see his nose looking like it's straight out of *Rocky*. Italian. Collette says that Italians aren't really white, that they're olive-skinned. Green-skinned, like a frog or lizard. Ain't that some shit. I decide to burst Collette's bubble on the phone tomorrow: "Collette, I met an Italian last night, and he wasn't olive. He was pale. Had to put my sunglasses on. I may have retina damage."

"Yeah, Pops?" Fat Man's his father? Dag, how did short and squat make tall and thin? Maybe Giovanni's adopted.

"She okay?" Pops says.

She? How he know a *she* is in the car? I have tinted windows on my Jetta. No way he can see me from there.

Giovanni turns to me. "Are you okay?"

Concerned about little old *she*, are we? But I can tell he's really concerned—something about his eyes—so I drop the attitude. "Yes. Thank you."

"Well good," he says. "We'll see you inside then?"

Maybe you will, and maybe you won't. But dag, I am starving, and I do smell me some hot bread. I swear they pipe the aroma out some vent in the roof or something, because the whole neighborhood can smell the bread baking. In the middle of this struggle between my stomach and my pride, I start thinking weird stuff. I wonder if Giovanni's bald under that ugly-ass cap, wonder if his eyes are really dark brown, wonder if his hair really smells like a wet puppy. But mostly I wonder if he's going to wash his stank hands before he serves me. That's the first damn thing he better do.

I sit in the car collecting myself, wishing R. J. was still around. Yeah, he dogged me out, but on nights like these . . . It's still hard for me to admit that he used me, but I have to face facts. I talked him into looking outside Roanoke for a job to go with his electrical engineering degree from Virginia Tech since GE wasn't hiring. I bought that *Business Employment Weekly* and circled all the possibilities. I updated and printed out his resume. I mailed the resumes to all those damn box numbers. Then, I helped him pack up his shit in a U-Haul and watched him go to D.C. last August.

"You're coming to visit me next weekend, right?" R. J. asked.

"Sure," I said.

The next week, however, the Jetta's power windows became possessed, rolling up and down on their own. No fun at all during late-summer thunderstorms. I could just see myself getting on I-66, bailing the Jetta while fighting traffic. Mama's hoopdy Buick never would have made it to D.C. and back, and I wasn't about to ride a bus for fifteen hours, with twenty stops along the way in one-house West Virginia towns like Whitesville, Paw Paw, or Odd.

"That's okay," he said when I told him. "I'm still getting settled. Why don't you try again next weekend?"

Don't think I didn't try. Reginald James Hodges was too fine to leave to the ladies in D.C. Educated. Single. Dressed sharp. No kids that I knew of. Paid out the ass to work for the government.

He said he couldn't tell me exactly what he did or he'd have to kill me. And he said he loved me.

But after that first weekend away, something would "come up" on his end to prevent my visit. "Oh, baby, they working me over-time," he'd say, or "We got a new project going now that's taking up all my time."

I just wasn't having this at all, so I decided to surprise him at his apartment in Arlington. I washed and waxed the Jetta, got my hair done right at Brand-Nubian Hair Designs, my nails done at Salon Du'Ta. Wore a brand-new mustard yellow outfit courtesy of the E-Style catalog, perfectly matching shoes, and all the necklaces, earrings, and rings he had given me. I literally bathed in CK1. I put the *butt* in *buttah* that day.

Then I got a pad of Post-it notes and wrote some suggestive somethin'-somethin's on them. I was going to stick them up all over his apartment, leading him to me in the bedroom. He was gonna have to really search for that last Post-it. . . .

It was a simple plan. I'd go to the apartment building manager, claim I was his fiancée, and say, "Could you possibly let me in so I can surprise my future husband?" Who could refuse little ol' me?

I took a day off from Star City Cable that Friday in September and made it to Arlington in under five hours. After making sure R. J.'s car wasn't around, I went to the office and found the man-ager, a sweet-faced Maya Angelou-looking woman named Dee, who was *easy* to convince.

We walked together up to apartment 215, each of us cheesing and laughing. She knew what was up.

Dee put the key into the lock, turned it, and pushed the door. The door chain was still hooked.

"Reggie? Is that you?" a female voice asked.

Dee's mouth dropped open. Mine just tightened up a notch. *This shit ain't happening*, I thought.

"Open up," Dee said. "It's the manager."

"Just a second," the ho in R. J.'s apartment *sang*. The bitch has the nerve to sing, like she's that Maria chick in *The Sound of Music*. Now there's an intelligent white movie: some crazy white Nazis are chasing your white singing asses, and you take time out to sing.

The chain rattled, the door opened, and there stood a five-foot-two, eyes-of-blue *white* bitch in a skimpy black silk kimono with an orange dragon on the back. This ho put the *tack* in *tacky*.

"May I help you?" she asked, looking from me to Dee and back again to me. She must have seen the smoke in my eyes.

Dee held me back and said, "Does R. J. Hodges live here?"

Blue Eyes flipped her fake-ass dirty-blond hair off her shoulders. "Yes. Reggie lives here."

I was thinking about where to shove the Post-its if Dee would just let me go.

"And you are?" Dee asked, planting her hip into my side.

"Dagney. Is there some sort of problem?" And then Dagney actually yawned!

Dagney? What the hell kind of name is that? Ain't it amazing what white folks name their children? My people would never name a child that. Dagneisha, maybe.

Dee shot me a look that said, "No, no, not now, sister." I was having a hard time with Dee's hip. I wanted to cry, I wanted to burn Dagney's hair off with four or five Golden Hots, slowly savoring the sizzle and the smoke.

"Uh, Miss—"

"Winston. Dagney Winston." She actually stuck out her hand for Dee to shake! Reach over here, I dared her with my eyes. I'll shake it and them fake-ass nails off!

"Miss Winston. You're not on Mr. Hodges's lease."

"Do I have to be to stay overnight with Reggie?"

That did it. She used the word "overnight" and the name "Reggie" in the same sentence, so I shrieked, and I don't mean one of them candy-ass screams in slasher movies, where the dumbass white girl runs out into the woods naked with no weapon saying

"Who's there?" and later tries to run from a guy walking 0.2 miles per hour and trips over the only pebble on a smooth road. I shrieked, and I'm sure that even the President looked up from his "ho of the week" and said, "What the hell was that, darlin'?"

But Dee was just too big-boned and too fast. She boxed me out like Dennis Rodman and kept me from that doorway. I couldn't see Dagney, but I could hear the skank crying. Of all the things I could have said, should have said, that shriek said it all. But I still wanted me some dirty-blond hair for a trophy.

I tried the "I'm-all-right-back-away-with-hands-up" technique, but Dee wasn't fooled. You can't fool a sister with a tired-ass move like that. Damn door was still open, too. If that was me in there, and someone was shrieking like that at me, that door would have been shut, locked, triple-bolted, chained, and every piece of furniture in the apartment would have been stacked against it. But not Dagney, oh no. She was in her "Can't-we-all-just-get-along?" mode.

"There must be some misunderstanding," she cried.

"Understand this, ho!" I shrieked and lunged for Dagney through Dee.

Dee's big-boned self didn't even flinch as I bounced off her. In a controlled voice, Dee said, "Dagney, you better shut this door and lock it."

"But I don't understand!" Dagney sobbed. "Reggie and I are going to be married! We've been dating since my freshman year at Tech!"

Boom. I started to say something but stopped. My heart fell, and the Croissanwich in my stomach rose.

Luckily for Dee, she stepped aside in time. Dagney, however, would later have to explain to R. J. how a semi-digested Croissanwich ended up plastered to her kimono, the door, the carpet, and I think even the coatrack just inside the door.

Dee helped me stagger back to my car, where I sat and cussed R. J. for half an hour. Dee patted my back and tried to comfort me.

"You okay now?" Dee asked. I shook my head. "Are you through?"

I knew what she meant. She could have asked, "Will there be a round two?" My people don't give up after only one round. I didn't answer, and the first tears began to fall. "Oh, child," Dee crooned. "Is he worth them tears?"

"No. These tears are for me."

"Good."

"Ain't nothin' good about this."

"Sure there is. I seen just about everything in this life, but I have never seen a sister throw up on a white woman." I wiped a tear off my nose and started laughing. "That shit will *never* come out," Dee said.

"I ought to go," I said.

"You sure, honey? If I know Dagney, she on the phone right now to R. J. She weak. She'll want to know what to do. I mean, R. J., this woman blew chunks on me, like, omigod!"

Why is it when life is at its absolute worst, my people can still laugh? Hell, we all ought to be comedians then. I was in tears laughing from listening to Dee's impersonation of Dagney.

"You really think R. J. will show up?"

Dee patted my stomach. "You got anything left in there?"

"I doubt it."

"Damn. I would have liked to see you throw up on him, too. But, I doubt R. J. will be by. He may have lost his damn mind by hurting a fine girl like you, but no man is gonna come runnin' if his current lady says a crazy black girl done thrown up on her."

"You're right."

"So, I'll ask you again: Are you through?"

"Yeah."

"Alright, then. Get yourself home and find you another man. Shouldn't take long. I'll keep an eye out tonight, see if R. J. makes an appearance."

"What for?"

"'Cause he deserves a scare. He needs someone in his face confronting his frontin' ass. I like to confront people. It's in my job description, you know. And, he gonna have to pay more rent."

"How much more?"

She checked out the ruined outfit I was wearing. "How much that outfit cost you?"

"A hundred and fifty."

She raised her eyebrows. "Hmm. Gonna cost him two hundred. A *month*." She hugged me again. "Now get yourself home. You drive fast enough, you may be able to get out to a club in time for the last dance."

I made it back to Roanoke by 11 P.M., but I didn't feel like going out. And since Mama was out bowling and Collette was out with Clyde, I had no one to talk to. I debated whether to call R. J. or not and decided on not. It wouldn't have done any good. He would have lied, I would have cussed his ass, maybe even broken something of Mama's. Still, it would have been interesting to hear his side of things. I mean, how do you lie yourself out of two years of two-timing?

That night, I decided that no way, no how was I ever going to let myself get hurt again. Never. I decided that a man wasn't worth all the investments I made: the weekly hair appointments, the clothes, the shoes—wait, shoes are always a good investment—the hours sitting in front of a mirror to make myself look . . . *exactly* like I did the last time I saw him. What's up with that? And while I was like a gerbil on a wheel at Woolworth's running in circles for R. J., my man was a worm out wriggling in another woman's mud.

My mud ain't been wriggled in for a long time since I've put a lock on my coochie. Some call it celibacy—I call it "coochie-lock." It's not that hard to practice since there are no men in my daily life anyway. My job doesn't allow much face-to-face, no man at Star City excites me, I live in a neighborhood full of old white folks, and I rarely go clubbing thanks to Collette's attempts at hooking me up. I guess church at High Holiness is my social highlight of the week. And all of this because of the "kimono ho."

At least I have Mama, and my mama has always been on a mission. She graduated near the top of her class at NC A&T, the first in the history of her family (as in from the beginning of time) to graduate college. She met a man, saw him long enough to get pregnant, then told him to take his narrow ass out the door. Mama is a single parent by choice, and for her it's the right choice. She's never felt the need to tell me who my daddy is, and I've never felt the need to ask her.

That's not entirely true. I've always had the desire, the wish to ask Mama about my daddy, but I've kept my mouth shut because my daddy is in my dreams, and I'd hate for Mama to prove me wrong about those dreams. My daddy is every great black man who ever lived; my daddy is every athlete on TV; my daddy is the one who wins all those Grammys and Olympic medals. My daddy gives inspiring speeches to me, he dunks for me, he plants gardens for me, he sings for me, and he always smells like Lagerfeld. People ask me, "Do you miss him?" Miss who? How can you miss what you've never had? Sure I'm curious, but I've never cried myself to sleep over him.

When I was five, I asked Mama where my daddy lived. "That man ain't never lived, child," she told me.

"He's dead?"

"No. He's alive. He just ain't livin'. And don't you ask me another thing about him ever."

From then on, my daddy has lived in my head, and since you can't lose what you never had either, my daddy will never die.

Mama, though, seems to want all men to die, especially any man who tries to get close to me. She warned me about R. J., but I wasn't hearing her. "A man that fine, Renee, you know he got some skeletons. He too pretty. It's the pretty ones you got to watch out for. You can't be around them twenty-four-seven to see who they're seeing, and believe me, girl, their eyes are connected directly to their dicks. Your daddy was the same way."

"He was?"

"Everywhere we went, women, some of 'em married even, were lookin' at him, up and down and stayin' down, if you know what I mean, while I was standin' there holding his damn hand. Even in church! I didn't need that shit."

"You could have married him."

"What for? So I could sit and wonder where he was and who he was with at what time of night? Child, I only wanted him to make me a pretty baby, to use him before he used me. I have my pretty baby, a good job, a house with a picket fence, and a car that runs most of the time. What more I need?"

I'm nothing like my mama. Her social life is always in full swing: secret lunches during the week, bowling on Fridays, the Black Angus on Saturdays, High Holiness on Sundays. And she's still gorgeous. She gets mad when she gets carded and flat-out refuses to admit she's forty-eight.

"I ain't too old to have men beggin' for more," she says, "and I love to see all them old dogs beg."

Mama has her rules, though. She never gives out her home number, just her pager number. She never brings them to our house, and she never sees them more than "once in a while."

"It's all a matter of protecting myself," she explains. "Besides, variety is the spice of life, and as long as he's spicy, I'll give him some variety."

At any rate, Mama's made me into an independent woman without even trying, and I wouldn't have it any other way. While she's out, I stay in, reading E. Lynn Harris novels to make my own messed-up life seem "normal" in comparison. I watch the NBA on TNT, *Girlfriends*, on UPN, and reruns of *227* and *Living Single*. On Black Thursdays, I disconnect the phone and watch WGN all night. Hell, Chicago's news is always more exciting than Roanoke's. If I get truly bored, I rearrange furniture in Mama's spotless house. I know I get more than nine hours of sleep every day. If I'm not sleeping, reading, or watching TV, I cook. I ain't talking about some of my friends like Collette, who only press "defrost" on their microwaves or boil some water. I *cook*. My dirty rice will burn the hair off your crusty toes, and just one slice of my pound cake will make you need to join Jenny Craig. Mama says when she retires, we'll start our own catering company.

"We'll call it 'Mama Renee's,'" she says.

"Why not 'Mama Shirl's'?"

"Your name is more exotic. 'Mama Shirl's' sounds like some disease children get."

"Well, I ain't likely to ever be a mama."

Mama always gets quiet when I talk like this. Then she says, "Child, the day you have a grandbaby for me is the day I'm officially old. You don't want your mama to be old now, do you?"

"You'll never be old, Mama."

"You got that right."

"And it takes a man to have a baby, right?"

"Or the miracle of modern science."

Mama says that if sperm banks had been around in Roanoke in the early seventies, she'd have been first in line. "Imagine," she says over a cup of Swiss Miss in the parlor. "No sweaty man on top of you. No worries about what he may give you in addition to a child. No having to fake nothin'. No sloppy man to worry you during the pregnancy. Just an ID number."

"But," I say, "that would take the romance out of sex."

"There's romance?" she says, deadpan serious. "Honey, ain't a romantic soul been born since Nat King Cole. You want romance, read all about it in those Harlequins, or watch the next Julia Roberts movie. Romance is dead and gone."

"But what about the men who send you flowers?"

"I know what they want, and I don't want no men if that's *all* they want."

"But Mama, I thought that *was* what you wanted." It's weird having a mama who gets more action than you do.

"Child, I enjoy gettin' some every now and then. I ain't too old to get a leg up, but I also enjoy simple conversation on subjects other than the weather, the perfume I'm wearing, or where have I been all his life. If I could find me a man who I could talk to, who would listen to me, maybe I'd believe in romance again."

"So there's hope for you."

"I said 'maybe.' "

No matter how anti-romantic Mama is, I'm still hopeless. I actually enjoyed *Sleepless in Seattle*, though Meg Ryan reminds me of Dagney. (Tom Hanks should have pushed that ho off the Empire State Building.) I know shit like that never happens, but romance is about the impossible, the unpredictable, the improbable, isn't it? *Pretty Woman* is pretty far-fetched, like a bimbo is going to: 1. look like Julia Roberts; 2. meet a guy as fine as Richard Gere; 3. *not* sleep with him; and 4. eventually go off with his rich ass into the sunset. But damnit, I cry every time I see that movie. Hell, I'd settle for a single flower, and I wouldn't care at all if someone stole it from a cemetery or pulled it from someone's yard.

But my heart doesn't mend easily. I had an intense year-long crush on a senior, Jermaine Holmes, during my sophomore year in high school. Jermaine was supposed to be the shit in football and basketball but didn't get much playing time because he fumbled every other time he carried the ball and couldn't dribble a basketball without tripping over a painted line. But . . . he had a killer smile, serious dark-brown eyes, a thin moustache and a goatee, and the softest laugh; and since I was young and dumb, I pursued his ass relentlessly until he asked me to the prom—where I found him to be just as clumsy in the cheap hotel room on Orange Avenue afterward. There I was, finally ready to lose my virginity to the boy of my dreams, when Jermaine came with an "Oh Nelly!" before my head hit the pillow. He then had the nerve to say something like, "So was it good for you, too?" I almost said "What was?" (and almost asked who Nelly was), but I didn't because I was in love and Jermaine Holmes could do no wrong.

The prom was our only date. Jermaine never spoke to me again. I'd call his house, and he was "not-at-home-can-I-take-a-message?" for three weeks. I had given him my heart, and he had shit on it. The moment he made me a woman, I started to hate boys, and for the next two years of high school, I was in boy-hate mode. Any boy that dared step to me got some heavy shit.

"Yo, yo, girlie," a boy would say from where he slouched against a locker with his homeboys. A boy never seemed to have the guts to step to me alone. He had to have his homies there for backup. "How 'bout comin' over my crib?"

I'd fix him with a deadly stare and ask, "What you got that I can't live without, boy?"

"Oh, girl, I got what you *need*."

"You do?" He'd nod. "And what's that?"

By this time, we would have drawn a crowd. This kind of shit was more entertaining than going to class. "Well, uh, you know."

I'd bat my eyes and play innocent. "No, I *don't* know. Why don't you tell me? Tell everybody." I'd point at some girls in the crowd. "Maybe you got what they need, too. You got enough to go around for everyone here? Maybe you even got enough for your boys here."

After that I'd hear "Fuck you, bitch!" or get called a "stuck-up dyke," but I didn't care. I had my standards, and I had had it with boys.

I expected to meet a nice man at Roanoke College (where 95 percent of the 2.1 percent African-American population played basketball), but I didn't. The white girls from places like Connecticut and Massachusetts flocked to the brothers like white on rice, and the white boys who spoke to me were usually fat, drunk preppies who had nicknames like "Slobbo" and "Gunner" from pissant Northeastern towns no one ever heard of.

One overgrown beer fart named Oz (as in "land of") wearing a blue do-rag (like he was a Crip from his 'hood in New Hampshire) cornered me at the first frat party I attended as a freshman to tell me how much of a racist he *wasn't*. "I'm not prejudiced at all. My best friend back home, Luther, he's black, and I really dig black chicks."

How "Mod Squad" of you to say so, I had thought. If I had lit a match near his lips, he would have exploded and I would have been covered by preppie white goo. "You really dig black chicks?"

"Yeah," he whispered. "So I was wondering, if, like, maybe you and I could . . . you know." He pointed upstairs with the fattest finger attached to the fattest hand attached to the stubbiest arm that I had ever seen. Daa-em, I had thought at the time, how does he wipe his ass?

Instead of being nice, I smiled and shouted, "Oz, do you want to fuck me?" The frat party suddenly quieted. The *F* word is especially powerful among white people. Seems to arrest all thought and motion, I have no idea why. Hell, they invented the word.

Oz blinked and tried to shush me. No one does that and lives.

"Oh, I see. You're not prejudiced as long as we keep it quiet." I paused and whispered loudly, "So, Oz, you still want to fuck me?"

I wasn't invited to any more frat parties after that.

Then R. J. happened. I was at Mac 'N' Bob's, taking a study break from finals during my junior year (and eating the best damn hot wings on earth), when he walked in—alone—and stood next to me, all six-foot-three, 230 pounds of him. "This seat taken?" he asked in a sexy voice.

I looked at all the empty tables around me then looked up at him. The man was a mountain, a carved-onyx mountain, an African warrior. I couldn't speak and barely shook my head "no." My nose began to sweat.

He sat. "What's good here?"

I nodded at the wings on my plate.

"Got to get me some of them, then. They must be good, girl. Your nose is sweating."

Yeah, I thought at the time, and so's my coochie. "It isn't the wings," I said, finally finding my voice and my attitude. "My mama says it's because I'm so mean."

"Are you?"

I stared hard at my plate. "I can be."

He leaned forward, and I looked up. He locked eyes with mine. "Are you even mean to someone you've just met?"

"*Especially* to someone I've just met."

He nodded and licked his bottom lip ever so slowly. "Should I move to another table?"

"If you want to."

"That's not what I asked. Do *you* want me to move to another table?"

I had to test him. "Yes."

"Okay," he said, and he stood. "Sorry to have bothered you."

I let him take a step. "You didn't."

"Hmm?"

"You didn't bother me." Just my coochie and my tighty-whitey draws. "And . . . you can sit with me, but only if you want to."

He sat with no hesitation. "What's your name?"

"Who's askin'?"

"Reginald James Hodges the third, but you, and you alone, can call me R. J."

Damn, he could be romantic, and despite all the shit he put me through, I'm still a romantic. But here I am, twenty-six, in the prime of my life, wasting a snowy Friday night outside an Italian restaurant run by a kitchen match and a butcher block. I believe in God, but sometimes I think He's laughing His cosmic ass off at me.

When I'm finally collected enough, I enter Luchesi's and smell me some hot bread calling my name.

Pops bum-rushes me and says, "What can I get for you, gal?"

Gal? Is that Italian for something? What's this "gal" shit?

Giovanni, minus the hat, steps up to me, his dark brown eyes staring at my feet. "Would you like to be seated?"

What I'd like is for your Pops to quit calling me "gal." What if I call him "dago" or "wop"? How he like that? I'm in a fightin' mood, and I almost ask Giovanni if he washed his hands.

Pencil and order book already in hand, he leads me away from the door to a table for four near a country picture of some bull-cows chewing on grass and eyeing some female cows in the next pasture. White people and their "art." He snatches the little card that says "Reserved for three or more, please" and lays a simple menu on the table.

"Would you care for something hot to drink?"

I can't remember what Connie says is good. "What do you recommend?"

"Everything here is good!" Pops yells across the room, and I notice Giovanni wince.

"Well, uh, like he said, everything here is good."

With the possible exception of your Pops and your hair. Dark hairs shoot every which way. I watch him spin his pencil for a moment or two until he notices me noticing and stops. "Well," I say, sliding my coat onto the back of my chair, "why don't you surprise me."

His Opie smile from outside returns. "Okay. I'll be back in a few minutes."

He walks away, and I take a peek at his ass. The word "narrow" comes to mind, but it has possibilities. I laugh because that's exactly what my mama might say.

The menu is simple. Soups and appetizers at the top, sandwiches in the middle, desserts and drinks at the bottom. All on one side on the paper. Prices are reasonable. Only graphic is another damn cow. Maybe it's a picture of Pops's wife. Hell, maybe it's Pops's baby picture. No, the cow's smaller.

Just as I decide on the Italian sandwich and look up, there's Giovanni with a steaming mug of something that smells wonderful. "That was quick," I say. "What is it?"

"Mocha cappuccino with a dash of amaretto."

The words slide off his tongue like water. "Say that again."

"Mocha cappuccino with a dash of amaretto." I could get used to that accent. I mean, I *could*, not that I *would*. "Are you ready to order?"

"What's on the Italian?" I ask, purposely leaving out the "sandwich" part.

He doesn't miss a beat. "Honey-baked ham, Genoa salami, provolone, tomato, lettuce, onions, mayo, Italian dressing, and banana peppers."

"On what kind of bread?"

"Your choice."

"What you got?"

"Our sandwich bread is good—well, all our breads are good."

"Do you . . . make it . . . yourself?" I am a devil.

"Yes ma'am."

What's up with this "ma'am" shit? People say I still look sixteen. At least he's polite. It worked before, so I say, "Surprise me."

"Do you want it served cold . . . or *hot?*"

That gets me. I know he probably says that to every customer, but the way he says it! "Most definitely . . . hot," I say. "Steaming."

"Okay. It'll be ready in a few minutes. I'll bring out some bread sticks."

As I wait, I check out Luchesi's. The blue-and-white-checked floor is spotless. Either business is terrible or Italians are neat people. The tables are wooden and shiny, and although the flowers are silk, at least they match the yellow grain of the wood. Life should be accessorized, you know. Fans and lamps hang from the wooden ceiling, and all the metalwork matches the blue of the tiles. Except for the horny cows on the walls, Luchesi's is a pretty classy joint.

But the music has *got* to go. A mixture of singing, violins, and saxophone. Very depressing. I'm sure it's an Italian thing, but, as Collette might say, "It ain't got no beat."

I see Pops pulling what looks like a flat wooden shovel out of the oven. On the shovel are two round loaves of bread. Meanwhile, Giovanni is pushing something back and forth, surrounded by a bunch of huge white machines.

The mocha cappuccino is delicious. I don't know what amaretto is, but I'm feeling warmer down to my wet Nikes. When Giovanni returns with a basket bursting with bread, I ask him, "What's amaretto?"

"It's a liqueur."

I have way too much of my mama in me, and I can't resist asking, "Trying to get me drunk?"

"No, no," he says, his face turning red. It is not an attractive color on him. "It's just a flavoring."

"Oh," I say, taking another sip, making puppy eyes at him above the rim of the mug.

"But, if you want the real thing, I could—"

"Would you?" I interrupt.

"Sure. Uh, I have to run next door to get it."

Hold on. Next door? "There isn't a liquor store in this neighborhood," I say.

"Oh," he says. "That's where we live."

On Allison Avenue. Dag, we neighbors. Why haven't I ever seen this guy? Oh yeah—he white. "If it's not too much trouble," I purr.

"No, no trouble. Enjoy your bread sticks."

I pull back the napkin from the basket and count at least a dozen bread sticks—hot, buttery, and garlicky. But a dozen? Who's doin' the flirting here? If the sandwich is as good as these bread sticks, I'm going to become a regular customer. Hot, spicy, and hittin' the spot. I don't smell them before eating them like some people. I can't stand people who put their noses over food and take deep sniffs. I mean, a booger could fall out, right? And you'd never catch me sticking my finger in anyone's sauce or on anyone's cake. That's just plain nasty. My people would never do any of that. In public, anyway.

I watch Giovanni leave in a hurry. Mama would say he's just a dog in "fetch" mode. What would I say back? Maybe he's just trying to please me, Mama. No harm in that. I mean, it's not like he's bringing me flowers. Yet.

I'm just biting into my third bread stick when Pops waddles over and asks, "How is everything?"

I hate it when waiters and waitresses do that. I think they wait until you take a bite to ask most of their questions. My mouth is full, and unlike some people, I do not talk with my mouth full. It's probably historical. I mean, my starving people have been eating on the run and keeping quiet for four-hundred years. I don't care if it's a matter of life or death. I have more class than that.

After chewing and drinking some mocha cappuccino, I reply, "Fine."

"If you need anything, just-a yell." Then he waddles back behind the counter, perches his bubble butt on a stool, and stares at me, his hands clasped on his gut.

I've gotten used to white folks staring at me. They follow me around in the mall asking "May I help you?" when I know they're just out to harass me while white kids rob them blind. But Pops isn't staring at me like that. And it isn't like he's staring through me, like I'm not there. I'm used to that, too. It's something . . . well, odd. Must be an Italian thing I wouldn't understand.

"You live around here?" he asks. Dag, his voice carries.

No mouthful this time. "Yes." I notice he has all his hair. Silver. Maybe it's a toupee. Damn thing looks like a gray squirrel.

"How come you never come in before?"

A fair question, but damn he's nosy. "I don't know. I like to cook for myself, I guess."

"Ah," he says and smiles. "It's-a good to cook." What do you reply to that? Do you say "No shit!" or "Yeah, it's-a good to eat, too"? He shifts his body toward me and says, "You live alone?"

Waaait just a damn minute, Mr. Man. I saw *Goodfellas* and all three *Godfathers*. I am staring hard at my next bread stick when Giovanni comes through the back door with a bottle. He shows it to me kind of like those anorexic models on *The Price Is Right* show those little products on the tray, then he points in the direction of some machine.

I don't look at Pops and just hope he doesn't keep trying to get all up in my business. Now if Giovanni asks me, well . . . I'll have to think about that.

I look up and smile my wincing smile when Giovanni returns

with a fresh mug. "I haven't put any amaretto in it yet," he says, "so you tell me when." I let him fill that mug to the brim. He whispers, "Sorry about my father. He can be, uh—"

"Nosy."

"Well, uh, I'm sorry anyway. I'll have your sandwich out to you soon. Would you like some more bread?"

"No."

"I'll be with you shortly."

I shouldn't have said "nosy." I should have just kept my mouth shut and asked for more bread sticks. I don't know what it is with me sometimes. I just slam shut and get cold-hearted in a heartbeat. You piss me off and you take your chances. Giovanni is just trying to be nice.

He's over making my sandwich now, his head and eyes looking down at his hands. Fierce concentration. I notice his two eyebrows become one, or does he only have one eyebrow? That's gross. He looks up, and I look back into my mug.

Before I know it, I'm finishing my second mug. Caffeine and alcohol, what a concept. I'd feel better if . . . daa-em, I have to get a hold of myself. My sandwich must be done. I have to make it up to him, maybe tip him extra. I never do that.

He presents the sandwich to me with a mound of chips and says, "If you need anything, just ask."

I pick up my mug. "How about another one of these?"

"Sure. Uh, same amount of—?"

"Surprise me."

I've eaten lots of sandwiches in my lifetime; most I've made myself, but this is the best sandwich I've ever eaten. Maybe it's the amaretto, maybe it's because I'm hungry as a mug, or maybe it's the goofy cows watching me eat. Whatever the reason, I am satisfied, even if the tomatoes keep falling out on my plate every time I take a bite. I want to order dessert, but there's no way I'm going to finish this sandwich after all the bread sticks I've eaten. Maybe I'll just get a slice of carrot cake to go.

31

Giovanni appears in front of me with another hot mug. I feel like a real boozer, but that amaretto shit is good. "Is everything okay?"

"Okay?" I say a little too loudly. "This is delicious!" I can almost hear an echo.

Then the music gets louder, and I mean there's dust floating down from the speakers hooked to the wall. At first I react like I suppose all my people react when we hear "white" music. We scrunch toes-es and noses and grab onto anything bolted down.

Giovanni leans in, and I can't help but taking a whiff of him. I *will* smell people. He's kind of yeasty, but it's not stank, if you know what I mean. "That's Pops's favorite," he says. "Faure's 'Pavane.' Reminds him of Mama. He'll turn it down after it's over."

A saxophone fills the air, and his Italian words roll around my head. "Well, this is delicious."

"Good," he says, and as he turns to leave, I grab his hand.

I can't believe I'm doing this. I've lost my freakin' mind, putting my black hand on his ashy white hand in Old Southwest, Roanoke, Virginia, "Star City of the South."

"Have you eaten yet?" The amaretto must be kicking my ass.

Either my hand is hot, or he's been spending way too much time in the freezer. "Uh, no. I usually eat after we close up."

I pull on his hand, directing him into the chair across from me. "Do you mind maybe eating now?"

My eyes are glued to his, my grip loosening, but I am not letting go. "Sure. I'd like that," he says, and he leans back in his chair.

"Giovanni!" Pops yells over the music, and I let go.

"I'll be back in a minute," he says as he stands, nearly knocking over his chair. "What's your name?"

I mouth "Renee" but not loud enough for him to hear. I want him to lean in and get a good whiff of me. Hell, all he'll smell is the amaretto.

"What?" he asks.

"Renee," I say, just above a whisper.

"Pretty. I'll be right back."

Damn right, you'll be back. I don't let just anyone smell me in public. Now, I'll be the first to tell you that I do not believe in love at first sight. No way, José, Larry, Curly, or *Mo' Better Blues*. It's the amaretto, I swear. I mean, he's decent-looking, but he ain't fine. His hair needs a cut. Badly. I could bald him and start his ass over. And his nose could use major reduction, but I can't imagine his face without it. Seems to make his eyes deeper and darker. And talk about facial hair! He should have been the guy in that old shaving commercial, the one with the credit card. Probably has to shave twice a day. Lips are thin. Strong chin. Potato-chip ears. One eyebrow. Ashy as the snow outside.

But back to his eyes. I don't know how to explain them, but they aren't lying eyes. R. J. had a pair of *them*. Giovanni looks directly at me the entire time he speaks to me. No cutting side to side, no looking down, no looking over my head. I'm not saying he has diamond-cutting eyes. They're . . . honest. I have a moment of doubt and look for the *Candid Camera* crew. A nice, honest white boy? I have never had that thought in my life. It ain't in my culture.

I have to ask him, though, what he means by "pretty." Is it my name or me? Boys have always said I have a pretty name, but this boy isn't like anyone I've ever met before. He's *definitely* not from around here. But I do like his game. Yes, I do like that Italian boy's game. If I were country, I'd say, "Who'd of thunk it? We just might could have somethin' goin' on here down yonder in the holler called Ol' Southwest." But I'm not country. I'm a city girl, so I'd never say that. And what is *yonder* all about anyway? I say something like, "You go to that sale down yonder?" to Collette, and she knows exactly which yonder I'm talking about. People who ain't from here just don't get it.

Amaretto is the bomb! But I better slow down, and what's taking Giovanni so long? I decide to get my tip money counted out, but I can't find my purse. I must have left it in the car (I never do that), so I go out to get it.

I pick up my coat and head for the door. The snow is so thick I can't even see my car. In fact, I can't see anything except my arms. So, I'm standing in the middle of 4th Street waving my arms, trying to make a snow angel in mid-air. The lights of Luchesi's hit me just right, and I can almost see the angels. And for some reason, it's not as cold as it was before. So I'm just standing in the snow in the middle of the street, making angels and eating snow. Mama never said nothin' about eating white snow.

I turn to see Giovanni in a nice brown bomber jacket, standing just outside the door, his apron flapping below the jacket in the wind. Smiling. For some reason, I'm not embarrassed at all.

"Come here," I say.

He doesn't move. "Aren't you cold?"

"Come here," I say again, and I start humming Toni Braxton's "Un-Break My Heart." Yeah, I'm trippin'.

Giovanni walks over and stands beside me. I turn him to face me, and I'm staring at his chin. "You need to shave."

"Toni Braxton," he says.

"What?"

"You were humming a Toni Braxton song."

"Yeah." I look up. "Where's your hat?"

"You like the hat?"

"No."

"Well, that's where it is."

He has an answer for everything. "Your father doesn't like me."

We turn to look through the windows. Sure enough, Pops is sitting on his stool behind the counter watching us.

"Emilio Franco Luchesi doesn't want to lose Giovanni Anthony Luchesi to a pretty woman," he says.

So "pretty" means me. But what a long freakin' name. "Gee-oh-vah-nee Lou-case-ee," I say slowly.

"That's me."

"Can I call you 'G'?"

"Can we go inside? I don't want you to catch cold."

I got amaretto in my veins, boy. "Answer the question."

He presses his hand into the small of my back, gently pushing me towards Luchesi's door. I look around to see if anyone sees a white boy touching me, but there's no one out in this blizzard tonight. "Well, my friends sometimes call me Jay, but Renee, you can call me whatever you like."

When we get back inside, we shake off like a couple of dogs. Pops is acting like he isn't watching, like Mama does sometimes, so I know he's watching. He ain't slick. "What's up, Mr. Luchesi?" I say. I like the way that name feels on my tongue.

All Pops does is nod and cut his eyes over to our table. On it are two plates, mine and another where Giovanni was sitting, a lit candle, two steaming mugs, the bottle of amaretto . . . and there's my purse hanging off the back of my chair where I left it.

"Enjoy," is all Pops says as he leaves his stool, gets his coat, and walks out the back door.

"Still hungry?" Giovanni asks. I nod. "I better close us," he says, and flips the *Open/Closed* sign, turns off the outside lights, and dims the interior lights to highlight the glow of the candle. All I can think is, Daa-em. These Italians know romance.

For a second I think all this has been planned from the get-go. Say two Italians need customers on a snowy night. Say they throw buckets of water on the street in front of their restaurant or shovel their sidewalk into the street, knowing that will stop traffic. What, a car's stuck? Oh no! Let's go play *Rescue 911*. What? It's an attractive sistuh, alone on a night like this? Hmm. Let's warm her up with, say, a love potion like Spanish fly slipped into her drink. Oh, it's taking effect? Let's leave the woman with the fairly handsome son while we close early. Dim the lights, light a candle, and play that sexy saxophone.

I'm sure they didn't plan it this way, but even if they did, I'm hooked. And Julia Roberts can kiss my black ass.

"After you," he says, motioning to the table.

I take two steps, turn, and say, "Are you?"

He doesn't answer and holds my chair for me, easing it and me closer to the table. I can't remember the last time a man did that for me. Usually I won't let any man do shit like that, you know, open doors, help me with my coat. I'm a grown black woman and don't need anyone waiting on my every need. My ancestors opened their own damn doors, thank you very much! . . . But you know I'm bull-shittin', right? I eat that shit up!

That's when I notice a fresh yellow rose on the table. "I feel like I've been set up," I say. Giovanni just sits there staring at the rose. And damn if he doesn't look like he's going to mist up on me. "Giovanni?"

"Huh?"

"You okay?"

"Yeah."

I normally can't stand it when a man ignores me, but this is different. "Are you sure?"

He shrugs his eyebrow. "That's Mama's rose."

"It's pretty." I discover that the remains of my sandwich have been warmed up; I take a bite.

"Mama died of cancer when I was fifteen." A dead woman's rose on the table? The sandwich becomes a lump in my mouth. "Pops still buys her a rose every day anyway, and here it is."

I finally swallow and take a swig from my mug. "That's sweet." He hasn't touched his food. "Aren't you going to eat?"

"Oh. Sorry."

Eating in public is where a man either makes or breaks himself with me. I can't stand a sloppy man who chews with his mouth open, picks his teeth, talks with his mouth full, takes huge bites, slurps his soup or his drink, uses a fork when he should use his hands (or vice versa), and doesn't realize he has food or sauce stuck to his face. His napkin *better* be in his lap, and his elbows better *not* be on the table.

I try not to be too obvious about it, peeking over the rim of my mug. He picks up the sandwich with both hands, takes a reasonable bite, and chews with his mouth closed, elbows where they should be. So far so good. Now for a little test.

"You never answered my question," I say. "Are you after me?"

He raises his napkin from his lap to his lips with one hand and holds up one finger on the other. He swallows first and says, "Maybe." That's what I would have said, too.

I watch him sip from his mug, cradling it in his hands. I strain to hear a stray slurp. Not a sound. "But you don't know me," I say.

"True."

"You only know my name."

"True."

"And it may not even be my real name."

He narrows his eyes for a moment. "Is it your real name?"

"Maybe."

"You said it twice when I asked you."

"And your point is?"

"I hope that proves it's your name." He takes another sip of his mocha cappuccino and still no slurp. "Even if it isn't, that's what I'm going to call you."

"When?"

"When what?"

"When you gonna call me, boy?"

"But you're right here."

Uh-duh. "I meant, will you call me, say, tomorrow?" I give him exactly one second to respond. "Don't think so long, now."

"I'll need your number," he says.

"I don't give out my number to strangers." I let him worry his little self for a few seconds. "But, since you're no stranger than anyone else I know, I might."

"I'll get some paper." He pushes back his chair and stands.

"Hurry," I say, pouting. "You keep leaving me."

"I'll hurry."

When he returns, I tell him, "Took you twenty seconds."

"Sorry." I watch him prepare to write my number down when I pluck the menu from him.

"I'll write it." But there's something already written on this paper. "What's this?" I can't believe what I'm reading. No one has ever written a poem to me. "Where's the title?" I ask.

He turns the paper and writes "My Song to Renee" at the top. "Want me to read it to you? My handwriting is pretty messy."

I had already read most of it just fine, but he seems so eager. "Please. But when did you do this?"

"I wrote it while your sandwich was cooking."

Then he stands . . . and *kneels* right next to me! My hands are sweating, and my heart is about to burst. Something about a man throwing himself at my feet just . . . isn't normal. And though I know Luchesi's is empty, I still look around. We are, after all, in Roanoke, Virginia.

Sweet sizzlin' soul sister,
silken soft-skinned sis-TUH!
Gimme some play.
Share soma-dat darkness
with a white boy today.
Rub soma your color on me
the old-fashioned way,
sweet mocha sis-TUH,
give a white boy some play.

I seen you out walkin',
out struttin' yo' stuff,
head high, shoulders square—
I can't get enough.

You cut your eyes on me,
you're playin' a game—

sexy soul sister
in the dark we're the same.

Don't care what your friends say,
don't care what folks whisper,
just gimme a chance
my sweet sepia sister.

Sweet smokin'-hot sister,
sexy, sultry, sweet sis-TUH!
Gimme some play.
Share soma your darkness
with this white boy today.
Grind soma your color on me
the passionate way.
Simmering, seductive sis-TUH,
give my whiteness some play.

And that's when I grab his face, bring it up to mine, and kiss the living shit out of him.

I have lost my freakin' mind.

He pulls back first and says, "Renee, I have a confession to make."

"Please don't say you have a blue-eyed girlfriend."

"I won't."

"Good." I kiss him again, mainly for not having a blue-eyed girl-friend. "So what's your confession? You aren't gay, are you?"

"No."

"Good." Once again, my lips meet his. "What's your confession?"

"Uh, I have only been kissed like that, uh, three times in my life."

Waaait just a damn minute! "But we just kissed three times." He says nothing and tries to stand, but I hold his face and therefore his body down. "Wait. Giovanni, you've never been kissed before?"

"Uh, well, not by a . . . uh, black girl."

I relax my grip on his neck. "So what are you trying to say?"

He smiles. "I don't know exactly."

I squint. "You got a problem with it?"

"No. Do you?"

"What do you think?" I plant another, longer, juicier kiss on him. I know the boy still has his tonsils because it's one of *those* kisses. Although it's nice to have a dog at my feet, I have to let Giovanni get up off the floor.

"Stand up," I command. He does. I have such power! "Give me your hands." He does. "Pull me to my feet." He does with ease, and I was letting him pick up my entire weight. Lotta muscle under that ugly-ass apron. "Let go of my hands and take off that apron," I order.

He shakes his head. "You do it."

Sneaky. A quick learner. I do as I'm told, but seductively, you know, slowly reaching around him to the tie in the back, pulling gently on the knot until it comes free. He looks into my eyes the entire time, then bows his head to let me pull the apron off.

I ball it up, then think of something better. I put that apron on me. "Your turn," I say, and I close my eyes so I can feel his hands better.

"Renee?"

"I'm getting cold, boy."

"Renee?"

I open my eyes. "What?"

"May I dim the lights more?"

"Any more and they'll be off." I smile. "You're nervous, aren't you?"

"Yes ma'am."

I laugh, stand on tiptoe, and kiss him on the cheek. "Go on," I say, and as he turns to go to the light switches, I swat him hard on the butt. Nice ass. Firm. Nice rebound. Oh God, everything about this guy is nice. I hope it's not an act . . . and he did say he hadn't kissed a black girl.

He turns off all the lights, and I'm left in a pool of amber yellow light by the table. I turn "Mama's rose" so it doesn't block as much light, and like a ghost he's back in front of me. He doesn't say a word. As he reaches around me, I lift my arms and latch my hands to the back of his neck. Then he kisses me, and each one of his kisses is better than the last. He's not mauling, or groping, or pawing me. He's holding me, cradling me.

We pause. "You look wonderful in that apron," he says.

My stomach flutters. "You should see me out of it."

He widens his eyes, his Adam's apple bobbing up and down. His "Will I?" comes out an octave higher.

"Depends," I say.

"On what?"

"On if you got a girlfriend or not."

His shoulders sag, so I know he has one. "I see a girl every now and then, but it's nothing serious."

"What's her name?"

"Julie."

She white. "And you ain't serious?"

"No."

He doesn't bat an eye. I believe him. "You want to start something serious with me?"

"Yes."

"Well, make your move."

I watch his Adam's apple spasm. "Uh, what should my next move be?"

I kiss that Adam's apple, but the spasms don't subside. "What you want it to be?"

"Renee?"

"Yes?" I hold that "yes" such a long time.

"Would it be all right if . . ."

I pull his head down to nibble on his right ear. "If what?"

"If I called time-out?"

"You're out of time-outs," I whisper, my hot breath on his ear.

"Oh," he wheezes.

"And there's no clock in this game. This could take all night."

"What I meant," he says as I switch to his left ear, "what I meant was—oh, don't do that—what I meant was—"

I put a finger to his lips. "You Italians talk entirely too much. Now shut up, kiss me, and do some talking with your hands."

I am a lady, and I do not tell my business to the world, especially if that business involves two people releasing their passions, and I happen to be one of the two doing the releasing. Understand? This ain't no talk show, and I ain't no trailer trash ho tellin' it *all* on national TV. *My* people don't do that shit. My *biz*-ness is *my* biz-ness.

Let's just say we find out a whole lot about each other in a short period of time, and I, for one, like what I find. A lot. All of Giovanni's parts work, and though I ain't Stella (Mama is), I think I've got my groove back.

And we don't even have sex.

And I ain't trippin'.

Chapter Two

I'm buzzin', but the amaretto wore off about an hour ago. I'm high on that Italian man on the other side of the restroom door. Damn, it's nice to feel like a woman again. I miss his strong, soft hands already. Whew, that boy can roll my dough twenty-four-seven. He's gentle, tender, and curious, all at the same time. He kept asking if it was okay. Imagine, a man wanting to know if it's okay with me. I look in the mirror and see a happy, glowing, twenty-six-year-old woman, hair flying every which way, with a big, stuuu-pid grin on her face. And Julia Roberts can still kiss my black ass.

When I walk out, he's waiting in his chair at "our" table. "Good morning," he says.

I check my watch: 1:15. "Wow" is all I can manage before I kiss him and curl up in his lap. The candle on the table is almost a puddle, and I can barely see the cows. We sit there, all wrapped up in each other, watching the snow fall outside the windows until the candle goes out with a little hiss. I don't want to move, and the way he's nuzzling and nibbling my ears, putting his lips on that little spot at the back of my neck, I'd be a damn fool to get up and go out in a blizzard. I briefly think of Mama and where she might be, but I gave up worrying about Mama when I was younger. She didn't abandon me or anything like that, but once I hit thirteen, I was home alone or sleeping over at Collette's while she was painting the town black. Mama always came home, occasionally at a decent hour, and *I* was the one waiting up for *her*. Sometimes I just don't know who raised whom at our house.

"Where do you live?" Giovanni asks.

"Allison Avenue."

He laughs. "No kidding?" I use his hand to cross my heart. He sighs. "If you keep doing stuff like that, we may never get home. Which house?"

"Four-forty-three. But, do you really want to go out in that"—I point at the windows—"when you can be with this?" I put his hand under my blouse and rest it on my stomach.

"I see your point."

"No you don't," I say, rubbing my hands on his thighs. "It's too dark."

"You have anyone at home you want to call, let them know where you are?"

"No."

"You live alone?"

"Just about."

"What's that supposed to mean?"

I tell him enough about Mama to explain her absences, and Giovanni doesn't pry. He may have a big nose, but he ain't nosy.

"Mama would like you."

"Why?"

"For one, you're a good listener."

"It's-a part of my job," he says in that sexy Italian accent.

"Mine, too." I describe my job and tell him about Mr. Williams, and he just listens and laughs. "I also don't mind the silences."

"The silences?"

I say nothing for a few moments. "Did you hear anything loud?" I ask.

"No."

"Sometimes when two people get together, the silences get loud, like one person always has to be saying something. Kind of like chit-chat. Kind of like I'm doing now, but not really. I mean, we're saying nothing and saying everything at the same time, right?" If Collette was here, she'd say, "Girl, you trippin'." I am getting sleepy, and when I get sleepy, I trip.

"I understand," he says holding me tighter. "Pops and I have ESP or something while we're working. We can go a whole day saying only a few words to each other."

"That's not quite what I mean. What I mean is . . . oh, I'm not sure what I mean either."

"Okay, what are you thinking right now?"

"How nice this feels." And how I *shouldn't* be feeling this way about a white boy. I mean, I have *never* liked a white boy, nor did I ever think *any* of them were cute or sexy. Mel Gibson wasn't hot to me—he just had a funny accent and big hair. The white boys I went to school with were spoiled rich kids who pulled my pigtails in first grade, who called me "Renee *cow*ard" instead of "Renee Howard" when I went through a chubby stage during middle school, who were always trying to copy my homework in high school—and I was the only sister in the class. The only white boy I can even re-member by name to this day—Travis Preston—was the stankest, NASCAR-hat-and-shit-kicker-boot-wearing-est redneck I have ever known. So what am I doing now? Daa-em. I'm snuggling with the enemy! And yet . . . it does feel nice to be held. I squeeze Giovanni's arms around me tighter. "This feels nice."

"I'm thinking the same thing."

"That doesn't mean we have ESP."

"Well, what does it mean we have?"

Dag, Giovanni on a serious tip all of a sudden. Slow your roll, boy. But he does have a point. What do we have here? "We have each other," I say. For now, I think. I need to change the subject. "Are you going to give me flowers?"

"It's-a family tradition," he says mimicking his Pops.

"You have to send them to where I work. One dozen minimum."

"I'd rather grow you some."

"In January?"

"No. This spring."

I roll my head and neck. "I ain't waitin' till spring."

"Does that hurt?"

"Does what hurt?"

"When you move your head like that."

I laugh. "No. Does it hurt when you shrug your eyebrow? You should pluck that thing."

Then he tickles me in all the right places and, well, we lose a few more hours in the dark.

When I wake up, I'm still in his arms. The sky is a dark gray, and I can't tell if the snow has stopped. Giovanni's asleep, and despite his nose, he isn't snoring. In fact, he's hardly making a sound. Did I kill him? No, his chest is rising and falling just fine.

But I know his breath and mine are kickin'. I don't see how those movie people can be kissing on each other the next morning. You know they have the dragon, and how is their hair and makeup still perfect? No bed head, no smears. Hollywood needs a reality check. People's breath is stank when the alarm goes off.

I remove myself from our "bed" (a couple of chairs placed together), grab my purse, and slip into the ladies' room. That's when I realize I'm barefoot. Where are my socks? And for that matter, where are my draws? Oh, yeah. Just the memory is natural caffeine. I use the pink soap to wash my hands and face (it's better than nothing), pull my hair back into a ponytail, and brush my teeth with a little traveler set I keep in my purse. I'm about to leave when something cold taps my breast. A memento. I examine the silver medal and chain in the morning light and see some knight with a sword and a dragon. St. George? I prefer gold, but I earned this. I rubbed some of my color all over that boy all through the night. And at least I'll have something to remember him by. I had a white knight for a night, but I know this can't last. Sure, the black boys at my high school could experiment with the white girls, and maybe two or three white boys could mess with black girls, but that was high school, not real life. This is probably it. Though my heart hurts a little, I have to face the facts. In the cold, crisp light of morning, he'll see me for what I am: a black woman. I'll see him for what he his: an albino white boy. Then we'll go our separate ways with a hug and some nice memories that we'll never tell anyone about. . . . These thoughts make me shiver, so I close my eyes and feel his warm breath on my ear, hear him whispering my name, feel his hot hands caressing my neck. I squeeze the medal and give St. George a kiss. Maybe he'll see me simply as a woman. I smile. Yes. That would be nice.

I go out to search for what's missing from my body and hear the espresso machine whirring to life. "Good morning," I call out. No answer. I decide to sneak up on Giovanni and go behind the counter, but instead of Giovanni, I run straight into Pops.

"Morning," Pops says as he checks me out from head to toe, his arms behind his back. "What you like for breakfast?" I feel naked without socks or shoes and wonder how long he's been sneaking around. When I don't answer, he asks, "How about some sour-dough toast, bacon, and eggs?"

I manage a weak "Sounds great."

"How you like your eggs? With-a cheese? Scrambled? Sunny side up? Down? Maybe you like an omelet?"

I see Giovanni out of the corner of my eye. Sleeping like a little boy. Wake up! I scream in my head, but the ESP must not be working. "Um, whatever Giovanni usually eats, I guess."

He laughs. "Oh, Giovanni, he doesn't eat the breakfast. A real breakfast. He eats those Pop-Tart things or nothing at all. Why he's so skinny."

Do I detect sincerity in Mr. Luchesi's voice this morning? And what's up with his hands behind his back? I hope he's not holding my draws! But he doesn't seem angry. "Do you need any help?"

He smiles. He has all his teeth, too. "I thought you'd never ask. Come. Let us make the boy a real breakfast, put some meat on his bones. But first, you might want to put these on."

I brace for the worst, but in one hand he has my socks, the other my Nikes. And they're clean, as in laundered, and dry.

As I slip them on, he says, "The other 'unmentionables' will be done in a little while."

Shitshitshit. "Thanks."

He tosses me an apron and leads me to a huge grill. On the wooden shelf in front are a carton of eggs, some grated cheddar, a plastic container of spices, a mixing bowl and whisk, and a package of bacon. "You want the bacon or the eggs?"

"I can manage both," I say, slipping the apron on. "If it's all right."

He nods. "Go easy on the spices. I have a funny stomach. As for him"—he shoots a thumb in the direction of Giovanni—"he just funny in the head. Make eggs *Parmigiana al dente*." I just blink at him. Speak American, Pops. "Sprinkle lots of Parmesan and cook them enough to be firm. Don't want them runny like my son's head."

Am I expected to laugh here or what? I smile and begin cracking eggs into the mixing bowl. He watches me for a moment, then disappears towards the counter. You funny in the head, Mr. Man. I hope the condition's not genetic. But I'll give you eggs par-me-gee-aw-nuh all-den-tay. I don't make runny eggs or rubbery bacon. I cook everything until it's dead. Well-done doesn't mean burnt, but I won't have anything pink in my meat. White folks seem to like food bloody, which kind of explains the history of their race. The ability to blush makes you superior? Hmm. Okay, you think that way. Least I won't have ten pounds of undigested, impacted, un-cooked, raw red meat in my colon. I'm with Oprah.

As I cook, I'm trying not to think of Giovanni's hands. All those years of making bread, rolling dough. He gave me a massage last night, and while at first I felt like dough, by the end I was putty. He

48

started with my temples and worked his way down, down, down. Slowly. In circular motions. Hot fingertips on my glowing skin. I don't sweat; I glow, and I was glowing last night.

I could make Luchesi's fancier. First, I'd put matches or air freshener in the bathrooms. Those stickups have been arrested. Second, I'd get rid of the cows. Makes the customers feel like they're grazing in a pasture. I don't want any competition when I'm getting my grub on.

And speaking of grub, why is the only black woman cooking this morning? Is this all part of the plan? Say two Italians get a sistuh to spend the night in their bakery. In the morning, they trick her into making them breakfast by holding her draws for ransom. Hey, I say to myself, it's-a small price to pay for passion. And I'm hungry as a mug. Where is Giovanni?

"Looking good." It's Pops, and he surprises me. Dag, he's smooth, sneaky, and quiet for a lardass. "Why don't you go sit down. I'll be the waiter."

I tighten up my apron a couple notches before I return to the table. I like to make an entrance, and with this crisp, white apron against my sepia, curvaceous body—hell, I am mocha cappuccino with a dash of amaretto in the morning.

Giovanni is sitting at our table, clean-shaven and . . . dag, the boy has shaving cream in his ears. Someone needs to teach that boy to pay attention to himself. "*Ciao bella,*" he says.

I dig the lather out of his ears, wiping it on a napkin, and look into his eyes. He doesn't look away. Daa-em. The boy is looking at me just like last night. He actually sees me. "Good morning," I say, and I kiss him on the cheek instead of the lips. I'm taking no chances on a dragon-breath kiss this morning. "Doesn't *ciao* mean good-bye?" I say as I sit next to him. We'll give Pops all the room he needs across from us.

"It's both hello and good-bye."

"Kind of like *aloha?*"

"Yeah. It comes from *schiavo* which means 'I am your slave.'"

"Slave" is not a word I want to be hearin' at the breakfast table. I'm about to hit him with an attitude but check myself. "And *bella* is something good?"

He kisses me on the lips. Minty. "It means *beautiful.*"

First he looks right at me and then he kisses me? Shit, this might not be a memory after all. "How do you say, 'kiss me again'?"

He cradles my face and lays one on me, long and slow, Cresty not crusty. He says a whole bunch of Italian after that, something like "fah-tee mah-she," et cetera.

"All that for 'kiss me again'?"

"No." He squeezes my hands. "It means that deeds are more . . . effective than words, you know, like 'actions speak louder than words.'"

"A-hem," Pops says. The man must have some Native American in him. I'm supposed to have some Cherokee in me, but I can't glide around unnoticed like this guy. But the way Giovanni looks at me and I look at him—as a man—Godzilla could sneak up on us.

"*Buon appetito,*" Pops says. I know what that means. He places plates bursting with eggs, bacon, and toast, and steaming mugs of *cafe* something on the table.

Giovanni says something like "all-tray-tah-no" in reply.

I blink and raise my eyebrows repeatedly, but he ignores me. Must be another Italian thing I wouldn't understand.

I can't eat all this, but before I take my first bite, I notice both of them with their heads bowed. Praying. I immediately feel guilty and put my fork down. I used to pray with Mama before every meal, so I bow my head and pray for what I think is a long time. When you're hungry, there ain't no time for a testifying prayer. Say "God is Great" and get grubbin'. I look up, and they're still praying. I don't know much about being Catholic, but God has to get tired of listening sometimes.

"You know what today is?" Pops asks when they finally finish.

"January twenty-first," I say. I take a huge bite of eggs Parmi-

50

giana and say "mmm." That shit is buttah, which doesn't make sense, but it's an Ebonics thing.

"Isn't it the feast of Saint . . . Agnes?" Giovanni asks.

Pops smiles. Giovanni winces. Neither one speaks.

"Who was Saint Agnes?" I ask.

Pops leans forward while Giovanni leans back. "Saint Agnes was this woman—"

"Pops, please."

"The lady asks a question, I give an answer. Saint Agnes is a saint because she—"

Then they started running Italian phrases together, gesturing like they do in *Goodfellas* (except for grabbing their crotches, which is nasty) and literally yelling across the table at each other. Damn, arguing over bacon, eggs, and St. Agnes.

Giovanni is still steaming and has his arms crossed in front of him, but Pops continues. "On the eve of Saint Agnes, a woman is supposed to spend the night in a different district or part of town before going home." Daa-em. I was in a whole new world last night. "Before going to bed, she is to knit her stockings together."

"Sounds painful," I say to be funny.

"No, she sews them together *after* she takes them off," Pops says. I feel like checking my socks for stitching. "Then, she's supposed to sing a song. Wanna hear it?"

"Oh, come on, Pops!" Giovanni is pissed!

"Sure," I say. "I want to hear it." I love it when white people *try* to sing.

Pops clears his throat, does a few *mi-mi's*, and sings: "I knit this knot, this knot I knit, to know the thing I know not yet, that I may see the man that shall my husband be." Kind of catchy, but the rhymes are weak. "After singing, she is to go to sleep lying on her back with her hands under her head. If she has done everything right, her future husband will come to her in her dreams and press a warm kiss to her lips."

O-kaaaay. I know how I fit into this myth, and now I know why Giovanni is pissed.

"It's just superstition," Giovanni says.

"There are many who believe," Pops says.

I am not that superstitious. Okay, maybe I don't like brooms hitting me in the legs, and I hate splitting a pole. And that itchy palm thing? It's called dry skin. And I'm not even Catholic, so this St. Agnes stuff doesn't apply to me, right? But since I can't remember what I dreamed last night, I can't be sure that my future husband didn't kiss me. Last night was magical. Maybe . . . and this time I can't say "naah."

"Giovanni, are you my future husband?" Pops drops his fork and coughs. I cut my eyes from Pops to Giovanni. "Just play along," I mouth.

"Oh," Giovanni says. "Yes, Renee, I kissed you while you slept."

Pops takes a long gulp of his coffee.

"Did you dream about me, too?" This is fun.

"Yes."

"Well then, when do we get married?"

Pops's hands begin to tremble, so he puts them in his lap. We have his undivided attention.

"How about . . . Saint Bridget's Day?" Giovanni says with a smile.

"When's that?"

"February—February first. It's also called the Festival of the Bride."

"Perfect," I say. Pops's fat face falls another foot. Giovanni starts laughing.

"What you laughin' for, Giovanni?" I ask. "This is a serious moment in our lives, a serious moment in our relationship. I mean, it's not every day a girl becomes engaged."

Giovanni drops his fork. Gravity certainly is working at Luchesi's this morning. "You're serious?"

"Damn right I am. Where's my ring?"

I am having fun, and I am serious in a sort of let's-see-what-happens way. I don't know if it's proper to be a devil at a Catholic breakfast table, but I am having one hell of a time.

Giovanni excuses himself without saying anything, Pops is still frozen where he sits, and I continue to get my grub on. I know I'm sticking a fork in their master plan, if there even is one, but I've always gotten a kick out of sweatin' white folks. They turn so many colors.

"The eggs are delicious," I say. "The toast is just right." Pops grumbles something harsh in Italian. Man better not be cursing me. "Can we have the wedding reception here?" I don't know when to stop.

Giovanni saves Pops from another grumble, sits, grabs my hand tenderly, and slips a . . . white twist tie around my left ring finger. Oh no, he didn't! He twists it and says, "Will you marry me?"

Oh, so now it's on me. I think I've just found "far" as in "you've gone too far." It's a scary place. Now you know I love this boy's game. I really do. And we just click, you know? Like his poem says, "In the dark we're the same." Just now, though, Luchesi's is too damn bright.

"On your knees," I command. I have to put it back on him, make him say it again. I mean, he can back out if he wants to. He ain't putting all this on me.

But he drops like a rock to the ground. "Renee . . . what's your last name?"

I hear Pops gasp. I hope he doesn't have a history of heart trouble. They don't make ambulances big enough for people like him. "Howard," I say.

He takes my cold hands and warms them with his. "Renee Howard, will you be my wife?"

Oh damn. He said the W word. I've had a silly look on my face until now. Doesn't he know I've been playing? Oh, right. He's only known me for a night. I mean, a little while ago I was ready to take my medal and go home. I try not to look into Giovanni's eyes, because I get lost in them and do and say strange things, so I focus on the largest thing in the room—Pops's nose. I shiver. His people must keep the tissue folks in business. Pores big enough to put my pinkie finger through, hairs sprouting out that are long enough to roll up with a Golden Hot. My eyes gladly drift back to Giovanni's eyes, those sensitive, loving eyes, that cute face, that nose. Smaller pores. I'd thank his mama if I could. Bet she was a pointy-nosed woman, and why am I thinking of this shit when I have a man at my feet who really seems to love me?

But how does anyone know *for sure* about love? I mean, I thought I loved R. J., and look what happened. It's obvious the man kneeling in front of me is sure of himself. Do I love him? Or rather, *will* I love him? I love everything about him so far. We'll just have to see. I mean, he's quick, sneaky, curious—like me. Maybe I've found someone just like me after all this time. My soul mate is white, lives a few doors down, and works at a restaurant?

I'm still worried about the love part, so I whisper, "Are you serious?" One more chance for him to let it slide.

He doesn't hesitate. "Yes."

I look at the twist tie and turn it. Not exactly what I expected when I was a girl. My man turns out to be a white knight. St. George himself. I don't want to hurt him by telling him my doubts, and when I look into his eyes, I know it feels right.

Those eyes would never hurt me.

I feel misty; I know Pops is about to have a brain fart, and I know Giovanni's knee is getting tired, but I still can't quite . . . "Giovanni, you hardly know me."

Pops lets out a long sigh, so long that at first I think he did have a brain fart. "You're right, Renee. You two hardly know each other." Pops wipes his brow with his napkin. "Thank you for saying that. You are a sensible girl."

Giovanni won't budge from the floor. "I love what I know, and I'd love to find out more."

Pops scowls and says that "fah-tee mah-she" line again.

I have a good memory. "Deeds are more effective than words?"

Pops looks at me and laughs, showing all of his teeth. He is not a pretty man. "Is that what he told you?"

Now I'm confused.

Giovanni bows his head. "The phrase has more than one meaning."

"It means this exactly: 'deeds are males, words are females,'" Pops says.

I lift Giovanni's chin. He nods.

Deeds are males, and words are females. Deeds are for manly men, mere words for us weak, defenseless, unintelligent women. If there's anything I hate more than racism, it's sexism. Let's see you have a baby, Pops. The very thought kills my appetite. Let's see you squeeze an eight-pounder out your little hole. Let's see you get cramps. Knowing men, they'd probably make an Olympic event out of it: "the two-hundred-meter dash for men with cramps." I can hear some basketball announcer saying, "He's been in a scoring slump the past few days (nudge, nudge), but he's sure to come out of that slump tonight. Unfortunately, the other shooting guard is feeling bloated . . ." I know, in the middle of all this, how can I think of this shit?

"Giovanni," I say finally, trying to ignore Pops across the table, "I like your translation a lot better than his."

Giovanni lifts his head. "Thank you."

I look in his eyes. "I don't know if I love you or not, but I want to." The words leave my mouth, and I realize I've just pledged my love to a white boy. My ancestors are rolling over in their graves. "Maybe this Saint Agnes thing is the real deal."

"But you just heard him say it was superstition!" Pops yells.

"I believe, Giovanni." I don't cry, and though my eyes are heavy, my heart is light. "Ask me again."

"But—" Pops begins, but I shut him off with my hand. Evidently, Italians know what "the hand" is all about.

"Renee Howard, will you marry me?"

Instead of using mere womanly words, I pull Giovanni to his feet and give him the longest kiss in the history of Luchesi's.

And that's how I become engaged.

I've got a twist tie on my finger, a white man I've known for twelve hours in my arms, his father over in his chair having a heart attack, and I've just decided to get married on St. Bridget's Day.

I've lost my freakin' mind.

Why am I doing this? Is it because I can't back down from a fight? Because of what Pops says and represents? Because maybe deep down I actually love Giovanni? Or is it because I'm twenty-six years old and should be married by now? I feel like Buster Douglas (before he became a lardass), the boxer who "shocked the world" by beating Mike Tyson in Tokyo—only I'm shocking my own freakin' world. I want to say "Time out"; I want to say "Waaait just a damn minute, Mr. Man"; I want to rewind the past twelve hours and find out what went wrong.

But, damnit, it feels so right! I feel right, my heart feels right, the doubts I had in the bathroom were wrong, and I feel warm all over (even though I'm not wearing draws) because I have found me a quiet, passionate man who can cook and clean (in oh, so many wicked ways); a man who holds me with his eyes and doesn't have to squint like Richard Gere; a romantic man who speaks a real-life Romance language; a man who takes my breath away and it's not because he's overweight . . . Daa-em. Maybe Julia Roberts doesn't have to kiss my black ass anymore.

Pops looks like a zombie from one of those really bad black-and-white voodoo movies—you know, the movies where us "natives" are crazy and only the great white Bwana has any sense. I feel like I'm the priestess responsible, so I break away from Giovanni's embrace and kneel beside Pops. "Are you all right, Mr. Luchesi?"

His head turns slowly like that freaky girl's head turns in *The Exorcist*. "I will never be all right again."

He pushes himself back from the table to stand, but I grab his beefy left arm. He remains seated but gives me a sharp "no-you-didn't" look. I've seen better. "I didn't know this would happen, Mr. Luchesi. Please don't blame Giovanni, since I'm really the one to blame."

"That is a fact," Pops says.

"And we don't have to rush into it in ten days. Weddings take some planning, right?"

His face relaxes a little. "That is also a fact."

"And I suppose we'll need to get a caterer." I pause. "For the reception."

The lure of easy money (the bride pays, right?) doesn't affect him. "What will your family say about Giovanni?"

"Well, if I can get him past Mama—"

"Will she approve?" Pops interrupts. Anytime you want to get involved, Giovanni, feel free. "Will your mother approve of my son as your husband?"

A damn good question. Mama's open-minded, modern, her own woman. Maybe . . . and maybe not. "I'll let you know as soon as I do, okay?" I let go of his arm and stand.

"Is this what you want?" Pops says to Giovanni. "Is this what you've dreamed about?"

"*She* is what I want." Thank you, Giovanni. I don't feel like a "this."

"Does there have to be . . . a wedding?" He seems to choke on the word. "Why don't you take some time, get to know each other first? Your mother and I—"

"Knew each other for one month and eloped before you were supposed to be married by Father Mike!" Ba-boom.

"So we eloped. It was different in those days."

"Tell her why, Pops."

Uh-oh! Catholics getting busy with the rhythm method. I never understood that. Why call something the rhythm method that's used by people who are not known for having rhythm?

"No, you go ahead, you're so eager to tell."

"My mother was Jewish," Giovanni says.

I want to say, "And your point is?" but I don't. So Giovanni's Italian, Catholic, and Jewish. Big deal. Nobody's truly pure. I'm sure my own pedigree includes some Irish, English, or German. I grew up with kids hating me for my "white" nose and "good" hair even if I was darker than all of them. It didn't change the fact that I was an African-American.

After a short silence, Pops says, "At least I know her for more than a few hours before proposing marriage, the promise of a lifetime."

Time to calm Pops down. "I can wait a little longer."

"How long?" Pops is perking up.

I smile. "At least a month." He almost smiles back.

Giovanni whispers in my ear: "I've waited my whole life for you, Renee. I can wait." I know I'm blushing, so I try to rub the blood out of my cheeks.

Pops sighs again and does smile, but it's the kind of smile you use when you're either trying to hold back or squeeze out a poot. "What am I gonna do with you two? Huh? Huh? I leave you two alone for just one night, and you fall in love."

"You shouldn't have left," Giovanni says. I hope he's joking.

"Oh," I say quickly, "I don't know if—"

"You're in love! I can see it. Anyone can. It's written all over your faces."

I have to see this, so I drag Giovanni into the men's room. I see two people with big, stuuu-pid grins on their faces. Don't adjust your TV set, folks. The colors are right. "So this is what love looks like."

"Yeah. Uh, sorry about the ring."

"I like it," I say. Not really, but I don't want to hurt his feelings. A twist tie? Puh-lease!

"Really?"

"Blessed be the twist tie that binds."

He laughs. "I'll have to get you another one."

Reality check time. "Let's see what Mama says first, okay?" And let's also see how I feel about all this tomorrow. This fling could have some serious side effects.

He picks me up and places me on the sink ledge. I wrap my legs around him. He lowers his head and looks directly into my eyes. "Okay."

I look directly back. No one can outstare me. "And you have to find out what your father really thinks about us."

"I know what he thinks already. He told me last night."

"Last night?"

"It's his ESP thing. When he saw you, he said he knew."

"Knew what?"

"Just that he knew . . . something was going to happen."

Now that's some spooky shit. I bite my lower lip. "Well, what do you think?"

"I think something happened."

Something happened all right. I wish I knew what. "I really should be getting home."

"I'd rather do this."

"In the bathroom?"

He winces. "Yeah. Not very romantic."

"Yes, and I need my draws."

"Your what?"

"My underwear. My bra? My panties? Your father put them in the wash."

"He did?" He laughs, but I don't. No one messes with my draws but me.

"Get them for me," I order. "Now."

"Do you really need them?" He plays with the zipper of my jeans.

"Not with you around, but . . . I want to go home so I can get some sleep. You wear me out." I remove his roving hands from my jeans. "Don't you have to work today?"

"They haven't even plowed yet."

"Well," I say, grabbing and squeezing his butt, "it'll give you more time to convince your father that I am the bomb, and it will give me time to rest for tonight."

"What's happening tonight?"

I put my lips up to his right ear and switch to tease mode. "More. Much, much more."

He gulps. "How much more?"

I bite that ear and pull it. "How much you got?"

While Giovanni runs to rescue my Hanes, I ask to use the phone. "Sure," Pops says.

I dial home and get no answer (as expected) and then dial my voice mail. After the usual button pushing, I listen to my messages:

"Renee, honey, this is your mother. I'm staying out tonight. Stay warm!"

"Renee, this is Collette. Clyde and I are at Macado's. If you can, come by for a drink. There's this chocolate man sitting by hisself at the bar wearing a Rolex and an Armani suit. I'll keep him occupied till you get here. See ya!" I'll bet Chocolate Man had dreads, and the Rolex was fake.

"Renee, child, where the hell are you? I called your car phone and your pager. *(muffled)* Oh, she's probably out with Collette. *(louder)* Hope y'all have fun. I'll call you later." Mama still worries about her baby.

"Renee, Collette. Forget the Rolex man. *His* man showed up. Ain't' that some shit? Hardly anyone here anyway with the weather so bad. Clyde and I are gonna stay at the Patrick Henry, so I'll call you later with our room number." Ka-ching!

"Hello, Renee. Did you get my letter? Give me a call." I almost slam the phone down. R. J.? After all this time? Ain't this some shit! I notice Pops staring. I smile. Shitshitdoubleshit.

"Renee, honey, the roads are real bad now, so I'm going to assume you're safe somewhere. I'll give you a call."

"Renee, this is Collette. We in room 227. *(laughs)* Just like the show! Girl, I am wasted! *(not as loud)* Clyde lookin' good tonight! Gimme a call, but not before noon, you heifer! Later."

I erase all the messages and hang up. Pops is still staring. I suppose it looks funny to see someone listening a long time on the phone without speaking, but I'm too shook up by R. J. to explain.

"Thanks," I say weakly as I head to the ladies' room and shut the door. Goddamn R. J. and his sexy voice. Kimono ho Dagney probably dumped his ass. Either that or he wants something, probably the jewelry he gave me. Dagney's birthday must be coming up, the cheap ass. Oh, and there's probably a letter in my mailbox right now on the stationery I gave him. It's a good day to make a fire.

A knock on the door. Giovanni and my draws.

"You okay in there?" Pops asks.

Not really. "Yes." He *does* have ESP.

"Where's Giovanni?"

"Getting the laundry."

"What's keeping him?"

How the hell should I know? God, I hope he isn't trying them on.

I hear another knock a few minutes later. "Delivery for Renee Howard."

I open the door a crack, reach out a hand, and snatch at my clothes. I pull them in and close the door . . . but these are not my clothes. Zebra-striped underwear? A gray "Property of the New York Yankees" T-shirt? I open the door and grab Giovanni's shirt, dragging him in.

I close the door and lock it. "You have something you want to tell me?"

"I can explain," he says.

"No. Let me." My jeans flop to the floor.

"Hubba hubba," he says.

"You've had this underwear a long time, and you were just dying to give it to someone—"

"No—"

"Never interrupt a lady. Or, you wanted a reminder of last night, so you stole my draws like I stole your medal. You probably got a

61

collection of these somewhere." Slowly, oh so painfully, I ease into the striped underwear. "Maybe you're even wearing my draws right now."

He shakes his head but doesn't speak. I model for him, shaking the stripes just right. "My father ruined them," he says.

Off comes my shirt, Giovanni's medal hypnotizing him. "You like them?"

"What?"

I frown. "Come on, now. My titties aren't that small."

"They're perfect." I slip the T-shirt over that perfection and finish dressing. Giovanni turns on the water, saying, "Running water, running water."

"You are a trip," I say, giggling. "Did I get a rise out of you?"

"Oh yes." His face is beet red. He turns off the water.

"I'm ready to go. How do I look?"

"Perfect."

I tousle his hair. "You need a cut." Elvis sideburns, hair all uneven on the back of his neck, hair growing down his neck to his back. I'm no expert barber, but I can give a mean edge-up.

"I know," he says.

"I'll cut it tonight."

"You cut hair?"

"Yeah."

"You're amazing."

"I know."

He hugs me. "Is there anything you can't do?"

I kiss him. "I don't know. You'll just have to test me."

He turns on the water, but it doesn't help. I am such a tease, but men are such dogs. Giovanni's eyes bulge out, and you know what else. Running water can't help you when I'm in seduction mode.

And all this reminds me of R. J. *Damn.* I'm trying to forget his ass by showing some skin to Giovanni, and here he is again in my head. I took care of that dog, groomed his ebony self, kept him looking sharp . . . for the kimono ho.

"Ready?" Giovanni asks, putting on his bomber jacket.

"I can make it home all by myself, thanks," I say.

As he watches me zip up my coat, he gives me a puppy-dog look. Oh, he wants to go for a walk. How sweet. All men have that look, and Giovanni's is priceless. Big eyes, slight frown, eyes on the ground, the toe of one boot scuffing the ground, his hands deep in his front pockets.

"I wanna carry you," he says. Puppy dog wants to be St. Bernard. "It's not that far and—"

"What you tryin' to say?"

He hesitates. "Oh, I didn't mean you were too heavy. I meant, uh, in case, uh, you were worried about my back for tonight . . ."

"You're so considerate." Dag, the boy can talk. I'm about to get angry, and he makes me smile. "Okay, you can carry me."

"Be back in a little while," he yells to Pops, who only waves from the oven.

I wave at Pops and hug Giovanni to make sure he's real. I want to kiss Pops for making this guy, but just the thought . . .

I am not "light as a feather," but he manages to piggyback me home. The snow is high, the air cold, the streets unplowed, only one man out shoveling his walk. It seems we are alone in a universe of snow, the only sound an occasional giggle from me.

"Please tell me if you get tired," I say.

"I'm all right," he says. "I won't drop you."

Giovanni waves at the man shoveling, and the man waves back before *really* seeing us. He cuts that wave off and quickly looks away. So it begins, and yes, a white boy is carrying a black girl down Allison. Giovanni unlatches the white wooden gate at 443 and shoves hard until there is enough room for us to squeeze through. The steps of the porch are slippery, and he almost pitches me over the side into some snow-topped bushes. He is drenched in sweat . . . and *stank*.

"Do I need to carry you back?" I ask.

"I'm all right."

I pluck a letter (R. J.'s) out of the mailbox next to the front door, open the screen door, and insert my key into the deadbolt, then into the door knob. I open the door. "Come in," I say. Giovanni kicks off his boots and leaves them on the porch. "Bring them in, boy," I say, and I watch him carry them in. Who wants to wear cold boots? "Hang your coat in the closet. I'll go slip into something more comfortable." I leave him standing in the foyer as I walk up the stairs to my room, hips swaying. "Sorry it's so cold in here," I yell from my room as I slip on some moccasins. "Mama's rules."

"I'm all right," he yells.

I walk down the stairs. "You don't have to shout." I point at the moccasins. "Like them?"

"Yeah."

"I'm part Cherokee," I say.

"You're more American than I am."

Since Jamestown, honey. "Want the grand tour?"

"I'm afraid."

I take his arm. "Don't be. I'll dust all the prints after you leave." And I will, too: Mama checks. "You've seen the dining room and the sitting room. We hardly use either. They're just for show."

"So a dining room isn't for eating, and a sitting room isn't for sitting."

"That's right." We stroll down the hall past Mama's art collection. "Mama collects Beardens, Whites, and Porters."

"They're beautiful."

He stops at a detailed sketch titled "Awaken from Unknowing" and looks at me. Everyone does. "I know," I say, "looks just like me. Wish I had long hair like that." We peek into another room lined with bookshelves. "Mama's office." Antique rolltop desk, high-backed wooden chair on wheels, antique cherry secretary with beveled glass. I want her to buy some more modern furniture, but she refuses.

"Very classy," he says as he steps inside toward the clutter of pictures arranged on shelves around the room.

"Giovanni!"

"What?"

I grab his arm. "Come on. I hate having my picture taken."

"You're beautiful in every one of them."

"Come on!"

I pull him into the kitchen, and of course it's spotless, not a dish in the sink, nothing on the mirror-like counter. I lift the polished silver kettle from the stove. "Want some hot chocolate?" I ask.

"Yeah," he says, putting his hands in my back pockets. "Let's go to your room."

"Hubba hubba," I say, twisting away and taking two matching mugs from the cupboard. I've been watching Giovanni's reaction to the house, and unlike other folks who've visited, he's been pretty quiet. Of course, he's been one of the rare white visitors, so . . . I'm glad he noticed the White portrait and didn't make a big deal about it. That shit gets old. And contrary to popular white belief, we do not all look alike.

The kitchen is kind of small, and I begin to smell something ripe. I open the fridge and sniff. Nothing. I smell over the waste basket. No, that's not it. Then it hits me. "You are stank, boy."

"Huh?"

"Giovanni, you reek."

"I do?"

"You have odor. You do not smell nice."

He doesn't take it that badly and sniffs himself, grimacing. "Sorry. But, I do smell a little like you, right? What is your perfume?"

"CK-One. But that's not what you're smelling. You smellin' your own funk."

He blushes. "I need a shower, and I need to get back to work, so . . ."

Ah, he's so cute, but he has to go. I have so much to do: a letter to torch, phone calls to return, ten hours to sleep, a long, steamy bath to take, a meal to prepare. And we still have nothing in the house to eat!

"I'll see you later, then," he says, and he kisses me on the forehead.

"You missed."

"But I be stank, homegirl."

I give him my best "don't-go-there" look, but he doesn't get it. I can't stand white people who try to talk black, as if they're "down with us" or something. He is a pretty good mimic, though, so I let it pass. "Kiss me, Mr. Man." He does and I hold my breath. I may be falling for this man, but that doesn't mean I have to love every funky stank thing about him.

"Will I get the rest of the tour later?"

"You bet your ass," I say, and I swat his ass as he turns to go.

"Oh. Should I bring anything for our dinner?"

Just everything. "Bread sticks would be nice. Oh, and we're going to watch a movie."

"I thought—"

"There will be plenty of time for that, boy. But you need to be educated first."

"What are we going to watch?"

"You'll see."

After I kiss him good-bye at the door, I go down to the basement family room to make sure we still have the video. We do. Giovanni will learn an awful lot about black women tonight.

After spraying some air freshener in the kitchen and the foyer, I dial the Patrick Henry. The mail can wait. I need a little girl talk while I drink my Swiss Miss. I have never understood that sales pitch. A lily white girl selling brown cocoa? That would be like Wesley Snipes selling vanilla ice cream.

"Room two-two-seven, please."

After several rings, Collette picks up. "What?"

"Hey, girl."

"What time is it?"

I check my watch. "A little after ten-thirty."

"Heifer, I told you to call after twelve."

"I couldn't wait."

"Hold on a minute." Collette covers the phone, but she never covers it completely. I hear her tell Clyde to go out to anything that's open and get her some breakfast. "What couldn't wait?"

I take a deep breath. If I can do this with Collette, I can do this with Mama. Maybe. "I met somebody."

I know she's smiling. "It's about damn time. What's his name?"

Deeper breath. "Giovanni." Silence. I'm wincing.

"Wanna run that by me again, honey? I think I heard you say Gio-something."

It does sound ridiculous. "Giovanni Luchesi."

"Oh damn."

"Collette!"

She takes a deep breath. "Lord, what you gone and did?"

I describe most of the past evening and morning, and little by little, she softens. I leave out the part about the "ring" and us possibly getting married.

"But an Italian white boy? You didn't do the do, did you?"

"No."

"Didn't you want to?"

In the worst way. "I did. He didn't."

"He ain't gay, is he?"

"No. He just wants to take his time."

"Girl, you're liable to get pregnant the first time."

"I won't get pregnant."

"All those years them sperm been swimming around inside him? And he Catholic? He gonna be potent."

"We'll be careful, Collette." I am, after all, on the pill. Well, most of the time. When I remember.

More silence. "Do you love him?"

The million-dollar question. "I don't know, Collette. Maybe."

"Uh-oh. Your Mama gonna be pissed, or do she already know?"

"Shirl's still out," I say. "You're the first person I've told."

"You told me everything?"

Not quite. "Well, I'm wearing a ring and—"

She says a curse that I refuse to say (it begins with *M*). "Are you telling me that, and puh-lease stop me if I'm wrong. Are you telling me that you are engaged to be married to an Italian-Catholic-Jewish white man who works at a restaurant and who you've only known for fifteen hours?"

"Yes."

"Mama Shirl gonna kill that boy."

"Collette!"

"Is he Superman? Is he in the Mafia and got bodyguards?"

"No." Though Pops would make a good hit-man.

"Then Mama Shirl gonna kill that boy."

"She wouldn't."

"Bullshit. He'll be dead as soon as you say the word *white*."

"No he won't, Collette." I hope.

Another deep breath. "Well, shit, at least y'all will have pretty babies. Tell me again how he proposed."

We chat for a while, and I do my best to fill in the missing details. It's amazing how clear the previous evening is in my mind despite all the amaretto.

"Gonna send R. J. an invitation?" she asks. At the mention of R. J., I tell her about his phone call and letter. "What's the letter say?"

"I don't know. Haven't opened it yet."

"Well open it, girl. Oh, Clyde's back with some"—she says that word again—"McDonald's. Call me back after you read it. I gotta call room service."

I pity Clyde for a moment. Collette can be too hard on him sometimes. He gets no props for trying to please her.

And then I pick up R. J.'s letter from the kitchen table. More than a page. Scented with Fahrenheit. "Bastard," I say aloud, and the phone rings. I freeze. It can't be him, can it? After the events of the past fifteen hours, anything's possible. I push the button on the cordless phone. "Hello?"

"Is it *Roots*, because if it is, I've already seen it."

"No, Giovanni, it's not *Roots*." Is this the only movie white people have ever seen about my people?

"Oh. I'll try again later. *Ciao.*"

"*Ciao.*" I like the way that sounds.

Full of confidence, I tear open and read R. J.'s letter:

> *My dearest Renee,*
>
> *I have spent the last six months reevaluating my life and have come to a few important decisions:*
>
> *1) I need you.*
>
> *2) I need you.*
>
> *3) I need you.*

I nearly say that nasty word. This is not what I expected. And where'd he learn to write so . . . Caucasian?

> *I know I hurt you, and I'm sorry. I was a fool. After your visit, I told Dagney about you, and she moved out the next day.*

"Yes!" Kimono ho hit the door!

> *I haven't been seeing anyone, and if there's still a glimmer of hope for us, please give me a call. I miss you, Renee, for what we had, for what I foolishly threw away. Please give me another chance.*
>
> *Love,*
> *R. J.*
>
> *P.S. I'll be in town visiting the weekend of the 27th. I'll give you a call.*

In less than a week. The plot thickens. I call Collette. "R. J. wants to get back with me."

She's munching something on the other end. "No shit. What your horoscope say today, girl? It has to be something amazing."

My stars are, indeed, crossed. God, if You're really up there, stop trying out Your new material with me.

I read the letter to Collette. "At least he sounds like a sincere dog," she says. "What you gonna do?"

"Well, I'm not going back with him."

"Why not?"

"You know why."

"And your reasons are?"

"One, he dogged me out."

"Forgive and forget."

"Never. Grudges last forever." It's the divine right of the black woman. "Two, I've found someone new."

"Who's white and will die the second he meets Shirl."

"Thanks a lot! Three, ... " Three?

"Look Renee, all you have to do is tell Giovanni, 'Yo, Rocko, it was nice, but it ain't gonna work.' And you know it ain't. Then, you hook up with R. J. and tell him you'll cut his dick off if he ever dogs you out again."

I hate to admit that Collette makes a whole lot of sense sometimes. I loved R. J. once. We made a nice couple. We were two educated, professional black folks who would have had our wedding picture in *Jet* and one day might have appeared on the pages of *Black Enterprise*. But mainly, I looked *good* in public with that man, I felt *good* about myself in public with that man. Mama the man-hater even tolerated him, and R. J. was always polite to Mama. As for Giovanni, well, it's all new, exciting, and potentially fatal if Collette is right. My head says "R. J.," but my heart says "Giovanni."

"Renee?"

"I'm thinking."

"Well, at least test it out."

"Collette! I am not that type of girl." Though I *will* be that type of girl tonight.

"I better let you go get ready. Let me know what you decide."

I hang up and decide on a long, hot shower and a long nap. Maybe all this will be clearer to me when I wake up.

And then again, maybe not.

I try not to think about the letter, but I can't get R. J. out of my head. I'm in the shower, and it reminds me of some of our better moments. You spend two years with a person, you can't just remove him forever from your mind. I thought I could, but here he is again with me in the shower, washing my back, making sure the shower spray doesn't get into my hair, making nasty comments about my body. . . . I try to focus on the letter. Short and sweet. I almost believe him, but he probably only wrote it because he's coming to town and wants some. Yeah, it's probably a "gimme-some-lovin'-'cause-I-ain't-gonna-be-around-long" letter. What an asshole! Like I'm going to drop whatever or whomever I'm doing for his, for his . . . *fine* chocolate mountain of a body. I turn off the hot water and scream as the cold water blasts me. Except for some really bad titty hard-ons, both nipples looking like little thumbs threatening to fly off my body, that shit works.

But how do I respond? Or should I respond at all? If I don't tell him something, he'll drop in at the wrong time. Okay, what about a letter? It'd get there by Tuesday or Wednesday if I mailed it today, but the post office closes at noon, and I'll never get through this snow to the post office in time. Besides, he'd claim he never got it. E-mail's out for that reason, too. "I didn't get your message, baby; something's wrong with my modem. So, why don't we just sit down and talk over the old times?" Call him back? I'd have to talk fast so I don't get taken by his Barry White voice and smooth lines. What would I say? Should I cuss him? He deserves it. Should I say, "I've met someone, I don't want to see you, stay away from me, no means no . . ."? A part of me wants to see him crawl, would love to see him sick to his stomach at my front door. Maybe I'll just let him *think* I want him back, then hurt him bad, but that would be lowering myself to his level. It'd give me a whole lot of satisfaction, but I'm not that type of girl either. Most of the time.

After I dry off and put on some lotion, I slip into some ratty sweatpants and a T-shirt and snuggle under my blankets. I try to focus on Giovanni, I really do. But history is hard to forget and has a way of repeating itself. Though R. J. disrespected me, I truly did love him. And though Giovanni hasn't disrespected me yet, I truly don't know if I love him. To think Giovanni says he's been waiting for me, Renee Lynnette Howard, his entire life . . . I just hope I don't let him down.

I'm almost drifting to sleep, when the phone rings. "Hello?"

"Is it *Boomerang*?"

"Hi Giovanni. No, it's not *Boomerang*." Giovanni's voice is more Barry Manilow than Barry White. "Do you think Halle Berry's pretty?" I ask.

"No," he says immediately.

"You're lying."

"I prefer shorter, darker, and sexier."

Good answer. The "Is-she-pretty?" test gives me a reason to be angry at my man, like I don't already have an endless supply of reasons. No matter how he answers, I can be mad. If he says, "Yes," I rip his ass and tell him to go find Halle. If he says, "No," I tell him he's lying.

"I'm not that short, dark, or sexy."

"You are to me."

"Hey, aren't you supposed to be working?"

"Yeah, but I can't concentrate. Nearly lost a finger in the cheese slicer. Renee, I can't get you out of my mind." I want to return the favor, but my mind is kind of crowded right now. "I should let you sleep," he says.

"You should."

"I won't call again until I'm ready to come over."

"You won't?"

"I will if you want me to."

Such a puppy. "I need some rest, so don't call until, oh, after four."

"Can I ask you one more question?"

As long as you don't ask me if I love you. "Sure."

"Is it *Mississippi Masala, Guess Who's Coming to Dinner?, She's Gotta Have It,* or *The Learning Tree*?"

"No to all of the above. Have you seen all those?"

"Yeah. I've even seen the Poitier and Glover versions of *A Raisin in the Sun.* Oh, and I took Pops to see *X* when it first opened."

"You were outnumbered, weren't you?"

"Yeah."

"What else have you seen?" I'm worried he's already seen the movie I want to show him.

"I've seen hundreds of movies, but one in particular I never understood was *Daughters of the Dust.*"

"I haven't seen it, but I heard it was good. What didn't you understand?"

"You haven't seen it?"

I roll my eyes. "I don't get out much." And my people don't see every movie made about our people.

"Well, maybe we can see it together, and you can explain it to me."

I'm about to be harsh but stop. I got tired of college professors zeroing in on me when it came to black history and African-Americans in general. White people assume we know everything about being black, and let me tell you, there's a hell of a lot to know. I mean, we are history itself. I like amazing white people with my knowledge of them. I mean, damn, it's in the history books they write. If my people want to graduate anything, we have to know all about white folks.

"Maybe," I say, gritting my teeth.

"Okay. Well, I'll let you sleep."

"Thanks."

"Renee?"

"Yes?"

"I can't wait to see you."

"I know." I should have echoed him, but I am damn tired.

A few hours into my nap, the phone rings again. "What?"

"Is it *Jungle Fever*?"

"Yes," I say sleepily, "but it ain't the movie, boy. It's the real thing." Run some more water, boy, and stop calling!

I'm almost asleep again when the phone rings. This boy is getting on my nerves. "What?" I say harshly.

"Girl, where you been? You get my messages?"

Oops. I sit up. "Yes, Mama."

"You sound tired. You in bed?"

"Yes, Mama."

"You sick?"

"Just tired."

"What'd you do last night? When'd you get home? I know it wasn't last night. You meet somebody?"

Here we go. "Which question do you want me to answer first?"

"You *must* be sick, sassin' me like that."

"No, Mama." Think! "I got stuck on Fourth Street."

"And it kept you out all night? What you doin' on Fourth Street anyway?"

"Walnut Avenue looked pretty clear, so I thought I'd cut over—"

"Where's your car?"

"Near Luchesi's."

"They plow over there yet? Twenty inches, can you believe it?"

"No. Where are you?"

"I'll tell you all about it tomorrow."

No she won't. Mama's business is her own. "Are you coming home tonight?" Please say "No"!

"No. I'm snowed in. I gotta go. I'll get a taxi tomorrow and pick you up for church at ten-thirty sharp. Be ready."

"I'll be ready."

"Okay, bye."

I should have moved out years ago, but I didn't. Collette invited me to move in with her after I graduated from college, but I turned her down because I needed every available penny to pay off my student loans. Besides, I just couldn't see myself living with Collette. We'd have been the black "Odd Couple." She's flashy, trashy, and ashy, and I'm dignified, sanitized, and moisturized. She collects these figurines and places them everywhere, and I mean everywhere. You sit down to use the toilet in her bathroom, and a family of fat Caucasian Hummels smiles at you from the sink. Ruins my concentration. I can't even turn them around since they'll still be watching me through the mirror. And her kitchen? The word *icky* comes close to describing it: two soup cans full of drippings on the stove, a ratty washcloth that smells like ammonia, stacks of dirty dishes in the sink, crumbs to feed every rat in Roanoke on the counters, unknown gobs of goo on the floor and in her microwave, a month's worth of garbage stacked on *top* of a full trash can. Look in her fridge and you'll see her staple foods: bacon, sour cream, and fatback. She even eats Beanie-Wienies right out of the can! She rarely, if ever, irons anything, and her closets are so crammed that anything she pulls out looks like an accordion. Yeah, she's my best friend, but someone once told me that you should never live with your best friend if you want to remain best friends.

So, putting up with Mama's interrogations is part of the mortgage payment. Her absence, though, will give Giovanni plenty of time to see if we click in the light, too.

I sleep off and on for a few hours before showering, lotioning my body all over, and splashing myself with CK1. I'm sitting at my makeup table in a white terry-cloth robe preparing my hair when Giovanni calls again. *"Ciao, bella,"* he says, and I smile.

"What are you wearing?" I ask.

"A towel and a smile," he says. "You?"

Seduction time. "Nothing."

I know his Adam's apple is bobbing. "Aren't you cold?"

"I'm dressed, Giovanni. I'm doing my hair."

75

"When do you want me to come over?"

"Around seven-thirty."

"Why so late?"

"I need to get ready." I don't have time to explain in detail, and I still don't have a main dish for our dinner. So, will it be Pizza Hut or Domino's? Decisions, decisions. "You like anchovies?"

"Sometimes. Why?"

I shudder. White folks and their nasty fish. "Just wondering."

"Are you making pizza, Renee?"

"You could say that."

"Cool." How Richie Cunningham of him to say so. "I'm bringing some bread sticks, carrot cake, and a bottle of Chianti."

He's providing most of this meal. I don't know exactly what Chianti is, but if it's anything like amaretto, he's in trouble. "Don't forget the amaretto."

"You have any Coke?"

"Say what?"

"We can mix the amaretto with Coke and make Camaros."

As in *Coca-Cola*. Whew. "Yeah, I'm sure we have some Coca-Cola." I will not mess with a man who does that other shit.

"Seven-thirty, then?"

"See you at seven-thirty."

"*Ciao.*"

I hang up and look in the mirror at my do. I love my hair. Not. It looks good, but I have to sweat to keep it looking good. I home perm my hair over the sink every six weeks or so, looking for the "pink" using two mirrors. Then, I dry it and put it up in my blue Crips do-rag.

No man may see me in this condition.

After applying orange Marcel curl wax, I clip 'n' burn 'n' turn my Golden Hot for thirty minutes, hoping that the curling iron's spring won't pop out of place. Damn things are made to break. I know it's a conspiracy against black women. And while others are getting weaves, I won't. Too many horror stories. I once watched a high-school basketball game where this girl lost her weave while grabbing a rebound. Instead of calling time-out, she picked up her hair and dribbled the ball down the court.

I check out the scar tissue on the tips of my ears and at my hairline. I've burned myself more times than I can remember. And that's why, after all my suffering, I do not allow any man to touch my hair. Only I am allowed to run my fingers through my hair.

My hair as close to perfect as I can manage, I open my closet and try to figure out what to wear. Do I go skintight, low-cut, lotta leg, open midriff, hoochie mama? Or do I leave something to Giovanni's imagination? I decide on something in between because I have to be comfortable. I choose a Victoria's Secret purple low-cut bra and high-cut panties, and draw-stringed brown, green, and orange Skidz. Skidz may be out of style, but they're easy on, easy off. Next, I put on a brown plunging-neck sweater that doesn't quite reach my navel, some gold hoop earrings, necklace, and bracelet, and my moccasins with no socks. I look at myself in the full-length mirror in the bathroom and smile. I am the bomb. I could take out Iraq.

And now for dinner. I punch seven digits and order a large pepperoni, green peppers, onions, bacon, and banana peppers pizza using a coupon. They tell me it could be up to two hours because of the snow. "I'm a big tipper," I say.

"Maybe sooner," he replies.

"Five-dollar tip if it arrives by eight."

"It'll be there by eight."

Of course it will. Money is power.

I place candles of all sizes in every nook and cranny of my room and turn on some UNV. I hear the doorbell and check the time. Dag, they really want their five bucks. I open the door, and there's Giovanni holding most of our meal.

"Hi."

"You're early."

He checks his watch. "I am?"

"Come in, it's cold out there."

I take the food, wine, and amaretto to the kitchen, and when I return, I check out his threads, and threads they are. Fuzz balls on his sweater, nothing ironed, jeans over-washed, pockets frayed, a gray T-shirt. I will not be seen in public with this man.

"Are those boots Timberlands?"

"I have no idea," he says as he kicks them one at a time into the closet. They obviously aren't. No one treats Timbos like that.

I step into him and get my kiss. "You smell nice," I say. Old Spice? Gonna have to get him some Lagerfeld.

"So do you," he says. He holds my hands and steps back. "And you look . . . stunning."

"Come on, let's do something about your hair."

I drag him to the kitchen. "Take your sweater off"—puh-lease!—"and sit there." I point at the chair in the middle of the kitchen floor.

He eyes the clippers, guards, and scissors on the table. "You're definitely prepared."

I wrap a towel around his neck. "Whatever you do, don't move or say anything. I am a stylist, and my work must not be interrupted."

"What if I can't keep my hands off you?"

"Then you're gonna leave with a few bald spots, boy."

I know what I'm doing, I really do. Sort of. This is my first white head of hair, and hair isn't hair. I shave the back and sides real close with a number-two guard and enjoy shaving his sideburns off. Elvis has left the building! His ears are tricky, big potato-chip-looking things, and he doesn't wince when I know the clippers are pulling. I scissor off a few inches from the front and blend everything else. That's when I notice how ashy his nose and face are.

"You need to put lotion on your face, boy," I say. "Looks like you got dried-up Elmer's glue on your nose."

"I have dry skin in the winter," he says.

I check a few spots, snip a bit here and there, then run my fingers through his hair. Nice. No gray yet, and a hairline that isn't about to recede any time soon. I ain't into bald.

"All finished. Go upstairs to the bathroom and shower off or you'll be itchy."

"I'll clean up," he says as he stands, shaking the towel, hairs falling to the floor.

"No. Go rinse off."

"Thanks," he says and gives me a kiss.

"What you thanking me for? You haven't seen it yet."

"Do you like it?"

"Yes."

"Then it must be good." He walks out of the kitchen.

"Hey! No peeking in my room!" I know he'll look now that I've warned him. And I want him to see all the candles everywhere, my queen-sized bed turned down, the big fluffy pillows, the mirrored headboard. Tonight is going to be very interesting.

When the pizza finally arrives, I give the overweight delivery driver the coupon and the check and set the pizza on the coffee table in the sitting room. I tell him to wait at the door while I check out my pizza. Everything seems to be in place, so I hand him a five-dollar bill.

"This is very generous," Fat Boy says.

"You're welcome." Now leave, Fat Boy.

"Most folks aren't nearly this generous."

You mean, most *black* folks. "Thank you," I say, my hand on the door.

"Good night," he says, and he finally leaves.

The nerve! Getting all that excited over a tip, like he's amazed my people tip. Most of the pizza joints in Roanoke don't deliver to the 'hood, so how would he know? Dag, we hungry too.

Giovanni comes down the stairs and sees the pizza. "Smells good," he says.

"I hope you like it. I worked on it all day."

79

We return to the kitchen and chow down. And I mean, we chow down. Twelve bread sticks, ten slices of pizza, two slices of carrot cake—gone. The bottle of Chianti—history. I look at my sweater and see bread and cake crumbs and a couple of dribbles of wine.

"You were hungry," he says.

I pat my stomach. "I've made a pig of myself. And I need to change."

"You look fine."

"I want to slip into something even more comfortable for the movie." I stand and flick a crumb off his chin.

"Can I take one more guess?"

I sit in his lap, my arms around his neck, my fingers fluttering through his hair. "Just one more. And if you're right, I'll give you a prize."

"What's the prize?"

"Me, of course."

"What if I'm wrong?"

"You will be. Guess."

"Is it . . . *The Color Purple*?"

"No. You lose. No coochie tonight."

"Huh?"

I stand slowly and burp. That Chianti is a gas! "Excuse me. And I'm only kidding about the coochie, boy. Make me a Camaro while I change."

"Okay, but . . . what's coochie?"

I'd laugh, but he *really* doesn't know. "Uh, I think your people call it 'making whoopee.' You know, sex."

"Oh."

"I won't be long."

I ease up the stairs and feel so fat. Five slices of pizza? This boy makes me hungry. I take off the sweater, locate my favorite flannel shirt with the most buttons, ditch the bra and the Skidz, and begin buttoning up in front of the mirror. I get three buttons from the top and stop. Then I add a thin line of CK1 from my neck to just below my navel, add a "Hubba hubba" to my reflection, and slink down the stairs.

We go down to the family room in the basement with our Camaros, which are incredibly sweet. There I go again, mixing caffeine and alcohol. I dim the lights and grab the remote, pointing at one corner of a soft black-leather couch. "You sit there." He does. I spread his legs and nestle my butt snugly in between them, wiggling just enough to make him squirm.

"You get one more guess."

"*Ghost?*"

"Ee-oo. Though Patrick Swayze is kind of cute." For a white man. I press a few buttons on the remote, and TV, VCR, and sound system come to life. "You're about to get schooled, Giovanni. You better take notes."

The title screen appears:

WAITING TO EXHALE.

"Have you seen it?" I whisper.

"No."

"Good. Feel free to ask any questions, and Giovanni, any time anyone gets kissed, you have to kiss me. And any time anybody gets busy, we have to get busy. But no sex. This is Mama's favorite couch. Understand?"

He reaches one hand under my shirt while the other caresses my thigh. "I understand."

For the next two hours, we get as busy as two people can get without having sex. I had his shirt off within seconds, and he eventually popped all but one of the buttons on my shirt. We'd pause, slurp our Camaros, and watch the good parts. And even though I know it's coming, I still bust a gut during the "Big Poppa!" scene.

"Geez," Giovanni says, after we come up for air during the garage sale. "Are all, uh, black women that spiteful?"

"You dog a sister, you get burned."

"Literally."

"Don't worry. You don't have a Beamer."

"I have a Cadillac."

"Say what?"

"A seventy-two Cadillac Fleetwood." Oh great—a boat on wheels. "It has a huge back seat." So it's a boat with a sleeping compartment. My man drives a hoopdy.

He tickles and caresses the area below my navel. I can't stand that. I arch my back and invite him lower. A few minutes later, I can't take it anymore. "It's time," I groan. "I'm going upstairs to my room. I want you to count to a hundred, then come up."

"Can I count by two's?"

"No."

He kisses a line from one of my nipples to the top of my panties. "Please?"

I catch my breath. "Count to fifty then."

I dash up two flights of stairs to my room and light all the candles. I let my panties fall to the floor. I put on a Keith Sweat CD. I am ready.

But mostly, I'm curious. This shit doesn't happen very often in Roanoke, Virginia.

He walks in and shuts the door. The candlelight softens all his edges. He is inches away as he unzips his pants. They clump to the floor. He kicks them away. He takes my hands and puts them on his Hanes. I ease them off and am not disappointed in what I see. I point at the remaining button near the bottom of my shirt. He gets on his knees and kisses all around it, his breath warm on my stomach. He fumbles only a moment, and the button is free. I shrug my shoulders and let the shirt fall to the floor. He's still kissing my stomach, his tongue circling lower. My legs shake, the butterflies in my stomach fluttering free.

"Giovanni," I whisper. He looks up. "Come up here."

He stands and kisses my forehead, my ears, my cheeks, my lips, my neck, my hands, and holds me for a long time, swaying slightly.

I lead him to the bed and slowly ease down, pulling him on top of me.

"Renee?" Do I need to give you instructions?

"Yes?"

"Do you mind if I . . . kiss you all over?"

"Yes."

His eyes drop. "Okay."

"I'm kidding. I will allow you to kiss me all over." I ain't crazy!

He pulls the covers over us and kisses me in every possible place, his soft lips igniting whatever they touch. He spends a long, long time exploring my inner thighs. He returns his lips to my face after what seems like forever and kisses my nose.

I look into his eyes. "I could get used to this." Who wouldn't?

"So could I. Did I miss any spots?"

I'm about to say "No," but stop. How often does a girl get a chance like this? "Yes. How could you?"

"Where?"

"There are so many places you missed! You might as well . . . kiss me all over again."

Fifteen minutes of nibbles and kisses later, I am in flames. "Giovanni!" I cry.

His head pops out in front of me. "Are you all right?"

I giggle and grab his ass. "Oh yes."

"You scared me."

I did? I'm not sorry. "I want you now."

"Uh, well, I have to, uh—"

"What's wrong?"

"Uh, Renee, I, uh, I have to pee."

I am angry, but I laugh. "Go on. I'll just stay out here and freeze." I hide under the covers. A few minutes later, Giovanni returns.

"Renee?"

I flip the comforter back to reveal only my head. "That was cruel."

"I'm sorry."

"Prove it."

"How?"

I throw back the comforter with such force it falls to the floor at the other end of the bed. "Make love to every inch of my body."

And then he devours me. I writhe, I moan, I guide his head to any spot he misses and make him linger in some areas much longer than others.

Then I start shouting, "Oh, Giovanni!" over and over again.

That's when we finally become one, and I see colors, lots of beautiful colors. They're here with me behind my eyes, every color of the rainbow exploding into the darkness. I don't want the light show to end, but I open my eyes and see Giovanni with tears streaming down his face.

I cradle his face. "What's wrong?"

A tear drops on my neck. "Nothing. Sorry."

"No, no," I say and hug him tight. "No, Giovanni. There's nothing to be sorry for. Really. I have never had anyone make me feel so wonderful."

"Really?"

Well, not for a long time anyway. R. J. made me see rainbows nearly every time, but it seemed like sex was a test of R. J.'s manhood. He *had* to make me come before he did, had to prove himself to me in bed, had to be the stud. Giovanni amazed me, not so much with his skills—the boy needs a little more rhythm and a *lot* more motion in my ocean. He amazed me with a single tear. A man shed a tear for me without shame. Sure he gave my coochie a workout, but I think my heart saw rainbows, too. I wipe away another tear from his cheek. "Really. You were wonderful, Giovanni."

He slides behind me and holds me in his arms. "I've been fantasizing about this for so long."

"You've only known me for a day, boy."

"Actually, I've known you since high school. We both had Mr. Jeffries."

"No shit? You've had a crush on me since high school?"

"Sort of. We, um, never spoke."

This boy is obsessive! "Boy, I didn't even know you in high school. Were you really thinking nasty thoughts about me all during class?"

"Not all the time."

"Well, did you do everything tonight that you fantasized then?"

He thrusts playfully against my ass. "No."

"Then what's stopping you?"

Chapter Three

I don't need to remember my dreams as long as my reality is like last night. A gentle man has come into my life, taking his sweet time with very slow hands and spicy kisses.

But in the morning, I'm alone and cold. Shit. I listen for proof of him somewhere in the house and hear nothing but the scrape of a shovel outside. No note anywhere in my room. Maybe he had to work and left me a note in the kitchen. I look at the clock: 10:05.

Mama will be here soon, and I'm not ready. Time to act sick.

I race to my closet, grab my robe, and tie it on as I slip barefoot down the stairs. The shovel sounds grow louder, so I peek through the eye-hole in the front door and see Giovanni. He's the sweetest . . . and the sweatiest. He looks tore up and tore down, face red, nose dripping, sweat flying. I know a mug of hot chocolate will warm him up, but if he expects me to hug him? Forget it. With Mama coming, it's "drink fast and get your funky ass a-steppin'."

I go to the kitchen, get out two mugs, and put water on to boil. I walk down the hall and sit on the ledge of the sitting-room window watching him work. He's so busy that he doesn't see me. That's okay. I'm tore up from the floor up, too. But what gets me the most is that he didn't have to be asked. He just up and does it. After last night, I can't think of how he keeps going. I guess I didn't work his ass enough. He holdin' back on me!

And then I see trouble in the form of a taxi pulling up to the curb. Mama's home early, and we're in shit as deep as the snow.

I want to run out there, but I'm barefoot and naked under my robe. I may care about Giovanni, but I'm not crazy. I snatch the phone and get ready to dial 911, but Giovanni doesn't even notice Mama. He just keeps shoveling away.

"What the hell you think you're doing?" Mama yells. That gets his attention. "I asked you a question!"

Giovanni winks at me (so he *does* know I'm here) then turns to Mama and smiles. *"Ciao, bella!"*

Mama comes through the gate and stands in front of Giovanni, her hair perfect as usual. "What you call me?"

"I say hello in my language."

Mama points at the house. "Is she paying you?"

"Is-a who?" he says like Pops.

"Is my daughter paying you to shovel our walk?"

"Your daughter? But you are, how you say, *bellisimo!* Surely you are her sister?"

Mama don't play that, but it was a nice try. "Answer my question."

"No, she no pay me. Your daughter, she get her car a-stuck at Luchesi's. I help her out by shoveling so she can get it today."

Mama squints. "All the way here?"

"Ah, your daughter, she is Renee? Renee is *belladonna* and give me a nice-a tip Friday night. I feel I must repay her kindness. I do it for free. And I am finished. Please thank your daughter again for me."

Mama's squint remains. "I will."

"Arrivederci," Giovanni says as he strolls away singing some Italian song.

I race to the kitchen and busy myself at the stove.

"Renee!" Mama yells as soon as she hits the hallway. "You ready?"

"I'm in the kitchen!" My voice cracks, and I can barely pour the water from the kettle.

"Girl, you ain't ready, and I got us a taxi waiting."

I turn to see her hands on her hips. I look away and see the top of the Chianti bottle sticking out of the garbage can. "I don't feel well."

"You got a fever?"

"I might." I was on fire just a few hours ago. I'm amazed the smoke alarms didn't go off.

She comes over and feels my forehead. "Girl, you hot and sweaty, stank and funky. Dag, girl, what you doin' in a robe with nothin' on your feet? Get on up to your bed."

Giovanni has sweet-talked her. She hasn't even mentioned him. I relax a little, but if she sees that bottle . . . "I just came downstairs to make some hot chocolate."

"With two mugs?"

Damn. "Uh, I put out an extra in case you wanted some." And Tupac Shakur is really alive.

"I'm not thirsty. You see that boy out there?"

Here it comes. How dumb can I play this and still get away with it? "What boy?"

"That Eye-talian from Luchesi's. Fool shoveled the sidewalk all the way from Luchesi's to our front door."

"He did? I didn't hear him." He shoveled an entire block? That boy *is* holding back on me!

"Said it was so you could get your car today. Boy barely spoke English. Said you were bell-uh-donna or something, said I was bell-ee-see-mo. And the boy had some serious funk, some serious funk. You eat there Friday?"

"Yes." I'm smiling inside. *Belladonna!*

"And you tipped him?"

Actually, I never paid, but . . . "Yes."

"How much?"

Shitshitshit. "The usual."

"Fifteen percent?"

"Yes."

"Boy went to a whole lot of trouble for an itty-bitty tip. Well, you just get back into bed, and I'll bring you some soup later. We got any soup in the house?"

"No."

"I'll bring you some." She holds my arms and looks hard at me. "I've never seen you look this sick, girl. You better get some sleep, baby." She pecks me on the cheek and takes a deep whiff. "And take a bath. I'll be back around two."

"I'll walk you to the door."

At the door she squints, and my stomach jumps. Mama doesn't squint unless she's trying to figure something out. "What?" I say.

She shakes her head and smiles. "For a minute there I . . . No. That's silly. A-reeve-uh-dare-chee!"

I nearly fall out.

As soon as the taxi disappears from view, the phone rings. It can only be one person. "Hello, Giovanni."

"How'd you know it would be me?"

"My people are psychic."

"Is she gone?"

"Yes."

"That was close."

"It could have gotten ugly. I was waiting for you inside with just my robe on."

"Just your robe? Nothing else?"

"Nothing else. I was going to be your breakfast." Not. "Can you imagine my mama surprising us in the kitchen?" I see a flashing steak knife in my mind. "On second thought, don't imagine it. And were you flirting with my mama?"

"She's beautiful, Renee."

"Well, I don't like it." I don't. That's even more twisted than what I'm doing with a white boy.

"When am I going to meet her for real?"

"Soon." I haven't worked that one out yet. "I have a lot of cleaning up to do before she gets home with my soup."

"Soup? Are you sick?"

"Why I gotta be sick? I might like soup!" I can't believe I'm yelling at him. It must be the tension of the moment. "She *thinks* I'm sick, Giovanni. That's all." Silence on the other end. "Giovanni?"

"I'm here." I know I hurt him. His voice is so soft.

"Why don't I come see you when I get my car? When do you close?"

"At seven on Sundays."

"I'll be by around, oh, seven-thirty."

"Okay!"

"And Giovanni?"

"Yeah?"

"I miss you." The boy's getting to me.

"I miss you, too."

For the next two hours, I repair the damage from the night before. I don't know how Mama didn't see the mess! I fill a garbage bag with the pizza box, the empty Chianti and amaretto bottles, the paper plates and napkins, and set it out back. Then I vacuum the kitchen floor for any stray "white" hairs I can't explain. After rearranging the family room and collecting all my buttons, I tackle my bedroom, replacing my funky sheets with fresh sheets, collecting and returning all the candles to their "correct" positions around the house.

Exhausted, I take a shower, put on some sweats, and call Collette's pager number. As soon as I flop onto my bed, the phone rings.

"Okay, girl, tell me everything, and I mean everything."

"Good morning, Collette."

"It's after one o' clock, heifer. Least I call at a decent hour."

"Where you calling from?"

"We still at the Patrick Henry."

"Poor Clyde."

"Forget Clyde. Now tell me everything."

Time to be dramatic. "There's nothing to tell," I say sadly.

"Oh, honey, that's too bad."

I giggle. "Actually, he was *very* bad! Wicked, in fact."

Silence for a moment. Sometimes it takes Collette a moment or two to figure things out. "Ooh, why you do me like that?"

"Because I can, Collette. Giovanni treated me like a queen."

"He rocked your world?"

My universe. "He rocked every inch of my body, Collette."

"Every inch?"

"Every single solitary square inch of this fine body."

"Damn. I'm jealous. He got any brothers?"

"Stop! There's only one, and he's only for me." I hope.

"Is he still there?"

"No."

"But you miss him, right?"

"Yeah."

"Well, well, well."

"Well-well-well what?"

"Well-well-well nothing. Has he met Shirl yet?"

"Sort of." I describe the encounter, and Collette laughs.

"Better watch him, Renee. He gets tired of you, he may go after your mama."

"Over my dead body."

"You never know. White boys is crazy that way, you know. Once they get a little cream in some coffee . . ."

Nasty way to put it. "Come on, Collette, help me out. What do I do?"

"You need my help?"

"Yes."

"All right. Is this lust or something more?"

"Both."

"Okay, do you see yourself saying 'I do' to Giovanni in front of a church full of your family and his?"

A segregated wedding? "Maybe."

"Maybe? Is this a definite maybe or an 'I'm-not-sure' maybe?"

"Somewhere in between."

"That's helpful."

"I mean, if Mama likes him, yes."

"Not a maybe?"

"A definite yes. But if Mama doesn't like him—"

"We'll be laying flowers on his casket."

"Stop!"

"Just keeping things in perspective. You know Shirl doesn't warm to your men easily. How long it take her to speak to R. J.?"

Mama never actually "warms up" to anyone but me. "Months."

"And you expect Shirl to—"

"No." This could take a lifetime. "What am I gonna do?"

"I have an idea."

"Tell me."

"It's kind of drastic."

"Tell me!"

"Okay. Take Shirl out to eat at Luchesi's."

"You're kidding."

"Think about it."

Mama and I being served by Giovanni. The wonderful food, the atmosphere, his smiling face. The cows watching us . . .

"Renee?"

"I'm thinking." Mainly about the cows. "But what if—"

"You can't know what if till it happens, right?"

"Right." I smile. "Right."

"I'm always right. So, when you gonna see him again?"

"Tonight."

"Dag, Renee. Give the boy time to recover!"

"No way. I'm just picking up my car."

"Uh-huh."

"After they close."

"I get the picture. Good-bye, Renee."

"*Arrivederci!*"

"Yeah, whatever."

I nestle back into my bed and wonder a whole lot of "what-ifs." What if I hadn't gotten stuck? For that matter, what if it hadn't snowed? I should be thanking VDOT and the city for *not* clearing the roads. But what if I didn't grab his hand? Is this fate or coincidence? Thinking like that can drive you crazy. How does anyone get together without some sort of magic or chance?

As I am drifting off to sleep, I whisper to the ceiling: "If loving Giovanni is wrong, I will never be right again."

"Soup's ready!" wakes me precisely at two. My body is pissed at me and doesn't want to move. Maybe I *am* sick.

"You get any rest?" Mama asks.

"A little." I sit up as she hands me a bowl of piping hot soup and a spoon. I blow on it and try not to slurp. "It's good."

"Hmm." She sits at the other end of the bed, staring and squinting. Oh shit. "You got stuck on Fourth Street the other night, right?" I nod. "And you weren't here to answer the phone, even when I called at two-thirty. Where'd you spend the night, Renee?" I'm busted, but I can't, just can't spill it all. "Don't spill your soup," she says.

I notice a little puddle on the comforter. "Sorry."

"You gonna tell me about it?"

It isn't a question, coming from Mama. She will sit there until I tell her about it. I set the soup bowl on my nightstand. "I met someone."

"And you're not sick."

"No ma'am."

She sighs heavily and shakes her head. Then she laughs! "Well, I'm glad." Say what? "'Bout time you stopped moping around here 'cause of R. J. 'Bout time you found somebody else."

She's actually happy! This isn't so bad at all. "I thought you'd be mad, Mama."

"I'm not, baby. So tell me, what's his name?" Damn, even names are hard in this situation. Wait, he said his friends sometimes call him . . . "You did get his name at least?"

I remember. "Jay."

"Jay. As in the letter or as in blue?" I spell it for her. "He have a last name?"

What is his middle name? "Anthony." Though technically a lie, it is partially true.

"Jay Anthony. Two first names. And how'd you meet?"

Time for a few half-truths. "After Giovanni—"

"Who?"

"The guy at Luchesi's."

"Oh, him." She frowns. "How you know his name?"

"He told me."

"Pushy Italian," she says, smoothing the comforter in front of me.

"Oh, he's not pushy. Just very outgoing."

"Yeah, outgoing for a tip. You see his nose? Daa-em. Like an elbow growing there. Boy had elephant ears, too. Throw in the few brain cells he has, and you've got Dumbo."

I scrunch up the covers but maintain my poise. I think Dumbo's cute. "Anyway, after Giovanni helped me out of the snow, I went into Luchesi's."

"And that's where you met Jay?"

"Yeah." And that is the truth.

"What's he look like?"

Oh joy. "Tall, muscular. Short hair, brown eyes." And white as the snow piled up outside.

"Handsome?"

"I think so."

"But not too handsome?"

"He's easy on my eyes, Mama."

"And how'd he treat you?"

"Like a queen."

"He got an older brother for me?"

Sometimes I wonder if Mama is really my sister. We have some of the deepest conversations, and from what I know of my friends and their mamas, we get a whole lot deeper than they do. She told me about sex when I was only eight, had me on the pill as soon as I hit puberty, and helped me through the messes with Jermaine and R. J. We borrow each other's clothes, fight over counter space in the bathroom, and are even mistaken for sisters in public—and sometimes *I'm* the older sister.

"I don't think he has any brothers, Mama."

"How old is he?"

"My age." I think.

"Divorced or single?"

"Single."

"Any kids?"

Good question. "None."

"Where's he work?" I hesitate. "He does work, doesn't he?"

"Yes. I just can't remember the name of the restaurant he manages."

This gets her attention. "A manager? Not a dishwasher or a busboy?"

Mama thinks he's black. For now, he'll just have to be black. "No."

"Where's he live?"

This is so aggravating! "Mama! I only just met him."

She stands. "You don't want to tell me, fine."

"It's not that I don't want to tell you, it's—"

"What? I want to know all about this man who stole your heart."

"He didn't steal my heart, Mama." I'm giving it to him. You should see the ring he gave me. It's sitting over on my dresser.

"Good. Never let a man take your heart. Makes you crazy when he jumps up and down on it later."

"Not all men are like that, Mama. Some are gentlemen."

She sits again. "Is Jay a gentleman?"

"Yes."

"So you two didn't do the nasty."

"Mama!"

She blinks and grabs her chest. She chuckles to herself. "If y'all didn't, he has got to be gay."

"Mama!"

She ignores me, stands, and crosses to the window. "We got to air out this room, girl. Bring a fan or something. . . ." And then she stops. Oh shit. "You did, didn't you? Right here." She digs her index finger into the bed. "This morning you only had that robe on. Did I just miss him? What'd you do, sneak him out the back? Or was he hiding in your closet? And these sheets are crisp and clean. Did some washing today instead of goin' to church, did you? And you was funky down there in the kitchen, girl. And on the first date? Child, haven't I raised you better than that?"

Stone cold busted. "It wasn't like that. Yes, he did spend the night, but—"

"Both nights?"

"We were at his place Friday and here Saturday, but he wasn't in the house this morning when you came in, I swear." He was in front of the house. You met him, Mama. You think he's Dumbo.

She doesn't speak for a long time. "And I was starting to like Jay."

"You will like Jay, Mama. You don't understand."

"Then explain it to me."

I am at a total loss when Mama's like this. "Mama, I think I'm falling in love with him."

She raises both hands to the ceiling. "Sweet Jesus! Didn't R. J. cure you of that?"

"I don't think I ever really loved R. J., Mama. Our relationship was never anything like this. Jay cares about me so much. That first night at his place, I wanted him so bad." I hear Mama's breath catch. "But he didn't want to," I say quickly.

"He must be gay or one of them bisexuals you read about in those sick and twisted novels of yours."

E. Lynn Harris may be twisted, but he ain't sick. "No. Jay just wanted it to be special."

"His place is a dump, isn't it?"

"No. It's nice. Lots of woodwork, blue and white everywhere with lots of prints on the walls." Of cows. "And clean. He keeps his place clean. And he even cooked for me." All true.

"He sounds gay to me."

"Mama, please."

"One, his shit matches. Two, he cooks. Three, his place is clean. He gay."

I show her my hand. "Please."

"Okay, so you think he ain't gay. All right. But two nights and you say you love him? Get real." She shakes her head. "And does he love you?"

"I think so."

"Did he say it?"

"No. But he doesn't have to. I can see it in his eyes, feel it in the way he kisses me, holds me." Makes love to me. Sheds a tear for me. Shovels a city block for me.

"You're making me sick. When am I going to meet him?"

"Well," I begin carefully, "he works almost every day, but I think his nights are free."

"Dinner, here, Thursday night, seven-thirty," she announces. Ba-boom! "I'll ask him if he's free."

She shakes her head. "This dinner is mandatory, Renee. I want to size up this Jay Anthony at the beginning, not somewhere in the middle like last time. And if I like what I see and hear—"

"You will."

"You *hope*," she says in a deadly tone. "Now, you gonna lie around in bed all day, or do I have to go get your car for you?"

"I'll get it later."

She hovers in the doorway. "I don't make half the payments on that car to have it sit in front of a restaurant all weekend. I don't trust Eye-talians. I want you to go get it now. And if you have trouble, get Gio-vanilli to help you."

"It's Giovanni."

"Whatever. Go get your car."

"Okay." I need to change the subject. "You gonna tell me about your weekend?"

"No."

"Mama, that's not fair! I just told you everything about Jay!" Okay, not everything.

"You didn't have to," she says with a smile, and she heads downstairs.

I need to tell Giovanni about the change in plans, but I'm afraid to make a call. Mama used to listen in on some of my calls when I was in high school. I never actually caught her, but I know she did. I pull on my Timbos and slip into a long, black wool coat.

"Wear a hat!" she yells from the kitchen. Mama's eyes are everywhere.

After pressing a white knit hat over my hair, I leave and race down the sidewalk Giovanni cleared especially for me. When I get to my car, I see mounds of "snow turds" blocking its exit. I breeze into Luchesi's and see Pops at the counter. Luchesi's is otherwise deserted. "Where's Giovanni?"

"Hello, Renee. How are you?"

How rude of me. "Oh, hello, Mr. Luchesi. I'm fine."

"Good. Giovanni's where you should be. Asleep in his bed."

So what are you trying to say? "Oh. I need his help moving my car."

"I'll help you."

I go out and get in my Jetta, starting it up after a few non-starts. I get out and knock some icicles off my fenders. Pops appears with two shovels and hands one to me. We work on the ice piles for a few minutes until he stops shoveling. "What are your intentions for my Giovanni?"

I stop. "My intentions?"

"Yes."

"We're still getting to know each other."

"So the marriage, it is not a sure thing?"

"I can't say for sure."

"Have you told your mama?"

"Not yet." And today would not be the best day to tell her. "I care about your son, Mr. Luchesi."

He scoops a large chunk of ice out of the way. "So you say."

"I do." If I say I care, I care. I know caring isn't love—yet—but I'm working on it, so give me a break, Mr. Man. "I care a great deal about him."

"Easy words to say. Hard words to mean."

He takes my shovel, and I can't find my voice right away. I stare at Mr. Luchesi's raggedy, flour-spattered shoes, then look him in the eye. "I'm not in the habit of saying things I don't mean, Mr. Luchesi."

"Hmm," he says and squints. He doesn't believe me. "I do not have this habit either." He stares hard at me, but I don't turn away. "Do not hurt him. He is all I got. Get in your car. I will finish."

Five minutes later, I'm pulling out into Fourth Street. I stop beside Pops and get out. "Thanks."

"It was nothing," he says.

"Tell Giovanni I'll call him later, okay?"

"Okay."

"Don't hurt him" echoes through my mind as I drive the short distance home. Don't hurt *him*?

After getting the Jetta, I try to avoid Mama as best I can by staying in my room. Of course I fall asleep, and when I wake up, Mama's got dinner on. We eat a meal of liver and onions (her "punishment" meal) and make small-talk about work. Neither one of us brings up Jay again, which is fine by me.

"I'll do the dishes, Mama," I say. I need to build up some brownie points.

"Go on. I'll do 'em."

"Okay."

At seven, I try to think up an excuse to see Giovanni but come up blank. I hate playing twenty questions with Mama, especially when I'm lying. I flip through a few channels, find nothing on, and return to my room. At half past seven, I fight the urge to run out the door to Luchesi's. Knowing Mama, she'd follow me. I hope Giovanni isn't pissed. A phone call will have to do. I dial Luchesi's.

"Luchesi's. We close at eight."

"Mr. Luchesi, this is Renee. May I speak to Giovanni?"

"He's with a customer. We stay open later tonight. Big business. You should come by."

"Uh, well, I can't."

"Want me to tell Giovanni for you?"

"No. I'll call back after eight. Thanks." I hang up and pout.

Mama sticks her head in. "You using the phone?"

"No."

Great. I wish I had a second line. Mama gets on the phone every Sunday night with her sister, Phyllis, and they talk for hours. Hmm. Maybe I can sneak over while she's on the phone. I wish we had a dog to walk. I'm twenty-six, and I still have to do things on the down low. Sneaking around that old house is difficult, but somehow I manage to get down the stairs without too much creaking. I hear Mama talking and check my watch: 7:35.

After closing the front door, I leap off the porch, bust through the gate, and run down the sidewalk. As I cross in front of the first big window of Luchesi's, I see Giovanni at the counter with a customer, a pale white female customer. I don't like the way he's looking at her, not one damn bit. And she's practically raping him with her eyes. I enter and stamp my boots real hard on the welcome mat, but Giovanni doesn't turn his head.

Pops notices. "Renee, so good of you to make it. Have a seat! Giovanni will be with you shortly."

Giovanni finally turns and looks at me, smiling that dopey grin of his. White Ghost walks past me with a smile on her face. I storm to "our" table and sit.

"Hi," he says as he slides a menu in front of me. "What kept you?" I ignore him. I know I'm late. "What was that about?"

"What was what about?" I point out the window at Pasty-Face waving to him from outside. He straightens the flower in the vase. "We were talking."

"About what?"

"The poetry reading Tuesday. Julie says she's going to read."

That was my competition? Giovanni's working both ends of the racial color line. "That was Julie?" He nods. "And it's nothing serious?" He shakes his head. "Uh-uh." I want to be mad, but he's looking right at me, not down at his feet or over my head like most guys do when they lie to me. Maybe this is a new trick. Maybe I'm overreacting, but I can't let it go. And now I know what night Mama and I will eat at Luchesi's. *Tuesday*. "Just friends?"

"Yes."

"No little Giovannis running around?" I shudder after saying it. Giovanni and Julie's kids would be light green. Yuck.

He smiles. "None."

"Well, I didn't want anything." I stand.

"Why don't you stay?"

I want to, but I'm angry. "You want me to stay?"

"Yes."

"Well, I'm tired." Mainly of sleeping all day.

"Are you feeling okay? You look, uh, pale."

"Say what?" This ebony woman will never look pale!

"I mean, the color in your face—"

"What about it?" My eyes are daggers, and he's the bleeding target.

"Nothing."

Damn straight it's nothing, Mr. Flirt-with-the-White-Girl. "I'm going." I start to leave.

He grabs my arm. "Please stay. I'll bring you some bread sticks."

I pull away from him. "Do I look hungry to you?"

He drops his eyes. "Sorry."

Shitshitshit. I sigh heavily. "It's been a long day. I'll call you later."

He writes down another number on a menu. "That's the apartment number in case there's no answer here."

I take the menu. "Thanks."

"I'll be up late," he says stepping closer and lowering his voice.

I feel a tightness in my chest. "Okay. Bye."

I walk out and look back at him standing in the same spot near our table and smile. He smiles, and I start to cry. And I mean, I cry like a baby all the way from Luchesi's to my house.

And I have no idea why.

I sit on our porch swing until my tears run out. They just come pouring out, and I can't do a damn thing to stop them. It's almost like they want to come out, have to come out. I don't feel any better, though. I'll probably get a cold and get sick for real.

The front door opens. "Renee?"

"Yeah, Mama?"

"What you doin' out there?"

"Just waiting till you get off the phone."

"Out in the cold? Get in here, girl. Phyllis wasn't home." She holds the door for me, and I try to look away. "You been cryin'?" I nod and take off my coat. "What for, baby?"

"No reason."

"Renee. Is it Jay?"

I sit on the edge of the coffee table in the sitting room. "Yeah. I miss him."

She sits next to me and fumbles with her hands before patting my back quickly. "Go call him. I'm going to bed." She stands and fumbles with her hands again, then smiles briefly and walks upstairs. What's up with her? And who was she talking to if it wasn't Phyllis? Mama actin' strange.

I dial Giovanni's apartment and get no answer. I dial Luchesi's, and after five rings, Pops answers. "Luchesi's."

"Mr. Luchesi, this is Renee."

"Giovanni! Phone!"

"Thanks."

"Thanks, Pops, I'll lock up," I hear Giovanni say. "Hi."

"Hi."

I listen to the static on the line for awhile. "Aren't you going to say anything?" I ask softly.

"I'm afraid to."

Deep breath. I hate this part. "I'm sorry for . . . going off."

"It's okay."

"It's just that I saw you smiling at her, and I want you to smile only for me."

"Julie's a friend, Renee."

"How much did she tip you?" The ho better not have over-tipped him.

"Fifteen percent exactly. It's in the tip jar."

"You still aren't going out with her?"

"Look, we used to go out. Now we don't as much."

"As much? Is she your girlfriend?"

"Not anymore. We're friends."

Do I believe him? I guess I'll have to. "Well, I'm sorry tonight didn't work out. Mama's acting stranger than usual, so I thought I'd better stick near the house. By the way, Mama and I will be eating at Luchesi's on Tuesday night. When's that poetry thing over?"

A moment of silence. "You and your mama are coming Tuesday?"

"Why? You and Julie got a date?" I've done it again. I gotta learn to put my attitude on hold.

"No. But it'll be packed. I'll have to serve the house by myself. I'll hardly have any time for you."

"That's okay. I just want Mama to meet you before you meet her on Thursday."

A longer pause. "What's Thursday?"

"You're coming to my house for dinner."

"I am?"

"Mama invited you."

"She did?"

"Yeah, and your name is Jay Anthony."

"Hold on, hold on. I'm coming to dinner on Thursday at what time?"

"Seven-thirty."

"And your mother thinks I'm Jay Anthony?"

"Right."

"What else should I know?"

"That I am scared shitless." And that's putting it mildly.

"Why?"

"Giovanni, I haven't told her that you're white."

"I am? I thought I was Italian."

"Be serious. This is a big deal. Your dad seems to understand—"

"No. Pops does not understand. He says, 'This kind of thing, it shouldn't happen.'"

"Why?"

"He's worried about our children."

"Our children? Dag, he's getting ahead of himself. And your dad

does like me. I can feel it." Not really. "Mama, though, she's difficult because she can be. Understand? I mean, she barely liked R. J."

"Who?"

"A guy I used to date. Anyway, he was black, and Mama barely
spoke to him."

"Did you love him?"

"I thought I did. Anyway, Mama—"

"Where is he now?"

"D.C. But that's not important right now."

"You brought him up."

"Oh, Giovanni, that was a long time ago."

"How long ago?"

As long ago as yesterday's mail. I still have to do something about
that. "Geez, get over it." More silence. "All right." I tell him about
R. J.'s two-year deception and leave out nothing. Okay, I don't tell
him about the showers . . . or the letter. "Look, it's late, and
Mondays are a bitch at work. I have to go in early to deal with all
the complaints from the weekend."

"Can I call you?"

"It's nearly impossible, but you can page me whenever you like.
I'll try to call you back when I can." I give him the number. "I'll see
you Tuesday at least, unless I can sneak away tomorrow night."

"I'd like that."

I hate good-byes. "Well, good night."

"I'll kiss you in your dreams tonight."

"Where?"

He breathes heavily. "Everywhere."

"Anywhere in particular?"

He whispers the place, and my nose starts to sweat. "Hubba
hubba."

Chapter Four

I have a little trouble getting into work because only two lanes of 581 have been cleared of the snow. Most of the side streets are still covered, and it will take until Friday for life to return to boring around Roanoke. Twenty-two inches of snow this weekend, and they're calling for more snow this coming weekend. Maybe I'll be snowed in with Giovanni again.

Unfortunately, I can't enjoy my weekend memories too much since we are getting slammed at Star City Cable. As soon as I answer one call and hang up, another comes in. Collette and I can only exchange hand signals. Maybe we'll do lunch somewhere. Giovanni, though, pages me every fifteen minutes, turning my pager into a vibrator. At first it's annoying because I keep wanting to check it, but then, well, it starts to feel nice. I hope the batteries hold out.

"Thank you for calling Star City Cable. May I have your name and account number?"

"I have a problem with my bill."

These are never fun. "I'll need your name and account number, ma'am."

"It's a quarter more than last month!"

Oh no! We can't have that! "Could I have your last name, please?"

"Martin."

"Okay, Mrs. Martin—"

"It's Miss."

I can see why, heifer. "Miss Martin, do you have your statement in front of you?"

"Yes."

"Please read off the numbers located in the upper left-hand corner." She does, and I pull up her account on the computer. "Okay, Miss Martin, we increased the monthly bill for basic cable with the new year, so that's why—"

"I wasn't aware of this."

Of course you weren't, you clueless wench. "It was sent to you with December's statement."

"Who reads those? What are you going to do about it? I'm on social security. Don't you people ever consider that?"

I check out Miss Martin's account and see she has all the premium channels. Social security my ass. And then, my pager goes off like a bee in my pants pocket.

"And channel forty-two is fuzzier than the rest of the channels." One of the country music stations. "Why should I have to pay an extra quarter if channel forty-two is fuzzy?"

What you need a clear picture for, bitch? All country singers look alike. I let the pager buzz and buzz.

"Hello?"

"Miss Martin, I'm going to take that quarter off your account. Will that be satisfactory?"

"Yes. But what about channel forty-two?"

"We'll send a technician out to you by the end of the week."

Miss Martin seems satisfied, but she's not as satisfied as I am. I log out and dial Luchesi's.

"Luchesi's, Giovanni speaking."

"Don't stop," I breathe. "Whatever you do, don't stop." I hang up, and a few seconds later, Giovanni is back in my pants.

Giovanni's buzzing gets me through to my lunch break. Collette and I hit Boomer's Deli, which used to be my favorite sandwich joint until I ate one of Giovanni's sandwiches. Usually one sandwich will hold me, but today I eat their Italian sub, a plate of fries, and two brownies, chasing it all down with three glasses of sweetened iced tea.

"Girl, you eat breakfast?"

I had two waffles with lots of syrup and butter, but I'm starving. "Giovanni took a lot out of me, and I'm just putting it back." I tell her about "Jay Anthony" and Thursday.

"You crazy? Y'all will need me there."

"This isn't *Guess Who's Coming to Dinner?*, Collette."

"It ain't? Sure sounds like it. You gonna need a referee."

"No we won't."

"And an enforcer. I'll bring Clyde to regulate."

"Clyde? Pul-lease. He puts the *bounce* in *bouncer*. It's just a simple dinner, Collette."

"Nothing simple about it. Your mama, you, and a white boy gonna sit down and eat. I'll be parked out in front. Wouldn't it be a trip if R. J. showed up early?"

"That's not funny."

"Have you called him yet?"

"I'll call him tonight. You gonna eat your fries?"

"Dag." She slides them over and checks her watch. "We gotta get back. Connie's looking evil today."

As soon as I sit down at my computer and hook up my headset, I get the kind of call I'm getting more frequently concerning illegal cable. Cable isn't all that expensive around here, but some folks get over by splicing into paying customers' lines or getting chips to put in their cable converters to get free pay-per-view. I'd be pissed if I was the only paying customer in an apartment building and all my neighbors got their cable free. I've even heard some hard-up fools, who get free pay-per-view because of the chip, inviting folks over and then charging them to watch boxing and wrestling matches.

Star City decided to crack down on all this last August, threatening anyone caught with up to a $1,500 fine, and now folks are calling in to rat each other out.

"I wish to remain anonymous," a white lady says. I know she's white. My people don't make these kinds of calls.

"How may I help you?"

"I just saw a young, black male climbing a telephone pole on Tenth Street."

Young, black male. Just like on *Cops*. I'm pissed, but the brother is wrong for playing with a junction box, so I still have to report it. "And what did you see him doing?"

"Well, I was at a light and saw a group of them looking up a pole. Naturally I was curious. Why don't they just pay like we do?"

I'm about to tell her that I'm one of them, but I don't because Miss Curious thinks I'm white because I can talk white. I decide to play along. "What happened next, ma'am? Were you scared?"

"Frightened, a little shaken, but I was in my Saab with all the doors locked. I knew he wasn't working for the phone company or for Star City Cable, because he didn't have a tool belt or a hard hat."

"Ma'am," I say using my most urgent tone, "were his jeans baggy?"

"Why, yes they were. Shameful."

"And was he wearing high-top, unlaced basketball shoes?"

"Now that you mention it, he did."

"And were his friends all smoking something, maybe something illegal?"

"Yes. Yes they were."

In confirming her prejudices, I try to push it. "And did you hear any loud, thumping jungle music playing?"

"Oh, yes! It was awful."

"Where exactly was the pole, ma'am?"

"I don't know those streets, do you? Does anyone? All I know is it was before I got to Orange Avenue."

One of the dividing lines from white to black in Roanoke. I type the approximate location into the computer and send the information to a file. It won't do any good, though. Weeks may pass before we get there and switch the junction box back. "Thank you for calling this in. Customers like you make our jobs worthwhile."

"You're very welcome. You will send someone over there right away?"

"Oh, right away, ma'am. We can't have those hoodlums stealing our cable, can we?"

"No we can't. Good-bye."

After the click, I'm about to kick the garbage can under my desk when another call jumps into my headset. "Thank you for calling Star City Cable. May I have your name and account number?"

"I don't have a complaint. You're black, right?"

Say what? "Yes."

"I knew it. Well, I am too, and I'm pregnant, see, and wanted to know what you thought about some possible names for my child."

I relax a little and save the garbage can from another scuff mark. Some people have no lives and assume we have all the time in the world to talk. It's always nice to have a relaxed conversation with a sister, though. I only hope Connie doesn't listen in on this particular call.

"If it's a boy, I'll name him Shontay Malik."

"That's pretty."

"And if it's a girl, I'll name her Shaniqua LaQuon." She has to spell that mouthful for me.

"They're both pretty."

"You have any children?"

"No."

"This'll be our first. My husband doesn't like either name. He likes Luther Junior and Barbara Anne."

"As in Ba-Ba-Ba, Ba-Barbara Anne?"

"Yeah," she giggles. "Isn't that funny? It was Luther's granny's name."

"I like your choices much better."

"Thanks. Ever thought about what you're going to name your children?"

I pause and remember Mr. Jeffries, my tenth-grade English teacher, who made us imagine what our lives would be like in ten years. And that was nearly ten years ago. We were all giggly about it, and everybody lied about everything. I was going to be a professional basketball player in the NBA, marry Big Daddy Kane, and drive a gold-plated BMW. Everybody was trippin', but when it came to the names of our future children, we were serious. My people take giving children names seriously, probably because we weren't allowed to choose our names for so long.

"Janae." I spell it for her and tell her where the accent goes.

"For a girl?"

"For both. I'm only having one child."

"Oh. You know, you could spell it Z-S-A-N-E with a hyphen after the A and an accent over the E."

I can't imagine sending my child through life with a typographical error for a name. "I could." *Not!*

"Well, that's all I called about. I know you think I'm weird."

Just bored and pregnant. "No, no."

"Well, have a nice day."

"Same to you."

Collette would love to hear this story, but since we're so busy, I log out and let the calls stack up while I write her a quick e-mail. I notice I have some new mail, probably some office memo I'll forget as soon as I read it.

But it's from R. J.:

> *Hey baby! I'm taking a few days off, so I'll be able to see you Wednesday. Give me a call so we can hook up somewhere.*
> *Love, R. J.*

And that's when I push back from my desk, run to the ladies room, and redecorate a stall with today's lunch. Twice I've puked because of R. J. I can hear God giggling as I sit fully clothed on the toilet trying to play it off in case anyone comes in. Wednesday night? No freakin' way!

The bathroom door opens, and Collette calls out, "You okay, Renee?"

"I'm fine," I say, leaving the stall.

"You sick." She wets a paper towel and presses it to my forehead. "I'll tell Connie you have to go home."

"I'm all right, Collette. Must have been something I ate."

"You look like you could just fall out right now. You going home."

I feel nasty and don't want to listen to any more calls, but I want to stay over so I can drop by Luchesi's and not have to explain why I'm late to Mama. "I worked over" is a good excuse for Mama. And anyway, I do have to put in a few extra hours the next couple of days so I can take off early to bake my spaghetti on Thursday. "I'll be all right, Collette. I'm fine."

"Can I get you anything? Some ginger ale?"

"Sure."

After I wash my hands, I walk back to my desk and take some deep breaths. Collette brings a can of ginger ale, sets it near my computer, and, nosy-body that she is, reads what's on my computer. "Oh shit," she says. "Sorry about what I said before. I didn't mean for it to come true."

"Yeah, you did say he'd show up early, didn't you?"

"Well, what you gonna do?"

"I don't know. I guess I'll e-mail him back and tell him off. Then later tonight, I'll call and tell him off in case he doesn't get the e-mail."

"What if it don't work?"

"Then . . . I'm gonna kill him."

"Can I watch?"

I bury my face in my hands. "This shit ain't happening."

"Oh, Connie's on the warpath. Gotta go. Write that e-mail!"

Collette hurries to her desk while I put on my headset. I write an e-mail to R. J. while half listening to some man complain about the sound quality of channel four:

R. J.: I do not want to ever see you again. DO NOT bring your rusty ass to my door or I will have Mama shoot it off. And you know she's been dying to do that for years. Renee

P. S. And I ain't your baby!

I worry that he's taking the entire week off and won't see the message until it's too late. I dread talking to him on the phone. I know, I'll have Mama tell him. She's been wanting to give him a piece of her mind since September, but I haven't let her. Yeah, Mama's going to make a very important phone call tonight.

I feel better, so I finish my shift without any trouble, planning to stay over two hours until 8:30. I want to make it to Luchesi's in time to order, then Giovanni and I can close the place in style. I can use a whole lot of hubba hubba right about now.

I take a break, call Mama from work at 6:15, and tell her not to make dinner for me.

"I wish you'd told me sooner," she says.

"Why?"

"Oh, never mind. I'm going out." *Click.*

What's up with her? I call her back. "Mama, what's wrong?"

"I'm almost out the door, Renee. Nothing's wrong."

"You didn't fix anything for me, did you?"

"No. I gotta go. Don't wait up for me."

"Where are you going?" I ask quickly. Mama has the quickest hang-up arm on earth.

"That's none of your damn business."

"Well, have a nice time, and tell him I said hello." *Click.*

Well, well. Mama's real serious about a man. And that could change my plans for the evening. Shit. She might not be home in time to call R. J. I call Luchesi's.

"Luchesi's," Pops says, a little out of breath.

"Hi, it's Renee."

"Call the apartment." *Click.*

Dag, everybody's in a hurry this evening. I dial the apartment. After seven rings, Giovanni picks up.

"Were you in the shower?" I ask.

"No. I was just a little busy. What's up?"

He sounds rushed. What's the big deal? Doesn't anyone have any time for *me* tonight? "I'm just calling to let you know, if you're not too busy, that I'll be by a little before nine."

"Great."

Something about that "great" simply isn't. "You do want to see me, right?"

"Of course."

"Okay then. I want another Italian sub with lots of banana peppers on our table, and I don't care if you have to kick people out, on *our table* at eight forty-five. Got it?"

"Got it."

"What are you doing, anyway?"

"I'm writing another poem."

And you couldn't pick up the damn phone for seven rings? "Is it about me?"

"Actually, yes."

"I want to read it. Put that on the table next to the sub."

"I may not have it finished. It's really for tomorrow night."

"Huh?"

"I'm reading a poem tomorrow night."

What's gotten into him? "Really?"

"Yeah. I've got a good subject."

A man reading a poem about *me* in public? "But what about Mama?"

He sighs. "I was hoping that maybe she'd be gone by then, and that you'd stay."

Mama isn't one for the "artsy-fartsy." She barely sat through my high school and college graduations. "Knowing Mama, she'll be out the door as soon as she's finished eating. When do the readings begin?"

"Around eight, usually."

"Oh, she'll be gone way before then. Can you read your poem to me now? I'm practically all alone here."

He laughs. "You've already heard it."

"Not—"

"Well, with your mama gone, I can get away with it."

I imagine what it will be like to see my man making love to me with words in front of a huge audience. "I may jump your bones right then and there."

"That's a risk I'll have to take."

"What's risky about it? Oh, I have a call coming in. Bye."

"*Ciao.*"

I don't really have a call. I have to use the bathroom, and Giovanni and I are not at that stage in our relationship where I can say, "I gotta pee." It wouldn't be ladylike. I'm peeing when my pager vibrates again. It's Giovanni. I dial Luchesi's when I get back to my desk.

"Hello, Renee?"

"What?"

"You okay?"

"Yes. What? I'm busy." Actually, I'm playing solitaire on my computer.

"Renee, uh, do you have the poem?"

"I thought you had it."

"Oh shit."

"Excuse me?" You do not swear in my presence, Mr. Man.

"I'm sorry. Okay, after you read it—"

"Don't put this on me."

"I'm not blaming you. Pops may know where it is since he cleaned up that morning. But it may be in the Dumpster out back by now."

"You let my poem go into the garbage?"

"I'm sorry, I'm sorry. I'll find it."

"You better."

"I'll try."

"And, you better wash your hands, check that. You better take a shower before you make my sandwich."

"Okay."

"Well, get to steppin'." And I hang up on his ass. Just like a man to mess things up.

Two moody hours of solitaire and only one phone call later, I drive to Luchesi's, walk in, and sit at our table. Pops delivers my meal to me at exactly fifteen minutes to nine, but when Giovanni comes over and smiles at me, I do not smile back because I have no reading material. He wisely moves away to the counter. I am the kind of hungry that doesn't want to be bothered, even by a smile. My stomach has been empty for six hours, and I do not want to be interrupted. And why are there only three bread sticks?

I see Giovanni out of the corner of my eye. He hasn't moved from the counter. Either he's getting smarter, or he's scared shitless. The sandwich is good, but I'll never tell him that.

Here he comes again. "Hi." I say nothing and push the empty bread stick basket toward him. "Oh, I'll get you some more." I do not acknowledge him. He returns with a full basket. I am still silent. "I found the poem. Pops saved it." I look up at him and blink. "Oh," he says, and pulls it out of a pants pocket. "Here it is." He lays it on the table.

My "wince-smile" sends him back to the counter. He's handling this fairly well. He hasn't thrown himself at my feet, begging for mercy . . . yet. I can play this role indefinitely. It's up to him to change me. I am the one who's in control here.

The sandwich is especially delicious, the bread sticks hot, the mocha cappuccino sweet. I am becoming myself again, but I'm still not through punishing him. After I take the last bite, he shuffles over and takes the plate without comment.

"Wait," I say, and he jumps. "One slice of that lemon pie over there, a fresh mug of mocha cappuccino, and the check."

He nods and goes. It's past nine, and Pops flips the sign on the door. He and Giovanni whisper about something, then Pops leaves through the back door. Giovanni brings the pie and the mug and hesitates before turning the check face-down. I do not react, he walks away, and I begin eating my pie. And it is buttah. I am smiling inside and try not to let it show. Giovanni needs to bring one of these to our dinner Thursday. It'll melt Mama's heart. I hope. I finish the pie and debate getting a slice to go. I flip over the check. "No Charge" is all it says. "Waiter," I say.

He appears. "Yes?"

I show him the check. "There's a mistake on this."

He sighs so heavily I think he's going to pass out. "Renee, please."

Almost begging, but not at my feet. "Give me your pen." I take the pen and scratch out "No Charge." He doesn't seem to be breathing. "Are we alone?" I ask.

He clears his throat. "Yes."

I write "One Hour of Passion" on the check and hand it to him. He just stands there. "You're on the clock, Mr. Man. Better get started."

"I want to show you something sometime," he says after we're both exhausted. I wipe sweat off his forehead.

"You already did."

I examine the fresh scratch marks on his chest as he carefully puts on his shirt. "It's my journal from Mister Jeffries's class."

I stop buttoning my blouse. "You kept it?"

He has trouble with his pants zipper. "Yeah."

"No way," I say, balling up my bra and putting it in my coat pocket. I hated those journals. I doodled more than I wrote. I didn't (and don't) want anyone to know my business.

"I still have mine, and you're in some of my entries." He pulls on his boots.

I tuck my blouse into my pants, smoothing out the wrinkles. "Where did you sit? I don't remember."

He hands my underwear to me, and it joins my bra in the coat pocket. "Last seat, last row near the window."

I pull on my socks. "You were the new kid."

"Yeah."

I smile as I tie my Nikes. The tall, pale, skinny kid with the funny accent who only spoke when he was forced to by Mr. Jeffries is my Giovanni? "What did you write about me?"

"I can show it to you."

"I don't have time. Mama's probably wondering where I am." I stand and put on my coat. "Well?"

"I wrote that you were the only person in the class with any class."

"Really?" I smile and kiss him lightly on the lips.

"You were the only one to clap after I read my poems."

I zip up my coat. "Oh, I clapped for everybody." No need to en-large his ego. "I'll have to look in my yearbook when I get home," I say, slipping on my brown leather gloves. "Gotta go." I give him the tiniest little peck on the cheek and move towards the door.

Giovanni reaches around me to unlock the door, and I turn to him, pulling his hot body into me. "Buzz me again tomorrow, okay?"

"Okay."

"And . . . don't freak when you see Mama and me tomorrow night. You can't give us away."

"I won't."

"And . . . thanks for dinner."

"You're welcome."

"And . . . I think I love you."

"You do?"

He needs to have his hearing checked. He puts up with my shit and gives me rainbows, and any man who can do that deserves to be loved. "That's what I said."

"I love you, too, Renee."

We kiss for real this time. Mini-kisses and pecks are what white women do.

Mama isn't home, but I feel confident I can control the situation with R. J. The past hour of passion has made me bold. I dial his number from the phone in my room, and he answers on the first ring. Fool's been waiting like a puppy by the phone.

"Hello?"

"You get my e-mail?" No manners tonight.

"Renee, how good it is to hear your—"

"I know. Did you get it?"

"No, I took the entire week off, you know, had to clean the—"

"Well this is what it said. Don't come to my house, don't call me, don't—"

"Still be in love with you?"

He's not supposed to say that. "Yeah, right. Mama's locked and loaded, and if you so much as step foot on our sidewalk—"

"So how is your mama? Still looking fine?"

He's playing a game he can't win tonight. "If you so much as drive by our house, there will be a drive-by in reverse and—"

"I dream about you every night, baby."

"I ain't your baby!"

"You were once."

I don't like the way this is going. "Leave me alone."

"Remember how I used to rub you down after a shower?"

I do. He doesn't play fair. The things he could do with those massive hands of his, the places they would go and go and go . . . Shit, it was better than foreplay since he hit all my erogenous zones at once leaving only my coochie crying out to be filled. I try to catch my breath. "You were probably thinking of Dagney."

"Remember how you would always squirm when I put the lotion on your—"

"Shut the hell up!" I've let him get to me. But oh, the places that lotion went, places I had never lotioned in my life! "Look, I am seeing a wonderful man right now, who I love a million times more than I ever even liked your rusty ass, who will tear off your arm and beat you with it if you ever bother me again!"

That shuts him up, but only for a moment. "Is he good to you, Renee? Does he give you what you need?"

There's that sexy voice again. "Always."

"Wasn't I good to you?"

At times, R. J. was wonderful. He could take my breath away with one touch, one caress, one whisper. After all that rubbing, all he'd have to do is breathe on my man-in-the-boat and I'd come. I fan my face and ignore his question. "That's all I have to say." *Click.*

My hands are sweating. Damn. I run to the bathroom and check my nose. Sure enough, it's sweating. Brother always could make me sweat. Big chocolate mountain who could melt me with his voice.

The phone rings. "Hello?"

"Remember that weekend in Myrtle Beach?" R. J. says.

I hang up. How could I forget? We spent the entire weekend in bed, or rather, *I* spent the entire weekend in bed. He went out and got us food, kept us supplied with towels, gave me some powerful good loving.

The phone rings. "What?"

"You remember, right?"

I slam the phone down this time.

He was my love slave for an entire weekend. Normally, he ran the show. For three days, I owned him, made him serve me like a queen. And he was better than good.

The phone rings. "What?!"

"Shit, girl, don't yell." Mama! "Just checking to see if you home. Damn."

"I'm home, Mama."

"What you yellin' for?"

"R. J.'s been calling."

"What he want?"

"He wants me back."

Mama's voice changes. "Give me his number."

"You gonna call him?" Thank you, Jesus!

"Uh-huh. I'll call him from here." I give her the number. "Then, you put call-block on that number, hear?"

Why didn't I think of that? "What are you going to say to him?" I want to hear her rag his ass.

"Plenty." Click.

God, thank you for my mama! Maybe this cosmic joke has a serious punch line.

The phone rings again. "Hello?"

"I can be that way all the time, girl."

This time I don't hang up. I feel like toying with him. "Will you provide my every need?"

"Yes."

"If I say 'jump,' will you jump?"

"Yes, baby. Oh, baby, I'll jump high for you, honey."

"Well, jump . . . off the tallest building in D.C.!"

"Huh? Oh, I have another call. Don't hang up—"

But I do. It's Mama's turn. I press star-sixty and follow the instructions to block R. J.'s number. If he calls again from a different phone, I'll block that one, too.

I change into some sweats and flip through a few yearbooks to check out Giovanni. He hasn't changed a whole lot in appearance since high school, so why didn't I like him then? I look at three yearbooks, and each index only lists him once. Even as a sophomore, I am all over that yearbook. I wasn't all that popular, just photogenic. I check out my senior picture, a few pages before his. I hated that drape thing, and I know the photographer was looking at my titties, but I look hot. Giovanni, on the other hand, looks stiff in his senior picture, but I get to see how he looks in a tuxedo. He cleans up nice.

I stare again at Giovanni's sophomore picture, and the word "homeboy" pops into my head. I smile and remember an amazing day in Mr. Jeffries's class. During the poetry unit, we occasionally had to write original poems and recite them to the class. I didn't mind doing them (mine were rhyming mush about my crush on Jermaine) and usually volunteered to go first. Giovanni, though, always went last. Always. His poems were usually short and didn't rhyme, and since he was last, no one really listened. I mean, you've just heard thirty of the *worst* poems on earth—why listen to the last one? Maybe I clapped because the readings were finally over. On the last day of the unit, we had to recite a "Who Am I?" poem based on Langston Hughes's "Theme for English B," and Giovanni volunteered to go *first*. That pissed me off because I always went first.

I remember the room getting really quiet as he unfolded a sheet of paper and smoothed it on the podium. "My poem is titled 'Homeboy,'" he said, and a few kids snickered . . . including me. He wasn't from the 'hood.

But then . . . he asked for a beat. "Slower," he said as a kid in the back started a funky beat using the top of his desk and the wall. Giovanni started nodding his head, and for a second I thought he was going to do some Vanilla Ice arm-flap dancing. Thankfully he didn't. He smiled . . . and *rapped* a poem to a Tribe Called Quest song that went something like "Back in the day on the boulevard in Huntington, I hung out with my homeboys, we thought we were the Mafia . . ." And he was *good*. I think I even clapped for real, and after he sat down, no one wanted to go next, not even me.

"My Giovanni's a homeboy," I whisper with a laugh as I get into bed, check my alarm, and begin to nod off when the phone rings again. Busy night for the phone company.

"Hello."

"Just wanted to give you a good-night kiss." Giovanni makes a nasty kissing sound.

"Thanks," I say, but instead of a kiss, I moan like I'm seeing rainbows. No one can out-nasty me!

"D-damn," he says.

"Sleep on that . . . homeboy," I say and hang up on his ass.

Chapter Five

Mama wakes me. "Get up," she says, parting the curtains to let in some sunlight.

"What time is it?"

"Seven. You gonna be late."

I roll over. "I don't have to be in till nine today."

"Oh. Just thought you'd want to give yourself extra time to get to work, and you up now. You hungry?"

Starving, actually. "I'll grab something on the way. When did you get home last night?" She puts her index finger to her lips and leaves. I sit up and yawn. Sunny outside already. Maybe we'll have a big melt and a flood. Giovanni is probably awake, so I give him a call while I'm brushing my teeth.

"Morning." Giovanni sounds cranky.

"Did I wake you?"

He groans. "Yes."

"Get used to it. Say, do you think you can reserve our table for around six-thirty tonight?"

"I doubt it. We rearrange everything so more chairs face the windows, but I'll try."

"Try hard, Giovanni. See you tonight."

"Bye."

"And don't forget to buzz me."

"I won't."

The shower water feels too good to leave, and it's half past seven before I put my hair up in a ponytail and get dressed. I don't feel like impressing anyone today.

Mama's got a bowl of cereal sitting at my place at the table. "I said I'd get something on the way."

"Sit and eat."

"You're going to be late, Mama," I say as I slurp my cereal.

"I'm taking a half day to go to the doctor."

I stop eating. "What for?"

"Get my plumbing checked out. It's my yearly. Appointment's at ten."

I continue eating. She's getting to that age where I have to worry about her every ache and pain. "What'd you say to Reginald James?"

She smiles and sips some hot tea. "Nothin' much. Just put him in his place."

"I want details."

"Okay. I asked him if his operation was successful."

"What operation?" I look down and find I've finished my cereal. And I hate cereal.

"His brain operation."

I laugh. "What did he say?"

"Nothing. I told him I heard that transplants like that are very painful."

"Like what?"

"Like moving a man's brain from his dick back to his head. It must be torture!"

"You didn't!"

She raises one hand and puts the other on her heart like she does at church. "I most certainly did. Then he tells me to hold on while he clicks over to his other line. I hung up on his ass. He ain't comin'." Mama seems awfully relaxed this morning, and she's looking over her mug into space. Mama the serene queen.

"Mama, when you gonna tell me about your new man?"

She doesn't look at me. "He's somethin' all right." I hold my breath. "Promise you won't tell a soul?" Mama leans in like a conspirator.

"I promise."

"I *like* him." I expect thunder to roll and lightning to flash, maybe even an earthquake to shake the house. This is serious shit, and I am speechless. "What?" she says. "Renee, close your mouth or flies will get up in there."

"You *like* a man?"

"He . . . moves me. Does something for my heart."

"Is it love?" She rolls her eyes and takes her mug to the sink, filling it with water. "Well, is it?"

"You gonna be late."

"We have plenty of time."

She holds herself and smiles. "Maybe!" Then my mama starts to giggle. My mama never giggles.

"Oh my God!"

"Shit, Renee, you soundin' like a white girl. Say what you feel!"

"Holy shit!"

"That's better. Had me worried."

A plan creeps into my head. "Let's celebrate. Let me take you out to dinner."

"Tonight? The roads are bad, honey."

"We can walk down to Luchesi's, make it a girls' night out."

"What about Jay?"

I giggle inside. "He'll just have to live one night without me. And Mama, why don't you have your man come over for dinner Thursday? It's only fair."

"I might."

"Come on, it'll be fun."

"It certainly will." She sighs and smiles. "What time we leavin' tonight?"

"Six-thirty."

"Okay. Now do something more with that hair. A ponytail with all that nice hair? You can do better than that. I mean, I don't want to be seen with you tonight if—"

"I'll fix it, Mama." I give her a kiss on the cheek and run upstairs.

"And get rid of them ashy elbows while you're at it!"

Ashy elbows lotioned, I drive to work past some new construction on 581. Why does everyone have to slow down so damn much? Ain't nothin' to see, y'all! And why they doing construction when only two lanes of road are cleared of ice and snow? Sometimes road work in Roanoke makes no sense at all.

Once I'm at my desk, the pager starts buzzing, and then the battery dies. Oh well. I can fantasize without it.

Star City is being nice to us today for surviving yesterday, the busiest day in company history. We answered over ten thousand calls for the first time ever, so we are being rewarded with lunch from Pete's Deli. While we're munching on a little bit of everything from the buffet, Collette and I watch white people being nasty with the food. Some are double-dipping chips, a few are using their unwashed fingers to "test" the dips or icings before putting them on their plates, and others have their noses millimeters above the food in the trays.

"The master race," Collette says.

"Not all of them have such bad manners."

"Oh, so now you're sticking up for them?"

"A little." I recap last evening's events with Collette.

"So you won't need me or Clyde. Damn. I was looking forward to a little drama. But there could be some drama at that poetry thing. What if your mama don't leave?"

"She will. She hates that kind of thing."

"She may surprise you. She surprised you with her new man, didn't she?"

She *has* been acting strangely. She is just too damn happy to be my mama, not that I'm angry about it. Back in the day, whenever she wasn't happy, *nobody* could be happy. If her car wouldn't start, she'd fuss with the neighbors: "I know y'all put some sugar in my gas tank!" If she got an overdue notice on a bill, she'd cuss the mailman the next day: "If you had just delivered the original bill on time, I wouldn't be getting shit like this!" If one of her pound cakes didn't turn out just right, she'd cuss the next person who'd call on the telephone, usually a telemarketer: "You gotta lot of damn nerve callin' me when I've just burnt a pound cake!" Maybe that's where I get all my moods.

"Trust me, Collette. I can't see Mama sitting around listening to white people talk pretty. She may not even last through dinner."

"Why not?"

"She may have another date."

Collette laughs then stops. "Girl, you see how much that heifer over there done put on her plate?" I look at my own plate and see almost as much. "Damn. I'd never do that. . . ." She looks at my plate. "Not that it's any of my business."

At home after work, I start to worry. Mama's late. It's nearly 6:45, so I call Luchesi's and leave a message with Pops.

"We're running late, Mr. Luchesi."

"I'll tell Giovanni."

Just as I hang up, Mama busts through the front door carrying a box. "Sorry I'm late, baby. Let me freshen up." She tosses her coat into the sitting room and runs upstairs.

Ten minutes later, she struts down the stairs wearing a jade silk pantsuit that knocks me out. She walks slowly, like she's Naomi Campbell. "You like it?"

"Damn, Mama, I'm underdressed." I'm only wearing a navy blue pantsuit with a white blouse.

"You look fine."

I rub her shoulders with my hands. Silk is sexy. "When did you get that?"

"Michael bought it for me."

"Michael?"

She puts on her coat. "I never told you his name?"

"No. And are those earrings new?" Huge diamond studs.

"Yes. Come on. We're already late."

"How'd it go at the doctor's?"

"He says my plumbing is just fine." I blink at her. "I'm fine, Renee. Everything is in perfect working order. Now come on."

We have no trouble on the sidewalks, thanks to Giovanni. Mama's smile never fades, even when we see the huge crowd outside Luchesi's waiting to get in. "Damn," I say. "Look at that crowd."

"Don't you have reservations?"

That gives me a jolt. Believe me, Mama, I have *plenty* of reservations about tonight. "No. They don't take them."

"I was kidding. I don't mind waiting."

I want to feel her forehead for a fever. Mama and I don't eat out that often, but when we do, she is the most impatient person on earth. If there's a line, we go somewhere else. If the waiter or waitress isn't at our table within seconds, we leave. If there's just one tiny spot on a glass, we leave. And God forbid there's something wrong with the food. She had the kitchen at one restaurant cook her steak four different ways—even shouted at the waitress, "Tell them to burn it!" We left.

"Renee, the Eye-talian is motioning to us."

"What?"

Giovanni is standing in the doorway waving to me. So much for not giving us away. "I have-a your table all ready." He turns to Mama. "You are a vision."

And instead of getting mad, Mama blushes and says, "Why, thank you."

"Please, follow me."

Mama shrugs her shoulders as we walk past a large group of

white women stamping their feet on the sidewalk. Giovanni holds the door open for us, and he winks at me as I enter. He leads us to an empty table in front of a stool and a microphone on a stand.

"We in the front row for something, girl," Mama says as Giovanni holds her chair for her.

"We have poetry reading tonight," Giovanni says in his thick Italian accent as he seats me. "I hope you enjoy." He hands us menus and disappears into the crowd.

"You sure you didn't tip that boy more than fifteen percent, Renee?"

I don't answer and look around Luchesi's since I already know what I'll be having. At the table right next to us is Pasty-Face Julie herself sipping a mug of something. She's so white you could shine a light behind her and use her for anatomy class. All her veins are showing. And that flaming red hair. Droolie is another wooden kitchen match.

But this joint is jumping! Pops and Giovanni are working it tonight. I notice a self-serve sign on a silver coffee dispenser. Smart move. Half the people are eating, half just drinking, and many have piles of paper on their laps. I watch one guy with a hook nose lip-reading a poem, and see one lady scratching out something on a napkin. And the noise almost drowns out the opera music.

"What's good?" Mama asks. "And what the hell is that sound?"

"I hear the Italian is good," I say, "and I think that's opera music."

"Sounds like someone butcherin' a pig." It does, sort of.

Giovanni appears. "How may I help you?"

I widen my eyes and mouth, "Where's the accent?"

Mama's head is buried in the menu so she doesn't see our little drama. "I can't decide," Mama says. "You'll have to come back."

"May I get you something to drink, a little mocha cappuccino perhaps?"

"I'll have one," I say quickly.

"Sounds good," Mama says.

"Be back in a moment."

I shoot eye daggers at Giovanni's back as he weaves a maze through the tables.

"I knew that accent was fake," Mama says, her eyes still on the menu. "He only uses it to flirt."

Gulp. "How you know he's flirting?"

She looks at me and drops the menu. "It's obvious, ain't it? He been flirting with me since I walked in." I smile inside. "And he was flirting with me in front of our house on Sunday, too."

I restrain a laugh. "How you know he isn't flirting with me?"

"Puh-lease, with you wearing *that*?"

I groan. "What are you going to have, Mama?" It's 7:15.

"Oh, I don't know. Probably a salad."

I see six salads to choose from. "Which one?"

"Probably the Luchesi, but without the olives and mushrooms."

Giovanni returns with two mugs, placing them carefully on the table. He withdraws his pad, winks at me, and says, "Are you ready?"

"Yes," I say quickly. "I'll have the Italian. And Mama will have the Luchesi salad."

"I can order for myself. What's your hurry?" She turns to Giovanni. "What are your dressings?"

"Italian vinaigrette, honey mustard, honey poppy seed, honey lemon—"

"That's a lot of honey," Mama says to me.

Giovanni continues. "Thousand island, ranch, and our own house recipe."

"Which is?" Give it up, Mama, please!

"A family secret."

"Right," she says. "Well, I'll try the house recipe, and it better be good."

"I made it myself," Giovanni says, and I want to strangle him. Leave my mama alone so we can get her out of here!

"You did? Well, in that case, I'll have the honey poppy seed."

"I made that one, too." I send out some ESP filled with four-letter words.

"You did? Which ones didn't you make?"

"The vinaigrette. My father makes that."

Mama sets her menu down. "I'll have that one."

He takes our menus, bows to Mama, raises his eyebrow at me and leaves.

"Why you playing with him like that, Mama?"

"Who says I was playing? Maybe I was flirting."

Puh-lease. "Try your drink. It's delicious."

She takes a sip. "Sweet." I taste mine. It isn't sweet. She takes a larger sip. "Got a little punch to it, too."

No, he *didn't!* "Let me taste yours."

She pulls the mug back. "You got your own. And we ain't white so don't try that shit with me." I check out some of the white people near us to see if they hear. Just what I need is to start a scene with my mama when we're the only black people up in here.

So, Giovanni's spiking my mama's mocha cappuccino with amaretto. She barely drinks at all. Or, it was meant for *me* and he got the mugs switched.

Five minutes pass, and Luchesi's is standing room only. I had no idea it would be this crowded.

"Are those cows in those pictures?" Mama asks, squinting.

With her attention across the room, I pick up her mug and take a quick sniff. It's amaretto alright. "Yeah."

She leans back and looks around. "Blue and white. Nice colors, and everything matches. Beautiful wood." She stops and downs the rest of her mug. "Gotta get me another one of these."

I see Giovanni going from table to table carrying a huge tray loaded with baskets of bread sticks. With dexterity and strength, he drops a full basket and picks up an empty, keeping that tray perfectly level. He gets to us and deposits the bread sticks with a flourish.

"May I get you another mocha cappuccino? Free refills tonight."

"Free refills?" Mama says. "I may take some home. Thank you, uh, what's your name?"

"Giovanni."

"Giovanni," Mama says perfectly.

"I'll be back with your order and another mug in a few minutes. Enjoy the bread sticks."

I tear into a bread stick and pout. My man is flirting with my mother and ignoring the hell out of me. I know I told him not to give us away, but this is too much. And, he's getting her drunk.

A few minutes later, Giovanni brings the mug. "Your order is almost ready."

"Take your time," Mama says, sipping deeply. "This is *so* good. What's in it?" Yes, what's in it, boy?

"A special blend of coffees we grind here ourselves," Giovanni says.

"You grind here?" Mama's trying to be nasty. That's where I get my nastiness from.

Giovanni looks directly at me. "Yes, we grind here. Just about every night." Do we *ever*! "To this we add a blend of chocolates and a dash of amaretto."

"Well, you just keep bringin' 'em, Giovanni."

"I will."

Giovanni leaves, and Mama is beaming. "What's amaretto?"

"It's a liqueur."

"Alcohol?"

Tonight it is. "No, it's just a flavoring, I'm sure."

"This ain't flavoring, honey. This is the real deal. I think Giovanni's sweet on me."

"I have to use the bathroom," I say, throwing my napkin on the table and walking toward the counter. I catch Giovanni's eye, and he comes over.

"Your order's almost ready," he says.

I lower my voice and nearly hiss at him. "What the hell you think you're doing?"

He whispers in my ear, "You look beautiful tonight."

I know, but . . . "Answer me."

He whispers again, his lips brushing my ear. "It loosened you up, didn't it?" I want to slap him, but I like his lips on my ear. "I've won your heart, right?" I growl, but I nod. "And now I have to win hers."

"She's going to hear you read *my* poem. Doesn't that thing start in fifteen minutes?"

"Yes."

"It'll give us away."

"It won't. Trust me."

"Order up!" Pops yells, and I nearly pee myself.

"Your dinner's ready. Do you want the extra ingredient in your next mug?"

"Yes." I widen my thumb and index finger three inches. "This much."

"It'll be out in a minute."

I return to Mama, and I swear she's singing along to the opera music, giving it a definite gospel flavor. Her second mug is empty. Mama gettin' drunk.

"Renee, did you know there was gonna be a poetry reading here tonight?"

"Uh, yeah. But I thought we'd be gone by then since I know you don't like them."

"Are you kiddin'? I can't wait to hear what all these white folks have to moan about." She leans in to whisper, and I smell the alcohol. "We integratin' the place, ain't we?"

I look over and see a few other people of color who have just come in. "We aren't the only ones, Mama."

"You talkin' bout them back there? They yellow."

Giovanni appears, deposits our meal, says *"Buon appetito,"* and sets a brimming mug in front of me. Another bow and he's gone.

"He has pretty eyes, don't he, Renee?"

I take a huge gulp from my mug. Much better. "Yeah, he does."

Pretty eyes for *me*, Mama, not you. She eats some of her salad while I devour my sub.

"This is delicious. And those bread sticks are addictive." She pats her mouth with a napkin. "Michael can cook, too."

"Oh?" I smile suggestively at her.

"Get your mind out the gutter. He can really cook. I've eaten a bunch of meals I can't pronounce, and they were all delicious."

Some tall, skinny lady straight out of an L. L. Bean catalog steps up to the mike precisely at eight and asks for quiet. "Welcome to another Artemis night. I'm Lisa Walters, and I'll be your emcee of sorts. But before we begin, let's all give a hand to the Luchesis!" They cheer my man, and Mama's clapping the loudest. "We don't have a set order for who reads," L. L. Cool Lisa continues as the applause dies down, "so, when the spirit moves you, stand and walk to the mike. Tell me who you are, and I'll introduce you. Who'll read first for us tonight?"

Mama is into this. Her head is on a swivel, swinging left and right to look for the first reader. "Mama, stop."

The man with the hook nose stands and keeps getting taller as he gets nearer the mike. "Dag, looks like a totem pole," Mama whispers. I kick her under the table, and she giggles.

"Please welcome Christopher Dunleavy," Lisa says, and she sits down on her own special chair. Everything about Lisa is so special.

Mr. Dunleavy sits on the stool, but his legs still reach the ground. He rattles his paper and clears his throat. "Hello. This is called 'The Saint of Elm Avenue.' " He clears his throat again and begins:

> *Donnie cruises Elm Ave. in an incense dream,*
> *buildings glowing like blood on black tar,*
> *white neon illuminating his search for Agnes.*
>
> *He floats in the shadows past*
> *the suits and their blind visions,*

the policemen hard to read as Sanskrit,
mother-clouds hovering
over their oceans of children,
the lover-strangers,
spurting sex into the air.

One foot planted on the sidewalk,
the other inching up the wall,
she waits,
a cigarette in her mouth.

"Lonely?" she asks.
"Are you Agnes?"
"I can be."

As they walk arm-in-arm to her ten-dollar-an-hour room,
he twists the blade in his pocket,
dreaming of unkind cuts and redemption.

"Thank you."

Mama starts the applause, and people start clapping here and there. What the hell for? Man just hooked up with a hooker. I see Giovanni behind the counter on his stool shrugging his shoulders.

"I have one more I'd like to share with you. It's called 'Nights of Red Neon.'"

Angry angels hover over silent sidewalks, airy
densities with cornfield faces, slimy fingers, skin
sisters with no time for details (like
names), paid to be silver linings on
cloudy days, unblessed virgins, ('lookin' for a
a good time honey?'), snipers trolling with
double-barrel shotguns, swimming with hearts of cold.

"Thank you." He returns to his seat to a scattering of applause, and this time, Mama is barely clapping.

"Was that about what I *think* it was about?" I nod. "Man needs hisself a steady girl," Mama says a little too loudly.

After Mr. Totem Pole, the rhymers get up and try to impress us with their rhyme and rhythms. They fail. These girls from Hollins University then follow in a pack formation and make every man cross his legs. Mama can't stop laughing. Why are white women so Lorena Bobbit-like? "The Dead Man in my Bed" isn't bad, but the rusty scissors are a bit much.

"I call this one 'Effigy,' " the last Hollins girl says.

I tune her out and snap my fingers near the floor as Giovanni returns to our table. He crouches down. "Two more," I whisper.

"Okay."

After "Effigy" ends in flames and Mama fans herself, M. C. Lisa announces, "Our next reader is W. B. Slaughter."

A white man, who could be Giovanni's older brother with his big nose and ashy skin, takes the microphone and centers himself in front of the Hollins girls. "This one is for you," he says to them. "This is my version of *The Wizard of Oz.*" He pauses and recites his poem from memory:

> *There was this girl Dorothy, a fairly plain child*
> *with an ugly dog in the plainly ugly state of Kansas,*
> *who lived with her Auntie M,*
> *who couldn't afford the rest of her name,*
> *and some manure-toting pansies.*

Daa-em. He's describing those Hollins girls like he knows them but ain't none of them from Kansas. They're from some place Northern and rich, some of them even bringing their horses with them . . . so they can get a college credit in being rich enough to have a horse, I guess.

One day the wind did blow on Dorothy and her poor rat-dog,
  Toto.
They should have been destroyed by that tornado,
but they weren't.
It was a nice tornado.
They flew straight up,
breaking all laws of physics flew Dorothy and her pup.

They landed on some nasty witch's head,
killing her on the spot.
Bet the witch didn't have that *kind of house insurance.*
Just think: there she is, ready to fling some magic snot
at some underdeveloped, vertically challenged Munchkin,
when a black-and-white house flattens her and her
  Technicolor hat.
I guess some days you just can't win.

Dorothy then swaps lollipops with the Little People
when Glenda the good witch
floats in and says,
"So you've killed the nasty stank bitch."

Mama chokes on her drink and slaps the table while the rest of the audience cracks up. An older white man, in Roanoke, has used the phrase "nasty stank bitch"? He must not be from here originally. The Hollins girls lookin' mad, too.

She really didn't say it that way exactly
because back in nineteen thirty-nine you had to say things nicely,
what with World War Two starting and all.

Dorothy follows a yellow brick road
and before she can get too durn far,
she sees this scarecrow hanging out,

so she torches him—hardy har har har.
She then sees this heartless, aluminum-sided dude,
and instead of WD-forty, she squirts him with hydrochloric acid.
Then this really hairy freak, obviously overdosing on Rogaine,
*   jumps her*
so she shreds him with her sawed-off, double-pump Winchester.

I always knew that ho Dorothy had a serial killer's heart. Bitch is runnin' around in red pumps on a yellow brick road talking to scarecrows, lions, tin men—bitch had to be out of her mind.

W. B. sighs and looks directly at the Hollins girls, his face slack, his eyes wide.

As you may have figured out, Dorothy had PMS,
and back then, there wasn't any Midol around . . .
or any man in Dorothy's life to put down
to make her feel better.
Like now.

Hollins girls be gettin' housed! Mama and I can't stop laughing—but then I do. Daa-em. W. B. just housed every woman in the room. I should be offended . . . but the shit's too true! What did women do back in the day when their "friend" came?

Finally, after target-shooting a few flying monkeys
that look suspiciously like Michael Jackson,

He got that right. That scene used to scare the shit out of me. Still does, as a matter of fact. Then Michael goes and plays the scarecrow (when he was still black) in *The Wiz.* I shouldn't rank on Michael. The man *is* talent, and as embarrassed as my people act where Michael is concerned, we all know his every word, his every squeal, and his every dance move.

*and after melting a green witch with some heavy water from
  Three Mile Island,
Dorothy meets an egotistical wizard with a really big head.
The Wizard tries to fly Dorothy home to Kansas in a hot air
  balloon,
but it blows up like the Hindenburg.
Dorothy survives. Toto doesn't.
The little people pull Toto's body out of the ground and use him for
  an accordion.*

*Eventually, Glenda comes in to save the day,
she could have done that in the first twenty minutes, if you asked
  me,
and has Dorothy click her insensible red shoes together to go back
  to Kansas
and all the manure-toting pansies.*

W. B. pauses again, his smile disappearing.

*I bet Dorothy wished she could have stayed in Oz
because because because
somewhere over the rainbow
she changed her name to Judy
and drank herself to death.
For real.
Death got you, my pretty.*

*And at night on the plains of Kansas,
if you're really quiet,
you can hear the ghost of Dorothy-Judy say:
"You can take that rainbow
and shove it up your Kansas."*

Everyone in the room is clapping, not cheering, just clapping—
except for the Hollins girls. They look like they wish they had a

pair of rusty scissors to use on W. B. right now. I liked the poem, but the last part got me. You can have it all—fame, money, success—and still have nothing.

W. B. bows to the Hollins girls (the man has guts!) and hands the microphone to Lisa, who looks like someone has yanked her jaw to the floor. "Uh, um, our next reader is . . ." But there's no one moving. "Uh, who would like to read next?" I see a white blur weaving through the chairs to Lisa, and it's Big Red herself, whispering in Lisa's ear. "Please welcome Julie Drake."

White girl lookin' scared to death. If she turns any whiter, they won't need lights in here. I wouldn't have gone right after W. B.'s poem, because folks are still talking about it.

"I'm a little nervous," she says, so I stare extra hard at her, hoping she falls out or spews on someone. "My poem is entitled 'Giovanni.' "

What the . . . *the bitch!* What's that ho up to?

Mama giggles. "This gonna be good. Oh, there he is. She's written one about her man. This is going to be so good—"

"Mama!"

Giovanni appears and places our mugs on the table. "Did you hear what she said?" I whisper to him.

"Yeah."

A few people near us say "Sh!" I give them the evil eye as Snow White reads:

> *Brown eyes*
> *so soft his hands*
> *sincere smile*
> *tender man*
> *he brings me food*
> *my hands sweat-shake*
> *he fills my cup*
> *I cannot speak*
> *dark brown eyes*

so swift his hands
I want his smile
I want this man.

The skank-bitch-ho-heifer! I imagine strangling her with her own hair. I want this man? Well, you gonna get this foot up your ass! And Giovanni said this shit was over? I got me some straightening to do!

At first, no one claps, which is fine by me since the poem sucked (*shake* and *speak* don't *even* rhyme), but then people start hooting and hollering and slapping tables. What is this shit?

And why is Giovanni going *next?*

Mama's sipping her drink again. "Told you this would be good. I like the way she described his eyes. I liked her poem the best so far. She wants that man, oh yes she does—"

"Mama!"

"What's wrong with you? Damn, I thought you liked that romantic shit."

If I were a cartoon character, I'd have smoke coming out my ears. If I weren't a lady, I'd go over to Pasty-Face and take a razor blade to all of her freckles.

"Our next reader is Giovanni Luchesi!"

Major applause, and he seems to be loving it. What the hell is going on?

"I wonder if he has a poem for her," Mama says. "Yeah, he sure does. That's the way they do it in them Julia Roberts movies. *She* reads one about him, then *he* reads—"

"Mama, hush!"

But then I remember what's coming and smile that soap-opera-bitch smile every woman has. Little Red Writing Hood is about to be *housed* by my man.

"Hi," he says. "I am Giovanni, and I'd like to thank my friend Julie for her wonderful poem. Let's give her another big hand!"

Oh, this is too much! Damn, doesn't he know he's embarrassing me? But he did say "friend." He made that clear to everyone. Okay, okay. I'm all right. Now it's my turn. Bring the love!

"I've written a poem without a title. Sorry. Oh, and Pops is signaling me that we're out of . . . carrot cake." A few people boo. "Hey," Giovanni says, "it's your fault!" He seems to be enjoying himself. That's *my* man. "Okay, now to my poem."

"Giovanni!" Pops yells. Now what?

"Yeah, Pops?"

"The carrot cake will be ready in ten minutes!"

And now people are cheering. *Just get on with it!*

"And now, my poem. But I'll need someone to read it to."

I straighten up. Damn, I wish I dressed up more nicely. I move my chair away from the table a bit. Okay, come to me.

He takes the mike out of the stand and moves toward our table and moves around my chair to stand next to . . . *Mama?*

"Oh, my Lord!" Mama says, both hands on her chest. "I'm so glad I stayed, Renee. Oh, my Lord!"

That's not what I would have said. Giovanni shoots me a look, and now I understand what he means by winning her heart. As much as I'm going to hate this, it makes sense. I smile at him and nod.

"Would you come up and sit on the stool for me?"

Mama giggles and says, "Why, I'd be delighted!"

"Go, Mama!" I shout, and everyone starts clapping and stomping feet.

She takes his hand and he leads her to the stool, where she sits looking so fine in that pantsuit.

"Ready?" he asks her.

"For what?" She grins at me.

"Wait a minute," he says. "What's your name?"

"Shirley."

"Then the title of my poem is 'My Song to Shirley.' " And then he kneels, oh God, he's kneeling, and says,

Sweet sizzlin' soul sister,
silken soft-skinned sis-TUH!
Gimme some play.
Share soma-dat darkness
with a white boy today.
Rub soma your color on me
the old-fashioned way,
sweet mocha sis-TUH,
give a white boy some play.

Mama looks like she's going to faint. The audience is loving it. I'm feeling warm all under.

I seen you out walkin',
out struttin' yo' stuff,
head high, shoulders square—
I can't get enough.
You cut your eyes on me,
you're playin' a game—
sexy soul sister
in the dark we're the same.

Someone in the crowd yells "Amen!" Mama is hypnotized. I want to tell her, "Girl, I know what you going through, and you just enjoy the ride."

Don't care what your friends say,
don't care what folks whisper,
just gimme a chance
my sweet sepia sister.

Some man in the back hollers, "Give him a chance!" Mama is cheesing.

Sweet smokin'-hot sister,
sexy, sultry, sweet sis-TUH!
Gimme some play.
Share soma your darkness
with this white boy today.
Grind soma your color on me
the passionate way.
Simmering, seductive sis-TUH,
give my whiteness some play.

And then Mama hugs him as the audience comes to its feet. Some are yelling "Encore, encore!" while others are slapping hands and jumping up and down. Giovanni leads Mama back to our table, and still the audience stands, the cries of "Encore, encore!" getting louder.

"You want to hear it again?" Giovanni asks. Uh-duh. He gets that big doofy grin on his face and says to Mama, "May I borrow your daughter for a moment?"

"Yessss," Mama says grabbing my hand. "It's your turn now, honey. Whoo!"

I feel his hand at my back as we go to the stool. My legs are jelly, my heart putty in his hands. "Please don't kneel," I whisper, but he shakes his head. He reads it to me, but this time it's deeper, hotter, sexier. With Mama he was having fun. With me, every word drips of love.

And in the end, instead of a quick hug like Mama, I hug him tightly. As the applause swells again, I look at Julie, but she claps harder than anyone. She is so clueless, but I don't hate her. I mean, how can I hate anyone who has such good taste?

Giovanni helps me back to my seat and hands the mike to Lisa before returning to his stool behind the counter. Mama isn't as lively as before for some reason.

I mouth, "Are you okay?" She nods. I whisper. "You want to go?"

"No. I'm all right. I'll tell you about it later."

"Okay."

"Are we having fun yet?" Lisa yells. I hate when someone says that. "Who'll be our next reader?"

The audience gets quiet, and a voice shouts from way in the back: "I'll go." Pops is making his way to the front! I look at Giovanni, but he only shrugs. Pops sits on the stool and takes out an order pad, of all things, and flips a few pages. A few people laugh. "What?" he says into the microphone. "You write on your paper, I write on mine." More laughter, but nice laughter. I can't believe he's up there. "My son Giovanni can do this, I can do this." He flips a few more pages and stops. "Here it is. It is called 'To Ruth.'" Pops looks over at me. "I wrote it to Giovanni's mother and my wife, God rest her soul." Luchesi's is completely silent. I hold my breath as he begins:

> *I still buy you a rose*
> *every day like I promise.*
> *You like it?*
> *Good.*
> *A rose is you,*
> *especially the thorns.*
>
> *You laugh?*
> *Good.*
> *Not as good as the original*
> *but an echo will do.*
>
> *Our son?*
> *A man.*
> *Also not as good as the original*
> *but an echo will do.*

Pops pauses as a few people laugh. Pops smiles and continues:

RENEE AND JAY

Our bakery?
Doing okay.
My life is still in the dough.

Me?
I don't know.
You still have my heart,
so you tell me.

Pops bows once, puts his order pad in his apron pocket, and makes his way through tables to the back. The applause is deafening. Mama and I both blow our noses in napkins, and we're not alone. Even men are clearing their throats.

"I'd like to go now," Mama says, so we gather our coats and purses and approach the counter.

Giovanni's eyes are red, bless his heart. He flips through his order books, finds our order, and rings it up, keeping his eyes glued to the register.

Mama pays him before I can get my money out and says, "Tell your father I liked his poem the best."

"I will."

"And your poem wasn't half bad either."

He looks at Mama and smiles. "Hope I didn't embarrass you."

"I wasn't embarrassed. But you didn't write that poem for *me*, now did you?"

Giovanni looks from her to me and drops his eyes. "No ma'am. I didn't."

Mama turns sharply to me. "You gonna say good night to him now, or you gonna call him later?"

Big gulp. "I—"

"We'll see you Thursday night, Jay." She's looking right at me, no smile, no frown.

"Yes, ma'am." At least Giovanni has a voice.

"We have much to discuss, don't we, *Jay?*"

147

"Yes ma'am, we do. May I bring something, some wine or bread?"

She turns to him. "A red wine, I think. Two bottles, no three. And lots of bread sticks. And one of those New York cheesecakes. Renee's making spaghetti enough for four." Four? "Michael will be in attendance." If I was Catholic, I'd say some "Hail Mary" prayer. "Seven-thirty sharp." She turns back to me with a frown on her face. "I'll be waiting outside." Then head up, shoulders square, my mama, the only real lady I've ever known, walks out of Luchesi's.

"I better not keep her waiting," I say.

"Right."

"I'll call you later."

"Please," he says.

"Okay. Bye."

I look back once and join Mama outside. We are almost to the door of our house when she finally speaks to me. "We need to talk."

"Yes, Mama."

"You are my only child, and I would do anything for you. You know that, don't you?"

"Yes, Mama."

"And you know I raised you on my own because I wanted to, not 'cause I had to."

"Yes."

"And you also know that I think ninety-nine percent of all men are dogs no matter their color."

"You've made that clear."

"This is no time for sarcasm."

"Sorry."

She caresses my cheek with her hand. "The only thing I've ever wanted for you was happiness. You been happy, haven't you?"

"Yes."

Mama swallows hard. "Then what the hell were you thinking? You think a white man in *this* city gonna make you happier?"

"Giovanni's not from around here."

"You know what I meant."

I'm not ready for this. "I don't know, Mama. I just want the chance to find out."

She takes a deep breath, and I see her steam. "They say sometimes a white face has a black mind, but do you really know this boy well enough? He could be playin' you like R. J. I mean, that white girl wants him *bad*. He had to have given her a reason, right?"

"They're friends."

Mama rolls her eyes. "Uh-huh. He tell you that?"

"Yes."

"He could be lying."

"He isn't."

She shakes her head. "And he isn't all that good-looking, Renee. I don't quite see the attraction yet, baby. You gonna have to help me there."

"You liked his eyes."

"He does have some eyes, doesn't he?"

"Yes." Mama's weakening. "What are you trying to tell me, Mama?"

"I'm not sure."

"You like him, right?"

She rubs her eyes. "Well, I didn't kill him, did I?"

"Oh, Mama!" I giggle and hug her hard.

She holds me back and squints. I shouldn't have hugged her. "Doesn't mean I like him. And this is more than just a fling, isn't it?" I nod. "Please don't tell me you want to marry the white boy."

"Please call him Giovanni." My teeth are chattering from the cold. "And I think I do want to marry him."

"How should I feel about this? You really want to marry the Eyetalian?"

"Yes."

She sighs. "Damn. I didn't know it was this serious."

"It is, Mama."

"Well, come on. Let's get in out of the cold."

I grab her elbow. "But Mama, does this mean—"

"That I give my permission for you to marry the white boy?" I let go of her elbow and nod. "Let me put it this way: tell Giovanni that I won't shoot him when he comes over for dinner."

"Mama, that's not a blessing."

She puts her key into the deadbolt. "I bet Giovanni would call it a blessing, but that's all you're getting from me tonight. You can't expect me to bless a marriage when I neither know nor like the man, especially after y'all have deceived me."

"Can you blame us?"

She opens the door and walks in. "And what should that tell you? If you gotta deceive even your own mother to have a relationship, what kind of relationship is that? This kind of shit *don't* happen around here."

I close the door behind me, slumping against it. "That's what his father says, too."

Mama smiles. "See, not everyone done lost their minds. His father is a smart man. Maybe we can talk you two out of this mess. Go call the—Giovanni."

I dial Luchesi's, and Giovanni answers on the second ring. "Hello?"

"Hi. How you doin'?"

"Terrible. What'd your mama say?"

"Mama says she won't shoot you when you come to dinner Thursday." I let that sink in. "She's pissed at both of us."

"I don't blame her."

"Me neither. So, do you still want to come?"

"Yes."

"You're sure?"

"Yes."

"It could get hostile."

"True. Should I bring Pops?"

Now that would be interesting. "Not yet. I wanna keep Pops and Mama apart. They think alike." One of the scariest thoughts I've ever had.

"So, it wouldn't be a good idea to see you until then, huh?"

"Probably not. Were you planning to see me tomorrow?"

"Yeah, but I can wait. I just wanted to take you to, uh, get a real ring."

"Let's hold off on that, okay? Wouldn't want you wasting your money."

"I wouldn't be wasting my money, Renee. What are you saying?"

I'm just now figuring this out myself. . . . "I'm saying that if Mama doesn't approve, then . . . I guess . . . that's it. Sorry."

"You're sorry? That's it? The last couple days don't mean anything to you?"

"They do, it's just—"

"So Thursday's the day, my one shot. If I blow it, it's over."

"That's not what I meant."

"Sounded like it."

"Look, I'm kind of confused right now."

"Join the party."

Daa-em, he can be a sarcastic ass sometimes. "Just . . . wait and see. Mama's been known to change her mind." Once, I think. I wanted a certain pair of shoes, she said no, I pouted, she changed her mind . . . when I was seven.

After an uncomfortable silence, he asks, "Did you ever, in your wildest dreams, think any of this would happen?"

My dreams are always in color, boy. "Never. What about you?"

"I never knew we'd get together, but this part . . . I knew this would happen. People are so closed-minded."

"We'll just need to open a few." He doesn't respond. "Just think: we really only have to convince, what, two people? How hard can that be?"

"Actually, it's only one. Pops is a romantic. He won't like it, but he'll accept it. I'll make him accept it."

I hear a clicking sound on the phone. "Listen, you two," Mama says. "I need to call Michael, so get off the damn phone!"

"Yes, Mama." Mama hangs up.

151

"Tell your mother I'm sorry."

"She's just playing." I think.

"She didn't sound like it."

"I'll teach you to know the difference, okay?"

"Okay. Good night."

"Hey, where's my kiss? And by the way, Mr. Man, when are you gonna send me roses?"

"Wouldn't I be wasting my money?"

Ooh, that sarcasm has *got* to go. I swallow a curse. "No. You promised."

He sighs. "Is tomorrow too late?"

"No. A dozen. Red. Long-stemmed. In a vase."

"Done."

"And one other thing."

"What?" Ooh, he's not a happy camper.

I don't say "I love you" because of his attitude. Instead I say, "I'll see you Thursday, okay?"

"Okay."

"And Giovanni?"

"What?" He says it softer this time.

"This is not a waste of time. Bye."

Chapter Six

I wake up to a vomit burp. Some people call them "vurps." Whatever they're called, they're nasty. I brush my teeth twice and gargle, but I still have this egg taste in my mouth. One too many Italians and too much amaretto last night.

Mama's already gone to work, and I'm running late. I didn't hear my alarm buzz at seven, and now it's nearly half past eight. Do I call in sick? I have plenty of sick days saved up. But then I won't get my flowers. I know he'll send them because he's kept every promise to me so far. How would it look to have a dozen roses arriving at my empty desk, everybody wanting to read the card, Collette calling me every half hour to see how I'm doing? Sick days are a real pain in the ass sometimes. So I shower and dress quickly, throw the 'do into another ponytail, and leave the house at ten minutes to nine. Plenty of time to get to work.

I hit what little rush-hour traffic Roanoke has to offer, eating a cherry Pop-Tart while I weave in and out of traffic going sixty-five on 581, all three lanes clear of snow. I am jamming, the sub-woofer in the trunk pumpin' out some bumpin' bass by DJ Kool. I'm almost to my exit at Hershberger Road when I see the little blue lights behind me.

I should have taken a sick day.

I pull onto the shoulder and root around in my purse for my license and registration as a jar-headed, red-faced white man comes to the window. "License and registration." I hand it to him and wait. I've got nothing else to do, so I eat the other Pop-Tart. This will cost me, oh, seventy-five or so. "Will you step out of the car, ma'am?"

Wait just a damn minute! "What?"

"Step out of the car."

"What's this about? I'm on my way to work."

"Step out of the car."

Damn, Eraserhead, cut me some slack. I zip up my coat and open my door, watching all sorts of fools staring at me as they pass. "Am I under arrest?"

"No ma'am."

He opens the passenger side door of his car, and I get in. He shuts the door, and I feel very claustrophobic. There's not much room on my side with all his cop shit on the dash. He gets in the other side.

"I clocked you at ten miles over the posted speed limit in a construction zone." Ain't nobody working though! "I also observed you weaving in and out of traffic without signaling. That's reckless driving." Uh-oh. But if it's "wreck-*less*," why am I being charged? "I'm also citing you for having your windows tinted too dark."

"But I had them done at the dealership!"

"That's not my concern. They are in violation. In addition, I'm citing you for a violation of the city noise ordinance." Holy shit! That's a $250 fine minimum! Something about playing music too loud, so you know it's aimed at my people. You never see them pull over anyone jamming to "Achy Breaky." He clicks the top of his pen. "Do you have anything to say?"

Just let me get started, I think, but I can only shake my head. "No."

He fills out the report in front of him as the minutes and my money tick away. He goes over everything in the report in detail, but I barely listen. "Sign here." I sign the document, he tears it off, hands it to me, and says, "Drive safely."

Back in my car, I shake with rage. A speeding ticket I can take. The tinted window thing, though, is a sham. The dealership and I are going to have a few words. The weaving? Hell, everyone does it. And that noise ordinance can kiss my black ass. He's just mad because he don't have no tunes in his ride.

I'm half an hour late to work. Connie gives me her standard "Where-have-you-been?" look but doesn't approach me. She sees the fire in my eyes. I'll get a nice little memo later from her that says, "You had a significant tardy today. Two more and you'll be on probation for six months." More bullshit. I got stuck in traffic on 581 because of a wreck last year and came in twenty minutes late, and no matter how much I explained, Connie still gave me a "significant tardy," saying I should have left earlier. Like I knew there'd be a wreck.

I clock in and trudge to Collette's desk, dropping the summons on her desk and continuing to mine. I want to scream, and I *don't* see a dozen long-stemmed red roses in a vase on my desk.

That's when I have another vurp and run to the bathroom.

Collette is close behind me this time. "I'll keep everybody out," she says as I head for a stall.

I vomit and see pieces of my Pop-Tart floating in the toilet. "Damn."

"You all right?" Collette asks.

"Yeah." I flush and go to the sink. I look like the sorry side of shit. Collette hands me a wet paper towel. "Thanks."

"I'll explain to Connie."

"No. I don't want her knowing my business. I'll just stay over a half hour or work through lunch."

"More ginger ale?"

"Please."

"I'll go get it. You just take your time, honey."

"I'll be out in a few minutes."

I wet another paper towel and wipe the back of my neck. The door opens, and it's Connie. "Are you all right, Renee?"

"Yeah. Just a bad cold, I guess." I wash and dry my hands.

"Well, why don't you go home? We're not very busy today."

"Will that get rid of my tardy?" Sometimes I feel like I'm in school at Star City.

"Uh, no."

Of course not, wench. "I'll be all right."

"Well, if you feel ill, you just clock out and go home, okay?" I nod, and she leaves with her plastic "I-feel-your-pain" smile.

I go out into the office and see everyone looking at me funny. Damn, I can't even barf around here without everyone . . .

And there's the vase of roses on my desk. One dozen. Long-stemmed. Red. In a vase. In spite of my queasy stomach, I smile. Collette winks at me as I strut to my desk, and I don't care who watches me open the card. I open it slowly, pissing off everyone around me. I love a little drama. The card reads:

Buzz, buzz.

I reach for my pager in my pants pocket, but it's not there. I must have left it on my dresser. No good vibrations today.

After settling into my chair, I log on and check my e-mail. I have thirty messages! I look to either side of my computer terminal and see a bunch of smiling faces. They all want to know the same thing. Instead of replying to each one, I stand and announce, "It's from my . . ." And then I hesitate. What, exactly, is Giovanni? He isn't my fiancé, and the twist tie is lying on my dresser. "It's from my boyfriend," I say finally.

Everyone logs out and comes to my desk (Collette has made them well aware of my man difficulties), asking questions, congratulating me, and just generally cheesing it up until Connie waddles by. "What's up?" she asks, trying to be down.

The others scatter as I explain.

"Oh, that's nice. Are there wedding bells in your future?"

Nosy. "No."

Connie moseys away (get along, you heifer), and somehow Collette keeps a straight face, mouthing, "Read mine."

I scroll down my e-mail list to find hers and see another e-mail from R. J. Is this a messed-up day, or what? Collette's e-mail is only one word: "Details?" So I write back "I'll tell you at lunch." Then, I pop up R. J.'s:

> *I will be at your house at 9:30 Wednesday night. You can't get rid of me that easily. R. J.*

Daa-em. We are going to need the troops. First I page Mama. Then I copy R. J.'s note and e-mail it to Collette. Collette is typing furiously. My calls are stacking up, but I want to see what she has to say. I see her look up with fire in her eyes. In a moment, her e-mail appears:

> *Clyde and I will be by around 8, and we will be packing. You call your mama yet? C.*

I nod my head, and a call comes over my private line. "Mama?"

"What's wrong?" she asks.

Where to begin? "R. J. is coming to our house at nine-thirty tonight."

She sighs heavily. "He is? Are you sure he said tonight?"

"Yeah. Oh, I also got a major ticket, Giovanni sent me a dozen roses, and I threw up a few minutes ago."

"And it's only ten-fifteen? Were the roses that ugly?"

"No, Mama. I threw up because of a bad Pop-Tart."

"Uh-huh. Bet the flowers were wilted. So what'd you call me for?"

"Mama, I need you to be home tonight."

"Oh, I will. Gotta go."

Clicking over to the customer line, I begin my work day with a guy asking me if we can put cable in his Winnebago.

Like the commercial says, "It doesn't get any better than this."

Collette and I order some carryout delivered by Hi-Wok and have a working lunch. While Collette picks through her pepper steak, I devour General Tso and all his chickens. The call volume picks up with folks wanting repairs or new service in time for the Super Bowl on Sunday. Collette and I exchange e-mails when we can about plans for a Super Bowl party, and since Mama's house is so large, it's the natural place to have it.

Every time I look at the roses on my desk, I smile inside. I could have told him two dozen, maybe more. Something strange about a man who actually does what he says he's going to do. He needs to be properly thanked. I log out and dial Luchesi's.

"Luchesi's Deli and Pizzeria?"

Deli and Pizzeria? "Mr. Luchesi?"

"Renee? How nice of you to call. How is my Giovanni's baby?"

I'm not mad about the "baby" part. "Fine. What's this about 'deli and pizzeria'?"

"Oh that. We make a few changes. Giovanni's idea. I'm just an old man, so he make-a the big decisions now. We gonna have to hire more people, maybe even get delivery going, but that's the price of progress. You want to talk to him?"

"Yes."

He pauses and clears his throat. "He's not here."

"Well, give him this number"—I give Pops the number to my private line—"and have him call me as soon as he gets back."

"I will be glad to. And Renee?"

"Yes?"

"Take care of yourself, and eat smaller meals—no grease!—some crackers and some milk."

Where the hell is this coming from? "What for?"

"Oh, I talk too much. *Ciao.*"

"Good-bye."

How's he know my stomach's hating me? He must have ESP, because General Tso is waging war down there right now. I sip some ginger ale in the hopes of calling a cease-fire, log back in, and take my next call.

"Thank you for calling Star City Cable. May I have your name and account number?"

"Must I? Don't you have caller I.D.?"

Clipped, precise tones of a wealthy white woman in Southwest Roanoke County. "Yes ma'am, we do, but that won't give us your account number."

She reads the numbers at an excruciatingly slow pace then repeats them for me. I repeat them back to her quickly. "Yes, yes. I'd like to cancel my account." Her voice reminds me of Mrs. Howell on *Gilligan's Island.*

"One moment, ma'am."

Any time a customer wants to cancel, I have to inform Connie to pick up on her master headset and listen in. I type in the correct commands and send them to Connie's computer.

"Oh, *really* now, what's the delay?"

"Our computers are a little slow today, ma'am." And people accept that lame excuse. We have computers to speed up business, then they're the perfect thing to blame when it takes too long.

Connie waves from her glassed-in cubicle at the other end of the office, so I continue. "I note you have an outstanding balance of—"

"The check is in the mail."

Standard procedure will not allow us to close any account with an outstanding balance. "One moment please."

"Oh, for Pete's sake!"

Connie leaves her cubicle with her headset on, the cord dangling, and comes to my desk, plugging her cord into my phone's second line. "Mrs. Wiseman, this is Connie Miller, Miss Howard's supervisor. How are you today?"

"I knew she couldn't handle it."

I'm not supposed to speak, just listen. This part of the job sucks.

"Mrs. Wiseman," Connie continues, "we have procedures that must be followed, and Miss Howard was just following procedures."

"She didn't sound very intelligent."

I have to bite my tongue. I want to say, "And your coochie got cobwebs in it!"

"Mrs. Wiseman, we are not allowed to cancel an account with an outstanding balance."

"I told that girl the check was in the mail. Didn't she believe me?"

"Like I said, Mrs. Wiseman, until we have a zero balance in your account, we cannot cancel your subscription. When did you mail the check?"

"Yesterday."

"Okay. We may get it today, we may get it tomorrow. In the meantime, you and Miss Howard can go over a questionnaire."

"What for?"

"Another standard procedure, Mrs. Wiseman. We like to know why people cancel so we can improve our service. I'm switching you back to Miss Howard now."

"Will my service be cut off by Sunday?"

"Oh, certainly, Mrs. Wiseman," Connie says.

"That's all I needed to know."

Connie unplugs and doesn't look at me before walking to her cubicle. I know the heifer will be listening in once she gets there, so I have to talk fast. "Mrs. Wiseman, I heard everything you said, and I want you to know that I am a college-educated African-American female with a degree in business administration from Roanoke College, and I am deeply offended that you would consider me unintelligent."

"I—"

Connie's in her cubicle. "First question, Mrs. Wiseman. Why are you canceling your subscription?" No answer. "Mrs. Wiseman?"

"I'm sorry." A moment of silence. "I'm canceling my subscription to punish my husband for ignoring me during football season."

I have nothing to check off on the form on my screen for "revenge," so I use the mouse to star "Other." I try not to laugh. "Mrs. Wiseman, of all the accounts I've canceled, yours is one of the best reasons so far. If your check arrives today or tomorrow, he will not be getting a clear picture of the Super Bowl." Though it would be on NBC, I had heard folks in mountainous Southwest County had trouble getting channel ten.

"Thank you, Miss Howard."

Time to make some money. "Will you be reconnecting after Sunday?"

"That's a wonderful idea," Mrs. Wiseman says. "Wait, do you mean to say that I can cancel my service for one or two or even three days a week?"

Ka-ching, ka-ching. "That will get pretty costly, Mrs. Wiseman. You'd have to keep paying reconnect charges at twenty-five dollars each."

"How many weeks do they play games?"

"Well, they start preseason in August and end around the end of January."

"That's roughly . . . thirty weeks." And $750! "Splendid."

Must be nice to have money. "As soon as we receive your check, your cable will be out. Let me give you my personal extension number"—I do—"so I can process your next call to reconnect."

"Is *Monday Night Football* over?"

"Yes, ma'am."

"Then I'll call you Monday morning. Thank you, Miss Howard."

I'm about to take my next call when I see Connie thundering toward me. Collette widens her eyes and mouths "uh-oh." I shake my head.

"Renee," says Connie, a little out of breath, "that was—that was just . . . miraculous! Do me a favor and write up what happened, and maybe we can make that part of our procedures."

"Sure." Yeah right, so maybe *you* can get credit for *my* idea. As Mama might say, "Ain't nothin' changed in the whole white world."

"Can you have it on my desk by six?"

Connie must be up for a raise. "Sure."

"Good job, Renee." She squeezes my shoulder with a beefy hand. "Way to go!" Yeah, and you're my favorite cheerleader, Connie. How about erasing my tardy? Oh no. That would be breaking procedure.

I check the clock. Four hours until R. J.'s visit. Strangest "hump day" I've ever had, and it ain't over yet. I call Luchesi's during another break and leave another message with Mr. Luchesi for Giovanni to call me.

A few minutes later, the phone rings. "Giovanni?"

"Yes?"

"Where have you been?"

"Out. What's up?"

He says "Out" to me? "Well, some wonderful guy sent me roses."

"Did he?"

"A dozen red ones, and they're beautiful."

"Good."

"Anything wrong?"

"No."

"You sure?"

"Yeah. Uh, I gotta get to work. See you." Click.

No one hangs up on me without an explanation, so after work I drive very slowly to Luchesi's and park on the street at 6:30. Giovanni sees me and opens the door. "You want me to bring the flowers in?" he asks as he holds the door.

"Oh, I left them at work. I want everybody there to be jealous."

Pops waves me over and pushes Giovanni away. "Girl-talk," he says. "Go wipe a few tables." After Giovanni leaves, Pops puts one of his fat hands on my face and stares into my eyes. "How are you feeling?" I stare at his hand and think, *Here's the beef!*

"Okay. Why?"

He drops his hand to his side. "I mean, how is your stomach?"

"Fine." His eyes twinkle, and I'm finally catching on. "Do you think I'm pregnant?"

"Yes! I have dream about my granddaughter last night, and she looked just like you, only not so dark. *Café au lait* and *bellisimo*. She say, 'Poppa, bring me the pizza!'"

This is getting creepy. I have been a little sick, but my period's not late . . . *or is it?* "I need to use the rest room," I say, and once I'm there, I check in my purse for my planner. I usually keep track of my period using little stars. I find it and flip to my last period in December. I count up the days and realize . . . I should have had my period on Sunday. Today's Wednesday. I should be bitchin' people up and down!

I'm late.

I've never been late before. Ever. My "friend" has been right on damn time every damn time since Mama put me on the pill when I was thirteen. Three things I can count on in this world; Mama, racism, and my period—and now one of them decides to go on Colored People's Time?

No. No way. I'm on the pill, we only did it . . . a couple of times . . . on my most fertile day . . . NO!

I leave the rest room and bump into . . . Julie?

"Excuse me," she says. I look down and see what looks like an application in her hand. "Are you applying to work here, too?"

"No." What the hell is going on today?

"Oh, sorry," Julie says, and she walks up to Giovanni, who's polishing a table. For some reason, I can't move. She hands the application to him . . . and touches his arm. Oh no she didn't!

I stalk over to Giovanni and Julie. "Giovanni," I say in a sweet voice.

"Uh, Julie, I'd like you to meet Renee," he says.

I smile. "Hi, Julie. Has Giovanni told you that we're engaged?"

"No." Julie's face pales even more. Daa-em, white girl, you keep that up you're gonna evaporate. "No. He didn't tell me." She crumples the application and clears her throat. "Um, congratulations."

I have just cut the girl down, messed up her dream of working alongside my man—and I get congratulated. I feel shitty, but I believe that if you have to be a bitch, be the best bitch you can be. I kiss Giovanni lightly on the cheek and move toward the door. "See you tomorrow night, Giovanni."

I should be in a soap opera.

On the one-block ride to my house, I wonder if I'm really pregnant. How in the world is this possible? I take my pill like Catholics take communion. No one's sperm is that potent . . . is it? I mean, Italian swimmers don't do shit in the Olympics, so it should follow that Italian *sperm* . . . that have been fermenting in my man for years and years like fine Italian wine . . . Giovanni will never need Viagra.

I park the Jetta behind Mama's car and do what I do best—I talk to myself. Okay, wench, you're probably pregnant. Not exactly where you want to be at this or any time in your life, but you're here. Pregnant. Such an ugly-sounding word, probably invented by a man, for what should be a blessed event. Preggers. With child. In a family way. A bun in the oven—and a real-life baker put it there! You've spent your entire life thinking you'd never be like your mama, and here you are, unmarried and pregnant like she was with you. You have a child inside of you right now.

Daa-em.

I hold my stomach. I have a child inside of *me* right now. *My* child. And there's a guy just down the street who's willing to be my husband. *My* man. I've got the ready-made family I've always dreamed of inside a city block. We could get us a house with a *black* picket fence and little *white* jockeys out in the yard and—

I see a curtain move. Mama knows I'm here.

I struggle inside, and Mama asks if I'm all right. "Fine," I say. Just maybe a little bit pregnant, that's all, Mama. Yeah, and my baby's daddy is a white man you don't like, but other than that . . .

I spend most of the evening in my room until Collette and Clyde show up at eight o'clock. The cavalry has arrived. Now all we need is R. J.

While Clyde stands at the sitting room window telling everybody "A car is coming!" for the next hour, Mama, Collette, and I play spades in the kitchen. I start to tell them about my messed-up day, but all they're interested in talking about is R. J. and what could happen.

"He won't show," Collette says. "Punk-ass gonna punk out."

"He might," Mama says. "He's coming to claim his bride."

"Mama, please. I'm already spoken for."

Mama touches Collette's arm. "You know all about her white boy, right?"

"Uh-huh."

"What you think of him?"

Collette shrugs. "Don't know. Haven't met him. Renee seems to think he's fine, so what's it matter what I think?"

Amen! I smile at Mama, who only rolls her eyes.

"You're gonna tell me you're okay with your best friend sleeping with the enemy?"

Collette winks. "Now that's different. I only thought they was tryin' to get married."

"Be serious," Mama says. "Don't you think they're asking for trouble? All these rednecks around here gonna give them shit for the rest of their lives."

"Our people, too, Mama," I say.

"Maybe," Mama says.

"What you mean, 'maybe'?" I say. "*You* have a problem with it, and last time I checked, *you* was my people."

"She's got a point," Collette says.

"No she don't," Mama snaps. "I'm your mama, Renee. I'm supposed to have a problem with everything you do. I just have more of a problem with this, that's all."

"Then why you gotta be a bitch about it?" I shouldn't have said that.

"What'd you say?" Mama shouts.

Time for a little deflection. "You're dismissing Giovanni totally on the basis of his race."

"You sayin' I'm a bitch *and* a racist, here, in *my* own house?" Collette tries to stand, but Mama holds her arm. "Stay, Collette. I want a witness in case I have to kill her."

"Now who's not being serious," I say. "Okay, Mama, tell Collette what you think of R. J."

"R. J. is . . . acceptable."

"Why?"

Mama looks away. "Because he is. Damn. I don't have to explain myself to you."

"And Giovanni isn't acceptable, right?"

"Right."

"Why?"

"Don't be questioning me like I'm some child, child. Giovanni is unacceptable because he's white. There. Is that what you've been waiting for me to say? I cannot accept Giovanni because he's white. End of discussion."

"Why you gotta be so close-minded? You don't even know Giovanni, Mama!"

"I invited him to dinner, didn't I?"

"So you can confirm what you've already decided, that you don't like him."

"What's wrong with that?"

Before we can continue, the phone rings. I get to the phone first,

166

but Mama's too quick for me, snatching it from behind. "Hello?" She motions me to sit. "Where you at? It's almost nine-thirty. . . . What? I thought you were coming over. . . . No, I don't think Renee would like to speak to you tonight. . . . You did?" She covers the mouthpiece. "He says he saw you going into Luchesi's." She hushes me with a finger to her lips. "So, fool, what you doin' stalkin' my baby? Huh? You a man and you can't come over here tonight, but you can follow her around like a chump? . . . I know he white! Hell, I knew that from the get-go." She's shaking her head "no" at me, but it wouldn't surprise me a bit if she did know from the start. "I'll ask her." She covers the mouthpiece again. "He's beggin' now. Pitiful. You want to get in the last word? You know I'll do it if you don't."

"I'll do it."

She hands me the phone, and she and Collette leave the kitchen. "What?" I say harshly.

"Renee, please don't throw your life away."

"I almost did that with you."

"Come on, girl. What your life gonna be like with that skinny white boy? He can't give you what I can."

"He's given me more in a few days than you did in two years. And what you doing following me?"

"Just wanted to see who my competition is. That boy looks soft, Renee."

"There ain't no competition. He's already won." He just hasn't defeated Mama yet.

"Hell, we ain't even gotten started yet. You're just givin' me shit, girl."

"You think I'm givin' *you* shit? Boy, if you think you're gettin' shit from people, you should stop talkin' it."

"I ain't the one talkin' shit here. You're just confused."

"Actually," I say as lightly as possible, "I haven't been confused since the day I met your albino bitch. How is Hagney, anyway?" He doesn't speak. "I was so happy that she dumped your ass."

167

"I'm the one who ended it, not her."

"Bullshit."

"No, it's true. She still wanted me after you puked on her. Can you believe that shit? She wasn't strong enough for me, Renee. She couldn't handle all the stares, all the rude comments. Girl, I need your strength."

"You need therapy, R. J. I'm giving all my strength to a man who says he loves me and means it."

"Love!" He says it like a curse. "How long you think your love gonna last when you can't pay the bills? I went in there tonight—"

"Why?"

"To see where you'll be spending the rest of your life."

"Oh, puh-lease."

"That old man ain't gonna last much longer, and no restaurant in this neighborhood is gonna pay all the bills. Fools don't even charge enough. You ain't lookin' at this sensibly, Renee."

"Love ain't always sensible, R. J. I mean, I thought I loved you, and I thought you loved me. How insensible can you get?"

"Well, how's it going to be when you can't go out in public be-cause you don't match! With me, at least, you could have a little pride in your damn race."

"Did pride in your race make you put your black dick in that white bitch?" No answer. "I didn't think so." I yawn loudly. "Are you finished?"

"Look, I ain't gonna beg."

"This ain't begging? Sure sounds like it."

"Nah. I ain't going out like that. You want to mess with a white boy, you go on. You're going to regret it, and deep down inside, you probably already do. And I wouldn't even want you after he's ruined you. That's all I have to say."

"Finally. Does that make you feel better?"

"Does what?"

"Saying you wouldn't want me because you *know* you can't have me? Just think, R. J. Every day you wake your tired ass up and look in the mirror, you're going to be looking at a man who lost the finest lady he's ever known or will ever know to a soft . . . white . . . man. What's that say about your sorry ass?"

"Fuck you."

"Does this mean you ain't comin' over tonight?"

"Yeah."

"Well, speaking of fucking, R. J., your stuff was weak. It was lame. An inchworm could give me more satisfaction."

Click.

I'm not mad he hung up on me. I don't quite get the last word in, but in this case, I think I come mighty close. I laugh my ass completely off, and after Mama comes running in, I tell her what I said.

"He's right, you know," she says, shuffling the cards. "Wanna play some rummy?"

I nod and sit. "Mama, I don't know how you can agree with him after he dogged me out with a white girl."

"See? You mess with white folks, and bad shit happens. Why don't you forgive him, Renee? Give him another chance."

I look past Mama into the hall. "Where are Collette and Clyde?"

"Gone. I sent them home. There's no need now that R. J. ain't coming."

Something strange is going on. Unless Mama was listening in, she wouldn't have known for sure. "How you know that?"

"I just figured."

Bells go off in my head. "Or you knew."

"Knew what?"

"Daa-em, Mama. You set all this up, didn't you? When you talked to R. J. the other night, you asked him to come. Didn't you?"

"What if I did? You can't tell me who to invite and who not to invite into my own house."

I am beyond stunned. "Why you do that, Mama?"

She starts dealing the cards. "Well, at the time, I thought, you know, maybe y'all could get back together. You still think about him, right?"

"No, I don't." More bells go off. "R. J. *was* supposed to come over here tonight, wasn't he? And you got to the phone first and somehow told him not to come. Why?"

"The truth?"

"Yes."

She arranges her hand. "Well, you weren't in the proper mood to see him tonight. Calling your own mama a bitch and a racist in front of company. If that's the effect this white boy havin' on you—"

"I said you were *being* a bitch, just like now." I throw my cards on the table and stand. "This is how it is, Mama. I do not want R. J. back, and I will see Giovanni whether you like it or not."

She doesn't look up. "That's how it is?"

"That's how it is."

Then, she looks up . . . and smiles. "I can handle that."

"Huh?"

"I said I can handle it. You playin' or not?"

I sit. "What you sayin', Mama?"

She collects my cards and slides them to me. "We playin' to five thousand?"

I pick up my cards. "Mama, I asked you a question."

"I said I can handle it, Renee. We need to get your hearing checked."

"Handle what, exactly?"

She shakes her head. "The fact that you . . . want . . . Giovanni. I had to be sure."

"So you arranged all this?"

"Yeah. Had to make it real so I could see how you really felt. I was and am still hoping this is all just a crush, but if it isn't . . . I think I can handle it."

I don't speak for the longest time. I don't know whether to be pissed because she tricked me or overjoyed because she says she can handle the idea of Giovanni and me. I pick up my cards and see a hand loaded with hearts, and my own heart relaxes a little. I peek

170

around my cards at the lady I hope to be someday. "Thank you, Mama."

"Don't mention it. Now, are you gonna play or what?"

Later that night I phone Luchesi's. "Luchesi's," Pops says. "We're closed."

"Mr. Luchesi, I—"

"I'll get him, Renee." After what sounds like a fight, Mr. Luchesi laughs. "He's had a lot to drink, Renee."

"Gimme the phone, Pops."

"Are you drunk, Giovanni?" I ask.

"Just a little. A little lot. But it's not my fault. It's the Chianti. You understand."

"No, I don't. And what you drinkin' for?"

"'Cause of what you said to Julie. She cried her eyes out."

"Did she? Y'all didn't hire her, did you?"

"No. She tore up the application into little bits."

Good. "And that's why you're drinking?"

"Not really. It's 'cause of something Pops told me after Julie left. Please don't laugh when you hear this. It's just so funny. Pops says that you might be pregnant. Isn't that hilarious?" I don't make a sound. "Renee? Did you hear me?"

"Yeah."

"Well, isn't that funny?"

It is if you're God playing a cosmic joke. I feel a nervous weight in my stomach. I know he loves me, but there's no telling how a man will react when you tell him you're pregnant. "Um, your Pops may be right, Giovanni."

He drops the phone. Eventually he whispers, "We're pregnant?"

"There ain't no *we* about it, boy. I'll know for sure tomorrow. I'm going to buy one of those home pregnancy tests at—"

"I'm going with you."

171

Daa-em. He wants to go? Don't most men run away from shit like that? "You don't have to. Really. I can handle it."

"I'm going, Renee."

The nervous weight in my stomach suddenly feels lighter. My baby daddy is nice, honest, *and* responsible? Now I won't have to go through this shit alone. "I'd like that, Giovanni." My eyes mist until a tear slides down my cheek. "I'd like that a lot."

"We are certainly *allegro*, eh?"

"What's *allegro?*"

"Fast."

"Oh. Yeah." Speak English, boy.

"Do you still love me?" he asks.

"Yes."

"I still love you, too, and if you are pregnant, I will marry you to-morrow."

Yeah, right. "Giovanni, weddings take lots—"

"I know, I know. But two of the three people in my family are here! I can call Christina, and she'll be down in no time."

"Who's Christina?" And don't you *ever* interrupt me again.

"Christina is my sister. She's beautiful. Oh, and she's a lesbian. Pops hasn't talked to her since Mama died."

This family keeps getting more and more interesting. "How old is she?"

"Thirty, I think. No, thirty-one."

"Will she like me?"

"She may hit on you. I'm kidding, I'm kidding. She and Alexis Meyer have been together since high school. We'll have to invite Alexis, too."

"Giovanni, stop talking about the wedding, okay?"

"Okay."

"And why hasn't your father talked to Christina in so long?"

"It's a long story. Messy, too. And loud. It'll be in Italian, but I'll translate for you."

The boy is shit-faced. "Well, you'll just have to tell me some other time."

"Okay."

"Good night, Giovanni."

"Arrivederci!"

I don't hear a click. "Giovanni, hang up the phone."

"Okay." *Click.*

Chapter Seven

Janae keeps me up most of the night, and this morning I'm look-ing for the Tidy-Bowl man again. Funny how an old Italian man notices before Mama or Collette. My people are supposed to be good at knowing when someone's pregnant. What did he say to eat and drink? I look for and find milk in the fridge. I will smell milk, and though the date is okay, I'm not taking any chances. The crack-ers are stale, and I'm not even going to attempt eggs or bacon. Another vurp creeps up my throat. Gimme a break, baby-girl, I'm hungry!

It's hard for me to imagine having a baby. A friend of mine had her first baby while she was in high school, and I watched as she grew and grew and then disappeared and dropped out. I see her around town with three chaps, all cute, all nicely dressed, but she looks nothing like she did in high school. She looks twice my age. "A baby will make you *old*," Mama told me when I first started tak-ing the pill. "You keep taking these, girl, and you will never grow old. Never."

I'm sure as hell feeling old this morning, but there's nothing safe to eat. I'll have to pick up something like a plain biscuit on the way to work, but first, I have to have an antacid. The bottle in my room is empty, so I go into Mama's bathroom and open the medicine cabinet over her sink. I shake her bottle and barely hear a rattle. I choke down one little, chipped, dusty antacid that I can barely taste as it slides down my throat.

As I replace the bottle, I see a home pregnancy kit. In Mama's medicine cabinet. In my forty-eight-year-old Mama's medicine cabinet. I freak. This joke ain't over. Life must be the joke that never ends. I pick up the box and see one unused tester in its wrapper. But the box says

Contents: 2 testers.

No way . . . but she did go to the doctor to have her plumbing checked out on Tuesday. . . . Holy shit! My mama's pregnant! And my daughter will be the same age as her aunt or uncle? Shit, we oughta be on *Oprah*!

I am very careful on the way to work, talking to myself the entire way. "Use turn signal . . . My mama's pregnant! . . . Check speedometer and keep it under fifty-five . . . My mama gonna be a mama and a grandma at the same time? . . . Keep the music at a reasonable, Caucasian level. . . . I'm going to have a daughter and a sister? . . . Wave to Mr. Pooper-Trooper . . . better not."

My tint is still too dark, and he may decide to bust me again. This tint deal is so racist. They say it's so cops can count how many people are in the car. White people are easy to see, no matter how dark the tint. My people? Not as easy unless they yellow. And around Roanoke, my people ain't the only ones packin'. I had a call from a lady one day who said her kids did something to the converter. It was the middle of November. What are they doing home from school? "Their school lets 'em out for the first week of huntin' season," she says. Pooper-Trooper ought to be pulling over anyone with a gun rack in his truck.

When I walk into Star City Cable, I skip to Collette's desk, say, "I know something you don't know," and sit in my chair. I am completely losing it. I never skip.

Collette can't resist and comes over. "What you know that I don't?"

Girlfriend, I know an awful lot. "I found something."

"What?"

"Something in Mama's medicine cabinet."

"No shit. You found . . . medicine?"

"No." I intend to piss her off, but she isn't in a playing mood. She just stares at me. "All right. I found a home pregnancy test."

"Daa-em. Shirl?"

"The box held two testers, but there was only one up in there."

"She too old to be having a baby!"

"Shh. I know that. Maybe it was negative. She did go to the doctor on Tuesday."

"Oh, this is too much. Your family messed up beyond belief! Y'all should be on the cover of the *Enquirer.*"

"I don't think she's pregnant, Collette, but just the idea." And then the antacid stops working, and I run to the bathroom. Hello, Mr. Toilet. Miss me? There can't be anything left in my stomach. Come on, girlfriend in my uterus, gimme a break!

"You need more ginger ale?" Collette calls out.

Same song, third verse. "No," I say, and I flush. I step out of the stall. "Better make it milk and crackers."

Collette doesn't react at first. Then she tilts her head forward and widens her eyes. "Oh, my Lord! I told you that boy's sperm would be potent. You pregnant! Does Shirl know?"

"No." I wipe my face with a wet towel and decide that we need softer towels in here. "Even I don't know for sure yet, but I'm pretty sure," I say as I'm washing my hands. She giggles and gives me a big hug. "Careful," I say, stepping back. "I'm a volcano these days."

"I'm so excited, Renee! I'm going to be an aunt!" She lowers her voice an octave. "You gonna have it, right?"

"Of course." That's not something my people do.

"Good. One of us ought to be having children." I laugh and hug her. "Not so close, Renee. Daa-em. I'll get you a mint." She fans the air in front of her. "Can I tell everybody?"

"No. Giovanni and I will get one of those kits today, see if it's positive, but you have to keep this quiet."

"I'll try, but, girl, when am I gonna meet him? I'm your best friend!"

"You have an hour lunch today?"

"Yeah."

"We'll eat at Luchesi's. I'm taking a half day to get ready for tonight."

"Can we play a little ol' trick on him?"

On the way there, Collette explains her "trick" to me, and I like it. Poor Giovanni.

A little after twelve, Collette busts into Luchesi's while I wait in the car outside. I can just imagine the look on Giovanni's face as a tall black woman in a bright, multicolored sweater and tight Guess jeans comes in wearing some impressive earrings that almost touch her shoulders. Giovanni is going to get the full "Black Woman with an Attitude" treatment.

I give Collette ten minutes to ruin Giovanni's day, then roll through the door and stroll up to the counter. "Good afternoon," I say to Giovanni. "I'm hungry."

Giovanni leads me to our table near the wall.

"I'm ready to order, boy!" Collette yells. This is too funny.

"Be back in a second," Giovanni says to me.

"Giovanni," I say. "My chair, please."

"Oh, sorry." He pulls back my chair, I sit, and he pushes me forward slightly.

"Thank you."

Giovanni rushes to Collette. "Are you ready to order?"

"That's what I said," Collette says loudly. "And why you didn't hold my chair for me?"

"Uh, I—"

"Never mind." She sucks her teeth so loudly my toes curl. "What's your soup of the day?"

"Minestrone."

"What that?"

"A rich, thick vegetable soup with dried beans, macaroni, and vermicelli, topped with grated mozzarella."

"Daa-em, all that in soup? Sounds like a meal."

"It is."

"Well, gimme a bowl of that and . . . maybe a salad."

Giovanni looks at me. I pat my tummy and give him the saddest pout. "I'll go get your soup ready. Be back in a minute."

"No, no. I'm ready. I'll have the house salad and . . . what kind of dressings you got?"

Giovanni points at the list at the top of the menu. "Oh," Collette says, "here they are. . . . I'll have . . . the ranch. No, the honey-poppy-seed. Real poppy seeds up in there?"

"I think so."

"I could get high!" Giovanni doesn't respond. "And for my sandwich, I'll have the Italian. I hear they're very, very good. What are banana peppers?"

"Mild green peppers."

"They hot?"

"A little."

"Hmm." I stamp my feet and tap my fingernails on the table. I try not to look amused, but I am tripping inside. "What kind of bread your sandwiches served on?"

Heavy sigh from Giovanni. "Our house bread."

"It good?"

"Yes. Baked fresh today."

"Well, I don't know about the Italian. Might be a little too spicy for me. Give me gas. I'll have the . . . oh, I can't decide."

"I can take the banana peppers off the Italian."

"No, no. I think . . . I think I'll have the Reuben. With lots of sauerkraut."

I begin making audible moans.

"Would you like that served hot or cold?"

"Steamy."

Giovanni takes Collette's menu. "It'll be ready in a few minutes." He starts to walk toward me.

"I want something to drink!" Collette yells.

I sigh heavily, as though I'm giving birth.

Giovanni turns back to Collette. "Sorry. What would you like?"

"You got the menu, so you tell me," Collette says, waving her killer fingernails at him. Giovanni has to run the entire list twice. "Oh, just get me some . . . water," she says.

By the time Giovanni gets back to me, I try to act pissed. "I should have eaten somewhere else," I say.

"Sorry."

I bite my lower lip to keep from laughing. "Make me a cheese sandwich. No butter, no chips, two pickles. A bowl of chicken soup, lots of crackers, and a glass of milk. Oh, and some chocolate ice cream."

"We don't have any ice cream."

I freeze him with a stare. "It's for the baby."

"Oh. But—"

"Get some!"

"Yo!" Collette hollers, snapping her fingers.

Giovanni tears off toward her. "Yes?"

"Could you change the station? This music ain't happening. Try W-J-J-S. One-oh-six-point-one. Oh, and add some bread sticks to my order. My best friend in the whole wide world says they're the *bomb*."

Giovanni takes our orders back to Pops, and Collette and I exchange "OK" signs under our tables. A few minutes later, Giovanni brings my order to me first . . . as he should.

Collette yells, "Oh, I see how it is." I simply smile at Giovanni and dig in.

Giovanni delivers Collette's order while I am stuffing my face to keep from laughing. "You got a girlfriend?" Collette asks. This should be fun.

"Huh?"

"You do understand English, don't you?"

"Yes."

"Well, do you got a girlfriend?"

"Yes."

"A serious girlfriend or one you dog out on the down low?"

"We're practically engaged."

Collette bites suggestively into a bread stick. "She nice?"

"Yes."

"Nice as me?"

"I don't know you."

"I can be very nice. Tell you what, if it don't work out, here's my number." Collette writes the number on a napkin and slides it to Giovanni.

"Uh, thanks for the offer, but—"

"Take it. You never know."

My soup spoon is frozen over my bowl. He better not take that number. Giovanni leans down and looks Collette in the eye. "The beautiful woman over there is my girlfriend."

"You don't say. A pretty sister like her going with a guy like you? I don't believe it."

"It's true. So you, uh, know why I can't take this napkin, right?"

"Right." She crumples up the napkin. "But when you get tired of that ho, you'll be wishing you had my number. Bitch eatin' like a real heifer."

He's handled Collette pretty well so far, but we're not through yet. After Giovanni leaves Collette to check on me, she turns to me and mouths "nice ass." I try not to giggle.

"Is everything okay?" Giovanni asks me.

I shove the rest of my cheese sandwich into my mouth to keep from laughing. I nearly choke. I nod while I'm sipping my milk. "Yes," I manage after I swallow. "But where's my chocolate ice cream?"

Collette starts snapping her fingers.

"Renee," he says, "we don't—"

"It's okay. It's okay." I fake a pout.

"Sorry."

"Yo, what's up with the music?" Collette yells. Giovanni jumps.

"She wants J-J-S," he says to me.

"You gonna change the station for that wench? That skeezer has absolutely no manners. Giovanni, I'm beginning to like Pops's music." Not. "Please don't change it."

Giovanni rolls his eyes. "It will only be until she leaves."

"Oh, so you'd change it for the skank ho but not for me?"

"Yeah, I mean, no."

"I'm waiting!" Collette yells.

Giovanni shakes his head and does something around the corner. A few moments later, we're listening to "Tyrone." Perfect! Collette loves to sing, and because she disagrees with the lyrics, she belts out her own words. Loudly. "So you've been to sorrow's kitchen and licked out every pan . . . I am tired of all your bitchin', go get yourself a man."

My stomach hurts from trying to restrain my laughter. I see Pops and Giovanni arguing behind the counter, with Pops trying to get past Giovanni to change the station. This could get ugly.

"All you do is badmouth brothers and complain," Collette sings. The front windows are rattling. "About how they dog you, give you so much pain. Girlfriend, you ain't no queen up on a throne, and if you keep this up you'll turn into a dried-up old crone, sure as you born . . . you better stop that moan."

I giggle and sing, "Stop, stop."

"And start actin' grown. . . . " I wave Collette over to my table. She dances up to Giovanni and Pops, does a little shimmy, then moonwalks to our table where she bows to them, then sits. Giovanni and Pops stop arguing, blank expressions on their faces. I know that's redundant—all white folks' faces are blank to me. Collette and I hold out for only a few seconds before we bust out laughing and slap hands. Giovanni forces a smile. Pops throws up his arms and begins spewing Italian, but his eyes are twinkling so I know he's not that mad.

Giovanni shuffles over, and Collette sticks out her hand. "I'm Collette," she says between giggles.

He shakes it once. "Nice to meet you, Collette."

"Oh," Collette says, not letting go of my man's hand, "your hands are so warm. Sure you don't want my number?"

"Let go, Collette," I say and she does. "Sorry, Giovanni. I couldn't resist."

"Nice surprise." His face is very red. "You got me."

"We are the best," Collette says to me.

"I'll, uh, bring your meal over here, Collette."

"Thank you," she says, "and get me a Coke while you're at it."

"Sure."

He goes around the corner to get a tray. "Be nice," I say.

"Oh, girl, he cute. And so patient!"

"I know."

"But what about the fat guy?"

"That's Pops, Giovanni's father. He's really a very sweet man."

"Thought he was gonna kill your boy."

Giovanni places Collette's meal and a Coke in front of her. "Will you be having dessert?" he asks.

"No," Collette says, "but I know *she* will."

"Stop," I say. "I wanted some chocolate ice cream, but he won't give me any."

"Shame on you, Giovanni."

"I guess," Giovanni says, settling into the chair next to me, "we'll have to add it to the menu."

I pull his visor off and look at his hair. I whisper into his ear, "Did you shower this morning?"

"No," he whispers back.

"Go shave, take a shower, and put on some sexy aftershave, not that Old Spice shit."

"What should I wear?"

"Nothing. I'll come over after I'm done eating."

"Hey y'all," Collette says, "it's rude to whisper at the table."

Giovanni stands. "It was nice to meet you, Collette."

"No it wasn't," she says and laughs.

"See you in a bit," he says to me, and he swoops down like he's going to kiss me. I lean way back. "Sorry," he whispers before he leaves.

Collette blinks at me. "He was about to kiss you, wasn't he?"

"Yeah."

"That boy ain't from around here." She sips her Coke. "You buying, right?"

"How you figure?"

"Dag, don't you eat here for free? I'm kidding, I'm kidding. Where's he going?"

"To get ready."

"For what?"

I finish my second pickle and stand. "Me."

"Daa-em," she says. "You leaving me with the check?"

"Uh-huh."

"All right. Just this once. Have fun, girl. Oh, and be careful. Wouldn't want you gettin' pregnant, now."

Before I leave, I approach Pops, who is washing some pans. "Collette will be paying, Mr. Luchesi."

"No," he says, smiling. "Don't worry about it."

"Thanks." I start for the door, but he clears his throat. I turn back.

"Payment is one kiss on the cheek for an old man." He turns his jowly cheek toward me, I hold my breath, I kiss him . . . and my lips don't shrivel up. They even tingle a little bit, and the Old Spice, well, it's not so bad. On an old guy. "Thank you. You are a good kisser. Giovanni, he has good taste." I laugh and kiss Pops's cheek again. "A tip, too?"

I know I'm blushing. "Yeah." Pops likes me!

"You are too generous." He wiggles his eyebrows. "Now, go make my son presentable for tonight. He does not know how to dress."

But I'm not thinking about dressing him as I walk up the circular iron stairs to the apartment. The door is unlocked, so I walk in.

The apartment is surprisingly neat though sparsely furnished, but the walls are far too blue. Dead ahead is a tiny living room with an antique sofa, chair, and . . . is that a black-and-white TV? No cable box. They probably have no time to watch TV. Small kitchenette off to my left, counters clean, no dishes in the sink. Mama would call the kitchen a "phone booth." You could stand in one place and touch every appliance. I walk down a hall and see a few faded photographs on the walls of some very Italian-looking people gathered in a bakery. They all look pissed. I hear shower water running at the other end of the hall and decide to be nosy. The first room contains antique bedding and a huge dresser. Pops's room. I skip that one. The second door must lead to Giovanni's room.

I don't know what I expected. I imagined clothes all over the place, uneaten food, a nasty smell. But what I see is scary. Bed made. Not a speck of dust. Nothing on the floor except a circular rug. Nothing on the walls, and I mean, nothing. No posters, prints, pictures, not even a mirror. A simple double bed with solid navy blue comforter. One nightstand with a lamp and a wind-up alarm clock. The only "busy" thing in his room is his desk, covered with stacks of loose-leaf paper and notebooks. Since the shower water is still flowing, I open a notebook on top of the stack and read a poem called "To My Daughter":

RENEE AND JAY

You will have
your mama's smile
my nose
mama's eyes
my toes
your mama's fingers
my hands
mama's softness
my sweaty glands
your mama's cheekbones
my skin's dryness
mama's laugh
my shyness

You will also have
our love.

"That's sweet," I whisper. Boy even pushes my buttons when he's not in the room. I turn the page to something untitled:

We could almost see
forever that snowy night
in the bakery. I
held you, your eyes

and smile visible in
the darkness, and I
must confess, it was
the first time I'd

ever been alone with
a black girl (though
you're definitely brown). Every
time you closed your

185

eyes and ceased your
smile, you disappeared for
a moment. That's a
gift I'll never possess.

I'm flattered that he wrote a poem about me, but . . . being black is a gift? The boy is trippin'. And anyway, it wasn't dark until the candle went out. What's he trying to say? The boy needs glasses. And is he going to write a poem about every aspect of our relationship? Daa-em. I flip another page and see a blank. Whew. He better not write a poem about our sex life. I'm going to have to check this notebook often.

I hear the water stop. Time for a little Renee surprise. I strip and slip under the covers. I hear feet slapping down the hall. "Renee?" I remain silent. He walks into his room and doesn't see me right away. Geez, I'm not *that* dark! I hope he's not always this clueless. His towel falls to the floor, and I can't help but scream.

My scream nearly knocks him to the floor. "Don't do that!" he yells.

"Get that thing away from me!" I scream, pulling the covers over my head. And then it's quiet. Too quiet. "Giovanni?" I pop my head out of the covers, and he's gone. But then I hear a scratchy record starting, and opera music fills the air. I don't know what the man is singing, but it's . . . beautiful.

Giovanni returns and lies beside me.

"What is that song?" I say as he begins stroking my back with warm hands.

"*Ave Maria.*"

"It's beautiful." It is.

"Best I could do."

"No," I say, pulling him on top of me, "*this* is the best you can do."

"Are you sure you want to do this?"

I guide him closer and have to strain my hand. "You sure feel sure." And now I'm not so sure. We have a long day ahead of us, and I don't want to be walking around with a sore coochie.

He backs out of my hand. "No, I mean, what if you aren't pregnant, and *this* time—"

I yank him back to me and ease him inside. Daa-em. I'm gonna be sore. "I know I'm pregnant, boy. Just"—I bite my lip as he starts to thrust—"just don't give the baby a third eye, okay?"

He tries to back out, but I squeeze the hell out of his ass and pull him back in. "But—"

I twist the skin on both of his cheeks until he winces. "I'm kidding, boy."

"Oh."

"Now keep doin' what you were doin', okay?"

"Okay." He starts his—daa-em, he's thick today—thrusts.

"And if you do it right, we might be havin' us some twins."

He freezes then smiles. "You're kidding, right?"

I slap his ass hard. "Boy, what I tell you about stoppin'?"

"I'm sorry, I—"

"You stop again, you'll be walkin' out of here with a third cheek!" He falls forward and starts laughing. "I ain't kiddin', boy! What you laughin' for?"

He kisses me on the chin. "I'm just laughing 'cause I had the stupidest thought."

I raise my hips to meet his. Come on, boy. Work with me! "This isn't the time for stupid thoughts." This is the time for the nastiest, most wicked thoughts—

He plunges deeply and I gasp. "I know." He leans back slightly and lifts my legs to his shoulders, massaging my feet (oh yes don't stop doing that please!) as he continues pounding my poor defenseless coochie. "But if you give me a third cheek, I'll be able to shit in stereo."

I laugh him out of me—the shit *was* funny—then pin him to the bed, straddling him and digging my nails into his chest. "Look here, Mr. Man. You gonna make love to me or think stupid thoughts?"

He reaches up to hold my face, but I grab his hands and pin them to the bed. "Well?"

Then he says that "fah-tee mah-she" thing again, pins *me*, and gives me—I swear—two sets of rainbows, one inside the other, each one as powerful as the other. His actions definitely make me come louder.

While he gets me some ice water, I apologize to my coochie. "I can't help myself, girl," I tell her. "Please forgive me."

He returns with the ice water. I take a sip and ask, "Will you still love me after I get fat?"

"Yes."

"Will you still think I'm sexy?"

"Always."

"I'm going to look like a bowling ball. And you'll still be skinny. Why can't you have Janae for us?"

"Will that be her name?"

"Yeah."

"It's pretty."

"So, you gonna have her for us?"

"How would I look pregnant?"

I pull back the covers and check out his equipment. "Very scary."

We take a quick shower, then dress. Giovanni pulls on an old pair of jeans and a Georgetown sweatshirt. "No," I say, and I search through his closet saying "no" often. "We need to buy you some clothes, boy." I throw out a blue-and-black flannel shirt and the bluest pair of blue jeans. "Where's your iron?"

"We don't own one."

"That doesn't surprise me," I say putting on my earrings. "Just get dressed and try not to stand too close to me while we shop."

And I am not kidding about that. When we arrive at Harris-Teeter, I hand him part of my shopping list, point to the dairy section, and take a cart to the fresh food section. "Meet you in aisle six," I say. In a few minutes, my cart contains lettuce, tomatoes, pasta, ground beef, two jars of spaghetti sauce, and fresh mushrooms. He returns a few minutes later with all the wrong stuff. "Let's see what you got. Take the sharp cheddar back and get mild. One of the eggs is broken. Get another dozen and check it this time. Take the milk back and get a jug from sometime *this* year."

"Sorry," he says.

When he returns with the correct items, I am reading the labels on the pregnancy tests. They all say about the same thing, so I toss one into the cart. "You're bringing cheesecake, wine, and bread, right?"

"Yes."

"Then this is all we need."

At the checkout, I watch the prices on the register until one pops up that I don't like. "Wait," I say to the cashier, a white girl chewing her gum way too loudly.

"Is there a problem?" the cashier asks.

"The sign back there says the ground beef's on special."

"It's an old sign," the girl says, and she continues to scan my purchases.

I roll my eyes at Giovanni. "Then you should change the sign."

The cashier looks from me to Giovanni and back to the head of lettuce in her hand. "You're right," she says, but I know the wench doesn't mean it. Something about the way she cracks her gum.

The last item is the pregnancy tester. The girl "tries" to scan it, but no matter how she "tries," it just will not scan. That's something white folks do to embarrass us. "How much was this?" she asks me, holding it up for all the world to see, turning it so the folks in line behind us can read the label.

I snatch the box and slide it under the red beam. It scans immediately. I point to the register. "It cost *that* much."

The cashier hits the "total" button and says, "That'll be twenty-three thirty-five."

I smile my fake white lady's smile. "He's paying."

Giovanni reaches into his pocket and hands the cashier a brand-new hundred.

189

"Dang," the girl says, "is it real?"

"As real as your nails, honey," I say, and I storm out of the store.

I stand beside the Cadillac, steaming. Why do they have to do that shit? All she had to do was her damn job. Harris-Teeter ain't paying her extra for being a racist, so why she gotta be one with me? Those experts who say racism is a "learned response," who say that we learn to be racists from our parents, who say that racism is inherent and therefore inevitable in every culture—those experts are full of shit. The practice of racism, like everything else in this life, is a damn choice. Bitch in there *chose* just now to be a racist all by her damn self. Wasn't no parent whisperin' in her ear. "Well, I was raised that way" is a bullshit excuse. Truth is, the bitch in there and anyone who uses that lame excuse were just raised wrong.

"She deserved it," Giovanni says, loading the bags into the trunk.

"Bitch," I hiss. "They treat us like shit sometimes."

Giovanni unlocks my door and opens it. "By 'they' you mean white people, right?"

I don't feel the need to explain at first, but once he is inside the Caddy, I take his hand. "I didn't mean you. You just don't know. They expect us all to use food stamps or something. And I hate getting overcharged. And then she acts like she can't get that box to scan. I stopped using checks at that place because they used to write B-F for *black female* next to their initials on my checks."

"Then why do you go there at all?"

I drop his hand. He may never understand. "Let's go."

He starts the car. "I mean, if they're so racist—"

"Just go."

"All right." He backs out and stops. "Are you mad at her or me?"

"Giovanni, please," I say, and I turn the radio all the way up.

On the ride to the house, I think about the exact moment when I really knew that I was black. I was only four and was wandering up and down the toy aisles at a K-Mart while Mama made a payment on a layaway. I found few dolls that looked like me, but that didn't bother me. I wasn't into dolls that much. But while I was hugging and talking to a fluffy black dog, a little white girl came over to me—and started rubbing on my arm. I pulled my arm away and said, "Don't touch me." The little girl just giggled and looked at her hand with the widest eyes. "Wow," she said. "It don't come off." She turned to her mother, who had watched the entire thing, and shouted, "Mama, it don't come off!" Her mother scowled—I thought at me—and yanked her daughter away, the little girl still shouting, "It don't come off!" When Mama found me, I was crying and wouldn't let go of the dog. I still have that dog. It sits on my dresser, silently reminding me that "it don't come off."

When we arrive at the house, I'm nearly in tears and rush inside while Giovanni carries the bags behind me. He dumps the bags on the kitchen counter, and I start taking items out of the bags and placing some on the counter, some in cupboards, some in the refrigerator. Last, I pick up the pregnancy test and walk past Giovanni with not so much as the glimmer of a smile, down the hall and up the stairs.

I hate admitting someone else is right. I even hate admitting that I hate admitting that. Giovanni *was* right—I shouldn't spend money at any store that treats me like shit—but he was also wrong because I shouldn't be *treated* that way at that store or any store in the first place. I know I shouldn't take it out on him; I know I shouldn't punish him for another white person's ignorance, but sometimes I just can't help it. Yes, I had wonderful teachers who happened to be white. Yes, I have white neighbors who I've known for most of my life who I consider friends. Yes, I know that not all white people are racists. But like the color of my skin, those day-after-day feelings of hatred and despair just do not wipe off, they can't be brushed away by someone saying "Get over it"; they can't be erased overnight by a man crying "Can't we all just get along?" And deep down in the blackest part of my heart, a scary place in the center of my being, I don't *ever* want those feelings to go away because they're my armor, my strength, my means of survival. I don't want to be hateful—I want to be hopeful. But there are just too many lines in this town that I didn't draw, too many walls in my world that I didn't build. And here Giovanni and I are, preparing to blur the lines and tear down some walls.

And though I'm nervous and scared to death about it, for some strange reason . . . I can't wait for it all to begin. It's like I'm finally getting the chance to rub that little white girl's arm in that aisle at K-Mart and say, "Look, it doesn't come off of you either. Now you go deal with that for twenty-two years."

I look at the box in my hand. The directions are simple. Unwrap, pee on the square, wait. If a red dot shows up, I'm pregnant. If not, I'm not. Simple. If only life were this easy. Then why am I shaking? Giovanni should be here.

"Giovanni!" I yell from the top of the stairs.

He runs to the bottom of the stairs. "What?"

"Come up here."

He takes the steps two at a time. "What's wrong?"

"Come here."

"Okay."

I point to my room. "Wait in my room on my bed."

I'm almost too nervous to pee. They need to put a plastic glove in with these things. It isn't easy to hit that little square when you're nervous. I pat it dry with some toilet tissue and bring it to my room like I'm carrying an egg that's about to hatch. I set it on my night-stand and sit on the bed, the tester an arm's length away. Giovanni's arm pulls me to him.

How'd he know that I needed to be held just now? "I'm sorry about before," I say. "Forgive me?"

"For what?" He kisses my cheek. "It's okay. I have a lot to learn, huh?"

"Yeah." And I'll be your teacher. He starts tapping his feet on the floor. "Don't do that."

"But I'm nervous."

"You, too?"

"I've wanted to be a father my whole life, and now . . ." We both lean forward. Nothing yet.

"You've *wanted* to be a father?" Giovanni nods. Most of the guys I know don't want kids and don't want to be with girls who have kids. R. J. always used a condom, which is a good thing, don't get me wrong, but a couple of times he refused to make love to me because he didn't have one. "I'm on the pill and won't have my period for two more weeks," I'd remind him, but he wasn't having it or me. "Why?"

"I . . . just think I'd be a good one. I like children. I like serving them, like seeing their eyes light up when I bring them their food."

"Children don't tip."

"Smiles and laughter can be tips, too." So can kisses. "When Mama died, it was like my family died a little, and I've wanted a complete family ever since." He squeezes my hand. "And here we are."

That's so sweet! But I have to test him. "You ever change a diaper?"

"No, but I will."

"Hmm," I growl. "You say that now, but at three-thirty in the morning on a cold night, you know that I'll be the one getting up."

"We'll get up together, then. Promise."

I like that word. Promise. "I'm going to hold you to that." I kiss his cheek and look at the tester. It hasn't changed. "The directions say it could take as long as fifteen minutes."

"Oh." Time passes. "How's your mama feel about us?"

"She *says* she can handle 'us,' but I'm still not sure, especially because I'm gonna be presenting her with a mixed baby."

"A what?"

"A biracial child. Our baby gonna be yellow." He lets go of my hand. "What?" He starts to say something and stops. "What?"

"Nothing."

Something's wrong. "Lots of mixed babies in Roanoke, Giovanni. Janae will fit right in." He still doesn't speak. "What's wrong?"

"I just don't like . . . mixed and yellow. They sound so . . . negative, like she's mixed up and sickly or something."

He has a point. "Well, what would you call Janae?"

"I'll call her 'Janae.' I'll call her by name. I'll call her my daughter. And she'll be golden, not yellow."

If more boys like Giovanni who weren't "from here" came here with attitudes like that, Roanoke would be a golden town. I take and hold his hand in both of mine. "Promise to keep thinking nice thoughts like that?"

"I promise."

More comfortable silence. We lean in. Nothing. "What are the chances of this happening?" I ask. "I'm on the pill, which is ninety-nine percent effective. One measly percent chance."

"Maybe Janae wanted to be born."

I lean in. Still nothing. "No. Your sperm were on steroids." Still nothing. "Okay," I say, "let's say we're pregnant. What happens next?"

Without batting an eye, Giovanni says, "I marry you. How's Sunday?"

"Be serious."

"I am. We get the license tomorrow, and I marry you on Sunday."

"Right." I check the tester. Nothing.

"Seriously. I have it all figured out."

"You do?"

"First, we get the license downtown. Then we get your flowers Saturday afternoon. Saturday night, we rehearse."

"And where will we be married?"

"At Luchesi's."

He's lost his damn mind! "I am not getting married at Luchesi's. No offense." I look. No change.

"Why not? What church will marry us on such short notice? For that matter, what church in Roanoke will *marry* us? All we need is a space and someone to marry us, right?"

"Well, what if I want a big wedding?"

194

"You do?"

When I was with R. J., I did. It would have been held at High Holiness in early spring. No hot June or July weddings for me. I only had to suffer through one of those as a flower girl (the flowers had wilted before I could hand them to the bride) to know an unair-conditioned church in Roanoke is no place to hold a summer wedding. The church would have been full of roses, and I mean *full* of roses in every color of the rainbow, windows open to breezes blowing the rose scent everywhere. Every guest would have had a rose, too. We would have had to buy so many roses that the reception would have been a potluck dinner in the church basement. "Every girl wants a big wedding, Giovanni."

"Oh." He checks this time. "Nothing."

"And what about music? Where am I going to get a dress? And who's going to marry us?"

"My sister sings, and Alexis plays guitar."

"Collette could sing," I say, and he rolls his eyes. "Hey, she can sing a lot better than she did today."

He checks again. Nothing. "As for the dress, you could wear my mama's."

"Huh? Didn't she elope?"

"Yeah. It's never been worn. Neither has Pops's tux."

"Pops has his own tux?" He must have gotten it at a tent sale. "It'll never fit you."

"Christina can fix it. And Father Mike could come down and marry us."

"Father Mike?" Sounds as bad as Sister Betty Sue.

"Father Michael Bellafiore, from Saint Pat's in Huntington. He and Pops are old friends. He'd love to marry us."

We both lean in. Something's happening. "Is that a red dot?" I whisper.

"Kind of pink," he says.

"It's red. But is that a dot?"

"Looks like a dot."

My stomach falls, but my heart gets . . . bigger. How is that possible? Is it because another heart will soon be beating in mine? When will that happen? Will I get as big as a house? How long will I be vurping? Should I see a doctor? There's so much I don't know! "Giovanni, I'm going to be a mama." Giovanni stands and paces. "Aren't you happy?" He stops by the window, mumbling something in Italian. "Answer me in English!"

"Where do you want to spend your honeymoon?" he asks suddenly, still looking out the window.

I ask "Aren't you happy?" then stop. "What honeymoon, Giovanni?"

He turns to me, his eyes wild. "We have to get tickets soon so we can fly out Monday."

"Are you crazy?"

He nods. "So where are we going?"

He has completely lost it. "I don't know. Will you sit down?" He sits, fumbling with his hands. "This is all too fast."

"I know. *Allegro!*"

"And you're enjoying this!"

"*Allegro!*"

"Speak English!"

He takes my hand. "Do you want to be married to me?"

"I think so, but—"

"I want to be married to you. Why wait a long time for what we want? I don't want to elope. Mama's side of the family doesn't talk to us because of that."

I grab his face. "*What is the rush?*"

He drops his eyes. I shouldn't have yelled. His eyes drift to mine, then back to his hands. "This is all so unreal, Renee. I don't want to wake up."

"I'm not going anywhere." I kiss him. "We can't be *allegro* all the time."

"Speak-a de English." I kill him with an evil stare. "Okay, okay. But dream a little. Where *would* you want to go on a honeymoon?"

196

"The Bahamas? Maybe." But not on a boat. I have this historical fear of big boats and the ocean. "I hear Maui is nice, especially this time of year. I don't know, Giovanni. It's not something I think about, and it's not something I want to think about right now. We're going to be parents. Let's think about that."

"Okay, you're right. We need to slow down."

Finally, he gets some sense. I squeeze his leg. "Shouldn't we tell your father?"

"In a minute. I have something to say." He kneels and lifts my shirt. "To my daughter." He kisses my stomach. "Sleep tight, *bella* Janae."

I give him a nice hug. "Come on," I say, and we race each other from the house to Luchesi's. We enter through the back and hear Pops singing something loud in Italian, and even when he sees us, he doesn't stop.

"Pops," Giovanni says, but the slaughtering of pigs continues. Giovanni shrugs, picks me up, and puts me on the counter until Pops squeals the last note and takes a bow.

"So," Pops says, "you two are to be the proud parents of a baby girl, yes?" We nod. "I knew it." He touches his temple. "I'm a smart guy. Just tell me when is the wedding, and I start cooking."

"We haven't set a date," I reply quickly. Someone needs to slow these Italians down!

"Any day is a good day for a wedding," Pops says. "Soon, though?"

"We'll see," I say, checking my watch. "Oh, I have so much to do, Giovanni. I've got to get home to cook!"

"May I help?"

"No. I want to cook for you this time."

"Sounds like a good deal to me," Pops says.

I try to get off the counter, but Giovanni steps in between my legs and puts his forehead to mine. "What are you doing?" I whisper.

"Kissing you in front of my father."

I am about to protest when he lays one on me. I don't kiss him back.

"Hey, you two!" Pops yells. "You scare away all the customers. Out, out!"

I drag Giovanni out of Luchesi's and confront him in front on the sidewalk. "What's wrong?" he says.

Oh, nothing. Just that a white man has kissed me full on my caramel lips in public. I am still too pissed to speak.

"Are you all right?" he asks. Seems I've been hearing that a lot these days.

"No." He tries to take my hand, but I put it in my pocket. "Don't do that."

"Do what?"

"Don't touch me or kiss me in public."

He doesn't speak right away. "Sorry."

"We're in Roanoke, Virginia, not Rome."

"I'm from Long Island."

"Whatever. That shit don't fly around here."

"May I hold your hand at least?"

I would like nothing more than to have us getting kissy-face in public. Really. He's good at it, and my lips and hands want to be appreciated. I want people to know that Giovanni is my man. If we were anywhere else in the world, that is. "Haven't you been listening?"

He looks away. "It won't happen again."

Against all that I've believed in since I was born, I slip my hand into his. "It's slippery. Help me across the street."

He smiles. "Okay."

I lead him across Fourth Street just as a rusty brown truck comes over the little hill. As it passes behind us, I hear a voice yell: "Nigger lover!" I drop Giovanni's hand and walk quickly to my car, but he doesn't follow. I turn back and see him, hands in his pockets, yelling something to the passenger in the truck. Oh, not today, Giovanni. Please just leave it be! The passenger's head is bobbing up and down, but Giovanni's is steady as he walks closer and closer to the truck. My hands are sweating, and my heart's about to break a few ribs. Let it go, Giovanni! They're just rednecks with a combined IQ of seven who can't even count to two. A car behind the truck is honking now. The passenger flips Giovanni off, then slams his hand against the truck door. Giovanni must have said something. Please, baby, just walk away! The truck burns rubber and takes off. Giovanni comes over to me with the biggest, doofiest smile on his face.

"What did you say to him?"

"First I told him that I hardly knew him."

"Huh?"

"He said what he said, then I said, 'But I hardly know you.'" Nice comeback. It's not everyday that a redneck gets called a nigger. "Then he questioned my ancestry and said I was a traitor to my race. I asked him what planet he was from. Then he flipped me off, and I said something like 'Is that the length of your penis?'—something like that. I guess I get too carried away sometimes."

Though I appreciate his courage, I'm afraid for him. "But if you keep doing that, you'll be carried away for real. In a hearse." And I'm not kidding about that. All a white boy did in my high school was dance *near* a group of black girls at an in-school dance, and the brothers banked his ass. I don't even think the boy ever returned to school. "Just don't do it again, okay?"

"I can't let that shit slide, Renee."

"You're gonna have to. Just tone it down around me, and don't touch me if you can help it."

"Why?"

"Because we clash, Giovanni. We turn heads. We are not socially acceptable. We are not a fashion statement. Black and white hands only hold each other on those Benetton ads in magazines."

He caresses my face. "But I have to touch you. I want people to know."

I love that strong, rough hand on my face; I really do. R. J. wasn't nearly as affectionate in public, and I'm sure that R. J. and I often looked more like friends than lovers to anyone seeing us in public.

"Well I don't want people to know." I duck away from his hand. "Let's just do all our touching in private from now on."

He shakes his head. "I can't help it. You're so . . . touchable. Is that even a word?"

"Giovanni, please understand—"

"No."

I blink. He interrupts and says "no" to me? Who does he think—

"I won't *not* touch you, Renee."

That almost makes sense. I get into my car. "You won't touch me."

"I will."

I sigh, my mouth dropping open. So stubborn! "You will not come near me, especially tonight. Understand?"

"I already said no. I can't help it. I like talking to you with my hands."

I shut the door, start the car, and roll down the window. "I like you talking to me with your hands, too, but tonight's dinner is too important. One little stolen kiss or squeeze of the hand could end us."

He shakes his head. "Like I said, I can't help it."

I roll my eyes. "Well, if you can't help it, I don't want you to come tonight."

"You mean that?"

I don't stutter. "Yes."

He shrugs. "Then I won't come. If I can't *be* myself around you and your mama, then I won't *be* around you and your mama."

I shake my head and grip the steering wheel. "Whatever. I gotta go."

And without another word, he walks away.

A few hours later, the sauce is simmering, the noodles are boiling, and the salad is cooling in the refrigerator. He'll come. He has to. And if he doesn't, we'll have lots of leftovers to eat tomorrow.

"Janae," I say as I'm working, "this is the kitchen where I will teach you how to make miracles." It's funny how being pregnant allows you to talk to yourself. I think it's in the pregnancy contract. Maybe I should call and talk to him instead.

The phone rings as I'm running cold water on the spaghetti. It has to be Giovanni calling to apologize. I pick up the phone and say, "I accept your apology."

"I ain't done nothin' to apologize for," Mama asks.

Oops. "Hi Mama."

She laughs. "How's it going, girl?"

"Just fine. It'll be in the oven in about twenty minutes. Is Michael coming?"

"He'll be there. I'm coming home early, so I ought to be there by six. Bye."

"Bye." And maybe a little bit later, say around seven-thirty, Mama's going to know she's a grandmama. . . . I'm going to find out if Mama's having my sister . . . and I'll know if I still have a boyfriend/fiancé.

After alternating layers of spaghetti, cheese, and sauce, I put the spaghetti bake in the oven. I have just enough time to take a quick shower, my third for the day.

But the phone rings again. "Well?" Collette asks.

"You'll be an aunt in October."

"Yes! Can I tell everyone here?"

"No."

"Why not?"

"Just don't, Collette."

"All right, all right. But congratulations anyway."

"Thanks."

I could not walk in there tomorrow if they knew. All that attention is nice, but people ask too many damn questions like, "Do you want a boy or a girl?" or "When's it due?" Like anyone can tell you that exactly. I want a healthy child . . . who just happens to be a beautiful girl. I need a free day after this messed-up week. I plan to sleep all day tomorrow.

Mama arrives while I'm in the shower. She comes into the bathroom without knocking, as usual. "That was quick!" I say.

"Well, I, uh . . . well." She sits on the toilet seat.

I stick my head out. "Something wrong?" She's fumbling with her hands again. Oh, shit.

"No. Nothing's wrong." She tries to smile. "I mean, yes."

"I'll be out in a—"

"I just want you to like Michael, that's all."

I close the curtain and rinse off. "Mama, if you like him, I'm sure to love him."

"What I mean, baby, is like him, not so much by what you see, but by what you feel." Hold up. Mama out with an ugly man? What am I gonna be seeing? A man with a hump? "He's worried you won't like him, and he almost didn't want to come."

I turn off the water and open the shower curtain. Mama hands me a towel, and I wrap myself quickly. "I'll love him, Mama. He's going to be kind of like my dad, sort of, right?"

"Right, right." She smiles. "But whatever you do, don't stare. He hates that. And I mean don't stare at nothing around this man, not what he's wearing, not his face, and especially not his teeth. He's very sensitive about his teeth."

Dag, Mama thinks I'm going to scare him away. But nasty teeth? Crooked, beige, missing? Gross. "Mama, I'll be a good little girl. Hand me the lotion."

She puts the lotion bottle in my hand but doesn't let go. "I'm serious, Renee. If he doesn't meet your approval, I don't know what he'll do."

I'm almost touched. "I promise I'll like him, Mama, if you promise to like Giovanni."

"I ain't promisin' that." She lets go of the bottle and scowls. "Girl, you need some serious lotion on them legs. You turnin' as white as Giovanni." It's true. I could play ticktacktoe on my thighs. "One more thing. Michael has this, um, odor." You've got to be kidding! "You won't notice it after a while—I mean, at first it was really strong, but after a while I stopped noticing it. Just don't scrunch up your nose around him, okay?"

I'll just put on extra CK1 then. "Okay. What time is it?"

"Almost six. When's Giovanni coming over?"

"I don't know. He . . . may not be coming."

She blinks once. "Really?"

"Don't look so happy. We had an argument. He can be such an asshole sometimes."

She leans forward. "Really? Hmm. So it might just be the three of us?"

"It might."

"I'll go check the food." And then she walks out and leaves the door wide open. The draft gives me goose pimples . . . or is it the thought of my mama seeing a smelly, badly dressed, toothless, stank man?

Ten minutes later, she's back up in my face as I sit in front of my mirror fixing my hair. "What you gonna wear?" she asks. I point at the Guess jeans and white sweater on the bed. "Oh, good, you won't be outdressing me."

"Mama!"

"Come on, baby. You'll fall in love with Michael and run off with him." I don't think so, Mama. I have my standards, and a funky body is not one of them. "Sure you want to wear a white sweater? We'll be eating spaghetti and drinking wine if Giovanni shows up."

Not this mother-to-be. I may eat a bite or two of the spaghetti bake and maybe a bread stick. My main meal will be a simple tossed salad. "I'm sure."

"Oh, and don't laugh at the way Michael talks. He's very self-conscious about that. He, uh, stutters a little and has a lisp. Nothing awful, mind you, but, well, it embarrasses him."

Where did you find this guy, Mama? Big Lots? "Anything else, Mama?"

"What do you mean, 'anything else'?"

"I'm trying to get ready."

"My talking ain't stopping you. What you mean by 'anything else'?"

I put down the Golden Hot. "Mama, you are worrying yourself to *death* over how I'll like him. And the more you tell me, the more I'm starting to get worried. Let me make up my own mind, okay? I'll say what I said before: if you like him, I'll like him. End of discussion."

Mama giggles a little then. "What you must be thinking! What am I worried about?"

The doorbell rings. We both look at the clock. "It's only six-thirty," I say. "Who could that be?"

Mama leaves and comes back a minute later with a long box of roses. "Look at these flowers. Where are yours, girl?"

I pout. "I left them at work. What's the card say?"

She reads the card to herself and holds it to her chest. "None of your damn business. I'll go put these in some water, put them in the middle of the table for everybody to see. Maybe the flowers will block out Giovanni entirely." I threaten her with the curling iron. "I'll check the food. Hurry up, okay?"

"Okay. Leave, already." I hear her giggling down the stairs. My mama's done lost her mind.

The doorbell rings again a few minutes later. This *has* to be Giovanni. "Mama, get the door, okay?"

I hear the door open and close. "Renee!" Mama yells.

I hate being rushed. "What?"

"Come to the top of the stairs!"

"I'm not dressed! What you want?"

"It's not what I want, it's what Giovanni wants!"

He's here? "Well, what's he want?"

"He wants to kiss me!"

I am down those stairs in a flash, fully dressed, hair perfect.

"I was just kidding," she says, laughing her way down the hall toward the kitchen, where Giovanni is unloading the bread sticks into the oven to warm next to the spaghetti bake.

"Hi," he says . . . and gives me a hug in front of my mama. So much for toning it down. "You look nice."

"Not as nice as me," Mama says as I break from his embrace. "Open up that wine, Jay, I mean, Giovanni. I need a drink." I watch as Giovanni expertly uncorks the bottle and pours a glass for Mama. She downs the entire glass in one gulp. If she's pregnant, that baby just got shit-faced. "What is this stuff?"

"Chianti," I say.

She squints, then rolls her eyes. "How you know?"

"I've had some."

She stares at Giovanni. "I'll bet you have. Good stuff, though. Hit me again, Giovanni." He pours her another. "Boy, you better get some more meat on your bones. You get any more bony, you'll be givin' folks splinters when you shake their hands."

Giovanni takes a deep breath. "Speaking of putting more weight on, Renee and I have a little surprise for you."

Mama looks dead at me with a don't-you-dare look. "Is this a 'you-had-better-sit-down' surprise?"

"Uh, Giovanni, may I speak with you for a moment?" I say with fire in my eyes.

"He's right here," Mama says, gulping some more Chianti.

"In private," I say, my teeth clenched together.

"Don't mind me," Mama says. "It's only *my* house."

I push him ahead of me down the stairs to the basement. I do not give him a chance to speak. "Boy, what you think you're doing? First you hug me right in front of my mama, then you start bringing up shit I'm supposed to tell her which will probably get your ass killed." He pulls me to him and kisses me. "Don't do that!"

"Just getting a last kiss before I die." He starts up the stairs. "You coming?"

I yank him back down. "You are *not* telling her, *not* tonight, *not* ever!"

"You'd rather deceive her some more?"

"No." Damn, I hate when he makes a good point. "I mean, yes.

Maybe the test was wrong. I'll wait a week and try it again. We'll just say the surprise is a lemon pie Pops is making."

"Your mama's smarter than that."

He's making all sorts of good points tonight. "Why'd you have to say something, Giovanni? Why you gotta come over here startin' shit?"

He smiles. "It's in my culture. We're telling her tonight, Renee."

"The hell we are!"

"Then . . . I'm leaving."

"Well, go on then!"

"Fine." He starts up the stairs again . . . and stops. He turns and looks at me.

I feel like crying, but I will not give him the satisfaction. "Well, go on if you want to. Don't let the front door hit you in your bony ass as you're leavin'."

"*Ciao.*"

I watch him open the door, and the damn tears start falling. That's when I *don't* hear the front door opening and closing and *do* hear a chair squeaking on the kitchen floor. Shitshitshit! I bust up the stairs and see Mama sitting at the table, Giovanni standing near the counter, neither one speaking.

"Y'all through arguin'?" Mama asks. "Or is this goin' on all night?"

"I'm through," Giovanni says. "I was just leaving."

"You said that," Mama says. "You haven't told me why."

"Ask Renee."

"I'm asking you. Sit down, Renee." I sit and turn away from both of them.

"I gotta go," Giovanni says, and he starts to leave.

"*No you ain't!*" Mama says in the voice that used to stop city buses when I was a kid. Giovanni stops. "You don't come into my house and make my baby cry without some kind of explanation." She points to the chair next to me. "Now sit down."

He sits. The kitchen is completely silent. Even the refrigerator stops humming. All I hear is the swish of the wine spinning around in Mama's glass.

"Mrs. Howard?"

"*What?*" Bet she stopped a train just then.

Giovanni looks at me. "What I was going to say is that . . . Renee has something important to tell you."

Mama drops her voice as low as it will go. "You ain't gettin' out of it that easy."

"I—"

I cut him off with my hand. "Mama," I say. Drumroll, please. "Mama, I may be—"

"Pregnant," Mama says, and she gulps the rest of her drink. She sets her glass on the table. "Now was that so hard? Giovanni, my glass is empty." The kitchen is just full of surprises today. Giovanni rises and gets the bottle of Chianti, filling her glass without shaking a bit. How can he be so calm? And why is he smiling so much? Mama takes a smaller sip. "So, you're pregnant," she says eventually.

"Yes, Mama."

She looks at Giovanni, but he's useless, with a big, doofy grin on his face. "You cheese any more in here, boy, we gonna have rats," Mama says, and Giovanni's smile vanishes.

"Mrs. Howard," he says, putting the bottle on the counter, "we didn't mean for it to happen."

"Neither did I," she says as she takes another sip.

What the— "What you mean by that, Mama?"

"Sit down, Giovanni," she says sternly, ignoring my question. He sits. Mama picks up her chair and moves it so it touches his. "You got my baby pregnant?"

His Adam's apple spasms. "Yes ma'am."

"Why you do a thing like that?" The air is getting heavier. I want to open a window, I want to rewind to before Giovanni arrived. "Huh? You listenin'? Why you gotta get my daughter pregnant?"

"I didn't mean to."

"Don't you know," she says in a deadly tone, "that if that child over there has a baby, then I'm officially old? *What the hell were you thinking?*"

Giovanni can't find his voice. "Mrs. Howard, I—"

"I ain't no Missus." She takes a sip of her wine. "Call me Shirl."

Giovanni blinks . . . and so do I. What's she up to? "Uh, Shirl, you will never be old."

"Too late," she says. "Now answer the damn question. What the hell were you thinking?"

His shoulders slump. He looks to me for help, but I'm no help. When Mama's like this, it's best to say nothing. "Mrs. —"

"Call me Shirl, now."

"Shirl, I was thinking . . . at the time . . . and now, for that matter—"

"*Spit it out, boy!*" Mama yells.

"I love your daughter very much. That's what I was thinking when we were—"

Mama slaps the table. "Oh, spare me the details. I get the picture." Mama stares me down, a smile forming in the corners of her mouth. "Can I kiss him, Renee?"

"What?" I ask. She can't be serious.

She looks me dead in the eye. "I said, can I kiss your man?"

I'm shaking. "I guess."

She kisses him dead on the lips. Giovanni's eyes widen a foot. "He's a good kisser, Renee. Lips a little thin, but he'll do. Pour me some more wine." Giovanni nearly knocks over his chair getting the wine off the counter.

Something is very strange here. I don't know what it is yet, but . . . daa-em. I just let my mama kiss my man in front of me!

She takes her third glass and smiles at me. "Did I shock you?"

"Yes." And you pissed me off, too. Heifer.

"Good. Now you know how I felt when I knew that you were pregnant on Tuesday."

Ba-BOOM. "What you talkin' about, Mama?"

"I knew you were pregnant on Tuesday."

"How?"

She traces a finger around the rim of the glass. "Girl, I been pregnant too, you know, and you looked and acted pregnant on Tuesday. Reminded me of me when I was pregnant with you. And the other day, I went out and bought one of them tester things, just to be sure. Want to know how I did the test?"

She bought a tester for *me?* What the— . . . So she's not— . . .Oh, no you didn't, Mama! And not in front of—

"One of Renee's little routines. My baby girl always, and I mean always, brushes her teeth the first thing after leaving her bed. Then she pees."

"Mama, I know how you did—"

"She interrupts a lot, doesn't she? Gets it from me." Giovanni is frozen. "Anyway, after she pees, she doesn't flush and gets in the shower. She says it brings all the hot water—"

"Cold water, Mama."

"Whatever. Anyway, that's when I did the test. Swished that little wand in the water. It took forever to turn to that itty-bitty pink dot, but there it was." She turns sharply to Giovanni. "You going to marry her, right?"

"Yes ma'am."

"When?"

Giovanni looks at me. "As soon as possible."

"How soon?" Mama asks.

"Sunday."

No, he most certainly did not—

"Fine by me," Mama says. "Okay with you, Renee?"

"What the hell is going on here?" I feel like throwing something at both of them. "Don't I have some say in all this?"

"Of course you do, baby, of course you do. Tell me again, Giovanni, how we gonna pull this off."

I look at Giovanni and see a traitor. "You've already told her?" I yell, but he only shrugs.

"I'm playing, I'm playing," Mama says, finishing her third glass of wine. "He hadn't told me a thing. I just get a kick out of seeing you pissed." I slump in my chair and pout. "So tell me, Giovanni, how we gonna pull this off."

"You're not serious, are you Mama?" I ask. She has to be drunk.

"You got anything else to do on Sunday, girl? I hate football, and so does Michael. That's one of the reasons I like him so much. He ought to be here any—"

"*Mama!*" I scream, almost as loudly as when I shrieked at Dagney.

"*Renee!*" She mimics my scream perfectly, and I start laughing so hard that I start crying. "Talk fast, Giovanni. When she's giggling, she can't interrupt."

Giovanni pours himself a large glass of Chianti and takes a gulp. "Y'all are crazy."

"Yup," Mama says . . . just like Giovanni!

I still can't speak. This is all too funny. I manage to say, "Ooh, the baby!" a couple of times between snorts. And when the doorbell rings, I nearly fall out of my chair.

"You can tell us over dinner, Giovanni. *My* man is here. Y'all just wait in here. I may have to suck some face first."

I recover enough to say, "Help me up from here!" as Mama leaves. Giovanni helps me off my chair and hugs me. And I'm still laughing. "Let's go meet Michael!" But when I see Michael for the first time, Giovanni has to catch me from falling out on the hallway floor.

Michael is a tall, sharply dressed, *handsome* black man. He's more than handsome. He's beautiful . . . and I know him somehow. I take Giovanni's hand and stand. "Hello, Michael." And then Mama yells, "Surprise!" and I fall on the floor laughing again. We help each other up and run upstairs like two giggly girls.

We sit and recover in my room, leaving the men alone in the hallway. After we calm down and use half a box of tissues, Mama says, "Gotcha!"

"Yes you did. But, shouldn't we be getting down to our guests? I mean, it's a little rude to go off when you have two men in your kitchen."

"They'll be all right." Mama sits on my bed. "Always keep a man waiting." She leans back on her elbows. "Tell me, honestly now, what you thought Michael looked like."

"I pictured him as bald, toothless, hairy, wearing high-water pants and white buck shoes, with an elephant's nose and a green cloud of funk following him."

"Then I *really* got you, huh?"

"Yeah. Why you do that?"

"You seemed to be having so much fun with your secrets, I thought I'd have some fun with mine. What surprised you most about him?"

"That he . . . looked so familiar. Where have I seen him before?"

She smiles. "Oh, lots of places."

"Like where?"

"Like . . . everywhere, I expect. You just ain't been looking." She lies back on the bed, her hands under her head. "I met him at the Black Angus back in December. We sat next to each other at the table and got to talking. Just talking. While everybody else was dancing and getting drunk, we just sat and talked."

"About what?"

"That night? I think everything on earth. My life, my job, Roanoke, but mostly we talked about you."

"Why me?"

She rolls her eyes. "Anyway, the party was winding down, and he asked me if I wanted to go out for coffee. I pointed at his wedding ring. He said, 'My wife died a few years ago. I just haven't found anyone to take it off for yet.'"

"That's so sweet."

"Best damn pickup line I ever heard. We drank coffee and ate pie at Gary's Little Chef on Williamson, and later we watched the sunrise on Mill Mountain. I've lived here all of my life, and I never did that before." She sits up. "Have I told you enough?"

"I guess."

She shakes her head. "You still don't know."

"Know what?"

"Who that man is, Renee. I thought you'd have figured it out by now."

Michael is tall, handsome, nicely dressed, beautiful . . . dear Jesus! With *my* eyes, *my* nose, *my* lips, and *my* little ears—"My . . . my daddy's here?"

"Uh-huh."

"Holy shit!" My daddy's here! He's downstairs talking to Giovanni, the man I want to marry, and I don't hear shit breaking, and Mama's right here smiling at me right after I've made her officially old and . . . Waaait just a damn minute! "What you bring him here for, Mama? After twenty-six years, you decide to hook up with my daddy? What's up with that shit? Or is Michael supposed to be talking Giovanni out of—"

"You watch your tone, little girl."

"How you expect me to feel?"

"Surprised again?"

The bombs are really falling tonight. " 'Surprised' ain't the word, Mama."

"No," she says, standing up. " 'Pissed' is more like it." She sighs. "Maybe this wasn't such a good idea. I'll ask him to leave."

"*No!*" I shout. Mama's eyes bug out. "No," I say more softly, "I just need a little time to collect myself, to let this sink in." I mean, it's not every day you meet your daddy. I may even change my clothes.

"Okay, but don't keep us waiting too long. I'm hungry." She closes the door behind her.

My daddy, who's as handsome as Mama has always said, who she says I've seen everywhere, is downstairs in my mama's house talking to my hopefully future husband while I'm up here pregnant and pissed off. The cosmic joke continues.

Wait. *My* daddy is here, and I'm his little girl . . . pouting up-stairs. Just like when I was little. I'd dream of him playing with me or carrying me or just simply smiling at me throughout the night, and then I'd wake up without him and run to my mirror to see him somewhere in my face. I could never quite see him in time. I look in my mirror now and see his face clearly. He's here! All those years I had to leave his name blank on all those forms and applications, all those years kids made fun of me—those kids who said my daddy was in prison or pointed out bums on the street and said, "That's Renee's daddy"—all those years when I couldn't attend High Holiness's father-daughter banquets . . . none of that matters any-more. None of it.

Daddy's home!

But the man downstairs is a handsome man . . . and I look right ugly. I can't let him see me like this! Geez, it's like I'm about to have a date with my daddy! What should I wear? No. I've waited too long for this. I primp a few minutes and walk down the stairs. No one's in the kitchen, so I call out, "Mama?"

"In the basement," she yells.

I throw back my shoulders and walk down the stairs, trying not to cheese too widely, but I can't help it. He's cheesing too. Daa-em, it's like looking in a mirror!

"Congratulations!" Michael/Daddy says immediately and gives me a sturdy hug.

"Thank you . . . Daddy." And that's when twenty-six years of being daddy-less fully hits me, and I start to sob. Just saying that word to the man that word matches opens the floodgates. I bury my head into his chest as Mama leads Giovanni up the stairs.

"Let's sit," Daddy says, and we do. His eyes are full of tears, too. "I have some explaining to do, huh?"

I can't take my eyes off him. His hair is graying slightly, but other than that, he looks so young. He's an African prince, a king! My dreams have come true!

"I'll start from the beginning. Your mama tells me she hasn't told you anything."

"Not much."

"Then I'll start at the beginning. Your mama and I met at a party in Greensboro. We hit it off and one thing led to another. . . . I came up to visit her over that summer and found out she was pregnant. I wanted to do right by her, but she wouldn't have it. Even went to church with her four consecutive Sundays, just hoping God would tell her something. She told me that God told her to tell me to vanish, and I was young, so I vanished. I later married, but we didn't have any children."

I clear my throat. "Mama says I've seen you everywhere."

He smiles. "Yeah, I helped you off quite a few slides way back when."

"You did?"

"Yeah. Pushed you in a few swings, too. Attended most of your birthdays. Stayed mostly in the background, though. Even saw you graduate from high school and college."

"Why didn't—no, I know why. Mama."

He nods. "It's not a good thing to cross your mama." He leans forward . . . and bites his bottom lip! "I just wanted you to know that I've never been too far away from you, Renee. Your mama tells me you always liked the gifts I sent you."

"What gifts?"

"The ones from Santa."

"You were Santa?" And they were always *exactly* what I wanted! "You gave me that bike I wanted, the blue one."

He nods. "Kind of surprised me you wanted a boy's bike."

"I've never liked pink." My mind is racing. "And—and that down jacket with all the zippers and pockets!"

"'Get the biggest size you can,' your mama told me. You could have lived in that thing, and you could probably still wear it."

"They're out of style now, but then . . ." I start to mist up. "And the . . ." I swallow hard. "And the sketch that looks like me."

"Yeah. Couldn't resist. It was almost like the artist was drawing the woman you'd turn out to be. You're much prettier, though, but I'm glad you like it."

I didn't always, but I'll love it now. "Thank you."

"I guess what I'm trying to say is that I *have* been a part of your life—not a big part, and I'm sorry about that—but I want to be a bigger part of it from now on."

I feel the tears again. "Are you, uh, and Mama gonna get married?"

He fixes me with *my* stare. "What you think?"

I wipe a tear and laugh. "I guess not." I look at my hands. "But you'll be around, right?"

"Right."

I look at the ceiling. "I wonder what they're talking about up there. Or if they're talking at all."

He clears his throat. "So, do you, uh, really like this Giovanni?"

"Yes . . . Daddy." I get goose bumps every time I say that word. "What do you think of him?"

He brushes some lint from his pants. "Does it matter?"

"Yes."

He sighs. "Tell you what. You will hear all about what I think of him while we eat. I've been dying to have some of my daughter's cooking for the longest time."

"Okay." He puts out his hand, I take it, and we return to the kitchen. And it's real quiet in the kitchen. Mama and Giovanni ain't been sayin' nothin'.

And no one says nothin' for the longest time while we eat. Except for an occasional "pass the pepper" or an "mmm" from Daddy, the only sound is the house settling.

Mama, though, can't keep quiet for long. "Giovanni, tell Michael about your Sunday wedding plans."

"Sunday?" Daddy says. "*This* Sunday? It's Super Bowl Sunday, man!"

Giovanni takes a long sip of his wine and nods at the same time. "Yes sir, it is."

Daddy looks at Mama. "He's serious?"

Mama smiles. "He says he is. Tell us all about Sunday, Giovanni. I think even Renee needs to know."

"He hasn't even told you?" Daddy asks me.

"Well, he did, but . . . I guess I could hear it again."

Giovanni squirms in his chair and speaks directly to me. "Picture this: you're in my mama's wedding dress, never been worn. You leave your house on Sunday with your mama and Collette. You walk down Allison Avenue to Luchesi's. Cars honk or stop. Neighbors come out to watch. Can you see that happening?"

"No," I say with a roll of my eyes. "So far I'm going to be badly dressed, cold, and embarrassed." Mama laughs. "But go on."

Giovanni's face is turning that unattractive shade of red. "You, uh, arrive at Luchesi's. You see many people inside because the wedding will be open to the public." Mama snorts. I would, too, but it's hard to snort when your mouth has dropped to the table next to your plate. "You, uh, you smell bread baking for the celebration afterwards. Suddenly, you hear a guitar playing 'The Wedding March.' It's your cue to walk in."

"Are you serious?" Daddy asks and turns to me. "Is he serious?"

"He sounds serious," Mama says.

I shake my head. "Giovanni, this is not what I had in mind."

Giovanni stands and moves around to me. "Your mother and father walk down the aisle with you. You see flowers everywhere, and I mean, everywhere."

No fair. He knows that I'm a sucker for flowers. "Roses?"

"Thousands of roses, all different colors. And at the other end of the aisle, you'll see a tall man."

"Who's that?" Mama asks laughing.

"Shh," I say, "you're ruining my wedding." Daddy laughs.

Giovanni kneels in front of me, right in front of my mama and daddy! The boy is definitely out his mind . . . but I'm weakening.

"It's me, Renee, and I'm standing there in my father's tuxedo with him at my elbow as my best man. The guitar music stops, and Christina sings 'Ave Maria' so beautifully that everyone cries." He takes my hand. "Even me."

I can't find my voice at first. "That's enough."

"It'll work," Giovanni says.

"The hell it will," Daddy says. "That ain't *no* kind of wedding for my daughter." Giovanni releases my hand and returns to his seat. I feel bad for him, but it was a completely lame idea.

"You can say that again," Mama says. "Wait a minute. What we talkin' 'bout a wedding for? This ain't a done deal yet. What you tryin' to say, Michael?"

Now it's Daddy's turn to squirm. "I, uh, met with Giovanni before coming over here tonight."

"You didn't!" Mama says. She throws her napkin on the table. "What you do a fool thing like that for?"

"To meet him," Daddy says. "No crime in that. And I even had to talk him into coming over here. He wasn't gonna come."

"You really weren't?" I ask Giovanni.

"No." Daa-em. He's hurt my feelings.

Mama jumps up from the table. "Oh, this shit is too much! Michael, you actually approve of what's been goin' on? I mean, this boy got your daughter pregnant!"

"And he wants to do right by her, like I wanted to twenty-six years ago," Daddy says. In the grand scheme of ba-BOOMs, this has to be one of the biggest.

Mama can't speak, though her lips are moving. Eventually she says, "You only saying all this to kiss up to the daughter you abandoned!"

"At your request, Shirl." Daddy's quick with the comebacks. I thought I inherited that ability from Mama.

"You could have stayed!"

"Really?"

"Hell no! I'm just saying you *could* have stayed or at least *tried* to!

217

But no, you just turned your ass around and went back to Greens-boro!"

Giovanni and I have "oh shit!" looks on our faces. And here I thought *we* would be the topic of dinner conversation.

"Shirl, you were very clear about me . . . vanishing. I was to be the absent father so your daughter would pity you for the rest of your life."

The shit's gettin' holy now! I kick Giovanni under the table so he'll pick his jaw up out of his spaghetti bake.

Mama's so furious she can only hum. "Pity *me?*"

"You probably been badmouthing me all these years. No wonder she wants a white boy."

Oh no he didn't! Mama rocks her chair forward. "You're blaming *me* for this? Get out my house, man!"

Daddy doesn't move. "You invited me, and I'm staying this time."

"Like hell you are! Get the hell out my house!"

"That I helped pay for." Holy shit. That explains so much! But why didn't Mama get a better car? Where the money at? Dag, when these bombs gonna stop falling? I want to break this up, but I'm learning so much!

Mama drops her eyes. "Michael, I'm asking you to leave."

"I will when I finish eating. Renee, could you pass me that bottle of wine?"

Mama's eyes tell me not to even think about touching that bottle of wine. "Uh, Daddy, how's the spaghetti bake?"

"Delicious, honey. Now could you pass the wine?"

"I'll get it," Mama says and snatches the bottle, holding it by the neck. Time stands still, and I hold my breath. Mama moves slower than slowly around to Daddy's glass and . . . pours a single drop. "That enough?"

"For now," Daddy says with a little smile. "Thank you, Shirl."

Mama's shoulders sag. I know she was expecting a smart remark. My daddy sure does know my mama.

218

He drinks that single drop, relishing every bit. I almost laugh as he smacks his lips. "Delicious." He holds his glass in the air. "I could use a little more now."

"Get it yourself." Mama sets the bottle down and leaves the room for the kitchen. We hear her slamming pots into the sink. I get up and go into the kitchen to see Mama weeping in front of the sink.

"Mama, please don't cry."

"You see?" she says just above a whisper. "You see what that white boy of yours is causing?"

Say what? "Giovanni isn't causing any of this."

She wipes a tear. "He isn't? Would we be fussin' like this if he wasn't in the picture? Huh? Y'all have ruined everything."

"Ruined what?"

She starts to wipe out a pan. "It was just gonna be the three of us, Renee. We was finally gonna be a family. Then you gotta go out and start one of your own with a white boy. I call that 'ruined.'"

Daa-em. "I didn't know you were planning all this. You didn't tell me."

"I wanted it to be a surprise."

"It still is, Mama. It's a nice surprise."

"Real nice. I'm in here cryin', your father's pissed off, Giovanni . . . I have no idea what Giovanni's thinking. He does think, doesn't he?"

"Yes, Mama." Just not when he's around me.

"And y'all *really* want to get married?"

"Yes."

"What is the rush, child?"

I touch her elbow. "We don't have to rush. I think we can wait."

She turns and looks at me. "How long?"

I gulp. I've said the magic words. "A month, maybe two."

"Make it six, and you'll have my blessing," she says way too quickly.

"I'll be showing at my wedding, Mama. Three months at the most."

"Five. It'll be a June wedding."

"Four. Four months, Mama." I feel like saying "going once, going twice . . ."

She resumes washing the same pan, which is already spotless. "Late May. It'll be pretty then."

"So . . . we can get married in May?"

"Dag, all I said was that it was pretty then," she scowls.

I kiss her cheek. "Thank you, Mama!"

"For what? I still haven't given my approval."

"Yes, you have."

She waves the dripping pan at me. "No, I haven't. This is a— what—a hundred-and-twenty-day trial period. Ain't nothing permanent about it. And I don't want y'all seeing each other for awhile."

Huh? "Why not?"

She drops the pan. "You say y'all love each other, right?" I nod. "Well, I don't believe it, and we gonna test it, see who breaks first."

"How long?"

"Oh, I don't know. How about . . . a hundred and twenty days?"

"Make it ten, Mama."

"You don't think your love is strong enough to last longer?"

She got me. "Okay, thirty."

"I was thinking more like . . . a hundred."

Daa-em. "Mama, that ain't fair."

"You wanna get my blessing?"

"Of course."

"Then you gonna have to take this test. You pass it, you get my blessing. You don't—*and you won't*—and all I get is a grandchild."

"Granddaughter."

"How you know?"

"Pops had a dream."

Mama rolls her eyes. "Tell that old man it's the garlic he eats. He had a dream."

"Can I tell Giovanni?"

Mama laughs. "Girl, you know they been listening. This house can't keep no secrets for very long."

And when I return to the dining room, I know they know. Giovanni and Daddy are cheesing. I lean against the door frame. "You've been eavesdropping."

"Yeah," Giovanni says. "Uh, Mr.—I don't know your last name."

"It's Keeling, but call me Michael." So I would have been Renee Lynette Keeling. That's a lot of E's.

"Uh, I have something important to ask you." Giovanni takes a deep breath. "Mr. Keeling, I'd like to ask for your daughter's hand in marriage."

"What about the rest of her?" Mama yells from the kitchen.

"Oh, uh, the rest of her, too."

Daddy laughs and pats him on the back. "You have my blessing."

Giovanni gulps and fishes in his pocket for . . . oh, it's a fuzzy, black ring box. "Renee, I, uh, have something for you."

I cannot and will not move. Behind me, Mama has dropped a pan. In front of me, Daddy is smiling broadly. And on the floor—kneeling—is Giovanni. And as God in His infinite humor is my witness, the *only* thing going through my head is "there's something wrong with this picture, I need to adjust the contrast button a little, pump up the color some. . . ." But when I look into Giovanni's eyes, I know that there is absolutely nothing wrong with this picture. Nothing.

"Renee Howard, will you be my wife?"

I shake—just a little—and nod.

He opens the ring box and takes out the ring. What the diamond lacks in size it makes up in brilliance. It's a beacon. It isn't all that flashy, it isn't a traffic-stopper, and the folks at Star City may not even notice I'm wearing it at first when I go to work on Monday. But, thank God, it's *mine!* This ring is mine! "Hope it's the right size." He slips it on . . . and it fits. Sort of.

My fingers tremble. "We can get it resized."

He stands, and I break all my rules, kissing him full on the lips as my mama and daddy watch.

And that's how I *really* become engaged.

And that's the last time I kiss Giovanni for twenty-four hundred hours.

Chapter Eight

I haven't been sleeping at all. I toss and turn all night, wondering about all the unknowns coming up. Can we really pull this wedding off in four months? I've been to weddings, up to a year in the making, that were complete disasters. Flowers showed up as late as the vows, ring bearers refused to budge, flower girls threw up on Grandma, the bride herself had to hush whiny children, the best man fainted, somebody started a fight at the reception, the caterer never showed up. Maybe weddings that are overplanned have more disasters.

And I'm worried about Giovanni. I know I shouldn't be, but this "no contact for one-hundred days" thing is scary. And Mama means absolutely no contact. No phone calls, letters, cards, visits—and Giovanni agreed! She even got a Bible out for him to swear on! I'm feeling miserable for weeks, especially since the boy only lives one measly block away from me, until Giovanni finally finds a loophole in Mama's "contract": he sends me flowers. Three roses: one white, one purplish, one golden.

"Only three?" Mama asked the first time. "He cheap, Renee. And he only got one of the colors right. You ain't purple, and his kinda white ain't this dark. And he better not have put anything on the card."

"He didn't, Mama." I showed the blank card to her. "But I know what it says."

Sometimes he'd send them to work, sometimes to my house, and once the weather turned springlike, I was finding them under the windshield wipers on my Jetta. I wanted so badly to thank him . . . and that's where Collette came in.

"Girl, I need your help."

Collette was reluctant at first. "No," she said. "I don't ever aim to piss Shirl off."

"You won't, if you don't get caught."

So, for one hundred days, Giovanni and I talk through Collette. At first, it was romantic. "That boy misses you *so* much," Collette would tell me. "I never seen a boy so passionate like that. Makes me wanna cry sometimes."

"Me too."

"And you know what he told me to do? This'll trip you out. He wants me to give you a hug and a kiss from him."

"So hug and kiss me then."

"I will not, 'cause that ain't all! He also wants me to give Janae a hug and a kiss. I mean, what would people say if I did that shit?"

Nights are the loneliest. Work during the week and getting to know Daddy on weekends (talking until all hours of the night, shopping, taking drives on the Blue Ridge Parkway, going for walks around Old Southwest) keep me pretty busy, but the nights are cold. And Mama ain't no kind of help. I think she purposely stays away from the house so I'll be lonelier. Sometimes I imagine that she's parked in her Buick farther up on Allison Avenue just waiting for me to bust out the house and run to Luchesi's.

But a deal's a deal, and though recently Giovanni (through Collette) isn't as passionate, I know he still loves me.

"Dag, girl," Collette tells me today while we eat at Boomer's. "If you don't marry him, I might."

"He been flirtin' with you?"

"No. It's just, well, when he talks to me, he isn't talking to me, you know? It's like you're sitting there. I feel . . . no, I shouldn't say that."

"What?"

"I feel . . . special, Renee. I mean, Clyde is nice, but he don't share much with me. This boy shared some shit with me last night."

"What?"

"It's a bit twisted. It's about his family."

"Tell me."

She checks her watch. "I can't tell it like him. Boy kept breaking into Italian. And I may not have time to finish it."

I put down my sandwich. "How long were you there last night?"

She took a long sip of her iced tea. "Not long." I stare her down. "Okay. Don't get mad. It was a little after midnight is all—"

"Midnight?"

"He had a lot to tell me. Dag, I won't do this no more if you gonna—"

"No, no. I'm sorry. This shit just isn't fair. I'm sorry. Go on."

"Okay. First, he listened to what you told me to say about Janae and your morning sickness. He says it isn't fair that she's *his* daughter when she makes you puke."

"She shits for him, she poo-poos pretty for me. That's the way it's gonna be."

"That ain't fair, girl."

"Sure it is. I have to put up with her shit inside me for nine months. He gets her the rest of her life on the outside. What else he say?"

"Some weird shit first, like how y'all are going to have eighteen thousand breakfasts together, something like that."

"You told him that he's doing the cooking, right?"

"He said you were a wonderful cook."

"That wasn't the point of the question. What'd he say about doing all the dishes?"

"He thinks you're kidding."

"Tell him next time that I'm not." I check my watch. "Look, we only have thirty minutes."

"Okay. I hope I can remember it all. He says there may be a minor little problem about the wedding."

"Well, if it's minor, why bring it up?"

"That's what I said, then he tells me some serious shit that ain't so minor."

My stomach turns over. "Like what?"

"You know Christina and Alexis will be coming, right?" I nod. "Well, it seems that Pops ain't too happy about that."

"He'll get over it," I say.

"I doubt it. Listen to this: his mama was diagnosed with breast cancer when he was twelve."

"But she died when he was—daa-em, three years of that?"

"Yeah. He said it wasn't so bad the first two years, but when he was fourteen, the doctors found a malignancy, said it was terminal. Pops refused to believe it, and Giovanni's mama acted like she didn't believe it for his sake. Christina was a senior in high school and was planning to go to Columbia. Uncle Johnny helped them as best he could—"

"Who's Uncle Johnny?"

"He's the rich Luchesi." There is one? "Anyway, they couldn't pay all Mama's bills *and* send Christina to college."

"Tough break." I would have been royally pissed. I'm lucky Mama started saving the day I was born.

"Oh, Christina wasn't worried. She got accepted to N-Y-U and had a part-time job."

"That family sure likes to work."

"Would you quit interrupting?"

"Sorry."

"Anyway, Christina visited Giovanni's mama every day after school all that year while Pops, Uncle Johnny, and Giovanni ran the first Luchesi's. And then, it was time for the prom. Christina wanted to go, but Pops said they couldn't afford it. Your man gave Christina his tip money for her dress *and* for Alexis's dress."

"That was sweet of him."

Collette shakes her head. "No it wasn't. All the shit hit the fan on prom night. Giovanni sneaked off from work to take their picture, his daddy followed him, and then all hell broke loose. I'll try to tell you this like Giovanni did. Scared the pee out of me."

It's doing a good job on me, too.

"Pops slams through the door and yells, 'I tell you not to go dancing!' Before Christina can go off, Giovanni tells Pops that he bought the material for the dresses. 'Dresses?' he asks. 'Why you need two?' Christina explains that she had extra material so she made Alexis one. Giovanni thought Pops would give her a kiss and that would be that. But that didn't happen. Pops sat in a chair by the door, said, 'I wait for your date. I wait to see if he is worthy of you.'"

"Oh shit."

"'Oh shit' is right. Giovanni tried to get Pops to leave, but he wouldn't leave. That's when Christina told him the truth. 'Alexis is my date,' she said. Pops says something like, 'Why you not tell me you couldn't get a date, Christina? I would understand.' Pops gave her a kiss and started to leave. But Christina, she says 'No.'"

I close my eyes. "She told him Alexis was her date. She told him she was a lesbian."

"Uh-huh. And Pops blamed Giovanni."

"Why?"

"Girl, I don't pretend to understand the logic. Pops said if Giovanni hadn't given her the money . . ." Collette shrugs.

"His sister wouldn't have been a lesbian? That is completely twisted." Giovanni's family should go on *The Jerry Springer Show*.

"Wait till you hear this. Pops threw Christina out the house over that."

"He didn't!"

227

Collette raises her hand. "Swear to God. Hasn't spoken to her in over to ten years."

"Daa-em."

"And this is where your man made me cry." She turns away. "Why I wish sometimes I wasn't doing this. I know too much shit I don't want to know. I better be your damn maid of honor for this, ho."

"You will be, Collette."

"Promise?"

"Yes."

She turns back and wipes a tear. "Christina killed Giovanni's mama."

"*What?*" The customers around us stare at me. I stare back until they turn away.

"It ain't like that, Renee."

"Why you say it like that then?"

Collette sighs. "Just listen. Christina moved in with Alexis's family, and the day before graduation, she told Giovanni that his mama wanted to see him."

"She was awake?"

"No. She was still in a coma and couldn't talk."

"Then why—oh."

"Giovanni says he kissed his mama one more time, then . . ."

"Daa-em." I can understand why Christina did what she did, but I doubt I can do it for my own mama. I believe there's always hope. But if my mama was in a lot of pain, and she asked me . . . I hope I never have to answer that question.

"There's only a little more to tell. Christina came to the funeral, but she stood way off because she didn't want a scene with Pops. Pops didn't even notice she was there. Then—and this is what makes Giovanni so mad—then Pops only cried one tear and was back at work the next day."

"Maybe that's how he works it out."

"Maybe. But your boy has never forgiven him for not crying more." She checks her watch. "We better go."

In the car, I ask her, "Did you ask him how he came to Roanoke in the first place?"

"Now *this* is some funny shit. They moved here because Roanoke was named an all-American city."

"No way!" That bullshit award actually serves a purpose?

"Giovanni said his neighborhood up there was gettin' gang-infested."

"And he came here?"

"Yeah." We're back at Star City. "Oh, before I forget. Christina did graduate college, worked her own ass through, and now she and Alexis are making dresses and selling them to Broadway actresses— and even an actor or two."

"I believe it. And all this was just a minor problem. I hope we never have a major problem."

Collette chuckles. "I asked the same thing. I'm becoming more and more like you every day."

"You can always use some improvement."

"Hmmph. Anyway, he says if there's ever a major problem, he will shout in Italian, throw things, and make passionate love to you afterward."

"We'll just skip the first two and go directly to the third."

"Y'all gonna be arguin' all the time when the hundred days is up, huh?"

"Morning, noon, and night."

On the ninety-ninth day, I start to get nervous . . . and I run out of places for all of the flowers Giovanni has sent me. I should have more, but I didn't get any flowers yesterday. I think someone at work stole them. I've been keeping them alive in vases all over the house. The first ones are shriveling, but I refuse to throw them away.

"Dag, girl, *please* start throwing these things out," Mama says. "They startin' to stink. We drawin' bugs in from outside."

I rearrange the bouquet on the kitchen table. "I will, Mama. Tomorrow." I smile at the calendar on the refrigerator. "My sentence will be up."

Mama sits at the table sipping some coffee. "Tomorrow's only day one hundred. You mean the day *after* tomorrow."

"What?"

"Today is ninety-nine, tomorrow is one hundred. I said you could see him *after* one hundred days."

I kick myself because she's right as usual. "Oh, come on, Mama. What's a day?"

"It's twenty-four hours. Lots of shit can happen in twenty-four hours, right?"

"What's that supposed to mean?"

"Well, y'all got this shit started in less than twenty-four hours, right? Just think what a whole day could do."

I take a very deep breath. She's been this way for the past few weeks, rarely leaving the house when I'm home. "You didn't think we'd make it this far, did you?"

"I *still* don't think you're gonna make it, girl. I mean, if what I saw the other night in front of Luchesi's is any indication, you ain't gonna make it."

She's getting to me. I don't want to ask. I know she's lying, but . . . I sit across from her. "What'd you see, Mama?"

She shrugs. "Nothin'. My eyes are gettin' bad. I didn't see anything."

She knows exactly what buttons to push. "Well, what do you *think* you saw?"

"Now what is that white girl's name? No, wait. It'll come to me."

I stand and stretch my back. "You're tellin' me another story, Mama."

"You'll never know. I think your white boy been busy."

"What's her name, then?" She's been calling Julie "the white girl" for the past ninety-nine days. Some days she guesses and says "Jennifer" or "Mary."

"Oh. I just remembered. It's Julie. Julie Drake."

I don't panic. "It took you nearly a hundred days to find that out, Mama. Congratulations. But it don't prove nothin'."

"You're right. It don't. But when Julie told me where she worked—"

I sit down quick. "You talked to Julie?"

"Did I say we talked? I did, didn't I? I meant to say that we had lunch. Yesterday, as a matter of fact. Julie was positively glowing."

I squint at her, but she's giving nothing away with her eyes. "Where she work?"

"Stritesky's. That's a florist, ain't it?" Giovanni has been using Stritesky's. Mama checks her watch. "Hmm, your delivery's late today. Wonder why?"

I hesitate. "It's been late before."

"It has, hasn't it, but not this late. Hmm. Usually arrives by noon on Saturday, right? What time is it now? Gettin' close to four. Nice, warm spring day. Oh, and you didn't get any flowers yesterday, did you? Hmm." I jump up and dial information, but Mama zips over and hangs it up. "Who you callin'?"

"Stritesky's."

"Thought you might." She dials the number for me. "Just ask for Julie."

"Stritesky's," a voice says.

"Yes, I'd like to speak to Julie Drake, please."

"Julie's out on a delivery. Can I take a message?"

I hang up. "She's out on a delivery."

Mama smiles. "Is *that* what they call it?"

I dial Luchesi's and hand the phone to Mama. "Ask for Pops. I can talk to him, right?"

Mama shrugs and takes the phone. "Hello, Mr. Luchesi. This is Shirley Howard. How you doin'?" I try to grab the phone. "Someone wants to speak to you."

I snatch the phone. "Mr. Luchesi?"

"Renee! How good it is to hear your voice."

Yeah, yeah, yeah. "Where's Giovanni?"

"You are allowed to speak to him now?"

"No. I just want to know where he *is* right now."

"Oh. Well, I don't know. He's supposed to be here by now."

"Where'd he go?"

He pauses. "If I knew, I would tell you. He got in the car and left."

"When?"

"Eleven, eleven-thirty. Big smile on his face. Maybe he is planning something wonderful for you."

Mama returns to the kitchen table and sips some more coffee. "Ask him about Julie."

"Oh, yeah. Has Julie Drake been around?"

"Julie? Oh yes, every day. Like clockwork. Always at eleven. She is so punctual. Why do you ask?"

"No reason." The rat!

"Giovanni will be back in time for the dinner rush, I'm sure. He's never been late for that, though recently . . . Do you want me to tell him you called?"

"No. I gotta go." I hang up.

"Well?"

Mama's way too confident about this, so I shouldn't trust what I think is going on. But it sounds like Giovanni is messing around. Sowin' some oats, boy? We'll see about that. "We're going to Luchesi's for dinner tonight."

"We are?"

"Yes."

"But, if you see or speak to him—"

I grit my teeth. "I won't see or speak to him, Mama."

"Huh?"

"I'm only going there to be seen."

"Why I gotta go?"

"So you can make sure I don't kill him." Or Droolie.

She stands. "I'll go change. When we goin'?"

"Six."

Two hours later I practically sprint to Luchesi's, Mama falling way behind. I bust through the door . . . and see R. J. sitting at "our" table. I turn . . . and I *don't* see Mama.

I've been set up. Mama's still tryin' to hook me up with R. J. I have to straighten this shit once and for all.

Pops waddles up to me. "Renee, so good to see you. And how is Janae?"

"Fine." R. J. stands and motions to the chair opposite him.

"I didn't expect to see you here for two days. What a nice surprise!" He steps closer. "Sorry your table is not available," he whispers. "He insisted that he sit there."

Figures. "Where's Giovanni?"

"Oh, he just called. He and Julie had some car trouble."

"Julie?"

"Did I say Julie? Wonder why I said that. I'm sure he'll be here shortly. May I offer you another seat?"

"No, thanks," I say, and I walk over to R. J.'s table and sit in a chair facing the front door.

"You look wonderful, Renee."

"I know."

He sits opposite me. "It's been so long—"

I hold up a hand. "Cut the shit, R. J. My mama set this up, and I ain't interested in your bullshit."

He slumps and sets his jaw, grinding his teeth. Always hated that. "Why you come over here, then? And where's your man?"

"We should know that shortly."

Pops appears. "What can I get you?"

"You in on this, too?" I ask.

"In on what?" Pops is a terrible actor.

"Don't give me that." I feel like crying. "Pops, I'm carrying your son's child. Why you and Mama gotta try to break us up like this?"

Pops doesn't look at me. "I'll bring you some bread sticks," he says, and he leaves just as I hear the back door open and close.

"Sorry I'm late, Pops," I hear Giovanni say. "Julie's car had a flat." Then I hear water running in the big sink.

So it's true. Shitshitshit. I stare hard at R. J. "Don't read anything into this, okay?" I grab his hand and turn it over, putting my tiny hand in his huge one. "Nothin' will ever happen again between us."

He squeezes my hand. "Maybe I can change your mind."

"Puh-lease."

Then Giovanni zips by and takes an order at a table near the front door. He didn't even notice me. Boy looks like he lost weight, and he needs another haircut. He finishes the order and takes two steps . . . and finally sees me. He blinks. His eyes leave mine and focus on R. J.'s hand holding . . . daa-em, my left hand, the one with the engagement ring. I try to pull my hand away, but R. J.'s grip is too strong.

Giovanni steps closer, and I see a smudge of grease on his forehead. Shit, he *was* changing a tire. Boy never looks in a mirror. He stops at our table, tapping his order book on the table. "How . . . how is everything?"

I try again to pull away from R. J. "Hold still, girl," he says. "I want to look at the ring your man got you." He reaches his free hand out to Giovanni. "Name's R. J. You Giovanni?"

"Yeah." They shake hands. I thought I'd never see the day.

R. J. lets go with his other hand, and I hide my hand in my lap. "You got good taste, man." He reaches into his suit jacket (he always did overdress) and pulls out a fuzzy, black ring box. "Want to see what I'm giving *my* girl?" He doesn't wait for an answer and opens the box . . . and there's the twist tie I keep on my dresser. What the hell's going on? R. J. removes the twist tie, holds it up, then hands it to Giovanni. "Happy engagement, man." Giovanni doesn't move, the twist tie just lying in his hand. "Go on, put it on her. It was made for her."

Then the scratchy sound of a record crackles from the speakers, and "Ave Maria" begins to play.

R. J. stands. "I think I'm sitting in your seat, Giovanni." I have never looked so wide-eyed at a man in my life. As Giovanni sits, R. J. smiles and reaches into his suit jacket again, this time removing a wedding band and sliding it onto his ring finger. I mouth "Dagney?" to him, and he nods and shrugs. "I wish you both the best," he says with a slight bow. Daa-em, R. J. has manners after all.

When R. J. moves aside, Julie appears, her hands behind her back. "Hi, Renee. Sorry about keeping Giovanni away from you." Say what? "That didn't come out right. I mean, I'm sorry, Renee, and you, too, Giovanni, for the flat tire. It was your mama's idea, Renee. All I did was let some air out of a tire. Oh, and I've really enjoyed delivering all those flowers to you." She slides an arm out and hands me a bouquet of roses. "This is for yesterday, today, and tomorrow. And, I wish you two all the best for yesterday, today, and tomorrow."

"Thank you," I say. And I'm *really* touched.

Giovanni still hasn't moved or spoken. I kick him under the table. "Yeah, thank you, Julie."

"Bye. Make sure you invite me to the wedding." Then Julie leaves as "Ave Maria" ends and Pops, Mama, and Daddy stroll over. They need a bell on that front door. Sneaky people shouldn't be able to sneak in so easily. Luchesi's is suddenly standing room only, and there's Collette and Clyde near the door.

And then I hear the dinging of glasses. Lots of glasses. The dinging stops. No one is making a sound.

"Ladies and gentlemen!" Pops shouts. "Thank you for coming to the engagement party of my son, Giovanni, and my future daughter, Renee. Ninety-nine days ago, Renee got stuck here, just like tonight." Some nice laughter. "One thing leads to another, and Renee and Giovanni fall in love. In twenty days, they marry... somewhere." He winks at me. "And the reception will be held here at Luchesi's. But tonight, we embarrass them, yes?" Thunderous laughter and applause. "So a toast!" A hundred glasses rise. "To Renee and Giovanni! Happy engagement!"

Giovanni finally finds his voice. "Did you know about this?" he asks me.

"Giovanni, I had no idea." I mouth "thank you" to Mama, and she mouths "gotcha!" I hear that clinking sound again, and all eyes are on us. "They don't expect us to kiss, do they?"

"Renee, if we don't kiss, we'll have a lot of glass to clean up." He slides the twist tie onto my finger. "Will you still marry me?"

"Yes, but don't kiss me, please, not in front of all these—"

And then, bammo, he holds my face and kisses me until my toes curl. The noise is window-shattering. "Thank you," he says.

When the noise dies down, I hear Mama say, "Y'all can do better than that!"

Giovanni smiles and pulls me to my feet. "How about an encore?"

I take a deep breath . . . and kiss the living shit out of him in the exact spot where we first kissed.

After that? I float. I thank people. I hug everybody, especially Pops. Mama's pretty transparent in her sneakiness, but Pops? He has to be the sneakiest man alive. My people respect sneakiness in a person. Maybe the Italians migrated from Africa. It is, after all, only a hop, skip, and an elephant ride over the Mediterranean.

The party starts breaking up at eleven, and instead of leaving, many people stay to help clean up. That rarely happens at a black-folks party. Folks will stay after, but only to make a few plates to take home.

Meanwhile, I count up all the "tip money" that Pops says is our engagement present.

"How much?" Giovanni asks.

"Almost fifteen hundred dollars."

He hugs me close to him. "Sounds like spending money for our honeymoon."

236

"Yeah." But one-third of that money goes to the City of Roanoke. I still haven't paid that bullshit ticket, and it's way past due.

"You look tired. May I carry you home?"

"Would you?"

"Sure. Let me tell Pops."

I bundle up and have a few more folks admire my ring *and* the twist tie. Mama and Daddy see me last. "You goin' home?" Mama asks.

"Yeah."

"Don't stay up too late. We all goin' to church tomorrow." Daddy whispers something in Mama's ear. "Oh. Maybe not."

They are so cute! "Where are you two going?"

Daddy shrugs. "I think we'll get some pie at Gary's Little Chef, maybe see the sunrise on Mill Mountain."

"Is *that* what they call it?" I say to Mama, and she cracks up. "Have fun."

Daddy and Mama kiss either side of my face at the same time. I wish I had a camera. Then they leave.

"Ready?" Giovanni asks.

"Are you? I've gained some weight since January."

"I'll manage."

When we step out of Luchesi's, I climb onto his back. "Why you so skinny?"

"Nervous, I guess."

"Well, please don't drop us. I don't want my child to have three ears or seven toes because you were clumsy." We make it, with some difficulty, and I announce, "You're staying the night" once we are inside.

"I am?"

"Yes. I've missed you. But first"—I sniff him—"you need a shower. You are not coming into my bed funky."

He sniffs my neck. "You're pretty ripe yourself."

"Then, let's go get un-ripened."

* * *

237

When I get up to heaven, I'm going to ask God how He made it possible that two people, completely exhausted after a busy day, can make love to each other with such passion. It doesn't make any sense. Maybe love never gets tired.

"Daa-em, Giovanni," I moan. "We gotta stop."

He nibbles my ear and runs his tongue down my back. "No."

"I can't believe you're saying 'No' to me."

"Get used to it. I don't want to stop."

I groan and say, "Then don't. Don't ever stop. . . ."

I look at the clock an hour later: 2:15. "Giovanni?"

"What?"

"We better stop."

He comes up for air and says, "See you in the morning?"

I burrow my head into his chest. "Nicest words anyone ever said to me. Now leave me alone, Mr. Man."

Giovanni, wearing only his underwear, is up first the next morning and goes to the bathroom. I hear Mama creeping down the hallway and sit up in bed. This should be good.

"Good morning," she says. "Busy night?"

Silence. "Uh, um, I didn't know you were, I thought you were—"

"Come on down; I'll fix you some coffee. Looks like you gonna need it."

"Uh, thanks."

"Nice ass," Mama says, and she creaks down the stairs.

When Giovanni comes in, I shut my eyes and pretend I'm asleep. As soon as he's dressed, I slip on a robe and sit at the top of the stairs, where I can hear everything going on in the kitchen. A second later, Daddy joins me in his pajamas and robe. "Shh," he says and puts his arm around me.

"Liked you better the other way," Mama says. Giovanni says nothing. "What are your plans for my daughter?"

"Plans?"

"I don't stutter. You've had one hundred days to plan something. Now what are your plans?"

Giovanni clears his throat. "I guess we'll look for a house after the honeymoon."

"Where you going?"

"I really don't know. Maui maybe." Yes!

Mama laughs. "You ain't supposed to tell anybody, boy."

"Sorry."

"So what kind of house will she and my grandchild be living in?"

"Renee's convinced it will be a granddaughter."

"So I've heard. Now answer the damn question." Never make conversation with my mama when she's asking questions.

"Well, I have enough money to put twenty percent down on a three-bedroom, two-bath with a nice yard." Where'd he get that kind of money? He ain't in the Mafia.

"Really?" He's impressed her. "That's some serious money."

Giovanni doesn't speak for a few moments. "It's money from my mama's life insurance. It ought to be more than enough."

Mama's a little speechless, too. "Uh, y'all gonna live nearby? If I know Renee, she won't want to move too far away."

"We haven't even discussed this," I whisper to Daddy.

"It'll be up to her," Giovanni says. "I'm flexible."

She laughs. "I'll bet. You can live here till you find a place. But tell me, what religion will my granddaughter be?"

"Whatever Janae decides."

Say what? "You're going to let a child choose her own religion?" That's right, Mama. Set him straight.

"Yes, ma'am."

"Never heard of that. What are you anyway?"

"I'm a Catholic Jew."

"Is that possible?"

"You're Baptist, right?"

"Yeah."

"And you read from both Old and New Testaments?"

"Sure."

"So do I."

Mama laughs. "Renee tells me you have an answer for everything. But why didn't you go to college?"

"Family first."

"You mean the restaurant?"

"The two are the same in my family. The family runs the restaurant, and the restaurant runs the family."

"You ever expect Renee to work there?"

"It's up to her."

Mama laughs. "Are you going to make *any* decisions in this marriage?"

"Probably not." I laugh to myself. You got that right, Mr. Man.

"Well, you may have to put your foot down every now and then. Renee's pretty spoiled, you know. But that's my fault, so you take it up with me."

"I'm not that spoiled," I whisper to Daddy.

"Yeah you are," Daddy whispers back. "And I've loved every minute of it."

"But let me warn you, boy," Mama says with an attitude. "If you hit her, hurt her, make her cry, or curse her, I will take you out!" Mama isn't kidding about that. "Drink your coffee, boy, it's getting cold."

I can hear Giovanni gulp the rest of his coffee. "I should be going."

"Please kiss her good-bye before you go. I don't want her moping 'cause she didn't get her 'good-morning' kiss. She's liable to be a pain in the ass all day today as it is."

Daddy and I dash back to our beds and slide under the covers. Giovanni kisses me gently on the forehead, nose, and lips, and slips out without a sound. I can definitely get used to that every morning.

As soon as he is down the stairs, I open my door and hear Mama say, "That was quick."

"Didn't want to wake her."

"She wasn't asleep, Giovanni." Mama! Don't ruin it! "And neither was her father."

"No, I think she was asleep."

"Right. Bye, Giovanni. We'll keep this conversation our little secret, okay? I wouldn't want to worry Renee."

I'm feeling good about myself, just tripping around my room, watching Giovanni walk home, when Janae decides to wake up. I run out of my room as Mama's coming up the stairs and barely make it to the toilet in time.

When I return to my room, she's making my bed. "I can do that," I say.

"You brush your teeth?"

"Yes."

"Okay. You can help. Get the other side."

I take my side of the sheet. "Does this mean I can't sleep all day?"

"It does." She tucks her side under, and I do the same.

"Uh, where's Giovanni?"

"Don't give me that. You were listening. And so was that man."

I roll my eyes. "Yeah."

"You really love Giovanni, don't you?"

We tighten the comforter and lay it flat. "You know I do, Mama. I waited for him for a hundred days."

"Ninety-nine, and that ain't nothin'. I waited twenty-six *years* for your father."

"You didn't have to," I say.

"Yeah, I did. I had to be sure of him." Huh? "Some men you can be sure of in, oh, a few days." I roll my eyes. "Your father took longer."

"You thinkin' 'bout maybe marrying him, Mama?" Hopehopehope.

"Hell no. The man snores too damn loud."

"Mama!" I change to a whisper. "He can hear you."

"I know he can. And I want him to know that he snores too damn loud. Thought the windows would break or something."

"Get earplugs."

"Girl, it's like an earthquake in there. Earplugs won't help. Does Giovanni snore?"

I shake my head. "He, uh, smacks his lips every once in a while."

Mama winces. "That shit would drive me crazy. Anyway, I *know* you love him. You'd have to, the way he looks in his draws. Lord have mercy!"

"He doesn't look that bad."

She tosses a pillow on one side of the bed. "He's kind of scrawny with them bird legs. But, he does have a nice ass. I do respect that." My pillow hits her squarely in the face. She ignores it. "Your breakfast will begin as soon as you take a shower."

Showered, lotioned, dressed but still groggy, I enter the kitchen and smell something I haven't smelled in years. "Oatmeal?"

Mama doesn't reply. I slip into a chair opposite Daddy. She slides a bowl of goo in front of me, a plate of bacon, eggs, and toast in front of him. "Eat," she says.

I try to steal Daddy's plate, but he pulls it away, waving his fork at me.

"Oatmeal. Yuck." But the first bite tastes okay. "What's in this?"

"Brown sugar."

The second, third, and fourth bites fly by. As soon as my bowl is empty, she dumps another mound of goo. "Could I have some butter, too?"

"Bad for the baby," she says, and handing me a glass of milk. "Daa-em, girl, it ain't that good."

"It is." For some reason, oatmeal is the shit this morning.

The phone rings, and Mama answers. "Hello, Collette," she says. I stuff another mound of oatmeal into my mouth and reach out a hand. "Yeah, she's up. To about a hundred and ninety pounds." I make a face. "Huh? Big news? Well, you can tell me." That did it. I swallow and stand. "Really? Well, I'll tell her." She makes like she's hanging up then hands me the phone.

"What did you tell Mama, Collette?"

"Nothing, nothing," Collette says. "Your Mama trippin'. Just wondering if you'd like some company this morning."

"That's not big news."

"Forget you, then." I hear a click.

"Collette? Collette?"

"What?"

"Don't do that. Yes, I'd like some company this morning." I catch Mama's eye. "Mama's already driving me crazy."

"Good. I'll be there as soon as I can. Oh, one more thing. I have something very gold, very circular, and very diamond-like to show you."

"You're engaged?" Mama comes to the phone and sticks her ear near the earphone.

"I'll tell you all about it, though there ain't much to tell. See you soon."

I hang up. "Collette's engaged!"

"It's about time," Mama says. "You finished?"

"Yeah."

"Good. Now go up and rest on your bed. I'll send Collette up when she gets here."

"But, Mama—"

"Go."

Wake up, throw up, eat, rest. Why do I feel like I'm binging?

I flip on my stereo and choose an Anita Baker CD, plug in the headphones, and listen for awhile. Then I slide the headphones over my stomach. Maybe it'll calm Janae down long enough to digest my oatmeal. I turn up the bass, and I feel a nice vibration. If Anita can do this, what can DJ Kool do? I don't get the chance to find out, because Collette has made unbelievably good time.

"Where you coming from?" I ask her from the top of the stairs.

"Your man," she says, walking down the hall into the kitchen. "Morning, Shirl. Oooh, is there enough oatmeal for little ol' me?"

I race down the stairs and stand in the kitchen doorway. "Collette!"

"Put them daggers away, girl. I called from Luchesi's. Thank you, Shirl." Collette takes a spoonful of oatmeal. "Hmm. Brown sugar."

"And what were you doing—"

"Let her eat, child," Mama says, handing my bowl to Daddy to rinse.

"It's okay," Collette says. "I stopped by to drop off Clyde's and my gift to y'all. Is that all right?"

I sit next to her and smile. "What is it?"

"You'll see it later. Pops is letting me have *my* engagement party there tonight."

"Tell me now!" Both women look at me, then Collette resumes eating, and Mama hands another dish to Daddy. I hate this secrecy shit. "If I guess what it is, will you tell me?" The way Mama's looking away, I know she knows what it is.

"If you guess what it is, I will be amazed," Collette says. "In fact, I will be right astonished, won't I, Shirl?"

"You know, Mama?"

"I know everything, baby. Remember?"

"Do you know, Daddy?"

"I know nothing," he says. "I just work here."

If Collette had to drop it off, then it has to be big. "Did Giovanni help unload it?"

"Yeah." Collette stuffs a huge spoonful into her mouth.

"So he knows what it is!"

Collette and Mama exchange looks. "I doubt it," Collette says. Mama brings her a cup of coffee. "Oh, and you only get one guess. I ain't hearin' this all day, okay?"

"Okay." Heavy. Giovanni doesn't know what it is. That doesn't narrow it down a bit. "I need some time to think." I sneak up the stairs and dial Luchesi's. "Giovanni?"

"Pops."

"Is Giovanni there?"

"He's in the shower."

Good. "Well, maybe you can help me. Collette unloaded a—"

"Dog."

"A . . . dog?"

"A dog. Pee everywhere. Gift that keeps on giving."

He doesn't sound pleased. "Oh. Um, do you know what kind of dog it is?"

"He's big, that's all I can say. And you want a name, I name him Stinky. You want me to give Giovanni a message?"

"No. Thank you."

A big, stinky, male puppy dog. I always wanted a puppy, but Mama wasn't big on pets. I hope it's not a pit bull or a rottweiler. Those dogs scare the shit out of me. German shepherds aren't that much better. Was Lassie a big dog? As long as it ain't Marmaduke . . .

I return to the kitchen, where Collette and Mama are drinking coffee. "It's a dog," I announce.

"Nope," Collette says.

"Yes it is! I just talked to Pops—"

"Who told you what I told him to tell you. 'The gift that keeps on giving,' right?" The sneaky, devious rats. "Give it up, Renee. Please! There are more important things to talk about, like this ring that's been on my finger since I came through that door that you ain't said shit about!"

I had completely forgotten. "Oh, I'm sorry, Collette."

"No," she says, covering her hand, "no, you just go on with your bad self, and I'll sit here and cry."

"Collette, I'm—"

"Apology accepted. Take a look at this!" It's beautiful, and gaudy, and definitely says "Collette." Big diamond, side rubies, shiny white gold. "Clyde wasn't any help. I had to pick it out by myself."

"What you complainin' for?" Mama says. "Least you got one." Daddy makes a face behind Mama, and I laugh. "What's up with that, Mr. Man? You gonna do right by me? We got us a child."

And that's Collette's and my cue to sneak upstairs. After a door slams, Mama joins us. "Where'd he go?"

"I hope to a jewelry store," Mama says.

"Really?"

"No. I think your daddy and I are way past that."

Whenever the three of us are together doing anything—playing cards, shopping, eating out—we have to fuss. It's what we do. It defines us. And when we are in my room planning the wedding, we fuss over the order of the service. Mama and Collette argue over who should be maid of honor. Collette says it should be her because she's the youngest. "Whoever heard of a forty-eight-year-old maid of honor? Besides, Renee already promised me I could be maid of honor." Mama says it should be her because "there ain't a rule about how old a maid is!"

"Mama, you and Daddy are escorting me down the aisle. You can't be maid of honor."

That doesn't settle it, so I leave them to fuss and dial Luchesi's. Giovanni answers. "Do you know what's in the crate Collette brought?"

"No. What could it be?"

He knows. He can't lie to me. "You know, don't you?"

"I have an idea."

"Well?"

"I'd rather not spoil the surprise. Oh, Pops needs your help planning the cake."

"Wonderful."

He laughs. "I'm not going to tell you what I think it is, Renee."

"Would you tell Janae?"

"No."

"Liar. Well, I don't want to know, and you're probably wrong anyway." Will reverse psychology work on him?

"I probably am." Nope. "When y'all coming for this shindig tonight?"

"'Shindig'? Dag, boy, speak English. You close at eight, right?"

"Right."

"I guess eight then, damn."

"Are you mad at me?"

"No. But I may have to kill Mama and Collette. Talk to you later."

I return to my room. "So who's maid of honor?"

"Collette," Mama says wearily, and she hands me a piece of paper. "These are some ideas."

"Most of them are mine," Collette says.

"I can tell. You wanna sing Michael Jackson's 'Black or White' at my wedding? That's tacky!"

"If we give out the words on little black-and-white napkins to all the white people and sing it real slow, it might not sound half bad," she says.

I shred that piece of paper, grab a clean sheet, and begin writing. Collette groans, but I freeze her with my best "don't-you-say-another-word" stare. She gets the message.

In a few minutes, my wedding is complete:

Prelude:	*Alexis*
Solo:	*"The Lord's Prayer"*
	Collette
Candle lighting:	*Daddy and Clyde*
Duet:	*"Always"*
	Collette/Mama
Processional:	*Alexis*
Invitation to	
Marriage:	*Father Mike and Rev. Noel*
Solo:	*"Ave Maria"*
	Christina
The Vows:	*Bride and Groom*

The Ring:	*Bride and Groom*
The Kiss:	*Bride and Groom*
Recessional:	*Alexis*
NOTE:	*Clyde escorts Big Mouth in for solo; Michael escorts Mama for duet; both Big Teeth and Mama escorted out to get me; Clyde goes to front to be with Giovanni/Pops; Mama and Daddy escort me in, Big Hair following a long, long, long way back—near the door if possible—AFTER we are presented . . . everybody party!*

I leave the order of my wedding on my bed and go downstairs for some Swiss Miss. When I return, they're still looking at the paper, though a few lines have been crossed out.

"Child, I haven't sung in public since I was twelve!" Mama cries.

"Mama, you have a beautiful voice. Everybody knows it. Besides, Collette gonna drown your ass out anyway, so—"

"I will not!" Collette yells.

"But I don't even know the words!" Mama yells even louder.

"Collette can just write the words down on some black-and-white napkins and sing real slow!"

Both of them crack up. "If it comes to that, we will write 'em down on napkins," Mama says.

"Don't worry, Shirl. We'll do it *a cappella* with a whole lot of bump. But shouldn't we be singing 'Suddenly' for these two?"

"And what we gonna sing at your wedding, Collette?" I crack. "Whenever that is. We ought to sing 'Someday We'll Be To-gether'!"

"Ha-ha. But what's this?" Collette points to Christina's song.

"I heard it once and liked it. Giovanni says she can sing like an angel."

"Is Alexis another one of his sisters?" Mama asks.

I hadn't told Mama yet, and I don't plan to. She's nosy enough to be able to figure it out for herself. "Just a good friend of Christina's who plays a guitar."

Mama says something about how it would be wrong to play a guitar instead of an organ at a wedding at a Holiness church, and Collette says, "We havin' a hoe-down."

"And what's up with a priest?" Mama asks.

"He's an old family friend, Mama. How bad can it be?"

"First a guitar at High Holiness, and now a priest," Mama says. "Honey, I want to be able to show my face there again."

"It's my wedding. And it'll be beautiful, really beautiful."

I spend most of Collette and Clyde's engagement party trying to figure out my present. It's all boarded up, about the size of a stove. What a . . . stupid gift to give a man who runs a bakery. It couldn't be a stove.

We play spades for a little while and eventually switch to penny poker. Giovanni and Daddy are sharks and clean everybody out, leaving just the two of them with a huge pile of change between them.

"One hand for the pot," Giovanni says. "Name your game."

Daddy hands the deck to me. "Stud."

"Where?" Mama says. "I don't see one." Mama's drunk on Camaros.

"Shuffle 'em good, girl, and deal 'em out one at a time, face-up," Daddy says, a little slurred. He been hittin' the Chianti hard.

I shuffle and offer Giovanni the cut. He cuts it "thin to win." He is so cornball sometimes . . . and he's drinking some Canadian beer. His breath is kickin'. I flip him an ace of hearts, Daddy a ten of clubs. I'm about to flip another to Giovanni when Pops waves a ten in the air, slamming it on the table. He's had quite a few shots of amaretto.

"I bet ten on my son. Any takers?"

Collette literally shoves Clyde. "Go on, now." She gulps her strawberry daiquiri, her third or fourth.

Clyde sets his gin and juice down, opens his wallet, pulls out a ten, and slams it on the table. "Ten on Michael."

I flip Giovanni a king of hearts, Daddy a ten of diamonds.

"Ten more on Michael!" Clyde shouts.

"Done!" Pops shouts. Two more slaps later, there's forty bucks lying on the table next to maybe twenty bucks in change.

Giovanni next gets a queen of clubs, Daddy a two of spades. I turn to Clyde, but he hesitates. "Go on," Collette says.

"I don't know," Clyde says.

"Twenty on my son!" Pops thunders.

Daa-em. "Twenty on Michael, then," Clyde says.

I look around before dealing the next two cards. I am the only sober person here. "There's eighty bucks on the side bet, y'all."

Then Daddy reaches into his pocket and takes out two bills. "Forty to stay, right?"

"Daddy!" Giovanni shrugs and digs in his pocket, withdrawing a wad of bills. He counts out forty and adds it to the wrong pile. "Giovanni, that's the wrong pile."

"Hell, put it all together," Mama says.

Hands shoot out to pile up the money. "Okay, a hundred eighty in the pot." I deal a ten of hearts to Giovanni, a two of clubs to Daddy. Daddy has two pair showing with a possibility for a full house, and all Giovanni can hope for is a jack to complete his straight. I look at Pops first.

"Fifty," he says and throws a brand-new Ulysses S. Grant onto the table.

"Holy shit," Collette says. "You crazy, old man? You need glasses or something?"

"No," Pops says. "My son will win."

"Bet him, Clyde!" Collette yells as Daddy and Giovanni add fifty bucks each to the pile.

"It's all I got, Collette," Clyde says.

She snatches the rest of the bills from his wallet. "No, it ain't. Don't front."

"Okay," I say, my own hands feeling kind of sweaty. "Three hundred and eighty in the pot."

"Don't deal yet," Daddy says. "Last one down, Giovanni?"

Giovanni nods. "Yup."

"Deal the last one down, Renee."

I slide a card to Giovanni, then Daddy. Pops leans over Giovanni to look and says, "Oy."

Clyde leans over Daddy to look and says, "Well . . ."

Daddy empties his wallet. "There's sixty here. You stay in, we'll have an even five hundred."

"And if you don't," Collette says, "we get the pot."

Giovanni and Pops fumble around for a few minutes and have to go to the cash register. "Sixty," Pops says. "You first."

Daddy smiles at me and flips over . . . a three of diamonds. "Two pair."

Pops starts shouting in Italian, and Giovanni flips over a jack of clubs.

Daddy nearly falls out of his chair, Clyde slumps to the floor, Mama shouts (just to shout, I think), Giovanni and Pops embrace, and Collette starts howling. "Renee," Giovanni says, "I'm no good with money. Here. This is yours."

"Half of it is mine!" Pops says. Giovanni whispers something in Italian. That shit is so rude. "Okay, okay. We give it to her. Geez." Okay, maybe it isn't all that rude.

I gather up the pile . . . and that's when Collette really goes off.

"See that, Clyde?" Collette snarls. "Did you? Huh? That's what you supposed to do with your money." She waves a finger in Clyde's face. Clyde backs up into the counter, Collette digging her long nails into his chest. "You saw that, right? You saw him give her all that money? You for-evuh holdin' back on me, Clyde Dunbar!"

"Kiss her, Clyde!" Pops yells.

"Y'all stay out of this, now. This between me and my—" And then Clyde does kiss Collette, dipping her nearly to the ground.

When they are finished, Pops says "Shh" again. I don't hear anything, and neither does anyone else. Mama mouths "What?" to me. Pops walks over to Clyde and pats him on the shoulder. "That's all you'll evuh have to do, Clyde."

Collette is half happy, half pissed. She towers over Pops and is about to say something evil, but instead she says, "Don't move, old man."

She races around the counter toward the office. In a moment, the orchestra music ends abruptly. When she returns, she's carrying a crowbar. What the hell? She goes to the crate. "You watching, old man?"

"Yes. I watch, loud woman."

"I ain't loud yet, old man." She digs the crowbar into the crate and pops off a board. I can't help but move toward the crate. I peek through the hole and start laughing.

"Clyde, Daddy, come help Collette!" I yell.

Daddy and Clyde pry a few more boards loose, and the gift is apparent to everyone.

A jukebox.

"This ain't just any jukebox, old man," Collette says, waving a finger at Pops. "No. This jukebox is guaranteed to play good music at all times of the day or night." Clyde plugs it in, and it lights up like a Christmas tree. "And I'll even let you choose the first song." Pops has to be pushed over by Giovanni, but he's smiling. Collette hands him a quarter. He drops it in and just stands there. "It don't matter what you choose, old man," Collette says. "It's all good, honey."

Pops closes his eyes and pushes two buttons. A moment later, Luchesi's is filled with the sounds of "Betcha By Golly, Wow" by the Stylistics.

"What are they saying?" Pops asks Collette. "It makes no sense! 'Betcha by golly, wow'? Is-a that English?"

"It's English, old man," Collette snaps.

"If you say so, loud woman," Pops snaps back.

"I expect you to know the lyrics to all these songs by the end of next week, old man."

"Or what, loud woman?"

She smiles. "Or I will come here every day for lunch. Every single day."

"Every day?" Pops asks.

"Every single, solitary day."

Pops groans and says, "I learn, I learn. Geez, some people are so pushy with their music."

I thank Collette and Clyde and grab Giovanni as the Dramatics' version of "In the Rain" begins. Pops dims the lights while we slow-drag. Collette and Clyde bump and grind over by the window, Mama and Daddy dance cheek to cheek near the counter, and Giovanni and I barely sway near our table.

"Giovanni?"

"Yes, Renee."

"We're getting married."

He holds me tighter and kisses my neck. "Yup. You still love me?"

"Yup."

When the song changes to "It's Your Thing" by the Isley Brothers and the others start bumpin' and grindin', we still slow-drag.

"We're not dancing to the music," Giovanni says, his forehead on mine.

"Have we ever?"

Chapter Nine

Over the next two weeks, I finally get to know my husband-to-be. Giovanni and I are inseparable, and in addition to loving him, I find I actually like him . . . most of the time. I know that makes no sense, but if you think about it long enough, you might understand.

We take Giovanni's hoopdy Cadillac on our first "date" in public to get our wedding bands at Fink's in Tanglewood Mall. A white woman with platinum blond hair sees us and smiles. "Hello again," she gushes to Giovanni. White women seem to gush a lot. "How may I help you?"

Giovanni's blushing. "We'd like to look at wedding bands."

She flashes a look at me. "Oh." Her eyes widen a bit. "So, is this Renee?"

"Yes ma'am." Giovanni raises his eyebrow.

"Well, um, this is your lucky day, Renee." His, too, heifer. She scurries around snatching at rings in the glass display case and places them on some black velvet. A band that is all diamonds catches my eye. "Beautiful, isn't it?" It is. "Try it on."

Giovanni picks it up and slides it onto my finger next to the engagement ring. I am shaking and blinded. This is the kind of ring combination that could reroute air traffic at night. "It looks like a perfect fit." I decide then and there that I will never take this ring off as long as I live. Oh, how it sparkles! Just snip off the tag . . . holy shit—$9,995?! I'd be wearing my Jetta on one finger! "It's one-point-five carats and nearly flawless. It looks exquisite on you."

I turn to Giovanni and whisper, "It's too much."

"I know," he says. "I just wanted you to see what I'm getting you in ten years."

I like a man who thinks ahead! We end up getting a nice ring wrap for me for under a thousand, and I find him a nice band with five diamonds for five hundred. We use our engagement "tip money" to pay it all in cash, and Platinum Blonde is too amazed to gush.

"You see how she was lookin' at me?" I ask Giovanni on our way to McDonald's. Janae's hungry already.

"No. I was only looking at you."

Instead of driving through like I wanted, Giovanni parks, and we have our first lunch date in public. While we wait in line, he asks me a bunch of questions: "What's your favorite color?"

"Blue," I whisper.

"Same here. How many kids do you want to have?"

Dag, boy, ask everybody. "Just one, and please whisper."

"Only one?"

He could have asked all this in the car. "Wait till we get to our table, boy."

At the counter, I recognize Chaunte, one of my friends from high school. She looks over and sees me. "That you, Renee?"

"Hey, Chaunte. How you doing?"

"Not as fine as you. Where you get that ring?"

Damn thing is a beacon. "We're engaged," Giovanni says before I can explain, and Chaunte blinks. Gonna be a lot of that today. I smile weakly and stare at Ronald McDonald. When he gonna change his hair color?

Chaunte says "oh" like we have a disease or something and gets back to work. Giovanni and I are gonna have a little talk about this.

255

I lead him to a booth where we can get a little privacy. "Giovanni, why you gotta be so loud? And what you doin' tellin' everybody our business?"

"They're going to know eventually, right?"

I lean in. "Not everybody. Our business is our own and nobody else's. Don't ask me personal shit in public and tell the world 'we're engaged' out loud."

"Why not? It's true."

I roll my eyes. "Well, the truth scares people, okay?"

"Sorry." He bites into his Big Mac. "So why do you only want one child?"

Doesn't he know I'm angry? That's *not* the question to ask a pregnant woman. "Don't tell me that you want more."

"I do. I like big families."

"There's only going to be one, because after I have Janae, you're going to get cut."

"Huh?"

"Snip, snip, and no more babies."

"Ouch!"

"A guy at work had it done." And we're real glad he won't be making any more babies like him. He's the kind of guy who butts into a conversation after everything's been said and says it *all* over again. "He said it didn't hurt." I tear into a fry for emphasis.

He winces and sips his Coke. "Why don't you want a boy?"

"It's not that I wouldn't be happy with a boy. It's just that, well, boys can be harder to raise."

"I turned out all right."

For the most part. "And anyway, whatever our child is, he or she will be considered black."

"Won't they be both?"

"No, and there ain't gonna be no 'they,' boy. Just one. A girl. And in this country, you are black until proven white. Besides, black women are kicking some serious ass now in books, movies, politics. Janae will one day be President."

"I really like that name. Almost sounds Italian, you know?"

"It ain't." I unwrap and eat half my double cheeseburger. "So, where are we going to live?"

"Where do you want to live?"

"Did you see *Sleeping with the Enemy*? I want the big white house with all those windows. Think it's on the beach somewhere."

"Seriously."

"I am serious." I sweat him a little. "Well, I guess I can settle for a three-bedroom, two-bath with a yard in Northwest until then."

"You were listening."

I nod. "But it has to be nice, with a garage. I'm tired of birds bombing the Jetta."

He takes a bite of his burger. "The birds don't bomb the Caddy, and it's a much bigger target."

"That boat needs a wash, boy. They only shit on clean cars." Giovanni laughs, and I notice folks staring at us. "Don't look, but we got folks grittin' on us."

"'Grittin'?"

"Starin' hard. Grittin' their teeth."

"It's these fries," Giovanni says. "They're overcooked."

"It's us, boy."

"They're just jealous." He finishes his meal and collects my trash. "Besides, I don't even see them. Like I said before, I only see you."

"Wait until I start showing more," I say. "We gonna pop out some contacts and break us some lenses then."

The next step of our "date" takes us to a drug store. We wander the aisles for awhile, but I know he's up to something. He's such a kid.

"I want to buy you something," he says, "and I want you to buy something for me."

"What?"

"That's just it. We don't know until we look. It's a surprise. Five-dollar limit."

"Can it be more than one item?"

"Sure, as long as the total is less than five dollars."

"Bet," I say, and I start my search. Five bucks isn't much, but I've shopped with less. The challenge is to find the right gift. I skip the tobacco section and barely check out the colognes. Any cologne that costs less than five bucks is *real* toilet water if you ask me. I bypass the women's sections at first, then backtrack and find the perfect gift for Giovanni: women's section, aisle two. I palm it in my hand, and since I have some money left over, I decide to get a card.

I roam the card aisle, giggling here and there. Should I be romantic or nasty? I decide on nasty. Then I notice Giovanni at the other end of the card aisle in my people's tiny section, stressing over his selections. I feel his pain. What, twelve percent of this country is African-American, and one percent (maybe less) is devoted to greeting cards that celebrate us? I hated having to give my mama a birthday card with some big ol' blond-headed woman on the front of the card. And unless my people are buying for someone's mama or grandma, we have only one choice for father or sister or cousin.

"Finished?" I say without looking down the aisle at him.

"Almost."

"I'll go pay for these." I love this spy shit.

"Okay."

The cashier looks at me a little strangely (oh, that's the way her face just *is*) but makes no comment. "Please put it in a bag," I tell her, "and may I borrow your pen?" I jot a little somethin'-somethin' on the card and slide it into the envelope. I do not seal envelopes that have been lying in a slot for who knows how long and have been fingered by who knows who. I tuck in the flap and take my bag. "Thank you."

Giovanni walks up to the cashier while I wait at the newspaper rack. He's trying to be sneaky. We need to do something about his walk. He walks like a white man, like he has to get somewhere when he really has nowhere to go. I mean, if you're going to go nowhere, at least go there in style. I watch as he, too, fills out a card and, after paying, carries a bigger bag to me.

"First, the receipts," he says. We compare, and both are under five dollars. "Tear receipt." We rip the receipt off the stapled white bag. "Now, switch." We do. My man trippin'.

His bag is heavier than mine, and it's double-bagged so I can't see through it. "You first," I say.

"Okay." He opens the top of his bag and looks inside. "What?" He tightens his eyebrow. "Is this what I think it is?" He pulls it out and laughs. "Eyebrow tweezers?"

I giggle. "You look like Brooke Shields."

"Gee, thanks." He holds them wrong as he tries to start plucking.

I pull his arm down. "Not now. Later. And I may remove some hair from another place, too."

"I'm not that hairy down there," he whispers.

"Yes you are, boy."

"But that'll hurt."

I croon, "It'll hurt so good." His face turns red. "Open the card."

"Oh." I watch his eyes reading the card. Sure enough, his Adam's apple starts bobbing. "Wow! Is that even possible?"

"Every bit of that is possible."

"Wow," he says again. At least he doesn't say "cool beans" or something extremely Caucasian like that.

"My turn," I say, and I tear open the top of my bag. Inside are a bottle of kids' bubble bath and a rubber ducky. "Gee. For me?" We *suck* at giving gifts! "I can't take baths in my condition."

"Oh. Sorry."

I open the envelope and see a completely blank white card. I turn it over as if the turning will make words magically appear. "I thought you wrote something on it."

He steps closer and whispers, oh too damn gently, "I'll fill it— *and you*—in later."

"Down, boy. We ain't doin' it again until the honeymoon."

"We're not?"

"You can wait. You waited a hundred days, didn't you?"

He pouts. "But we'll have the apartment all to ourselves."

"Boy, I am just too tired for that. But I will let you rub me down after a shower."

He smiles. "Okay."

When we get to Giovanni's apartment, we have some good, clean fun playing "hide the duck." We towel each other off, and I ask him for some lotion.

He looks under the sink and finds some no-name brand lotion. "Will this be okay?"

I roll my eyes. White people, ashiest race on the face of the earth, and their weak-ass lotion. "No, but if it's all you got, it'll have to do. Warm it up first."

"How?"

"Squeeze it in your hands. What'd you want to do, microwave it?"

He squeezes a literal pond onto his hands and starts rubbing them together. "Now what?"

I run my hands down my body on both sides. "Put it everywhere, but watch the hair." He starts with my legs, massaging the lotion in slowly. "Stop," I say, and I grab a towel. I wrap the towel around me and say, "I need to be lying down for this."

For the next hour Giovanni lotions me as I lie on his bed, massaging every surface of my body, even my feet. "Watch them hammertoes," I say.

"Your what?"

"My toes are little hammers. Yours are just long and scary."

"Thanks a lot."

"That feels so good," I say over and over. And it does feel damn good, but I can't keep my eyes open and "fall asleep." I'm only faking because I'm too pooped to go any further. I have it down to a science. I feel him kiss my nose and cover me with sheets, and then I really fall asleep.

When I wake up, I look around the dark room and locate Giovanni by the shadow of his nose. He's sitting in his desk chair, his chin bouncing off his chest. How uncomfortable. I find my clothes folded, sort of, on the nightstand. I slip into them and turn on the nightstand light. That's when I see a wedding dress in his closet. Is Giovanni hiding something from me? No, it's too pretty and not his size. Not very flashy, but pretty. After carefully removing the plastic covering, I examine the fabric. Silk. Créme. I look for a tag and don't find one. An original? Giovanni's mama had taste.

I carry the dress into the bathroom and try it on. It's snug here, a little loose there, but I look gorgeous. I look like *Ebony* Fashion Flair model Renee (with accents on *all* the E's, no last name) at a show. Thank you, thank you. They're throwing flowers at my feet. Thank you—

"Wow!"

The runway disappears. I have to talk fast to play this off. "It needs a little work, but it'll do."

Giovanni kisses the back of my neck. "Christina will fix it exactly the way you want it."

I check out how the dress hits my ass. "Your mama didn't have the same body I do. I mean, this fits a side-to-side person, not a front-to-back person like me."

"Huh?"

Time for a fashion lesson. "The women of my people," I begin, sounding like Maya on that United Negro College Fund commercial, "are built front-to-back. We have more front"—I smooth out my chest—"and a whole lot more back."

"So I've noticed."

"And I thought you only loved me for my eyes."

"Them, too. But get back to the back part."

"Unzip me. I don't want to wrinkle it." He does. "Most fashion designers use anorexic white girls with no titties to style their dresses. My people need a fashion designer with us completely in mind. Maybe I can interest Christina. I'll have to be CEO."

261

"Of course."

As we dress, I tell him I want a ten-tiered wedding cake.

"Ten!"

"Okay. I'll settle for seven."

He smiles. "You're kidding now, right?"

"No."

"Geez."

We go next door, and I let Giovanni hold my hand because it's a very short walk. "Hello, Mr. Luchesi." Giovanni doesn't say anything. What's up with that?

"It's in the walk-in," Mr. Luchesi says. He old, but he lookin' older today.

"How do you know—"

"What you're going to ask, Renee? I have ESP. Your cake is in the walk-in. I'll finish it tonight if you let me."

O-kaaaay. Take a pill, Pops. Giovanni shrugs and leads me into the walk-in freezer. I see seven circular cakes of various sizes with neutral créme icing. Yeah, it matches my dress perfectly. But seven? And it's not done yet?

Giovanni's warm hands reach around and rub my tummy. "How many?"

"I see seven."

"His record's fifteen."

No way. "What'd it look like?"

"The Leaning Tower of Pisa. For one of Uncle Johnny's weddings. Didn't fall, though."

"What's up with you and Pops?" I whisper.

"He's being an asshole."

"Huh?"

"He's nervous about seeing Christina."

"Can you blame him?"

He leads me out of the walk-in. "Yes, I can."

"Giovanni—"

He kisses me. "It's an Italian thing."

"Oh."

"Come on."

"Where?"

"I'm hungry!" he yells.

I pull him to me and whisper, "We're in a restaurant."

"Yeah, let's go to Shoney's, Renee!" he yells again, then leaves me and walks through the back door.

"See you later, Pops!" I yell, but I get no reply.

On the drive to Shoney's, I try to get Giovanni to talk, but he won't. "Fine," I say eventually. Italians and their moods.

We turn on Hershberger Road and make the left into a nearly full Shoney's parking lot. Inside we wait where it says to "Please Wait for Hostess," but no hostess shows up. Bitch is probably hiding from us.

A young white girl approaches, her hair stacked up on her head like kindling wood. "Uh, how many?" How many you see, bitch?

"Two," Giovanni says.

She takes two menus and leads us all the way to the other side of the dining room past two empty booths. Giving us a workout, Straw Head? After placing the menus on the table, she breezes away without a sound.

"Is this okay?" Giovanni asks.

"This will do," I say as I frown at the smiling Shoney Bear staring at me from the menu. I want a Philly steak 'n' cheese so bad, but Janae will have me hurling.

"What are you having?"

"Soup and sandwich, probably the club," I say.

He closes his menu. "I'll have the same." And then we wait. And wait. I rearrange the white, pink, and blue packets while Giovanni reads every word on the menu twice.

"Go see what's taking her so long," I say.

Giovanni walks to the front counter. He's back in a minute and sits. "You won't believe this," he says with a funny smile.

"Try me."

263

"We're sitting in *Sheila's* section, but *Sheila* isn't here yet, so we'll just have to wait until *Sheila* gets here. Let's go."

"No," I say. Normally, I'd be gone in a heartbeat. But not today.

"Huh?"

"Go back up there and demand service. Use the word 'lawsuit.'" He leaves and comes back a few minutes later. He doesn't look happy. "What happened?"

"Sheila *is* here. She'll will be with us shortly."

"Perfect." He squints. "We're going to do a little experiment on Sheila." I explain, and he finally smiles.

When Sheila, an older white woman, arrives ten minutes later, her hair in a terrible bun, we're ready. "You ready to order?" she asks Giovanni. She hasn't even taken so much as a peek at me.

Giovanni gives his order in Italian. Sheila nearly drops her pencil. I translate in broken English. "He zay he vant soup. He zay he vant sandvich. Club. And Coke-a no Pepsi."

Sheila writes it down. "And for you?" I don't respond because she doesn't even look at me. "And for you?"

"Are you talkink to me?" Weird, but I almost sound French.

She finally looks at me. "Yes."

"I have zame."

She takes our menus and rushes off. Giovanni breaks the silence first. "That was amazing. She wouldn't even look at you! Her whole body blocked you. She is *not* getting a tip."

"No. She'll get a tip."

The meal itself is uneventful. Sheila does her job, the vegetable soup hits the spot, the club is adequate, she refills our Cokes. She still won't look at me, but I've made my point with Giovanni.

When it's time for the check, Sheila lays it in front of Giovanni, who immediately waves his hands and chatters at her in Italian. I can tell she's afraid to ask, so I say, "He say I pay." But instead of sliding the check closer to me, she turns and walks away.

"God, what a bitch!" Giovanni says. "And you want to tip her?"

I flip over the check and calculate fifteen percent of our bill. "Give me five dollars."

"Renee!"

"I said, give me five dollars."

"She didn't earn it, and that's way over fifteen percent."

I smile. "Five dollars, please." He pulls it out of his wallet and tosses it on the table. "*Hand* it to me, please." He drops his eyes and hands me the five. "Thank you. Now watch."

I leave the table and pay the check, then I find Sheila near the salad bar. "Sheila," I say with my biggest smile. "Ve vant you to have zis, for all za trouble ve cause." I hold out the five and she grabs it, but I don't let go until she looks me in the eye. Then, in a steady American voice I say, "Thank you for your trouble." I release the bill, spin around, and return to Giovanni. He stands, I take his arm, and we walk out of Shoney's, heads high, shoulders square. We both turn and smile at Goldi-logs, the hostess standing behind a glass window, and take two suckers for our trouble.

"And what have we learned today?" I ask as we walk toward the car.

"Don't eat at Shoney's?"

I pat his hand. "No, no. We learned that the only color that really matters in this world is *green.*"

Near the end of our first date, we browse Books-A-Million. I comment on the *four* shelves devoted to my people out of the thousands of shelves in the store. He nods. I'm hoping he's storing away all this vital information.

Our date ends outside the front door of my house. "One little peck on the cheek," I tell him, turning my cheek to him.

"Oh, come on."

"Giovanni, this was our first date. I do not suck face on the first date."

"You've got to be kidding. We took a shower together." He steps away, his hands in his pockets.

"Okay, suit yourself." I turn to insert the key, and he spins me around and pecks me on the cheek. "Just wait until our second date."

"What do I get at the end of that one?"

I peck his cheek. "A handshake."

Our second real date involves two things I don't like to do: deal with the government and spend money—which are sometimes one and the same.

It's raining, so I hand Giovanni an umbrella. "You know how to work one of these?"

"Yup."

"Good," I say, and we head outside. "If just one drop of rain falls on my hair, no coochie till the baby's born."

That umbrella shoots out faster than Michael Johnson at the Olympics. And no, not one raindrop hits me anywhere as we get in the Cadillac. Withholding coochie is some powerful shit.

Heavy rain splashes the windshield as we head for 315 Church Street to get our marriage license. We find no parking nearby, so we settle for the garage across from the main library on Jefferson Street six blocks away. Giovanni gets a ticket from the attendant, and we park on the second floor, away from all that rain. He's ready with the umbrella, and we're off.

He's being exceptionally careful with that umbrella, and I get a strange vision in my head, don't ask me how. I see my ancestors smiling at us as he, a white man, holds an umbrella in heavy rain for little ol' black me.

At Church Avenue, we have to wait while an old Celica packed with brothers cruises by, bass thumpin'. I nod as they look back. Yes, a white man is holding an umbrella for a sister. Get over it. We cross First Street and step inside the building at 315. Now I'm nervous. I know this isn't the real thing, but going for a legal piece of paper that says you're married can tense you up. We go up to the second floor and follow the signs. Giovanni opens the door to a glassed-in room surrounded by a huge counter. No one comes to us immediately, though a few white women walk back and forth in front of us.

"Do you ring a bell?" Giovanni asks. I try to catch a few eyes, but no one's looking. "Excuse me," Giovanni says, slapping the counter.

A white woman stops what she's doing (which, as far as I can see, is nothing) and comes to him. "I'm sorry," she says. "So many people haven't made it in yet with all this rain. How may I help you?"

Giovanni says, "We'd like to get a marriage license."

She raises her eyebrows and blinks. "Okay." She places two clipboards and pencils in front of us. "Fill everything out as best as you can, and call me when you're finished."

We sit on some uncomfortable vinyl seats and fill out the forms. "This is like filling out an application for employment," I say to Giovanni.

"Never did that."

"Oh yeah." His résumé would be nearly blank.

The form is pretty simple, but having to write down my race pisses me off. Our vows will not be, "I, Renee the African-American, take thee Giovanni, the Italian-American."

We're zipping right along, cheesing at each other, and then I get to the space for my daddy's name. This is the first time I can write his name down as my daddy. I nearly giggle. I turn to Giovanni. "You ready?"

"Yes."

We hand the clipboards to the woman, and she types for a while before handing us a document. We check her work, and under number five (race) I'm "black." I prefer "brown," thank you very much.

"Looks okay to me," Giovanni says.

I roll my eyes. One day he'll get it. "Fine," I say.

We pay her twenty-five dollars and she hands Giovanni two forms. "You need to have the officiant—"

"The what?" Giovanni asks.

"The preacher," she says.

"Preacher *and* priest," Giovanni says. What this woman must be thinking!

"Okay. Have the preacher and the priest complete and sign both copies after the service. When's the wedding?"

"The twentieth," I say.

"Are you getting married at Saint Andrews?"

"No," I say, grabbing Giovanni's arm, "at High Holiness. Oh, and you're welcome to come to the reception at Luchesi's Deli and Pizzeria on Fourth Street. The public is invited."

We are still laughing as we leave the building, but Giovanni has that umbrella ready. If anything, the rain is getting heavier.

"Why'd you say all that?" he asks as we slosh through puddles to the car.

"She was nosy."

"Maybe she was just curious, or maybe she was just making conversation."

"I know my breed," I say. "We women are *nosy*." He pulls the Cadillac out of the garage and turns south on Jefferson. "Martin Travel?" I ask.

"Yup."

We pull into the Towers Mall parking lot, and the Cadillac swims along fine. We walk into Martin Travel, and an hour later we escape with a huge stack of brochures (to places *Ebony* says I should go), one travel itinerary, and plane tickets to Maui.

We also leave a couple of thousand dollars poorer. "Ka-ching, ka-ching," is all I can say as we ride out onto Colonial and read the itinerary. We fly out of Roanoke at 8 P.M. to Charlotte the day after the wedding. Since the second flight leaves for Chicago at ten, we may have to hustle. After a two-hour layover in Chicago, we'll fly nonstop to San Francisco before changing planes one more time after a short layover for a direct flight to Maui and a resort with a name full of vowels.

"I want to invite the entire office to the wedding." Except for Connie.

"You sound worried."

"You should see how some of those people eat!" *Your* people, boy.

After we turn onto Wonju Street, Giovanni asks, "What was the damage again?"

"Almost three thousand," I say. "I've never spent that much money in my entire life."

"Wait until we get to Stritesky's."

Instead of taking 581, which tends to be pinball alley across all three lanes in rainy weather, we take Franklin through the city up Williamson Road through a dozen lights (and past a couple dozen lighted signs with misspelled words) to Peters Creek Road and Stritesky's.

Inside Stritesky's, I'm struck by all the varieties of flowers. Every color, every size. Almost too many choices. And that's the way I like it. A white woman walks over wearing a green smock, kind of like what elementary-school art teachers wear with all the pockets. "Hell of a day, isn't it?"

"Yes, ma'am," Giovanni says. He's just too polite sometimes. "I'm Giovanni Luchesi. Ginny, right?"

"Yes. Nice to see you again. How are the silks holding out?" Ginny asks.

"Just fine. We dust them every night." Giovanni says.

"What can I do for you?"

Giovanni points at me. "This is my fiancée, Renee."

"Hello." A pleasant hello, not curious or nosy. I like Ginny.

"Hi," I say.

"Julie's told me all about you two. Do you want her to help you?"

This will be different. "Sure," I say.

"You sure?" Giovanni asks.

"Why wouldn't I be?" I mean, in a twisted way, this will give poor Julie a little closure, right?

Julie comes out with a notepad and pulls me aside. "Hello again. Uh, no offense to Giovanni," she whispers in the tiniest voice, "but he's color-blind. You better pick them out."

"Color-blind?" I whisper back.

"He and his father ordered the wrong flowers six times before getting them right." She explains to me how customers had complained, and how Pops had to eventually bring an entire table to Stritesky's to match the silk roses.

Giovanni is looking at candleholders and candle stands. It must be a Catholic thing. "What's our limit, Giovanni?" I ask him.

"Just be reasonable. Have her put it on our account."

Reasonable, huh? I don't know if I like the sound of that. But for the next half hour, Julie shows a rose, I say "Yes!" She asks how many, I ask, "How many do you have?" High Holiness will become a garden. "When do you want these delivered?" Julie asks Giovanni.

"By ten next Saturday morning," he says. "And could we have a pair of these candle stands?"

Julie scribbles a few more notes to herself. "We'll have everything at the church by ten. You'll just have to return the candle stands on Monday."

I can't believe what we've just ordered. "Are you sure you can deliver all that by ten?"

Julie smiles. She could be prettier if she tried. "I guarantee it. I'll deliver it all myself. Uh, can I stay for the wedding?"

The ultimate in closure. "Sure." I check my watch. "Dag, it's only eleven-thirty. What are we gonna do the rest of the day?"

"We *could* help Pops run the restaurant so he can work on the food for the reception."

Yeah, and we *could* take a nap. "Can I wait tables while you make the food?"

"Sure."

We formulate a plan and execute it flawlessly. Without a word we march into Luchesi's, storm behind the counter, grab aprons, strap them on, and salute Pops.

"What is this? Saluting a baker?" Pops asks.

"Privates Luchesi and Howard reporting for duty, sir!" Giovanni barks. He is trippin'!

"What do I say?" Pops asks.

"You say, 'At ease,' " Giovanni says.

"Okay. At ease." We relax and smile. "You two, crazy in love, now just crazy."

"Put us to work, Pops," Giovanni says.

"Oh, so you come over when you know there is no one here? Some help that is."

I take Pops by the hand and place him on the stool. "Take a load off, Pops," I say.

"You hear what she calls me?"

Giovanni picks up a hand towel and throws it to me. "I call you that all the time, Pops."

"But she's not family yet. What you gonna do about that?"

Giovanni winks at me and growls. "I put her to work. After I put her to work, I whip her silly with wet spaghetti."

"No, not the spaghetti," I laugh, and start shining already-shiny tables.

"I cannot watch, oy!" Pops waddles down the hall to his office.

A half an hour or so later, my first customer, a pale white woman who looks vaguely familiar shakes out her umbrella inside the doorway. I snatch an order book and pencil from Giovanni's apron pocket before he can blink.

"Welcome to Luchesi's Deli and Pizzeria," I say. "Won't you be seated?"

The woman goes to a table for two near the window. I look back to see Giovanni wide-eyed and about to say something. I can handle this. Chill, boy. I hand the woman her menu.

"Thanks. Oh, what a beautiful ring," she says, taking off her soaked rain jacket.

"Thank you. Do you want something to drink while you decide?" I've got this waitress shit down cold.

"Something hot," she says. "Breve, I guess."

I have no idea what she just ordered, but I write it down anyway. "Cup or mug?"

"Mug."

"Okay, I'll be back." I leave with her order and show Giovanni the ticket. He stares past me at the woman. "Giovanni," I say, waving the ticket in front of his eyes. "Make this."

Giovanni shakes his head and hops to it. So that's how he learned to move so fast. He brings a steaming mug and puts it on a tray the size of a pizza. His hands are shaking. "What's wrong?"

He stares at the woman again. "Nothing."

"I won't spill it. Promise." After analyzing the situation, I slide the tray off the counter onto my hand. No sweat. No drips or spills all the way to her table. "Here you go."

"Thank you." She takes a sip, and I whip out the order book. "Ready?"

"I'll have the red beans and rice and the bread of the day." I write everything down and reach for the menu. "I better keep it. I may have dessert."

"Okay. It'll be out in a few minutes."

I'm two steps away from her when she calls out, "And tell my little brother to get his ass over here to give me a hug."

Huh? I see Giovanni nod. Daa-em. I turn.

"Hi, I'm Christina. You must be Renee." I nod. "Yo, Giovanni, hop to it. I know you can read my lips. Chop chop!"

Now I am nervous. I don't know how to explain it exactly, but meeting Christina makes me very nervous, and not because she's a lesbian but because she's Giovanni's sister. It's a woman thing, I guess, like I have to especially impress her since I can't impress his mother.

And I'm not the only nervous person. I hear Giovanni dropping shit and making all kinds of noise back in the kitchen.

"I know how to make an entrance, huh? Come here. Take a load off."

She stands and holds out her arms. She's tall and thin with long, dark hair and absolutely no waist. She'd be a female version of Giovanni, except that she has bluish eyes and a thinner face. And those earrings! There must be thirty in her ears. She is very beautiful, though the clothes she wears do nothing for her: brown corduroys and black high-top Chucks? Fashion designers dress like shit!

I step into her embrace and get a fierce hug. I wince and sit opposite her. "I didn't hurt you, did I?"

"Well, I'm sure you know I'm pregnant."

"No shit! Giovanni didn't tell me that! Hell, he didn't even tell me you were black. Wonder why he didn't. I know, he didn't think it mattered. And it doesn't. Now, where is that Pops of mine?"

I like this person. Wish there were more like her in Roanoke. "He should be back in the office."

She smiles at me. "Damn, you're prettier than he described. Do you know what you're having yet?"

"Pops says it's a girl."

"You believe him?"

"Yes. Only a girl would get another girl up at four in the morning to go to the bathroom."

Christina laughs. "It's a girl, all right." Giovanni finally brings a tray, stumbling over the leg of a chair. "Careful, little brother, or I won't tip you."

He sets her plate on the table. "What are you *doing* here? The rehearsal's not until Friday."

"Nice to see you, too," she says. "Where's my kiss?"

He kisses her on the cheek. "And where's Alexis?"

"At the hotel. She drove us all the way here all by herself." She looks at me. "I never learned to drive. I had a helluva time finding this place. No one in this town knows where it is. I've been walking for almost an hour."

"Why didn't you call?" Giovanni asks. "I would have come to get you."

"And ruin the surprise?" She raises *her* eyebrow. She takes a bite of her red beans. "How's Pops?"

Giovanni sits. "Well, Pops—" The back door slams, and I jump. "Uh, Pops has just left."

Christina smiles. "He must have heard my voice. Good. He knows I'm here." She takes another quick bite and puts on her rain jacket. "Catch you later." And then she runs out the back door into the rain.

"What do we do now?" I ask after the echo from the back door fades.

Giovanni lays his head on the table. "We wait."

I massage his neck. "We're good at that."

And we don't have to wait long before the next customer walks in, and she's the all-American white girl: short, blond, and freckly, like she just stepped out on an ad for *Cover Girl*. Giovanni looks up, groans, and puts his head back down.

"Is Christina around?"

So this is Alexis. Wearing a soaked . . . Levi's jean jacket? I haven't seen one of them in years. "Uh, she just left," I say. "Out the back door."

"Chasing Pops, huh?" I nod. "Hi, Giovanni. Boy, you sure have grown."

Giovanni doesn't move. "Hi," he says, the table muffling his voice. "Want something to drink?" Nice manners. I pinch his neck, and he sits up. "What'll you have?"

"Anything with liquor in it," Alexis says.

"I know just the thing." I go behind the counter and get a bottle of amaretto and two shot glasses, returning and pouring Giovanni a tall one. "Drink," I say, but Giovanni only shakes his head and mumbles. "Drink it, boy." He downs it in one gulp.

"You must be Renee," Alexis says . . . and *hugs* me. A blond-haired, freckly white woman has just hugged me in Roanoke, Virginia. I need to move to New York. But I will *not* wear corduroys or jean jackets. I pour her a shot, and she sips it. "Hmm. I love this shit." She sips some more. "How long has Christina been gone?"

"Only a few minutes. Have a seat."

She sits opposite Giovanni. "Father Mike says hi. You'll love him, Renee. He is a giant, at least six-five and pushing three hundred easy. When he prays, God listens. And he is the funniest man. The things he says are just so . . . unexpected for a priest, you know?"

"Unexpected" is the key word today.

We chat awhile about her trip and how nice the Patrick Henry Hotel is, and all we hear is the ceaseless drumming of the rain. It's almost peaceful.

But that peace is shattered when Pops comes in arm in arm with Christina. They are both beyond torn up, dripping, smelling like all outdoors. He walks right up to Alexis and stops. I think I actually stop breathing.

Pops takes Alexis's face in his hands, leans in, kisses her forehead, and says, "Who is this vision? How are you? You should not be so much a stranger. Why you keep my daughter from me?" I slip my hand into Giovanni's as I start to cry. He kisses Alexis again, this time on the cheek. "I am so glad you came. Come. Let's go stand by the oven where it's warmer." Christina and Alexis each take one of Pops's arms and walk away.

"You're not supposed to cry until the wedding," Giovanni says.

I blow my nose on a napkin. "I'm just practicing."

He kisses away one salty tear. "Are you planning to cry at the wedding?"

"Yes. Especially . . . when you read me your vows."

He blinks. "What vows?"

"I've just decided that we would write our own vows." Just now, as a matter of fact.

"You did?"

"I did."

He hugs me. "But this is so unexpected."

I stare him down. "What isn't unexpected about your family?"

We have a wonderful rehearsal two days later at High Holiness. I have been dreading it, but everyone actually gets there on time. I think that's some kind of world record for my people. When Father Mike shows up, I am in awe. He is a giant, easily dwarfing Reverend Noel, who's closer to my height, and stands at least six-five and pushes three-hundred pounds—clean-shaven, white-haired, and definitely Italian. I guess when he prays, God does listen. But he doesn't wear his outfit or whatever you call it. He looks like an extra from *The Godfather* in a charcoal black suit.

I direct the three of them to the pulpit. "You three basically do nothing the entire time, so you just stand there."

Giovanni is barely paying attention to anyone but me during the rehearsal, which is as it should be. I line folks up, dress them down when they get out of line, and crack up when Collette does a very funky walk down the aisle. Alexis is playing something complex on her guitar while sitting in the first pew, Christina and Pops are inseparable, and I feel peace.

"It *will* be beautiful," Mama says afterward. "Now let's go have us a party!"

The front counter at Luchesi's becomes a bar as we all share a drink before going our separate ways. After Father Mike, Pops, Christina, and Giovanni down a shot of amaretto and say a whole bunch of Italian, Father Mike grabs the bottle and says, "This is mine."

Collette slaps the bar. "Hey, what's up with this bar? Where are the daiquiris?"

"We'll get the blender hummin' at our house, girl," Mama croons. "Don't you worry."

Pops starts ushering us toward the door. "It is time for you ladies to go. We men have important business."

Pops is in trouble now.

"Oh, really," Collette says, cutting her eyes at me. "You sayin' we ladies don't have important business, too?"

Pops smiles. "What I'm saying is that—"

"You want us to get out of here 'cause the stripper's coming."

Pops's eyes pop. "No, no! Not with the Father here." He checks to locate Father Mike over talking to Mama. "Last time something like that happened, Father Mike nearly left the priesthood."

Now Collette's eyes pop. "Really?"

Pops smiles and winks at me. "No," he says, and he walks away laughing.

I grab Giovanni and drag him into the restroom, locking the door behind us. "So, what will you men be doing?"

"As far as I know, eating, drinking, and playing cards."

"Sounds boring. No naked woman?"

He pins me to the door. "Only in my mind."

"Well, who is she?"

"Some girl I'm marrying tomorrow."

"Some girl?"

He kisses me tenderly, and I taste amaretto. "You'll never grow old, Renee."

Collette pounds on the door, interrupting our embrace. "Come on, Renee! We got food to cook!"

"Y'all go on!" I yell. I'm gettin' me some amaretto kisses.

"Renee! Christina's gonna show us some old home movies of your man!"

"Bye, Giovanni." A quick kiss and ten seconds later, I'm in my coat waiting for them by the door.

Christina and Giovanni argue in Italian all the way from the back to the front door, gesturing wildly with their hands. She kisses him on the cheek, points to her own, and he pecks her once.

"Enjoy the show," Giovanni says as we leave—five women marching down Allison Avenue lugging Alexis's and Christina's bags. Mama said she just couldn't have the two of them paying for an expensive hotel room when her basement had a sleeper sofa.

When we get inside, Mama takes charge, sending Christina and Alexis to the basement with their stuff and me upstairs to get the sheets and blankets for the sleeper sofa. Collette is already set up in Mama's office, which has a smaller sleeper sofa. "Meet in the kitchen in ten minutes," Mama orders.

I stand at the door to the basement and actually knock. I feel so silly.

"Come on down!" Christina yells.

I walk down and set their bedding on a side table. "That becomes a sleeper," I say.

"A leather couch that becomes a sleeper? We have to get one of these," Christina says, dropping onto the couch.

"And if it gets too cold, we have a few more blankets for you," I say.

Christina waves her hand. "Won't be necessary." Alexis joins her on the couch and they embrace. "We won't need them." I am embarrassed, and I'm sure it shows. I've hugged women before, but not the way they're hugging each other. Christina notices and looks up. "Your mama and Collette don't know, do they?"

"Collette does, but Mama doesn't."

"Hmm. Do we mind playing heterosexual women tonight for Giovanni's new mother-in-law?" Christina asks Alexis.

Alexis turns and dips Christina, deepening her voice. "Yo, bitch. You my woman."

"Guess not," Christina says, kissing Alexis firmly on the lips.

This should be a very interesting evening. "Uh, I'll be upstairs."

"Okay."

Mama, Collette, and I are in the kitchen getting pots and pans ready a few minutes later. "Where they at?" Mama asks me.

"Downstairs." Getting warmed up.

"It's getting a little chilly out. We should put that little space heater down there."

"It's okay, Mama," I say. "I don't think they're gonna need it."

Mama's little organizational meeting only lasts a few moments. Christina and Alexis draw dress duty with me in the basement. "Do something with it, please!" Mama says, laughing. Collette and Mama work the stove, preparing the chicken, greens, beans with salt pork and fresh tomatoes, and the sweet-potato pie for dessert. I feel a little left out when they have their premeal drinks of Chianti, but at least we have strawberry daiquiris planned for later.

I'm standing in the basement while two women pick and pin and tuck and shape and transform my dress to fit my body perfectly. Giovanni wasn't kidding about how good they are.

"How do I get out once I'm all pinned up?" I ask.

"Sorry, honey," Christina says, biting on a few straight pins, "you're in it until the honeymoon." She steps back and squints. "Turn around slowly."

"She's so beautiful," Alexis says. "Like a sculpture."

I'm not offended, because it's true.

Then they start taping the pins down with some sticky, thin gauze. "Now for the really hard part," Christina says. "Suck in a deep breath, let it all out, and don't breathe until we get this off. Not one breath or the dress will explode."

I suck in and exhale deeply. In a flash, the zipper's down and the dress is over my head. Alexis checks all the pins, and smiles. "Successful launch, captain."

I'm standing there in just my bra and underwear, but I don't feel self-conscious about it even though I'm starting to show. Christina tosses me my jeans and sweatshirt while Alexis gets immediately to work stitching, and I slip into my clothes.

"You don't have to do that now," I say to Alexis.

"It'll only take a sec." Her hands are flying.

Christina sits and drinks some more Chianti. "No charge. We couldn't think of what to get you two—"

"Oh, that's okay. The alterations are more than enough."

"But when you come to New York, we'll make you a Chrysalis original. Chrysalis is our label."

"That'd be so nice. But we better wait till a few months after the baby's born."

"Sure thing." Christina sniffs the air. "Something smells good."

"Let's go eat."

And we are some hungry women. Plates of cleaned chicken bones, empty pots and pans, and an empty pie tin litter the kitchen. Collette makes the daiquiris (virgin for me), and now we are in the basement getting silly with Marvin Gaye and Tammi Terrell, Diana Ross, the Temptations, and Smoky Robinson and all his Miracles. Collette and Mama practice their duet fairly well considering how drunk they are. They'll be fine tomorrow, as long as Collette tones it down a little. We'll just put short Mama in front of tall Collette.

We attempt to play spades upstairs, but neither Christina nor Alexis has a clue. And it's no fun playing spades with people who don't know what they're doing. "It ain't like hearts, y'all," Collette keeps saying.

Christina turns off the stereo right as Mama's finishing her Martha Reeves impersonation during "Jimmy Mack."

"No, you most certainly did not!" Mama says, but there isn't a trace of anger in her voice.

"Let's play a game," Christina says. "It's called 'I Never.' It's a lot of fun, and if you're really good, you'll get everyone *very* drunk."

All eyes turn to me. "It's okay with me. I'm gonna love seeing y'all throwing up instead of me."

Christina explains the rules. "All you have to do is say something you *never* did that you *know* someone in the room has done. The person who did what you *didn't* do has to drink."

"Want to run that by me again, honey?" Collette asks.

"It's easier just to play," Christina says, and everyone laughs. That's what Collette told her about playing spades. "And, if you can prove a person is lying, that person has to finish her drink. Everybody get comfortable." Mama, Collette, and Christina sit on the couch while Alexis and I lie out on the floor. "I'll begin. I never . . . lived in Roanoke."

"Oh, I get it," Collette says, and she takes a drink along with me and Mama. "My turn. I never lived in New York."

Christina and Alexis drink.

Alexis looks directly at me and Mama. "I've never been pregnant."

We take our sips, and Mama says, "I've never had long, blond hair."

Alexis giggles and drinks.

It's my turn, and I will get them all. "I've never been twenty-seven years old."

"Can she do that?" Collette asks.

"Yup," Christina says, just like Giovanni, and everyone drinks but me.

We go around a couple times until it comes back to Christina. "I have never slept with a man," she says. Mama looks at me then takes a big gulp. Collette giggles and drinks, and even Alexis takes a drink. Christina blinks at her. "You, too, Alexis?"

"I was scared," Alexis says, "so I crawled into bed with my mom and dad. You said *slept* with a man. You should have said *had sex* with a man."

Christina says, "Oops!" and downs the rest of her daiquiri. That had to give her a cold headache. Christina fills her glass with Chianti. Dag, I would have at least rinsed it out first. "Collette, your turn."

I can tell Collette is fighting herself. "Can I say I have never *not* done something?"

"Why not?" Christina says.

"Okay. I've never *not* had sex with a man."

Only Christina drinks.

"Alexis!" Christina shouts.

"Well, it was before I met you," Alexis says, twisting a lock of blond hair with a finger. "Remember Joey Talarico?"

"You slept with Joey the Fish?" Christina shouts. New Yorkers are definitely loud. "Not Joey the Fish! Oh my God!"

Alexis takes another sip of her daiquiri. "I was young."

"Who was Joey the Fish?" Mama asks.

"Let me tell you," Christina says, waving her hands. She's definitely more Italian than Giovanni. "Joey smelled like fish. I kid you not."

"He had a gland problem," Alexis says in a small voice.

"Glands? He never bathed!" Christina shouts.

"He did that night," Alexis says in a smaller voice.

Collette is into this. "Uh-oh! Tell us everything, Alexis!"

"Well, what was I, fourteen? I remember I was very nervous—"

Christina interrupts her with a wave of her hands. "Well, that's very nice. Who's next?"

Alexis spins around. "Me!"

"Oh shit," Christina says and slumps onto the couch.

"Let's see. I just want Christina to drink this time. So much to choose from."

"Make it juicy, honey," Collette yells.

"Oh, it will be." Alexis raises her eyebrows.

"Be nice," Christina moans.

"Okay. I have never . . . wanted to have sex with . . . Madonna."

"Bitch." Christina gulps the rest of her Chianti. "That was a long time ago. Who's next?"

Mama actually raises her hand! She must be bombed. "I have never had sex in my parents' house!"

Collette doesn't drink. Neither Alexis or Christina raise glasses. "Busted," I say, grabbing a bottle of Chianti and taking a swig before anyone can stop me.

Christina leans forward from the couch. "This I have to hear. My own brother doing the do in this very house?" She lifts her ass off the couch. "Maybe on this very couch?"

I take a much longer swig and shoot eye daggers at Mama. "I am a lady," I say. "I do not tell anyone my business."

"Well, if she don't, I will," Mama says. "You should have heard the racket they were making in there—"

"She's lying! She wasn't here!" Or was she?

"How would you know Miss *'Now-Giovanni-Now!'*? You were in no position to know!" Could she have sneaked in? Damn. "Anyway, I hear this ripping sound—"

"Mama!"

Mama rolls back in the couch and starts hitting Collette and laughing. Everyone is laughing but me. Mama recovers and says, "I'm just kidding you, baby. I didn't get in till four or five. You two were sound asleep." Whew. "But Christina your brother does have one fine ass. Let me tell you, one morning he came up out of the bathroom with only his draws on."

"Speaking of draws on and off, we ought to watch some home movies now," Christina says, saving me from further embarrassment.

After we freshen drinks and they tear the bottle of Chianti away from me, we dim the lights and watch the video.

"It's in color, right?" Collette asks.

"Mostly," Christina says. "There's no sound, so I'll stand and point if you want to know who's who."

For the next hour or so, we watch Giovanni grow up. While the others make funny and rude comments, I focus on my husband-to-be. Very pudgy baby with big ears. Clumsy and uncoordinated, falling over in nearly every shot. His sunny, toothless smile. His funny clothes and scuffed brown shoes. Lots of shots of him stuffing his face. His fearlessness around animals. One shot of him getting bitten on the finger by a rabbit. But the most moving shot is one of Giovanni's mother, Ruth, reading him a story while Giovanni tries to turn the pages to get to the end.

"He never let her finish a book," Christina explains. "He'd say 'The end!' and get another book."

His mother is short and pretty in a sad sort of way. Her smile never seems to complete itself, but her eyes smile. Giovanni definitely has her eyes, not Pops's.

Time flashes to when Giovanni is playing baseball. He is so much smaller than the other players, and his uniform hangs off him. I'm marrying Spanky from *Our Gang*.

"Was he any good?" Collette asks.

"Actually, he was sensational and made everything look easy," Christina says. "He had to give it up, though. Had to help run the bakery."

The last shots are of Christina's high school graduation. Alexis stands and points at herself.

"You haven't aged a day, child," Mama says.

"Thanks," Alexis says.

The final shot is of Giovanni hugging Christina at a distance. The camera zooms in, and I see him crying.

"Why's he crying?" Collette asks.

Christina looks away. "Just happy, I guess." No, he's not. She hits the off button, ejects the tape, and hands it to me. "For you and Giovanni to look at."

"Thank you." We lock eyes for a moment. Christina looks away first. She has to know that I know she pulled the plug on her mama.

Collette stands and stretches her back. "Are we out of wine?"

"You got plenty enough whine to go around for all of us," Mama says.

"Very funny," Collette says.

"There are at least four more bottles up there," Mama says.

Alexis grabs Mama's hand and pulls her off the couch. "Let's go get some, then," she says in an almost perfect Southern voice.

Christina and I are the last to leave the basement. She gently tugs my elbow, and I stop halfway up the stairs. "He told you?"

Not directly, but . . . "Yes."

"Good. He needed to." She takes a deep breath. "You okay with it?"

"I'm still working that out. I wouldn't have had the strength."

She squeezes my elbow. "It didn't take strength, Renee. All it took was love."

Chapter Ten

Writing my part of the vows the night before the wedding is easier than I thought it would be. I almost call Giovanni to compare, to make sure mine are longer (and better) than his. He gets to say his first, so I get the last word. I plan on bringing a pen to change mine while I'm up there, just in case.

I also sleep more than I thought I would. I thought I'd be too hyper or nervous, but I've had no time! If I had, say, six months to wait instead of twenty days, I know I'd be trippin'.

Janae is being kind this morning, so Mama is serving me my bride's breakfast of pancakes and bacon in bed. "Alexis says to come down after your shower for your final fitting," Mama says. For some reason, Mama looks like she's forty-eight this morning, worry lines wrinkling her face.

"It will only be nine o' clock, though."

"She just wants to make sure her alterations don't need alterations, I guess." Mama picks at her food. "You nervous?"

"No." I stuff a slice of bacon into my mouth whole. "Are you?" Ah, greasy food!

"Why should *I* be nervous? It's your wedding."

"I know." I slurp my coffee and watch Mama fumbling with her hands. She's nervous.

"I'm not the least bit worried." She watches me stuff a forkful of pancakes into my mouth. "But I am worried that you won't fit into your dress."

"I'm hungry! You wouldn't want me passing out, would you?"

"Come on," she says, grabbing my foot under the covers, "let's get you bathed."

After my shower, Alexis and Christina lower the dress over my head while Collette and Mama watch, their eyes as big as soup bowls. It is a perfect fit, but that doesn't stop Collette from running her mouth.

"She look like she ready to bust up on out of there. Don't bend over, Renee, or folks will think you a community chest."

"I thought you held that title, Miss Thing," I snap.

No one is very lively this morning. Christina is especially scary, looking like Morticia on *The Addams Family*.

"I'll be back in a little while," Christina says after we're done. "I gotta do something with Giovanni's tux."

"Do you need some help?" I ask. I'll just tag along, you know, just to pinch Giovanni, make sure he's still there.

Mama holds me from behind. "You'll see him soon enough. You go on upstairs and get nervous."

"I'm *not* nervous."

"Well, go on up and get that old, new, borrowed, blue thing going."

"I don't want to!"

Mama takes my hand. "I'll go with you."

We walk hand in hand up the stairs into my room. "Y'all may be breaking some traditions today," Mama says, "but you are not going to break these. Your dress is old and borrowed, so all you need are blue and new."

"I want your earrings, Mama."

287

"I knew it! But you're only borrowing them, right?" I nod sadly.

I look through my drawers for something blue and find nothing. But when I open my closet, I say, "I've found blue."

"You're not wearing those, Renee," Mama says. "That's tacky."

"They're blue," I say, holding up a pair of blue Nikes. "Besides, I do not want to fall on my ass on my wedding day. The dress will cover my feet."

Two hours of primping and waiting later, I am beyond bored. "What time is it? And why couldn't we have had a sunrise wedding?"

"You are driving me crazy, girl," Mama says. "It's two minutes since you asked me before." I stare hard at her. "Eleven-fifteen, Renee."

"We ought to be getting downstairs," I say, taking one more long look in the mirror at how beautiful Alexis and Christina have made me. My hair is gelled up with some baby's breath here and there, I have on just enough makeup to highlight my eyes, and the dress is the bomb. If Giovanni were black, we'd be on the Society Pages in *Jet*. Who knows? Maybe I'll send *Jet* a picture anyway.

"It doesn't take but twenty minutes to get to the church, girl! Dag, what's the rush? You'll just be sitting in that basement for an hour."

I hate that part. Why is it that a bride misses half of her wedding waiting somewhere?

"Sit with me," Mama says, smoothing out the bedspread beside her.

"I'll wrinkle the gown."

"Stand then, damn."

I look at Mama and drop my eyes. "Sorry, Mama."

"I know you're nervous, but damn."

"I just want to get there, you know? Why can't we just see if everybody's ready and get started? Who says we have to wait till a certain time?"

"You afraid he won't be there?"

"What? Puh-lease."

"So what you afraid of?"

"Nothing. I'm just impatient, that's all."

"You can say that again. Honey, that wedding is going to be over twenty minutes after you walk down that aisle. Hell, it can't start till you get there. Always keep a man waiting, right? And enjoy the moment, okay?"

"Okay."

Mama and I don't say anything for awhile. I'm standing, she's sitting, and I don't want to say anything that will make us cry.

"Well," she says, starting to get up, "if you're so all fired up about getting there early—"

"No. It's okay, Mama. Really."

"Make up your mind, damn," she says and sits.

More silence. "Mama?"

"What?"

"Thank you."

"For what?" She's trying to be so strong.

"For being my friend."

She starts to cry. "Now why you go and say something like that? Come here, you."

I go to her and we embrace. I try not to ruin my makeup and keep my face from hers. She catches on, and we do that cheek-to-cheek kiss the older ladies at High Holiness do every Sunday.

"Do I look all right?" she asks.

"Perfect. What about me?"

She primps in the mirror with me. "You look like me, so you have to be perfect."

"Mama," I say, taking her arm, "let's go for a walk."

"No, not today, baby. Let's just stay inside and drink hot chocolate all day."

Then I start to cry. "Daa-em, Mama. Why you say that?"

After ten minutes of starts and stops, we move out of my room and walk down the stairs. Only Collette waits for us. "Christina and Alexis have already gone over, and—oh, y'all look so beautiful."

Mama stops me on the stairs. "We are not beautiful, Miss Thing. We are *bellisimo*, and don't you *evuh* forget it."

"I won't," Collette says, " 'cause y'all remind me of that every damn day." She kisses my cheek. "Let's get to steppin'. I'll hold up Miss Renee's caboose here."

There isn't a cloud in a sky so blue I swear it's part of a Walt Disney cartoon. Three women, all fabulously dressed: one a bride, one a bride-to-be, one, well . . . my mama—all proud, dark-skinned sisters—walk down a sidewalk, nodding at people driving or walking by. We are queens, and they are our subjects. Mama and I hold hands, and Collette can't stop laughing once she sees my Nikes.

We somehow squeeze into Clyde's Lexus and take off to the church. When we get to High Holiness, they rush me to the basement . . . then they leave my ass on a cold folding chair to go find the photographer. I'm at my own damn wedding, and I'm all alone, listening as people tramp in above my head. I'm about to go on up and start a ruckus when I hear a deep, rumbling voice.

"Hello, beautiful," Daddy says. "So *this* is what I helped make."

I turn and see him with the photographer. "Hi, Daddy."

He kneels and kisses me on the cheek. "Mmm, you smell nice." He shakes his head. "No, no pictures now, man. This is a picture only I want to have."

"But they said to get one of the bride," the photographer stutters. Where'd Mama get this loser? He whiter than Giovanni!

"Hide in the bathroom, man. You can take 'em afterwards at the reception. The women will understand."

"Okay," the photographer says, and he bolts across the basement.

"You know they won't understand, Daddy."

He shrugs. "I know."

We both look up when we hear Alexis's guitar. "It's about time," I say.

"Yeah." He stands. "I'll come back for you in a little while, Renee."

I bite my lower lip to keep from crying. "You already did."

"Alexis is playing the prelude, y'all!" Collette yells from the other end of the basement. "It's show time!"

I am shivering, and it's not from the cold. In about ten minutes, I will be walking down an aisle to marry a man who has never been part of my dreams. Maybe that's why I love him. Dreams are supposed to be wishes, right? This wish has come true, and while it's nice to fantasize, you can't hug a wish. I know we'll be up against it, but as long as Giovanni's up against it with me, I'll be happy.

I listen to Collette bellow out "The Lord's Prayer" (she'll never need a microphone), and Mama and Collette sing "Always." When they finish, someone hollers, "Amen!" That's High Holiness for you. They'd "Amen!" the Barney song. Mama and Daddy are beaming when they come down to get me, and Mama doesn't say a word. She only smiles and fumbles with her hands. Daa-em. I think I've *finally* found out how to shut my mama up. She smooths down the dress and adjusts some of my baby's breath.

"You ready?" Daddy asks. I nod. "Then let's get it on."

It's kind of dark at first because the church is lit only by candles, but eventually my eyes drink in a thousand roses and countless candles. Mama's squeezing my arm something fierce, and I can't help but take a peek at who's looking at me as we cruise down the aisle as a family. Giovanni's side of the church is nearly empty, but my side is filled to bursting. Everybody is smiling, and so am I until I see Giovanni looking so buttah down by the pulpit. That's when I get a little jelly leg.

"I got ya, I got ya," Daddy whispers, steadying me.

Giovanni's cheesing so much he's just one big smile. I hope he put some lotion on his face, or that smile will crack his face in two.

That tux was made for my man. Pops is standing next to him, but he isn't cheesing. He's smiling, but his eyes are focused over my head. Maybe Giovanni's mama is here, too. I look up and thank her for the dress.

Suddenly we're stopping, and Father Mike, who *is* a mountain in his black robe, is talking, then Reverend Noel, but I can't hear a word they're saying. Giovanni and I are in eye-lock, and no amount of "Hail Mary" or "Blessed Jesus!" is going to break that. Those eyes! I've got to look away or I'm going to cry. But I can't.

Father Mike has finished blessing or praying or whatever, and now—is that Christina? No way! She's beautiful, wearing a long, black, sequiny dress, only two pearl earrings, and a pearl necklace. She walks past Father Mike and stands near Alexis, who's wearing an identical dress. Daa-em, they look good together, and I *never* thought I'd ever say that about two women.

Alexis strums a chord, and Christina's angelic voice fills the room with "Ave Maria":

> *Ave Maria, gratia plena;*
> *Dominus tecum:*
> *Benedicta tu in mulieribus et benedictus*
> *fructus ventris tui Jesus.*
> *Sancta Maria, Mater Dei,*
> *Ora pro nobis peccatoribus, nunc et in hora*
> *mortis nostrae. Amen.*

Mama, Collette, and I are crying. Father Mike is crying. Giovanni's eyes are dripping. And Pops is fighting it, fighting it . . . and then I see him wipe away a tear. Just one tear, and I doubt if anyone sees it but me. Ah, he's just an old softie.

Daddy hands us tissues. Thank God Collette snorts to lighten the mood. And I sure am glad we didn't videotape it, heifer snorting at *my* wedding.

"Giovanni and Renee will now exchange their own vows,"

Reverend Noel says, and Daddy slips a couple more tissues into my hand.

After wiping a stray tear off my cheek, Giovanni takes my hands in his. This time his hands are very warm, with only a slight tremble. We've come a long way since that first night four months ago. "You know I have to do this," he whispers, and then he kneels, looking full up into my face. I hear some fool in the back say, "Amen!"

"I, Giovanni Anthony Luchesi, take thee, Renee Lynnette Howard, to be my wife; to hold you tightly on long winter nights; to plant you flowers in springtime; to feed you bread sticks, and always more than three to a basket; to tell you the truth at all times; to surprise you at least once a day; to raise our children together." I roll my eyes. No tears yet, but I can feel them coming. "To respect you at all times; to grow old together and still hold hands; to listen to you with my eyes as well as my ears; and to love you always and forever until the end of time."

Just a few tears fall, and as Giovanni stands, I turn to Father Mike and whisper, "Can I kiss him now, please?" Father Mike shakes his head. I turn to Reverend Noel. "Please?" Reverend Noel shakes his head. Giovanni wipes what tears there are away, and I take a deep breath. It's my turn.

I am putty, I am putty. I reach out to Mama for my vows without taking my eyes off Giovanni. "Pen," I whisper, and Mama hands me the pen she has hidden under her corsage. I take my time, crossing out and adding, as people start laughing. I turn and stare them down, and they stop. A bride has power!

"Okay, I'm ready." I position the paper so I can hold his hands and read at the same time. "I, Renee Lynnette Howard, do take thee, Giovanni 'Jay Anthony' Luchesi, to be my husband; to wake you up every morning with a smile and a kiss—after you brush your teeth, of course." Nice laughter. Even Pops breaks into a broader smile. "To massage your shoulders and arms; to feed you dirty rice to cure your colds; to accept your flowers *daily*; to raise our *child* together; to grow *young* together and *occasionally* hold hands in public." A few more laughs, but none from Giovanni. He has that look in his eyes again . . . so I skip a few more digs and get to the end. "To love you with all I have for as long as I have . . . and then love you a little more."

"Thank you," Giovanni mouths and turns me toward Father Mike.

"It is now time to bless the rings," Father Mike says, and my heart leaps. Pops hands Giovanni my wedding band and ring, and then Mama slips something into my hand. Call it the punch line to God's cosmic joke.

"Place the ring on Renee's finger and repeat after me." Giovanni slides that band of gold on but doesn't let go. "With this ring."

I am swimming in his eyes. "With this ring," Giovanni repeats.

"I thee wed."

"I thee wed." He slides on the ring.

"Now Renee, place the ring on Giovanni's finger and repeat after me."

I can't help giggling as I slide the twist tie onto Giovanni's finger and tie it up slowly. Giovanni laughs out loud.

"With this ring," Father Mike says, also trying not to laugh.

"With this ring," I repeat.

"I thee wed."

"I thee wed." I slide it all the way down and squeeze his hand. We face Father Mike again, and as I turn, I catch Pops's eye. He raises his eyebrows like Groucho Marx. I've impressed Sir Sneakiness himself.

"With the power vested in me by almighty God, I pronounce you man and wife." Then Father Mike pauses so long we both look up at him. "But before I allow you two to kiss, I have a few words to say to everyone. I hope you don't mind. You can wait a few moments, right?" He has us, so we both nod our heads. "I arrived in Roanoke a few days ago. My task: to marry two people, one whom I've known since birth, the other whom I've known for less than three days. I have performed thousands of weddings, and I have to say, I have never joined two more beautiful people. They make a beautiful couple, don't they?"

Pops yells, "Here, here!" and the crowd joins in, some clapping, some whistling, and a whole lotta folks say, "Amen!"

After the noise dies down, Father Mike asks, "Giovanni, do you want to kiss your *wife* for the first time?"

Giovanni smiles at me. "Yes." So glad he didn't say, "Yup."

"Renee, do you want to kiss your *husband* for the first time?"

"Oh, yes."

Father Mike shrugs and looks first at Pops and then at Mama and Daddy. "Emilio, Shirley, Michael, look at your children. For two people in such a hurry to get married, *what are they waiting for?*"

Giovanni holds my face gently in his hands. "Are you ready for this?"

"Yes," I reply. "Are you?"

Giovanni nods.

And then we kiss until "Amens!" rattle the stained-glass windows.